THE BEAUTY

VOLUME FOUR

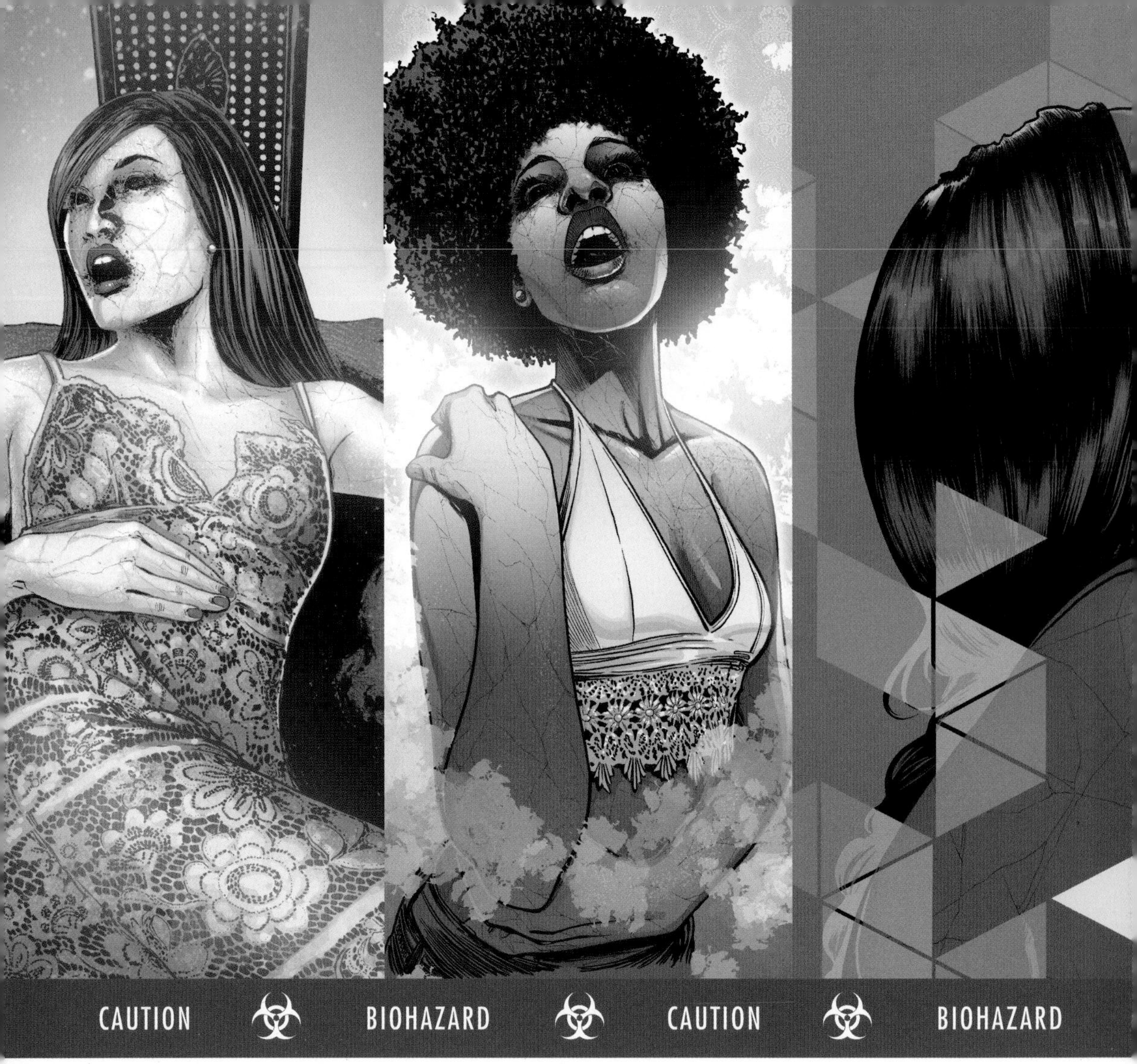
CAUTION
BIOHAZARD
CAUTION
BIOHAZARD

IMAGE COMICS, INC.

ROBERT KIRKMAN Chief Operating Officer • ERIK LARSEN Chief Financial Officer • TODD MCFARLANE President
MARC SILVESTRI Chief Executive Officer • JIM VALENTINO Vice President • ERIC STEPHENSON Publisher & Chief Creative Officer
COREY HART Director of Sales • JEFF BOISON Director of Publishing Planning & Book Trade Sales • CHRIS ROSS Director of Digital Sales
JEFF STANG Director of Specialty Sales • KAT SALAZAR Director of PR & Marketing • DREW GILL Art Director
HEATHER DOORNINK Production Director • NICOLE LAPALME Controller

www.imagecomics.com

THE BEAUTY, VOL. 4
ISBN: 978-1-5343-0653-0
First Printing. May 2018.

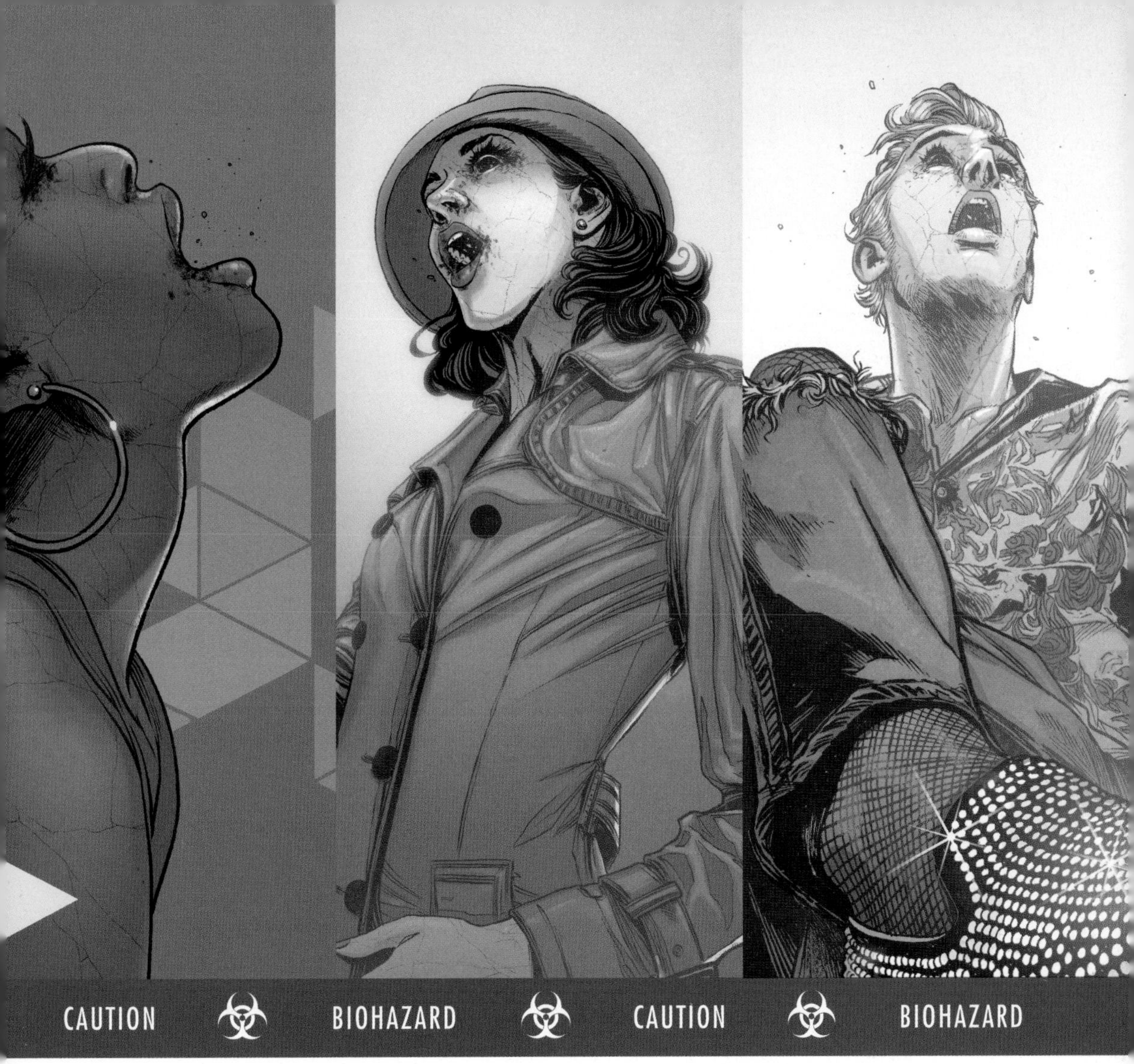
CAUTION
BIOHAZARD
CAUTION
BIOHAZARD

JEREMY HAUN & JASON A. HURLEY
story

MATTHEW DOW SMITH [CHAPTER 17]
THOMAS NACHLIK [CHAPTERS 18 – 21]
art

NAYOUNG KIM
color

THOMAS MAUER
lettering & design

JOEL ENOS
editor

CAREY HALL
production artist

CHAPTER

17

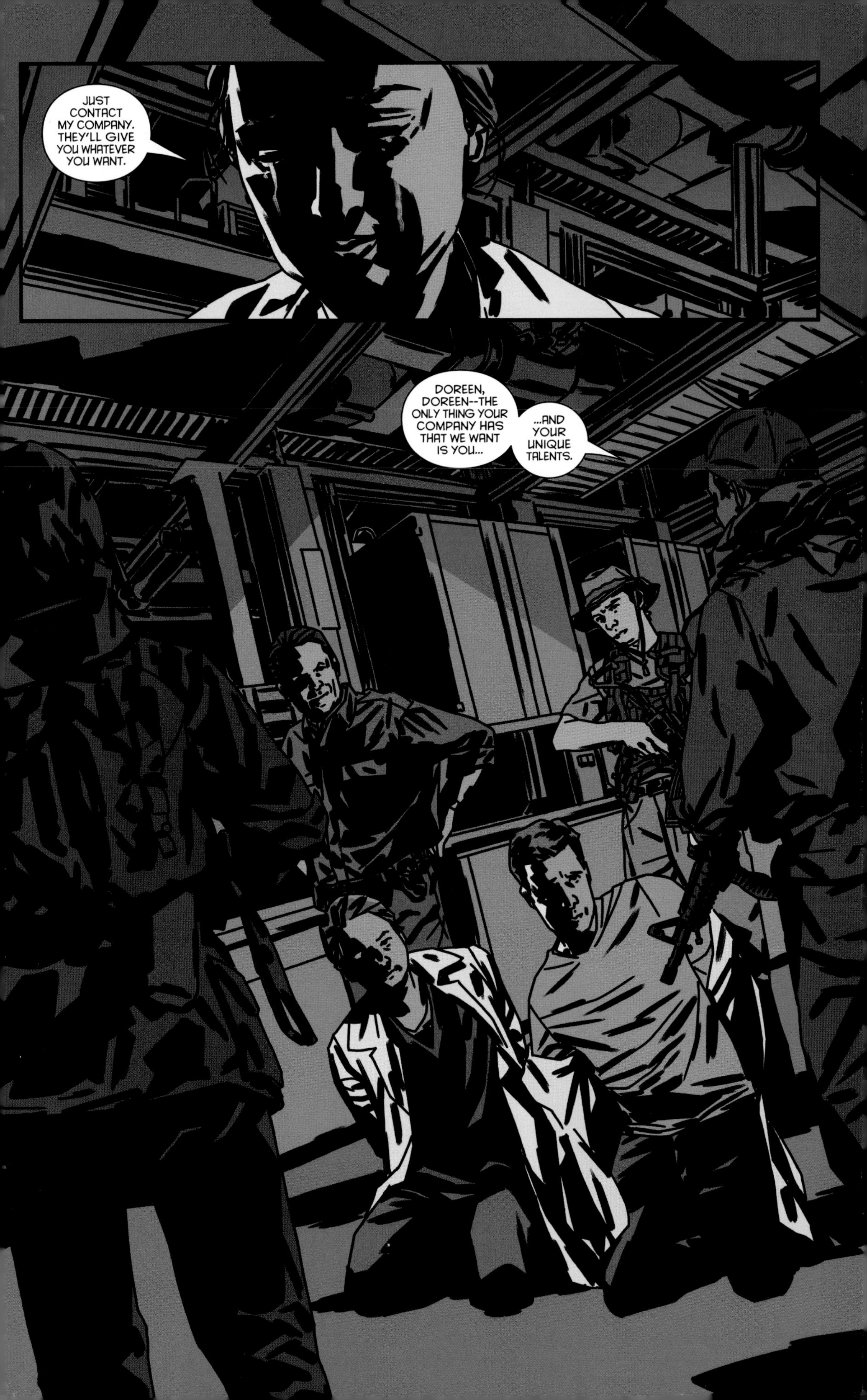
JUST CONTACT MY COMPANY. THEY'LL GIVE YOU WHATEVER YOU WANT.
DOREEN, DOREEN--THE ONLY THING YOUR COMPANY HAS THAT WE WANT IS YOU...
...AND YOUR UNIQUE TALENTS.

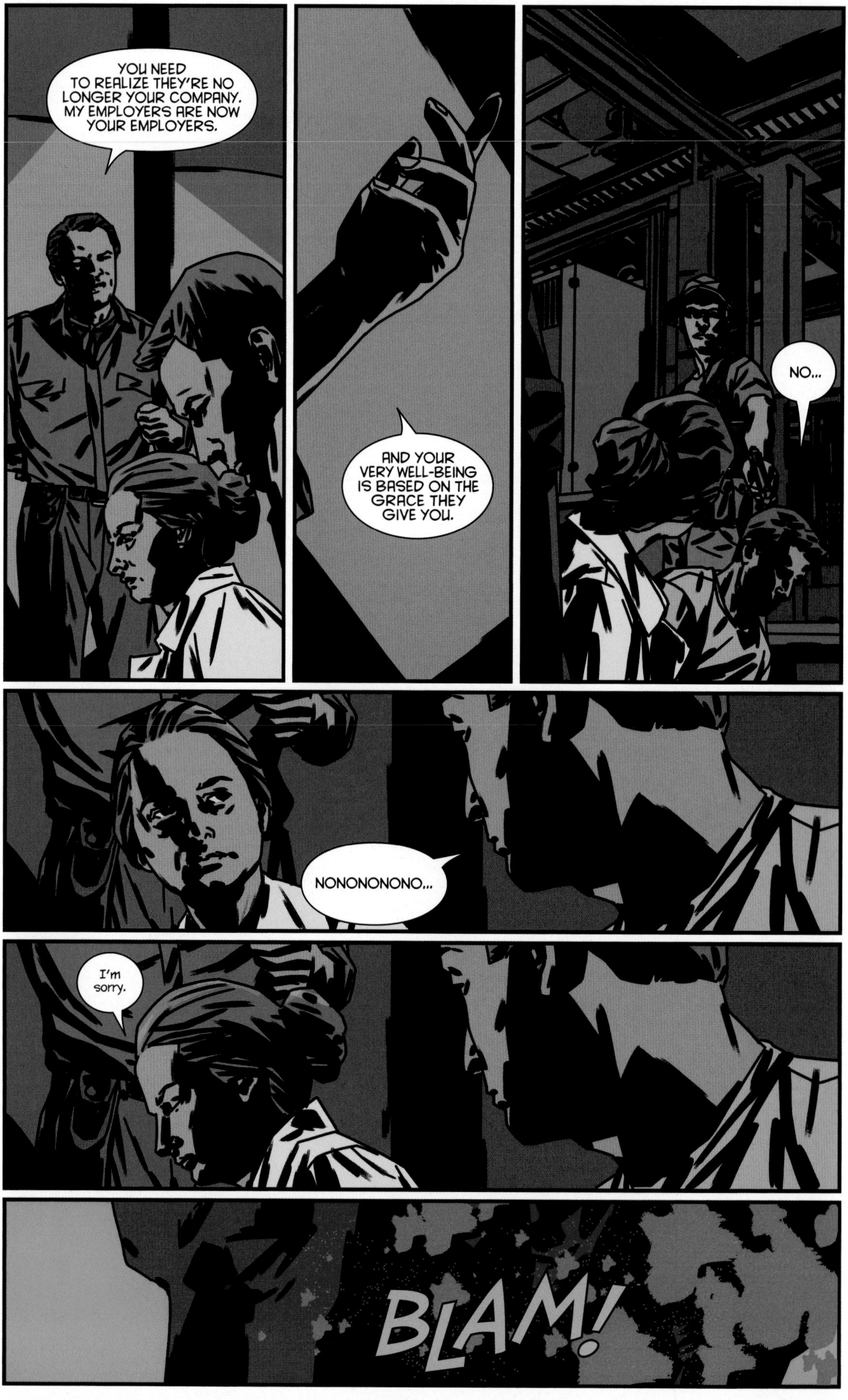
YOU NEED TO REALIZE THEY'RE NO LONGER YOUR COMPANY. MY EMPLOYERS ARE NOW YOUR EMPLOYERS.
AND YOUR VERY WELL-BEING IS BASED ON THE GRACE THEY GIVE YOU.
NO...
NONONONONO...
I'm sorry.
BLAM!

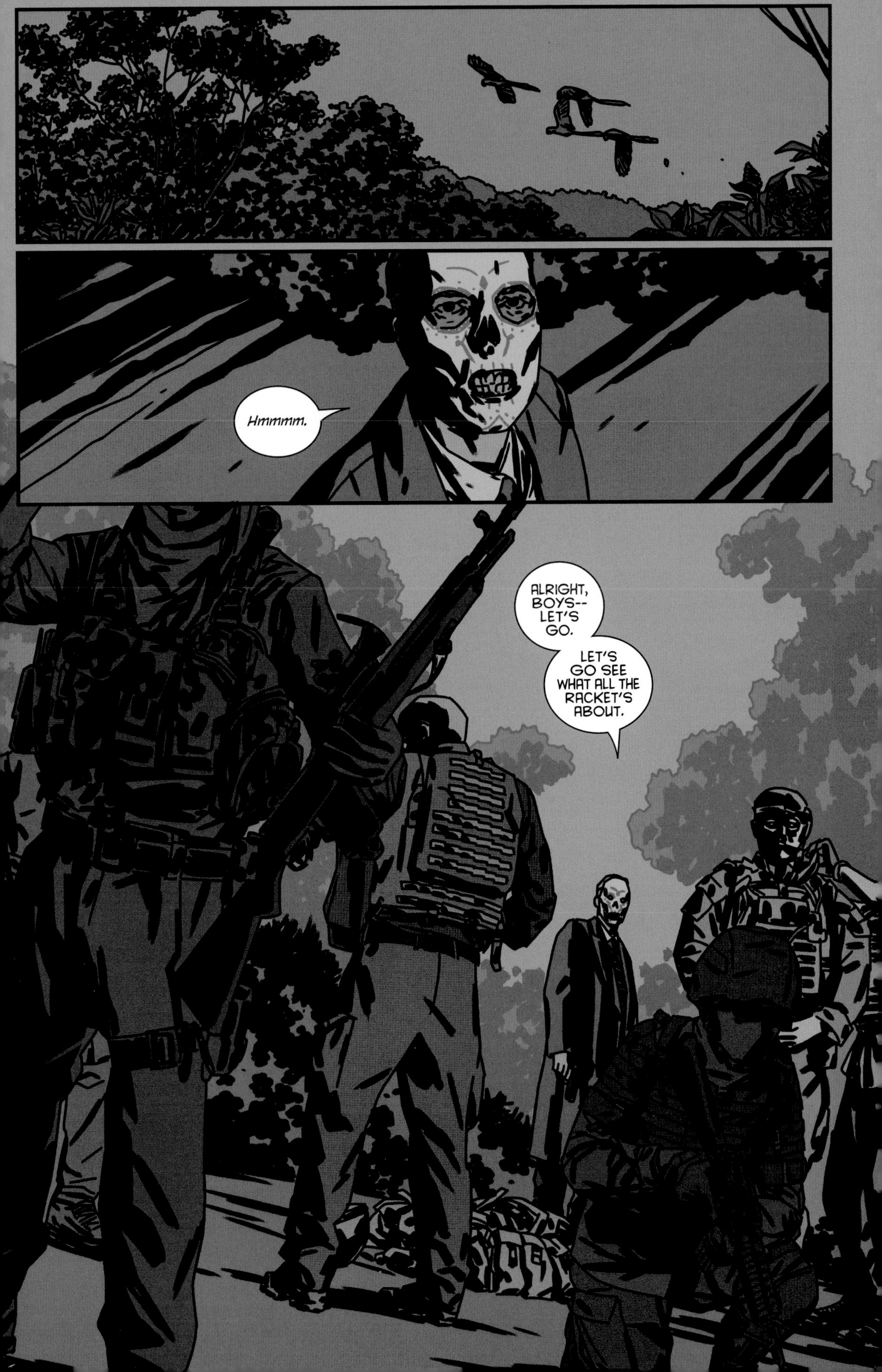
Hmmmm.
ALRIGHT, BOYS-- LET'S GO.
LET'S GO SEE WHAT ALL THE RACKET'S ABOUT.

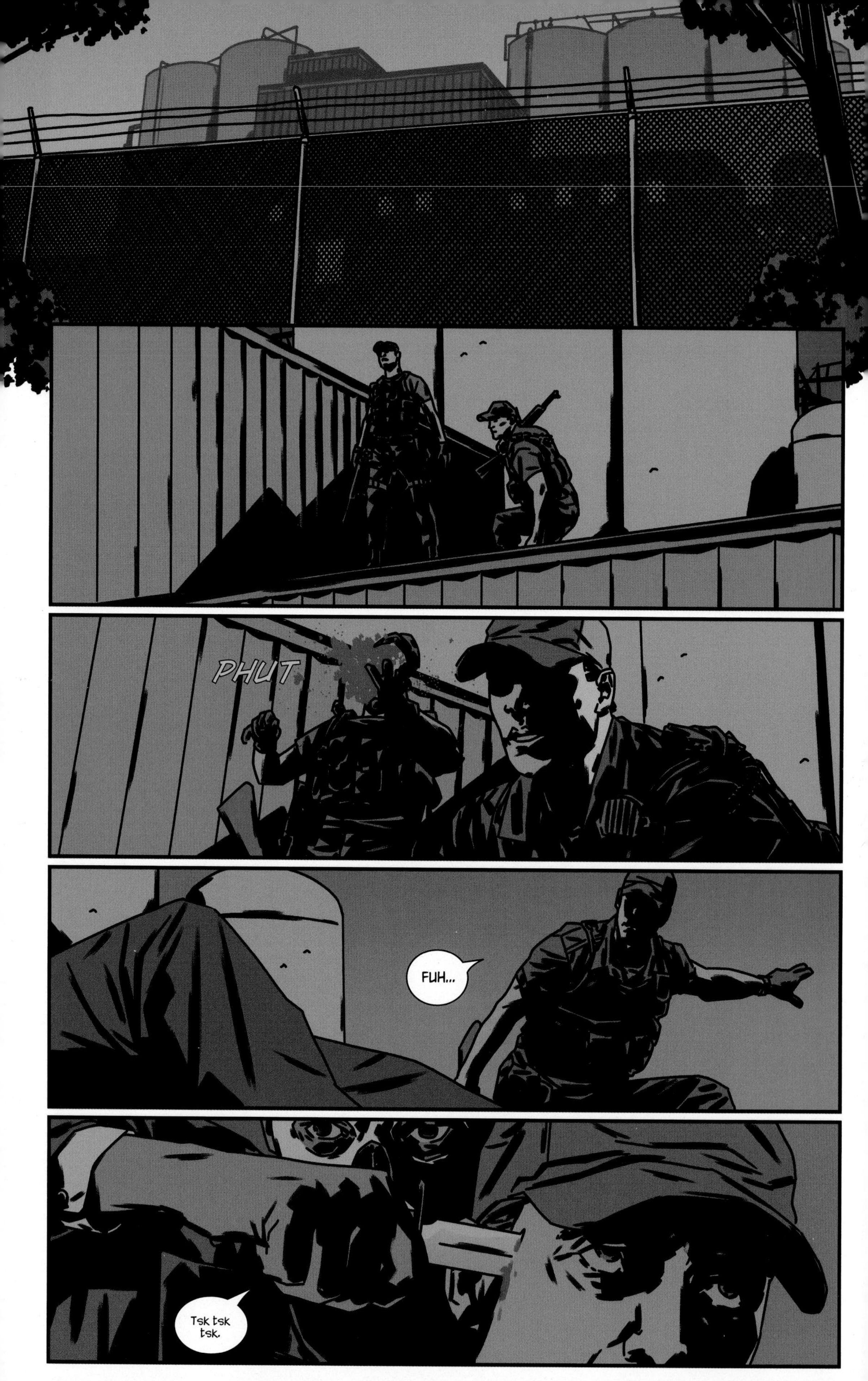
PHUT
FUH...
Tsk tsk tsk.

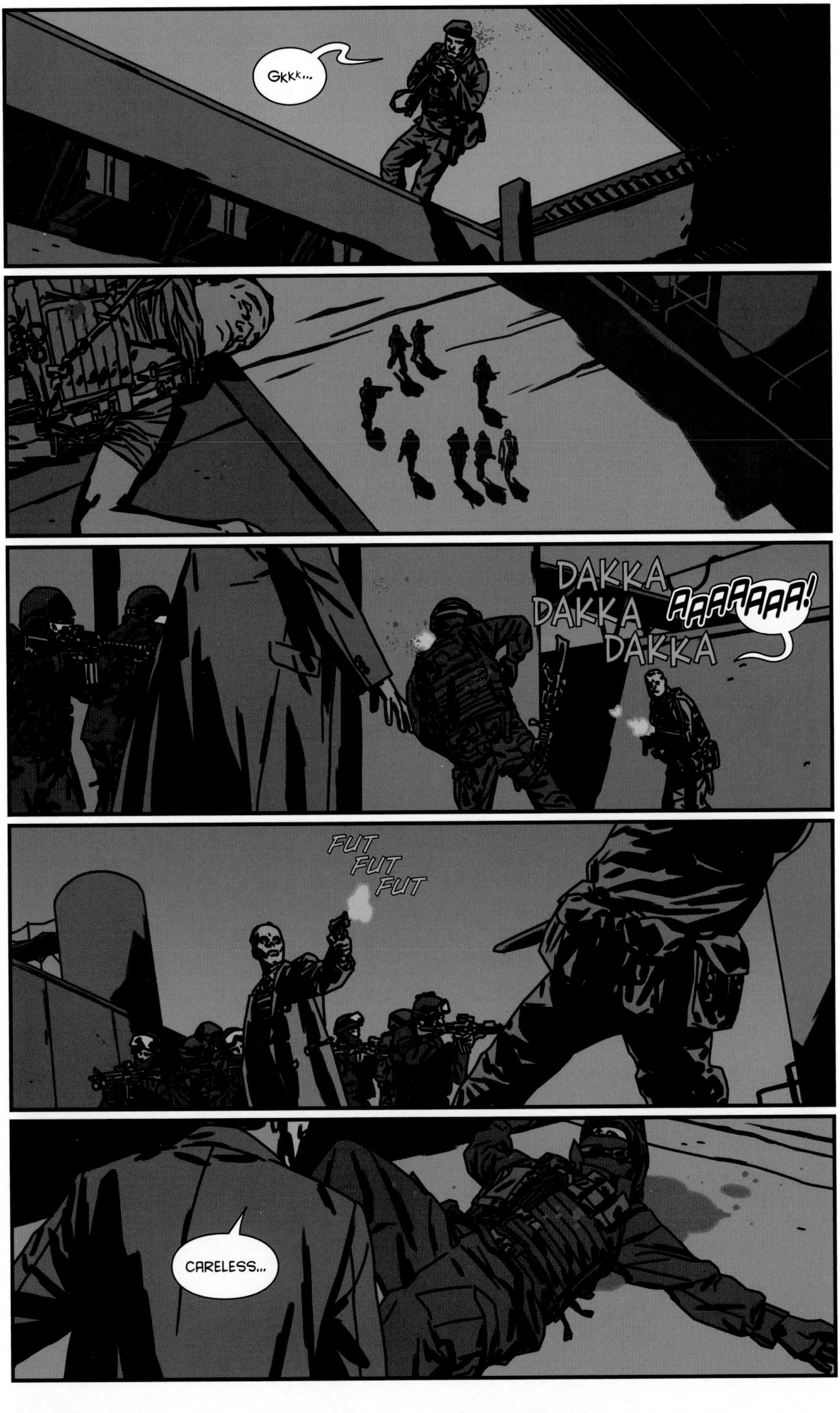
GKKK...
DAKKA DAKKA DAKKA
AAAAAAA!
FUT FUT FUT
CARELESS...

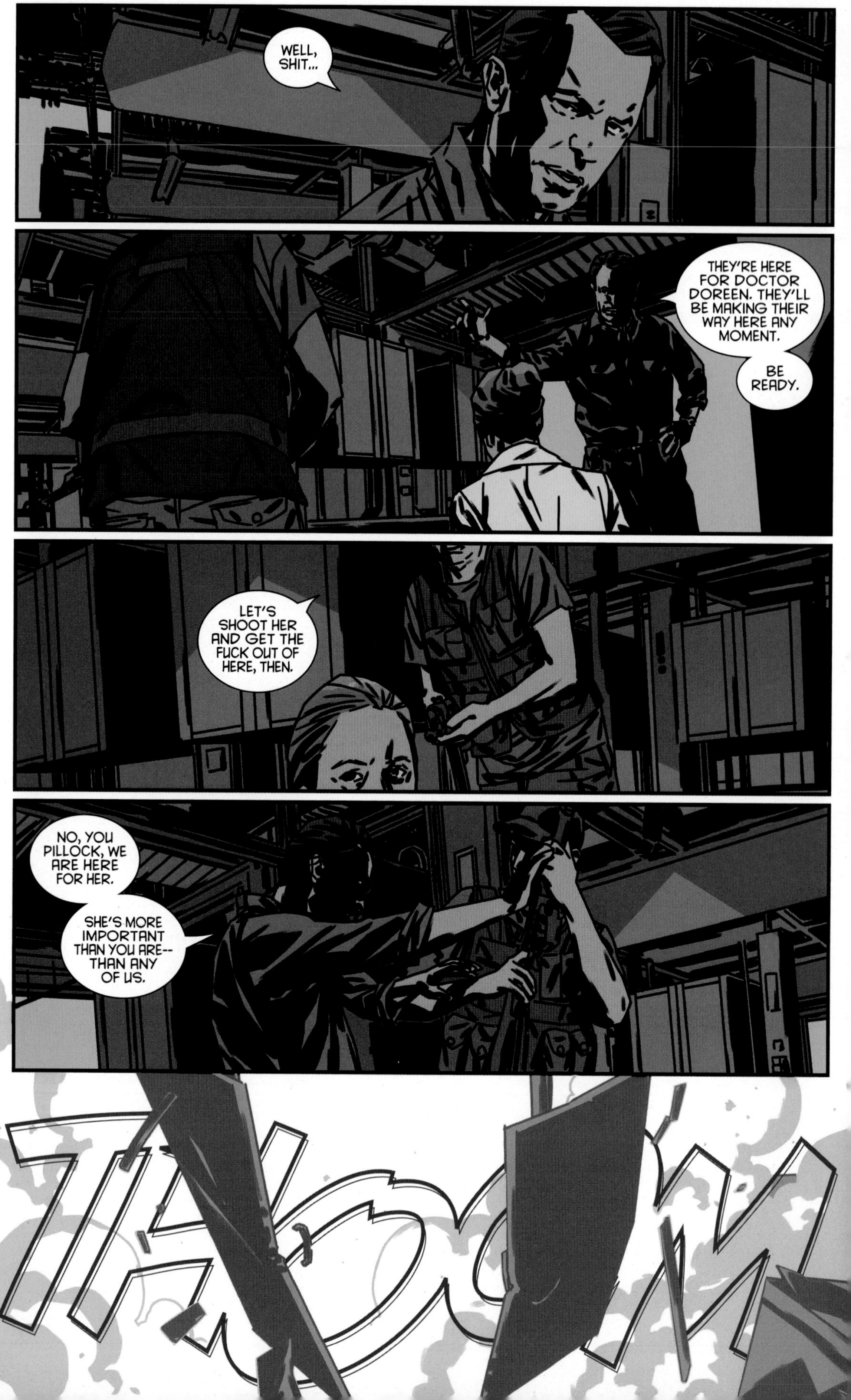
WELL, SHIT...
THEY'RE HERE FOR DOCTOR DOREEN. THEY'LL BE MAKING THEIR WAY HERE ANY MOMENT.
BE READY.
LET'S SHOOT HER AND GET THE FUCK OUT OF HERE, THEN.
NO, YOU PILLOCK, WE ARE HERE FOR HER.
SHE'S MORE IMPORTANT THAN YOU ARE-- THAN ANY OF US.
THOOM

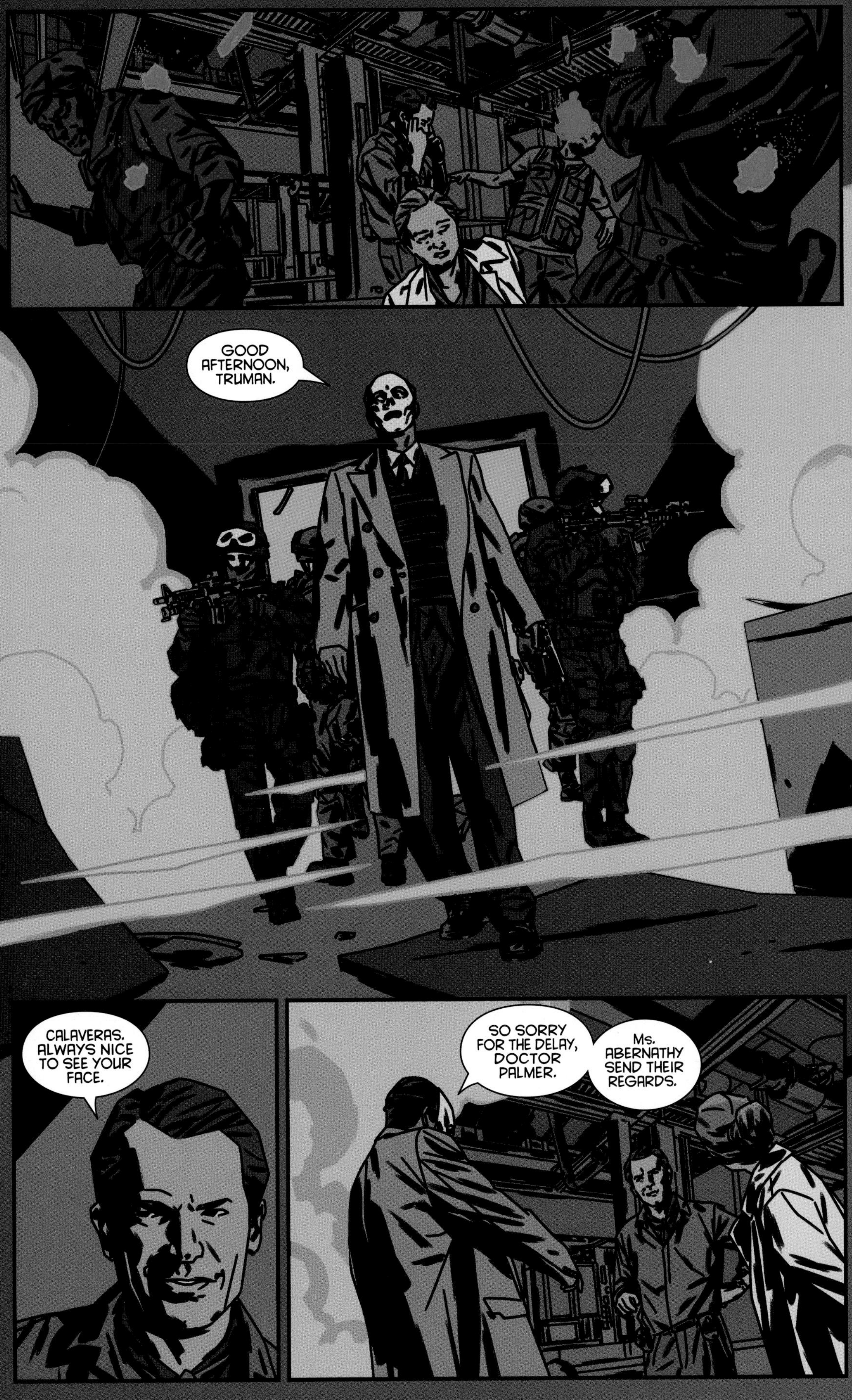
GOOD AFTERNOON, TRUMAN.
CALAVERAS. ALWAYS NICE TO SEE YOUR FACE.
SO SORRY FOR THE DELAY, DOCTOR PALMER.
Ms. ABERNATHY SEND THEIR REGARDS.

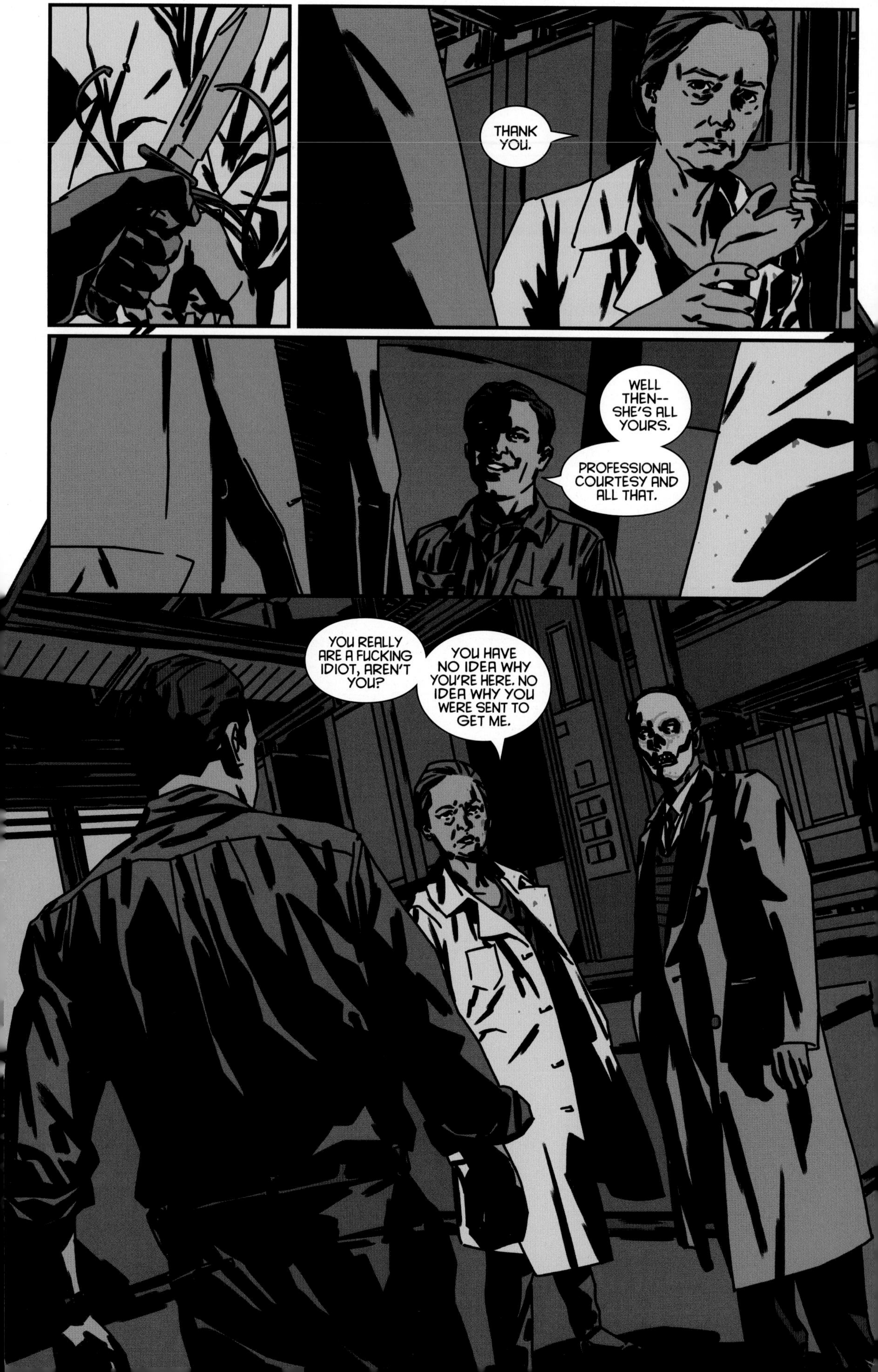

THANK YOU.
WELL THEN-- SHE'S ALL YOURS.
PROFESSIONAL COURTESY AND ALL THAT.
YOU REALLY ARE A FUCKING IDIOT, AREN'T YOU?
YOU HAVE NO IDEA WHY YOU'RE HERE. NO IDEA WHY YOU WERE SENT TO GET ME.

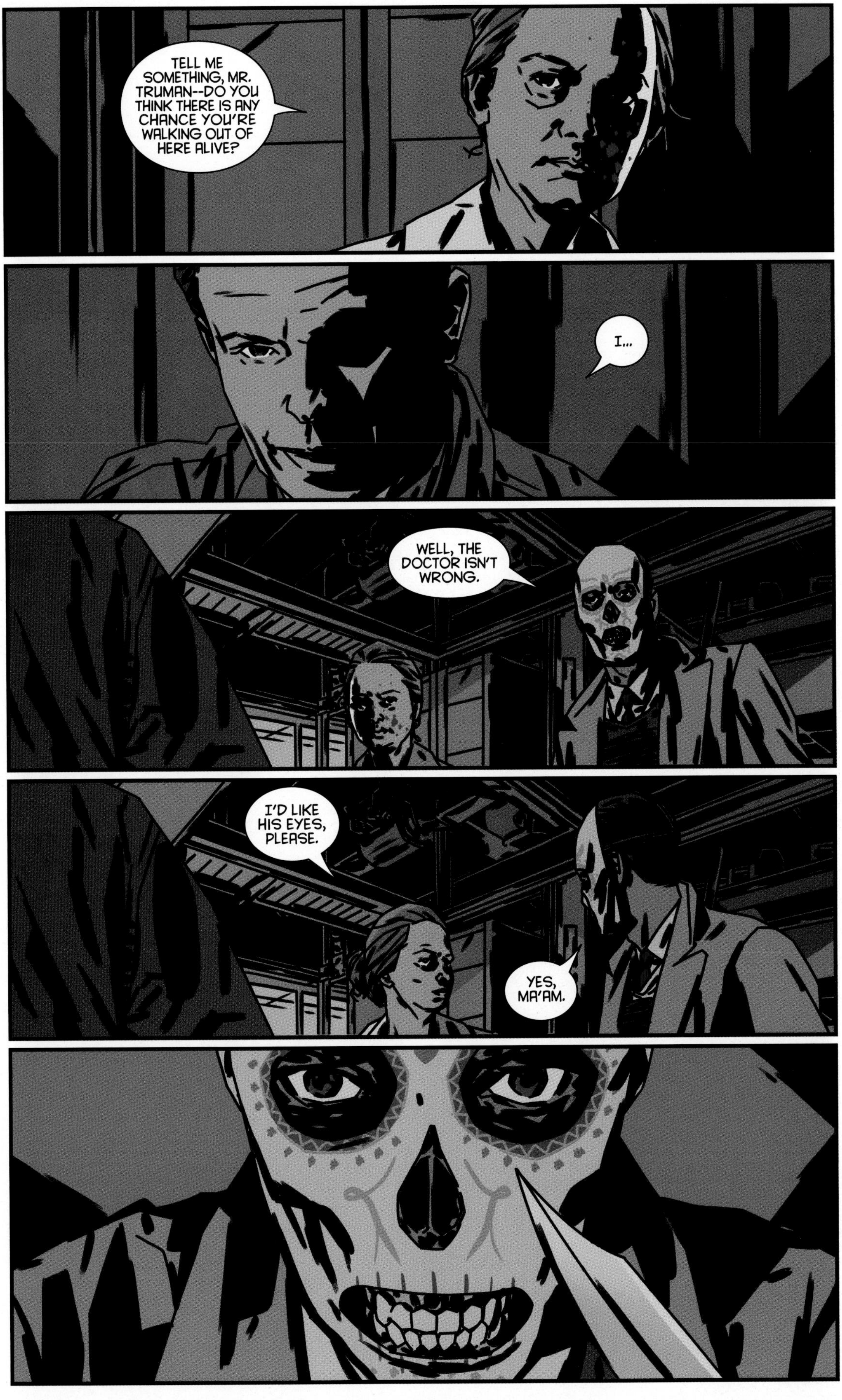
TELL ME SOMETHING, MR. TRUMAN--DO YOU THINK THERE IS ANY CHANCE YOU'RE WALKING OUT OF HERE ALIVE?
I...
WELL, THE DOCTOR ISN'T WRONG.
I'D LIKE HIS EYES, PLEASE.
YES, MA'AM.

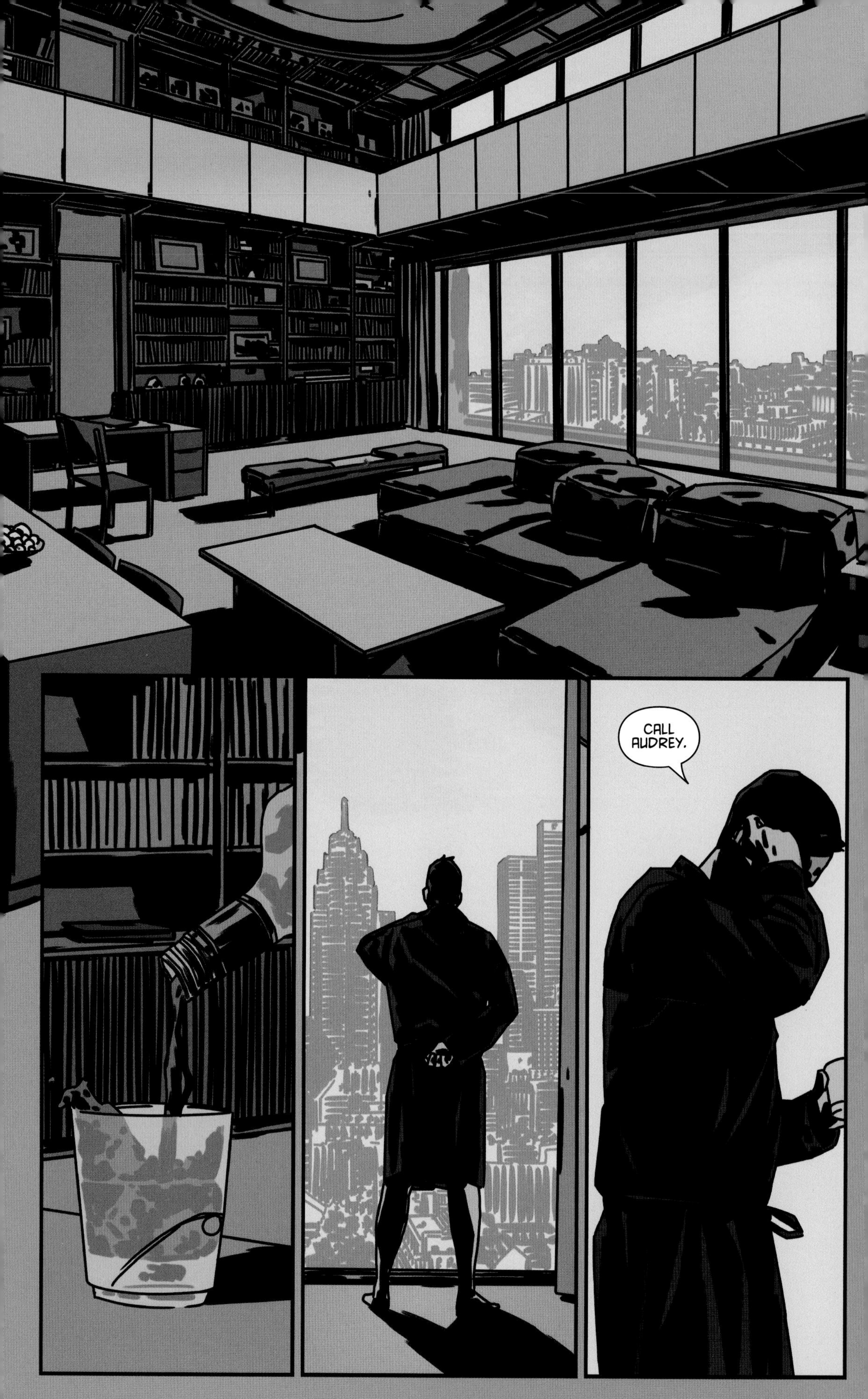
CALL AUDREY.

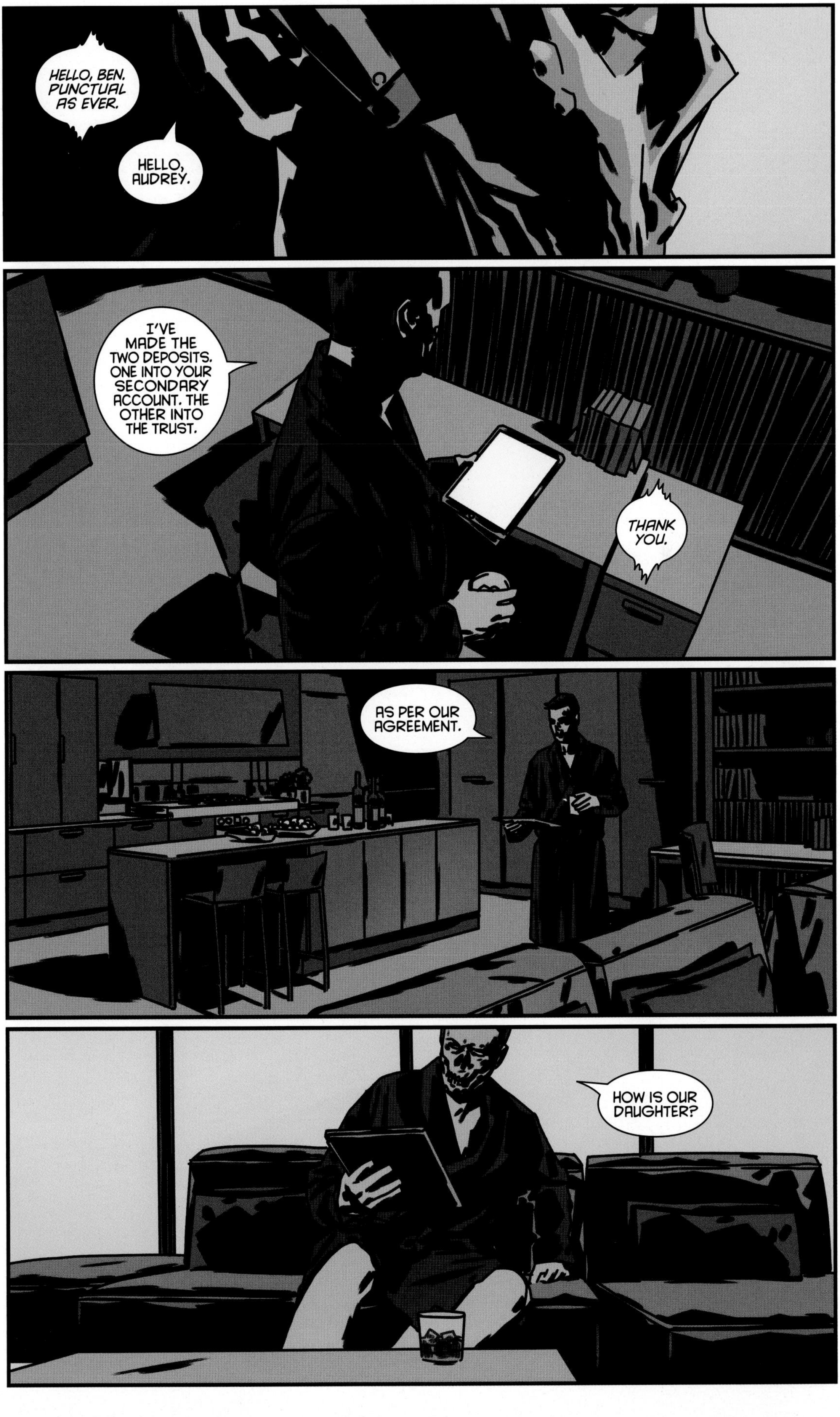
HELLO, BEN. PUNCTUAL AS EVER.
HELLO, AUDREY.
I'VE MADE THE TWO DEPOSITS. ONE INTO YOUR SECONDARY ACCOUNT. THE OTHER INTO THE TRUST.
THANK YOU.
AS PER OUR AGREEMENT.
HOW IS OUR DAUGHTER?

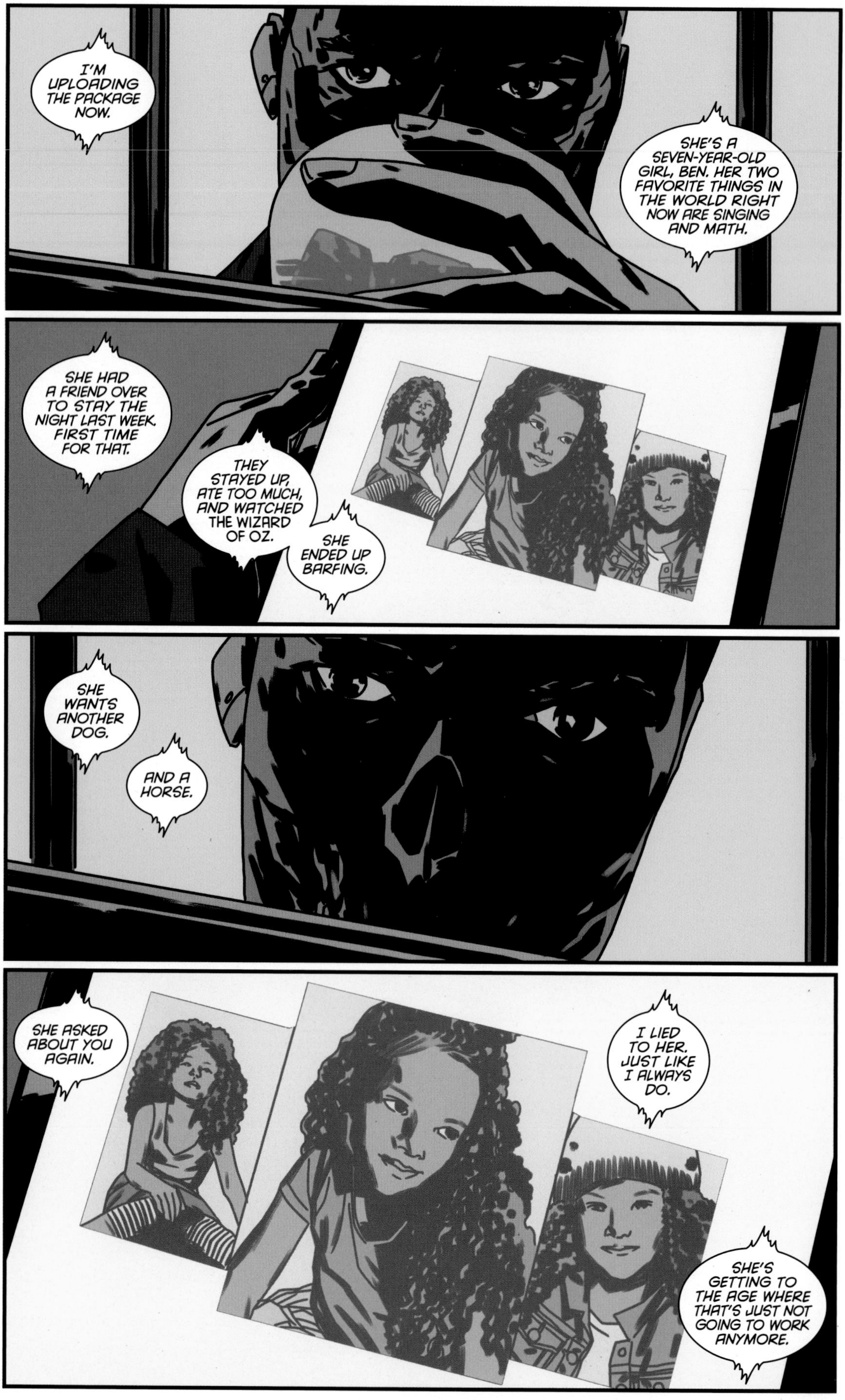

I'M UPLOADING THE PACKAGE NOW.
SHE'S A SEVEN-YEAR-OLD GIRL, BEN. HER TWO FAVORITE THINGS IN THE WORLD RIGHT NOW ARE SINGING AND MATH.
SHE HAD A FRIEND OVER TO STAY THE NIGHT LAST WEEK. FIRST TIME FOR THAT.
THEY STAYED UP, ATE TOO MUCH, AND WATCHED THE WIZARD OF OZ.
SHE ENDED UP BARFING.
SHE WANTS ANOTHER DOG.
AND A HORSE.
SHE ASKED ABOUT YOU AGAIN.
I LIED TO HER. JUST LIKE I ALWAYS DO.
SHE'S GETTING TO THE AGE WHERE THAT'S JUST NOT GOING TO WORK ANYMORE.

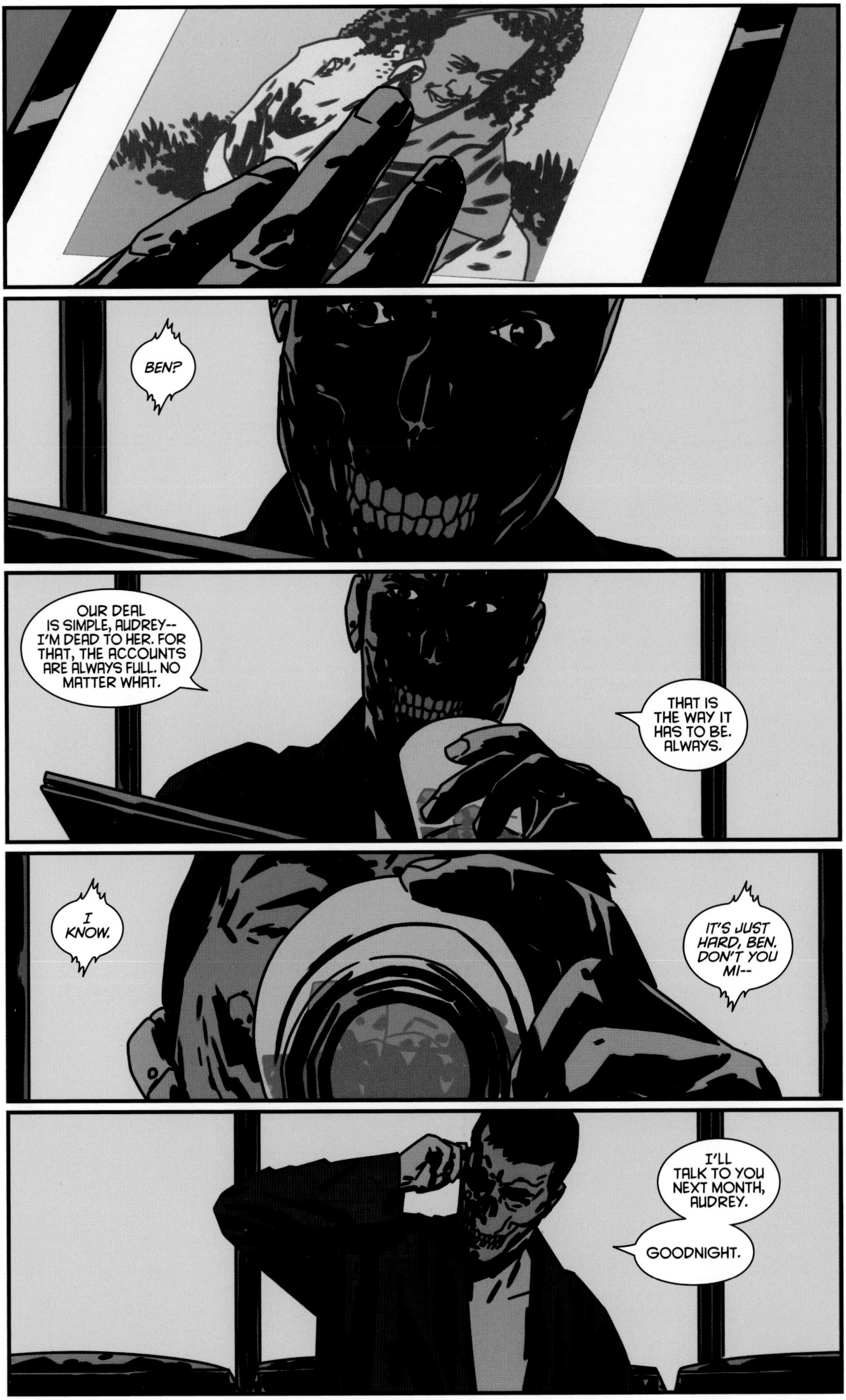
BEN?
OUR DEAL IS SIMPLE, AUDREY-- I'M DEAD TO HER. FOR THAT, THE ACCOUNTS ARE ALWAYS FULL. NO MATTER WHAT.
THAT IS THE WAY IT HAS TO BE. ALWAYS.
I KNOW.
IT'S JUST HARD, BEN. DON'T YOU MI--
I'LL TALK TO YOU NEXT MONTH, AUDREY.
GOODNIGHT.

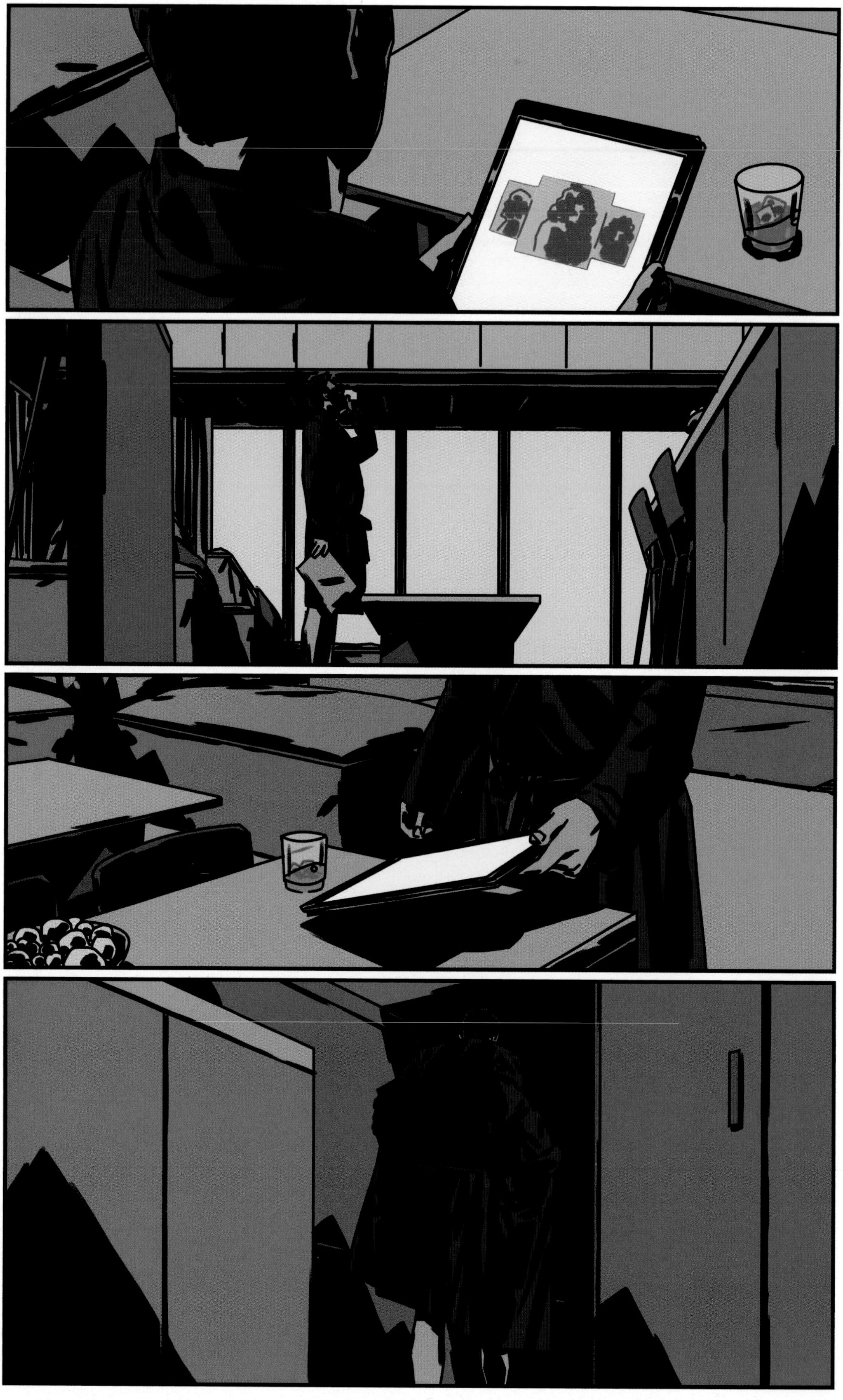

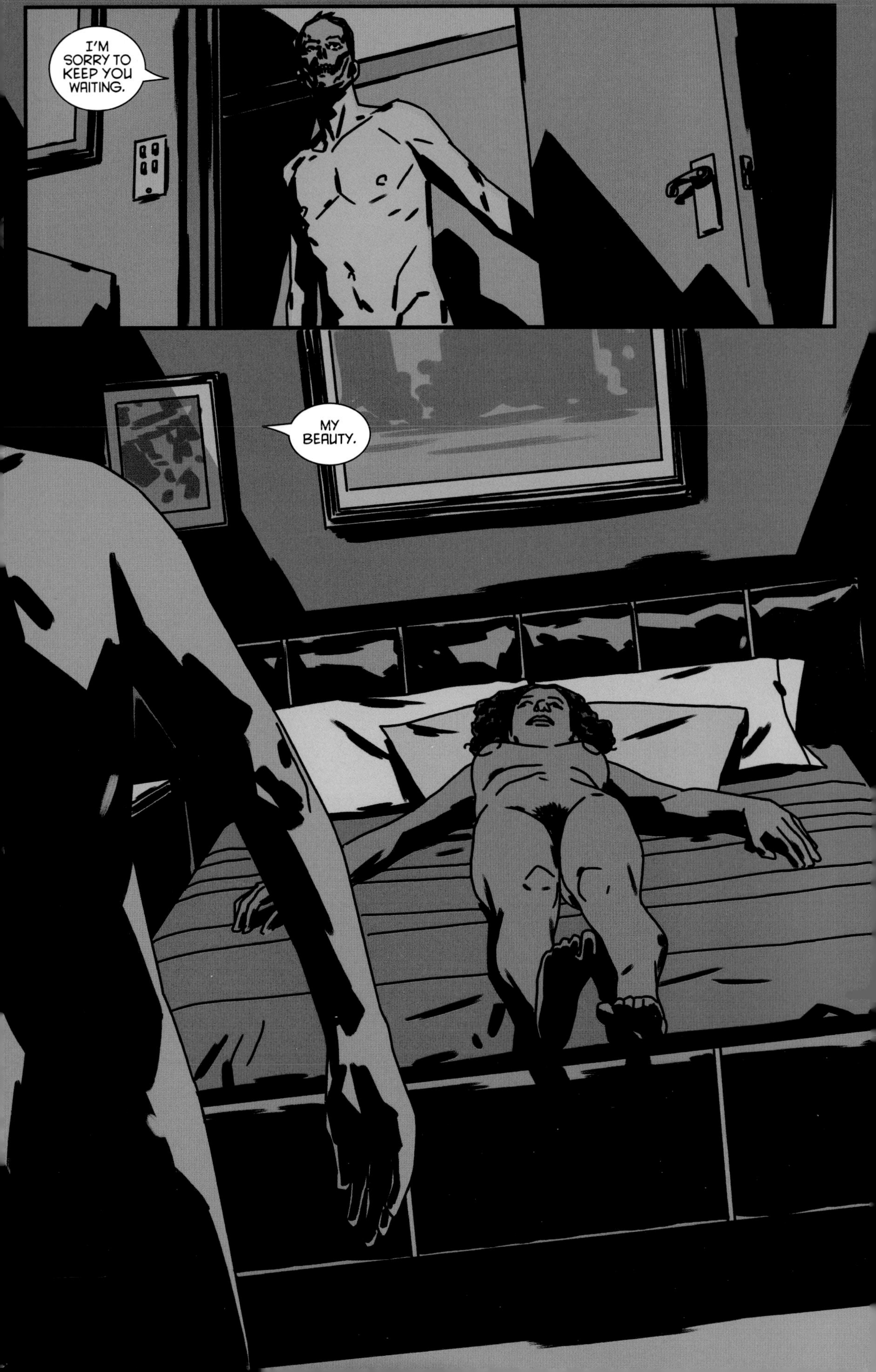
I'M SORRY TO KEEP YOU WAITING.
MY BEAUTY.

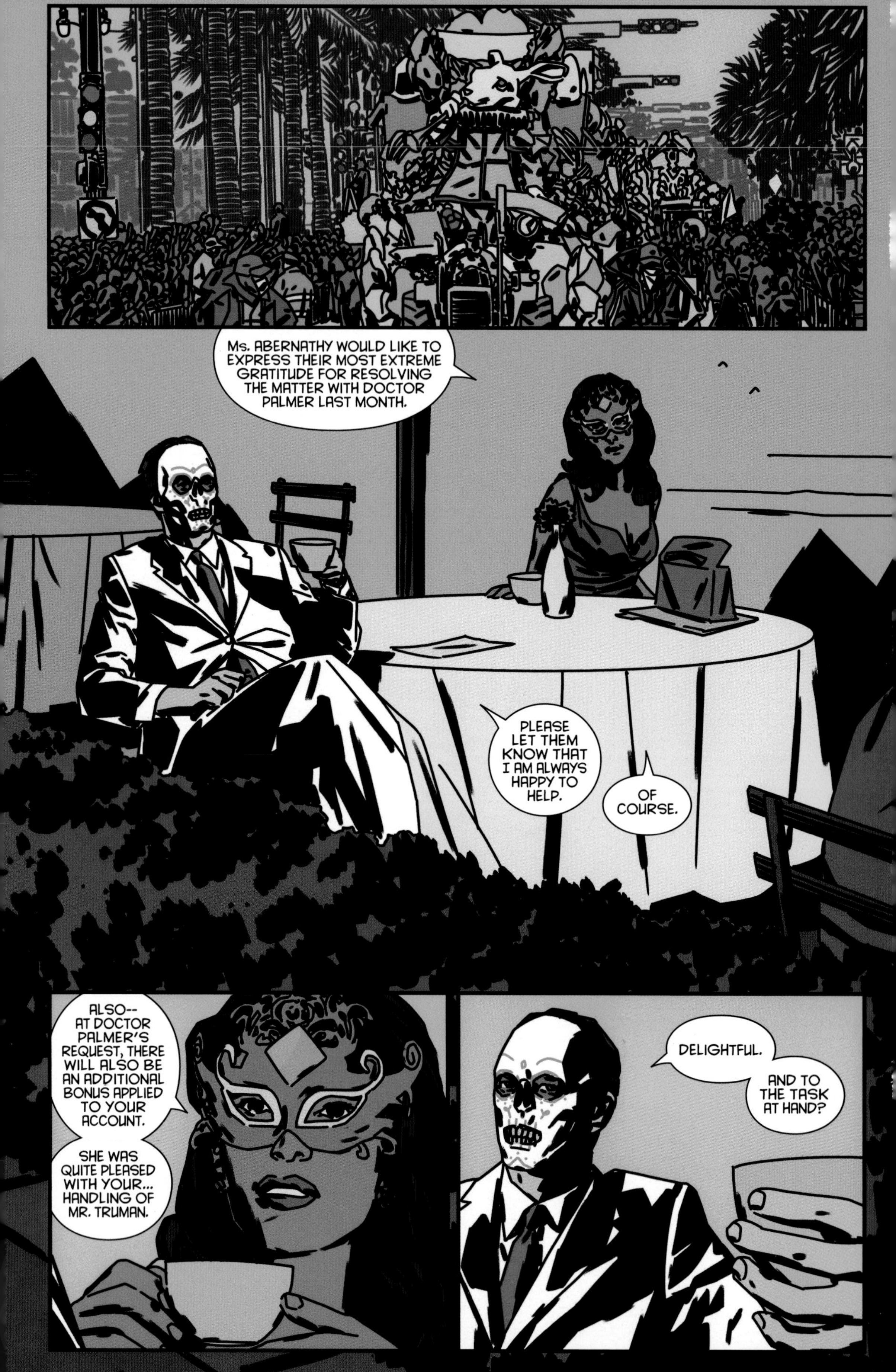
Ms. ABERNATHY WOULD LIKE TO EXPRESS THEIR MOST EXTREME GRATITUDE FOR RESOLVING THE MATTER WITH DOCTOR PALMER LAST MONTH.
PLEASE LET THEM KNOW THAT I AM ALWAYS HAPPY TO HELP.
OF COURSE.
ALSO-- AT DOCTOR PALMER'S REQUEST, THERE WILL ALSO BE AN ADDITIONAL BONUS APPLIED TO YOUR ACCOUNT.
SHE WAS QUITE PLEASED WITH YOUR... HANDLING OF MR. TRUMAN.
DELIGHTFUL.
AND TO THE TASK AT HAND?

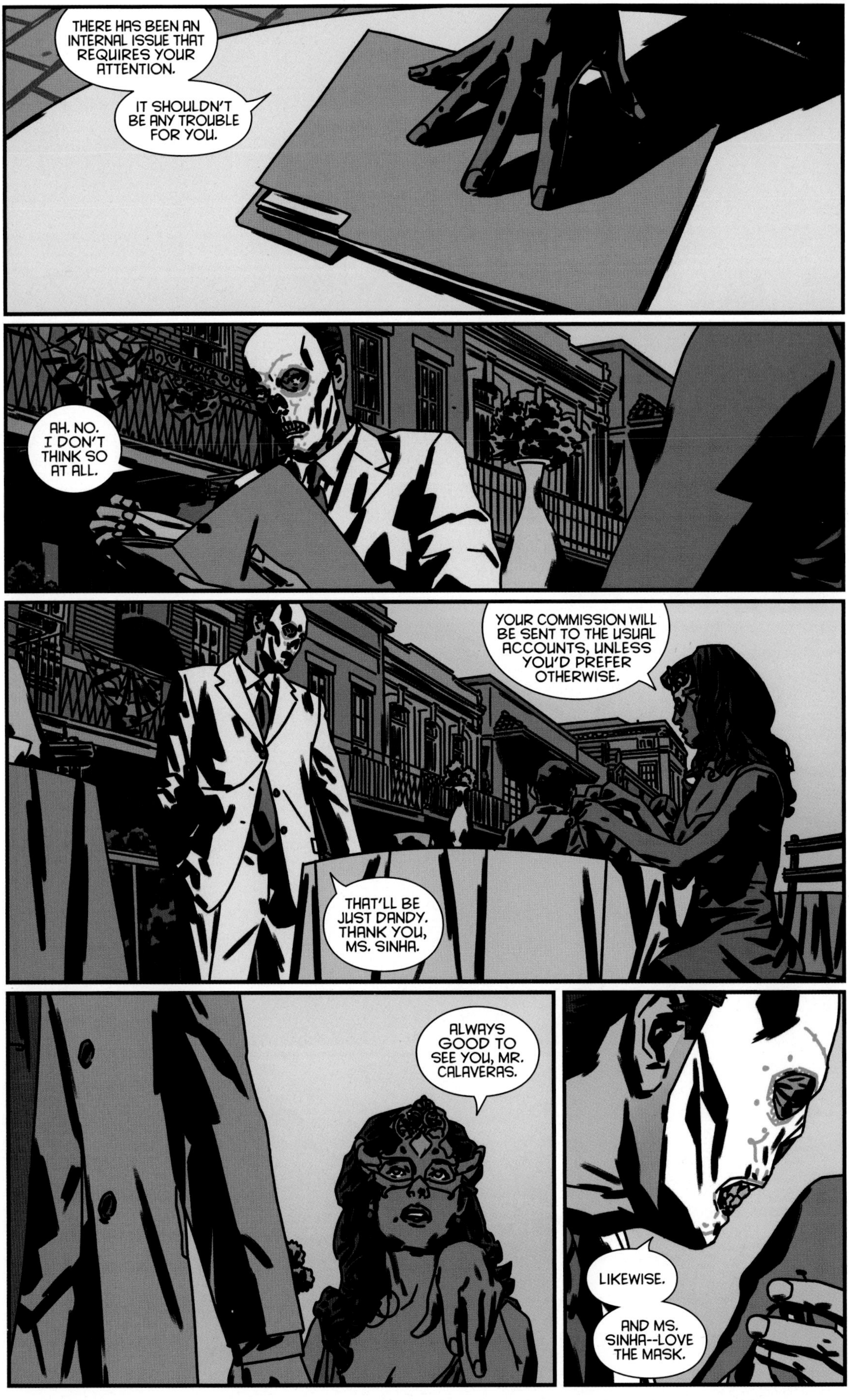
THERE HAS BEEN AN INTERNAL ISSUE THAT REQUIRES YOUR ATTENTION.
IT SHOULDN'T BE ANY TROUBLE FOR YOU.
AH. NO. I DON'T THINK SO AT ALL.
YOUR COMMISSION WILL BE SENT TO THE USUAL ACCOUNTS, UNLESS YOU'D PREFER OTHERWISE.
THAT'LL BE JUST DANDY. THANK YOU, MS. SINHA.
ALWAYS GOOD TO SEE YOU, MR. CALAVERAS.
LIKEWISE.
AND MS. SINHA--LOVE THE MASK.

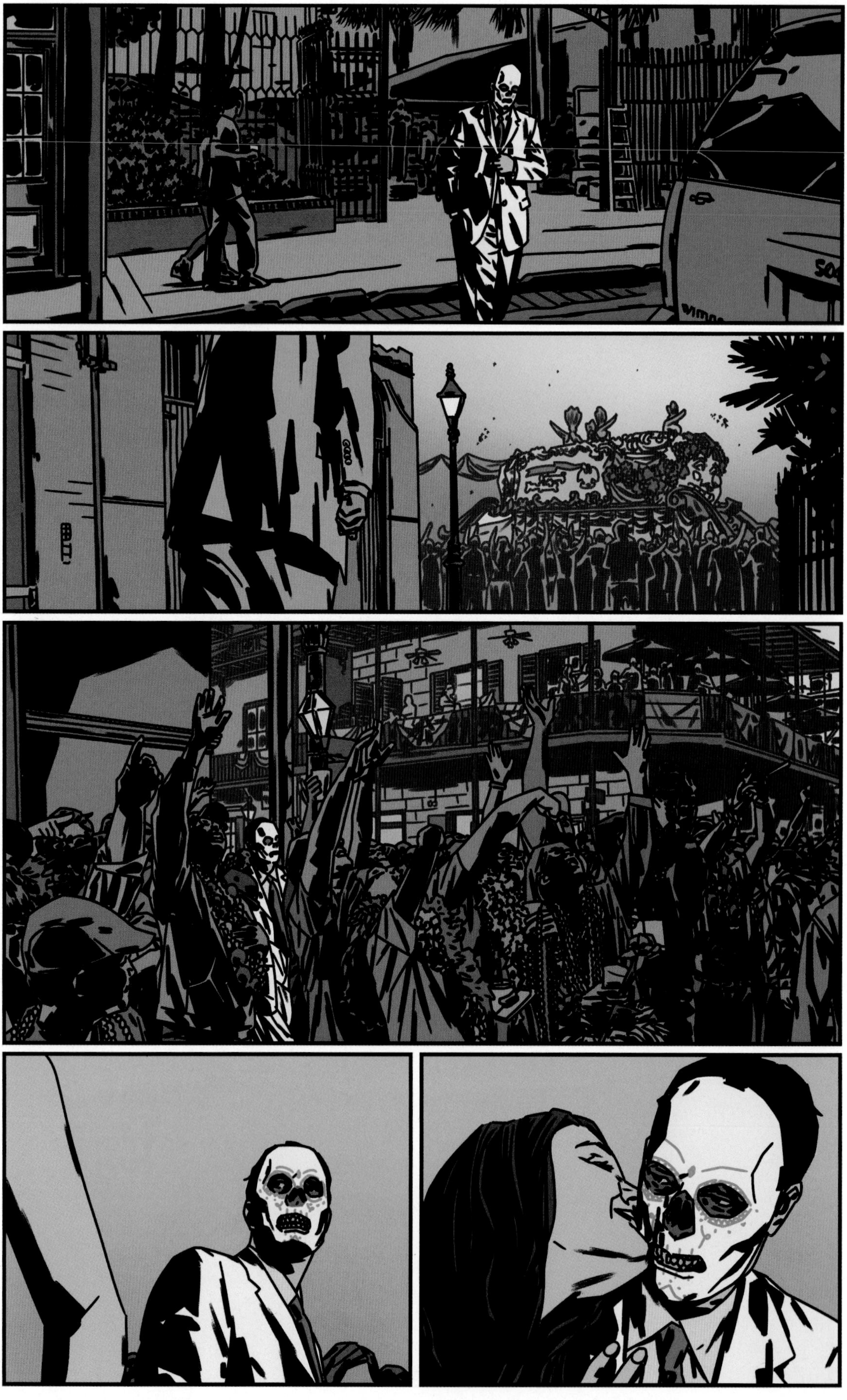

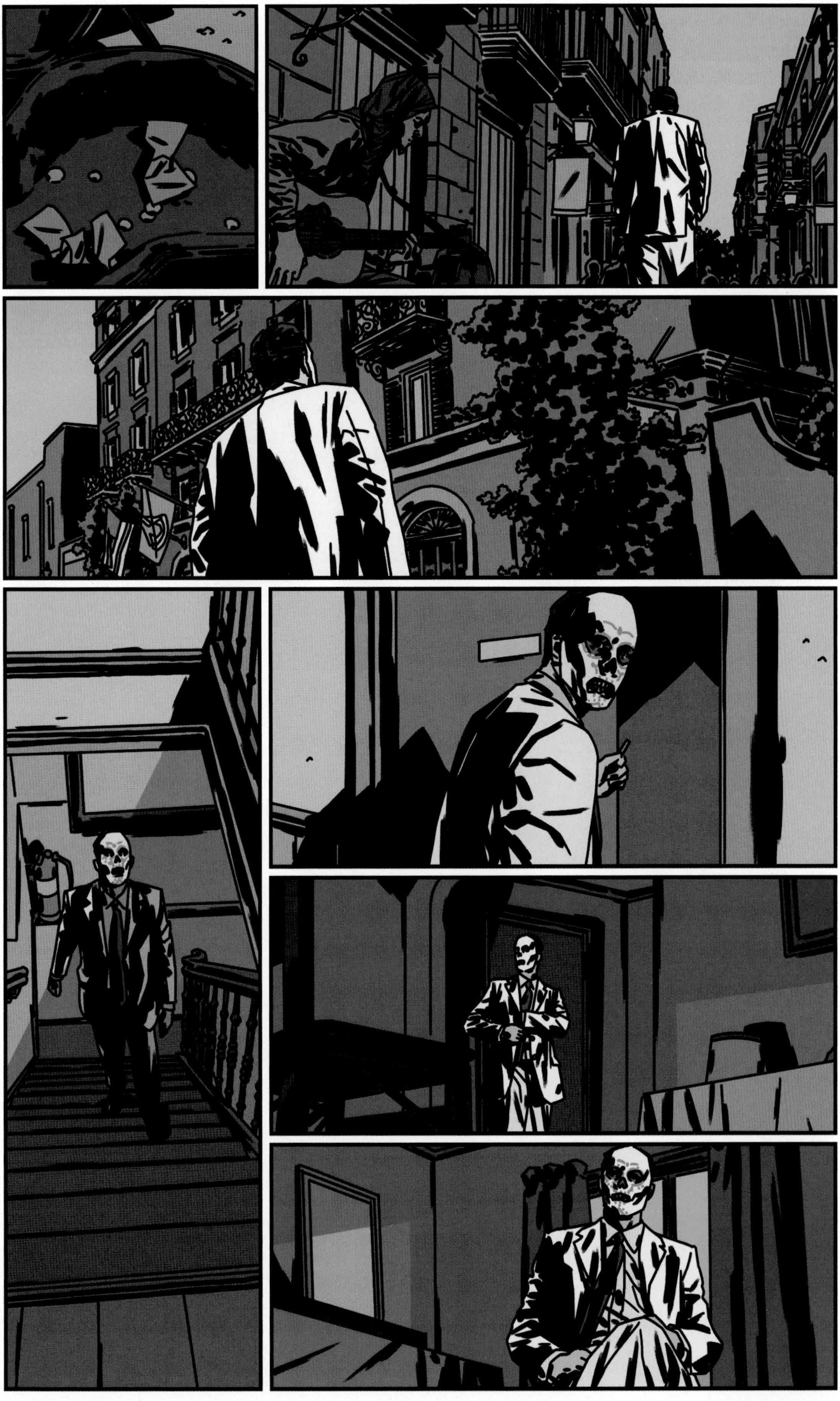

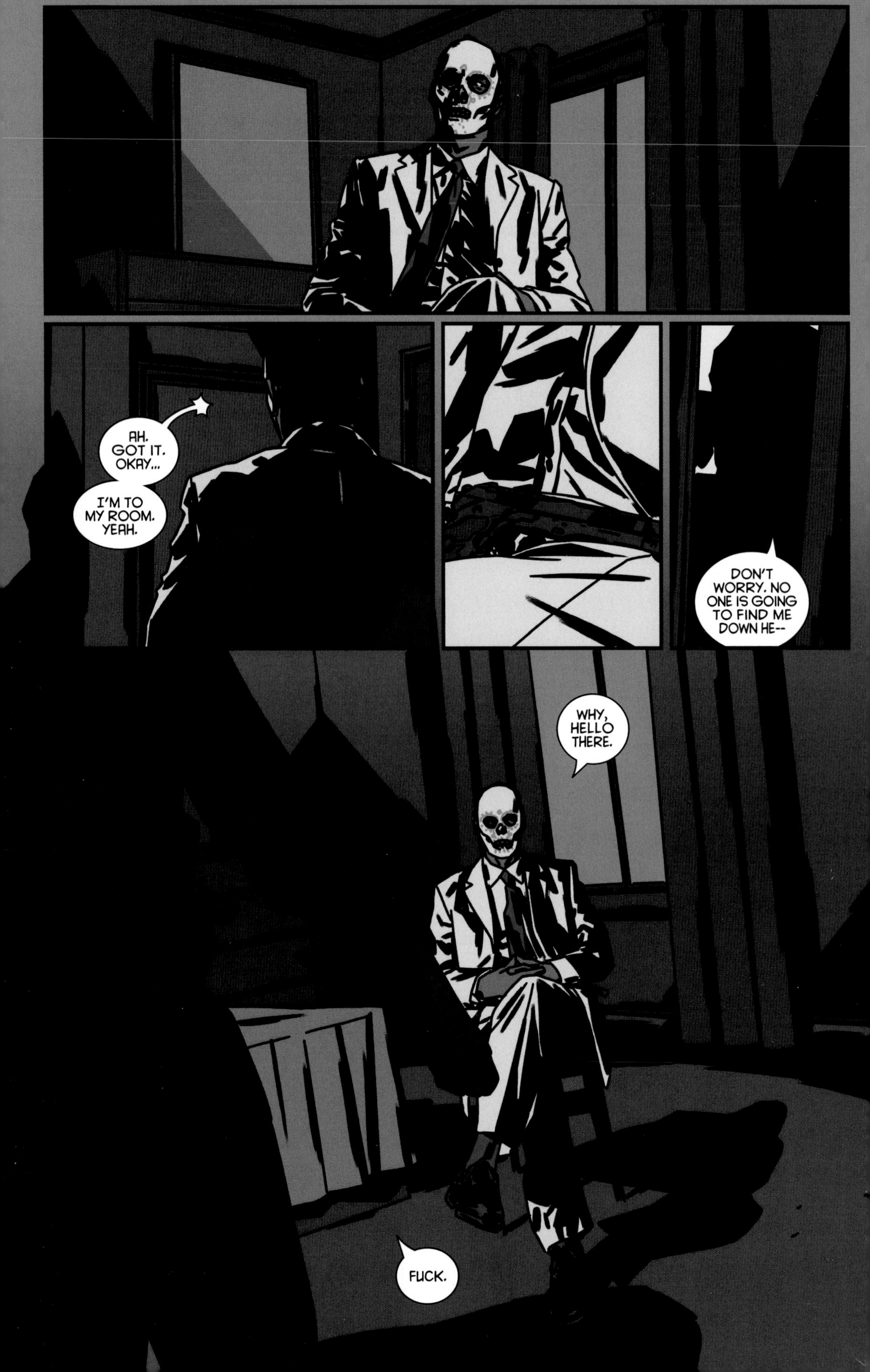
AH. GOT IT. OKAY...
I'M TO MY ROOM. YEAH.
DON'T WORRY. NO ONE IS GOING TO FIND ME DOWN HE--
WHY, HELLO THERE.
FUCK.

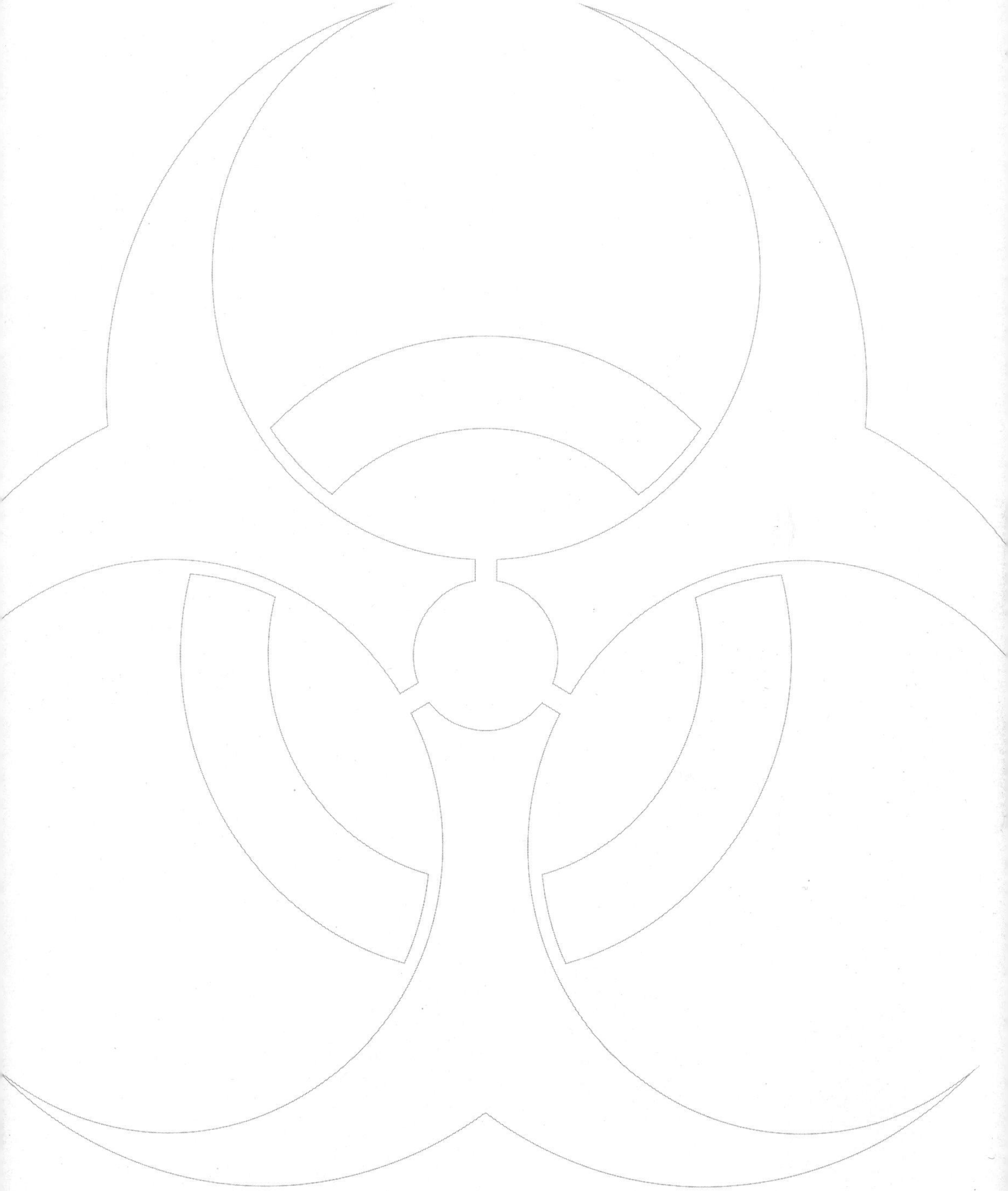

CHAPTER

18

"...AND SO, AFTER HUNDREDS OF HOURS OF INTERVIEWS, RESEARCH, AND REPORTING, AND A YEAR OF PRODUCING THIS PODCAST, WHAT DO WE KNOW FOR CERTAIN?"

WE KNOW THAT JANEY LIED ABOUT THAT EVENING. A LOT. SHE LIED TO HER FRIENDS AND FAMILY, TO US, AND SHE EVEN LIED IN COURT. THAT MAKES HER GUILTY OF PERJURY, BUT DOES IT MAKE HER GUILTY OF MORE?

"TO ME, IT'S NOT ENOUGH. I WOULDN'T CONVICT HER ON THE EVIDENCE THAT EXISTS. I CAN'T. I DON'T SEE HOW ANYONE COULD.

"WHICH MAKES THE FACT THAT SHE'S SITTING IN JAIL RIGHT NOW ALL THE MORE BAFFLING."

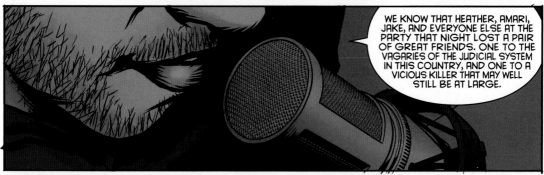

WE KNOW THAT HEATHER, AMARI, JAKE, AND EVERYONE ELSE AT THE PARTY THAT NIGHT LOST A PAIR OF GREAT FRIENDS. ONE TO THE VAGARIES OF THE JUDICIAL SYSTEM IN THIS COUNTRY, AND ONE TO A VICIOUS KILLER THAT MAY WELL STILL BE AT LARGE.

"ABOVE ALL ELSE THOUGH, WE KNOW THAT TARA HARTLEY IS MISSED. NOT JUST BY THOSE FRIENDS, OR HER FAMILY, BUT BY A COMMUNITY SHE HELPED MOLD INTO THE THRIVING CITY IT IS TODAY.

"AND WE KNOW THAT EVERYONE HERE AT THE OFFENSE WISHES PEACE AND CLOSURE TO ALL OF THOSE AFFECTED BY HER DEATH.

"..."

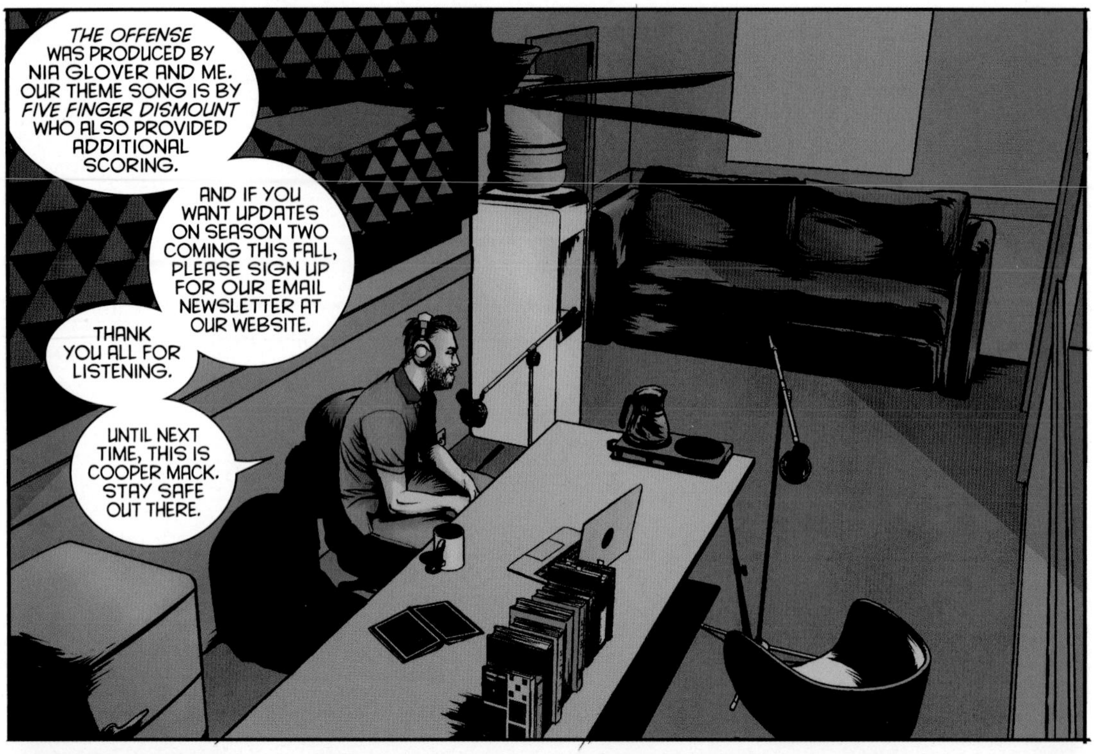
THE OFFENSE WAS PRODUCED BY NIA GLOVER AND ME. OUR THEME SONG IS BY *FIVE FINGER DISMOUNT* WHO ALSO PROVIDED ADDITIONAL SCORING.
AND IF YOU WANT UPDATES ON SEASON TWO COMING THIS FALL, PLEASE SIGN UP FOR OUR EMAIL NEWSLETTER AT OUR WEBSITE.
THANK YOU ALL FOR LISTENING.
UNTIL NEXT TIME, THIS IS COOPER MACK. STAY SAFE OUT THERE.

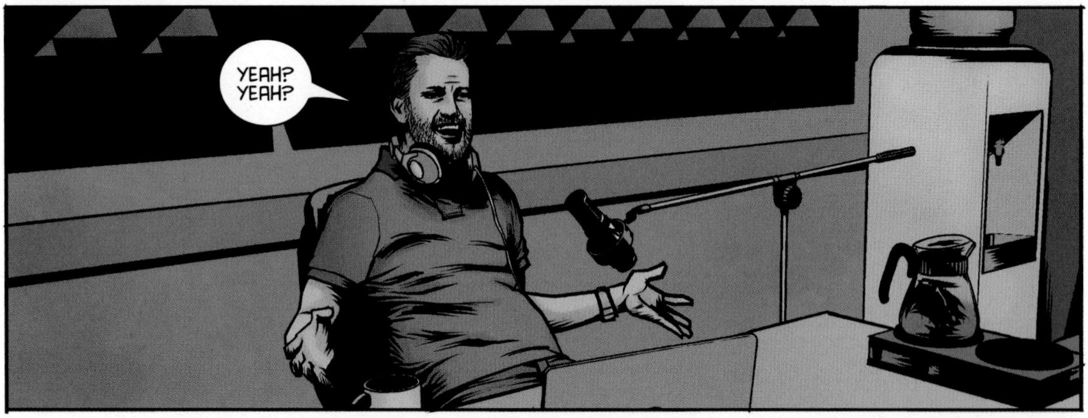
YEAH? YEAH?

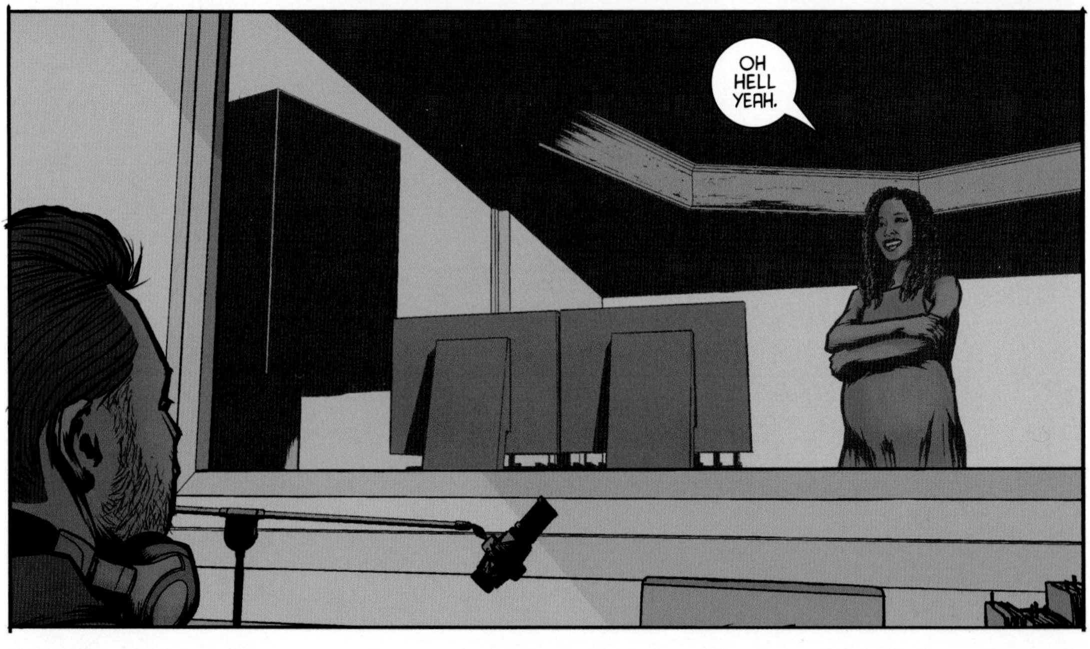
OH HELL YEAH.

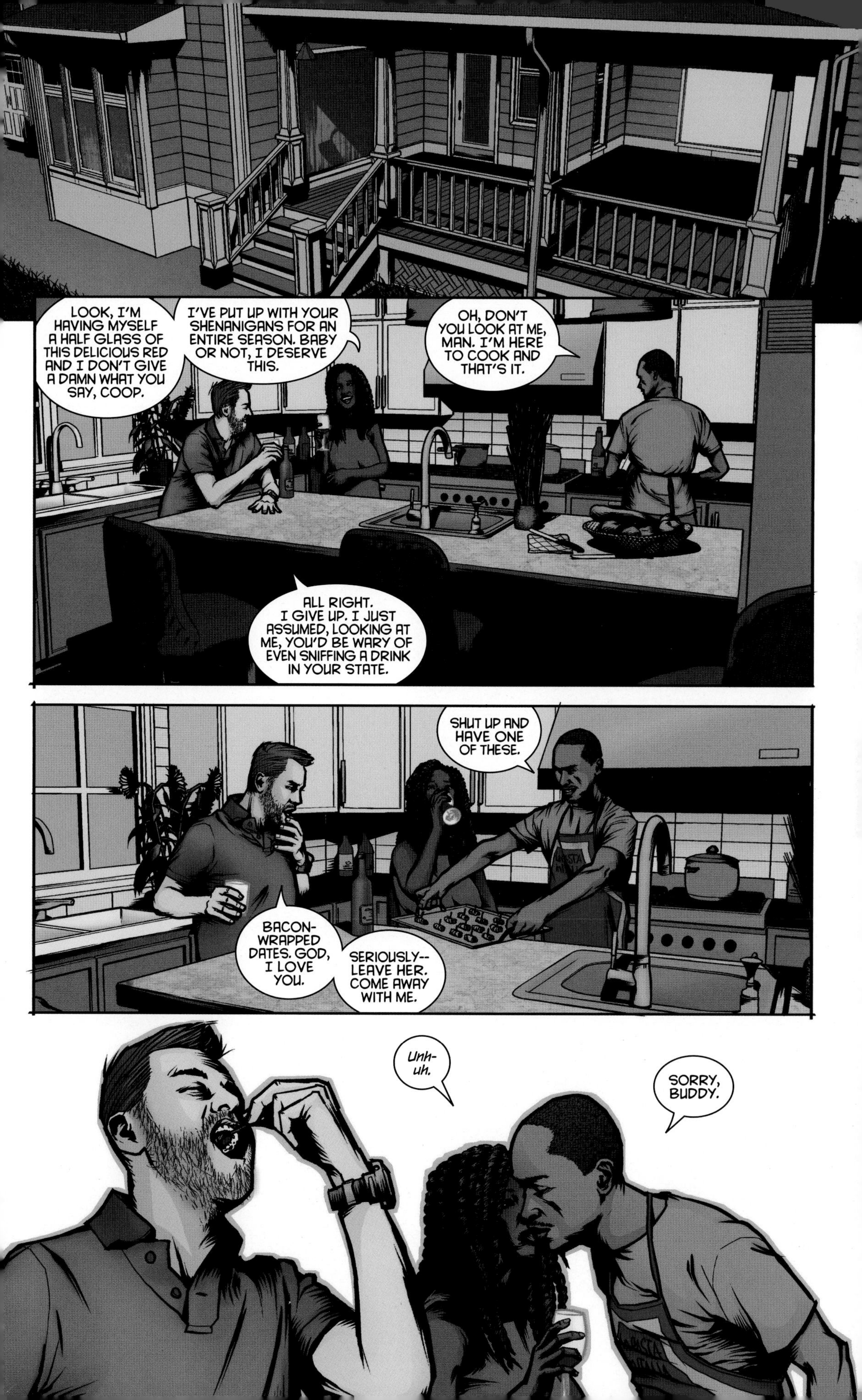
LOOK, I'M HAVING MYSELF A HALF GLASS OF THIS DELICIOUS RED AND I DON'T GIVE A DAMN WHAT YOU SAY, COOP.
I'VE PUT UP WITH YOUR SHENANIGANS FOR AN ENTIRE SEASON. BABY OR NOT, I DESERVE THIS.
OH, DON'T YOU LOOK AT ME, MAN. I'M HERE TO COOK AND THAT'S IT.
ALL RIGHT. I GIVE UP. I JUST ASSUMED, LOOKING AT ME, YOU'D BE WARY OF EVEN SNIFFING A DRINK IN YOUR STATE.
SHUT UP AND HAVE ONE OF THESE.
BACON-WRAPPED DATES. GOD, I LOVE YOU.
SERIOUSLY--LEAVE HER. COME AWAY WITH ME.
Unh-uh.
SORRY, BUDDY.

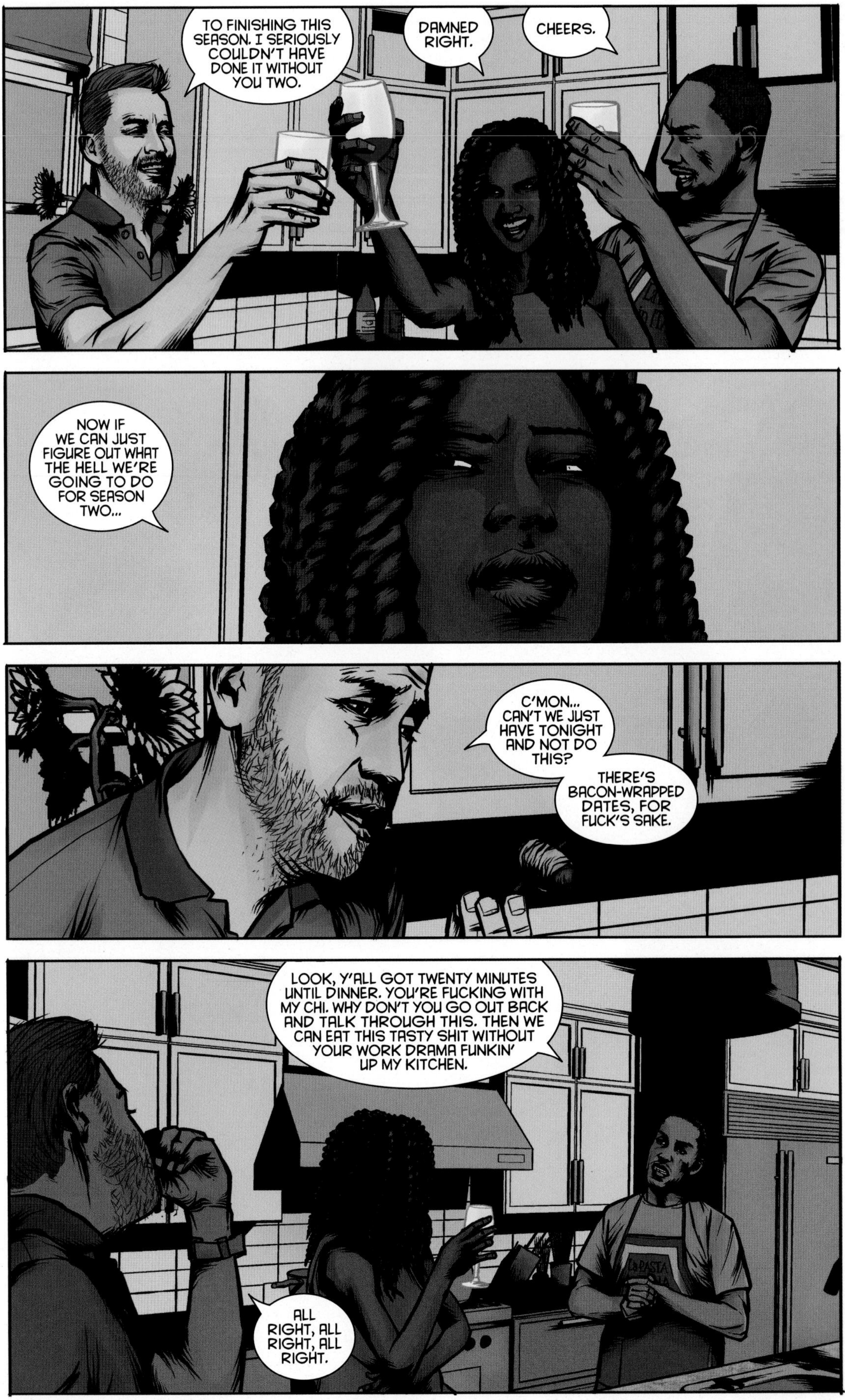
TO FINISHING THIS SEASON. I SERIOUSLY COULDN'T HAVE DONE IT WITHOUT YOU TWO.
DAMNED RIGHT.
CHEERS.
NOW IF WE CAN JUST FIGURE OUT WHAT THE HELL WE'RE GOING TO DO FOR SEASON TWO...
C'MON... CAN'T WE JUST HAVE TONIGHT AND NOT DO THIS?
THERE'S BACON-WRAPPED DATES, FOR FUCK'S SAKE.
LOOK, Y'ALL GOT TWENTY MINUTES UNTIL DINNER. YOU'RE FUCKING WITH MY CHI. WHY DON'T YOU GO OUT BACK AND TALK THROUGH THIS. THEN WE CAN EAT THIS TASTY SHIT WITHOUT YOUR WORK DRAMA FUNKIN' UP MY KITCHEN.
ALL RIGHT, ALL RIGHT, ALL RIGHT.

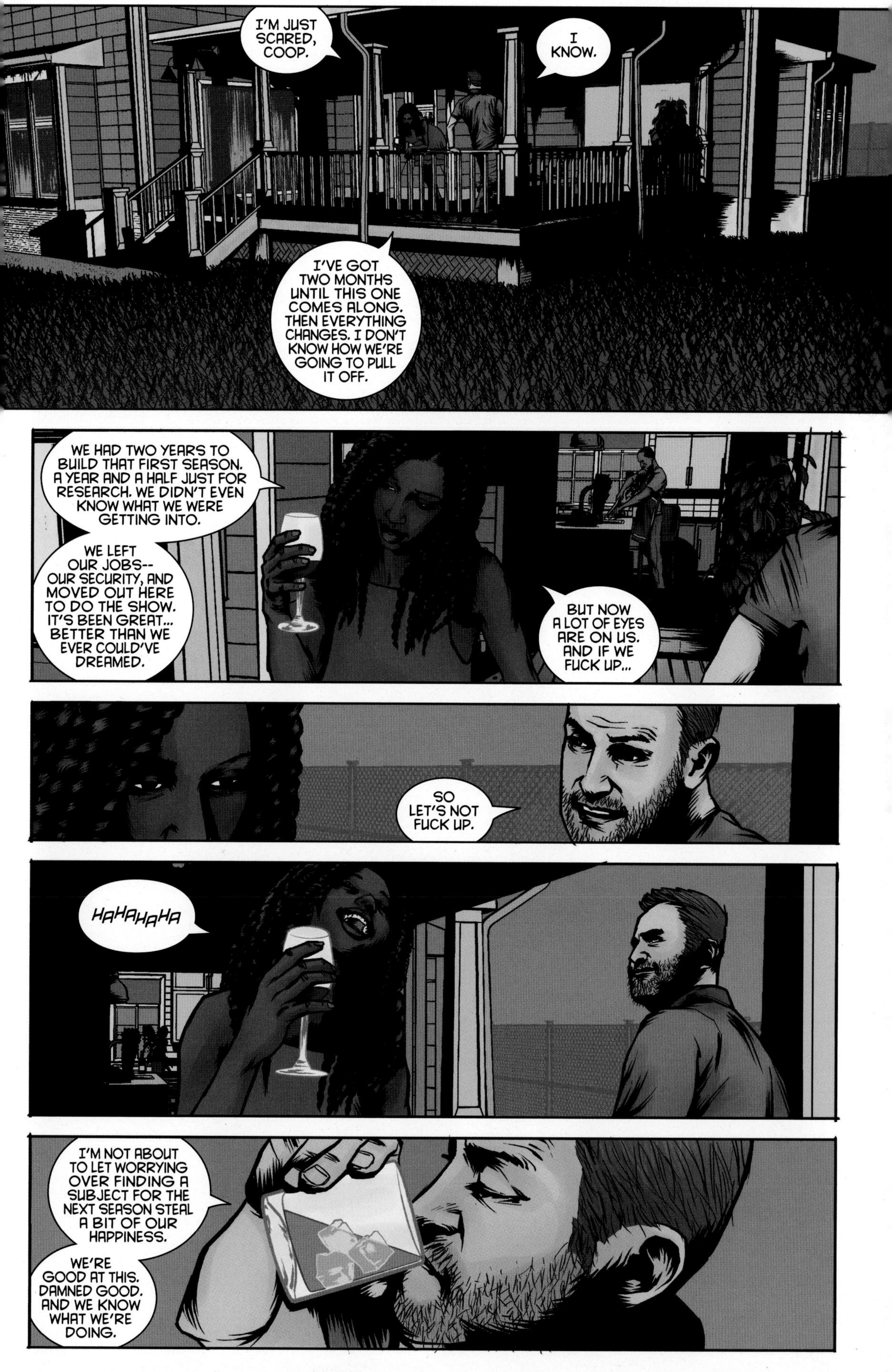
I'M JUST SCARED, COOP.
I KNOW.
I'VE GOT TWO MONTHS UNTIL THIS ONE COMES ALONG. THEN EVERYTHING CHANGES. I DON'T KNOW HOW WE'RE GOING TO PULL IT OFF.
WE HAD TWO YEARS TO BUILD THAT FIRST SEASON. A YEAR AND A HALF JUST FOR RESEARCH. WE DIDN'T EVEN KNOW WHAT WE WERE GETTING INTO.
WE LEFT OUR JOBS-- OUR SECURITY, AND MOVED OUT HERE TO DO THE SHOW. IT'S BEEN GREAT... BETTER THAN WE EVER COULD'VE DREAMED.
BUT NOW A LOT OF EYES ARE ON US. AND IF WE FUCK UP...
SO LET'S NOT FUCK UP.
HAHAHAHAHA
I'M NOT ABOUT TO LET WORRYING OVER FINDING A SUBJECT FOR THE NEXT SEASON STEAL A BIT OF OUR HAPPINESS.
WE'RE GOOD AT THIS. DAMNED GOOD. AND WE KNOW WHAT WE'RE DOING.

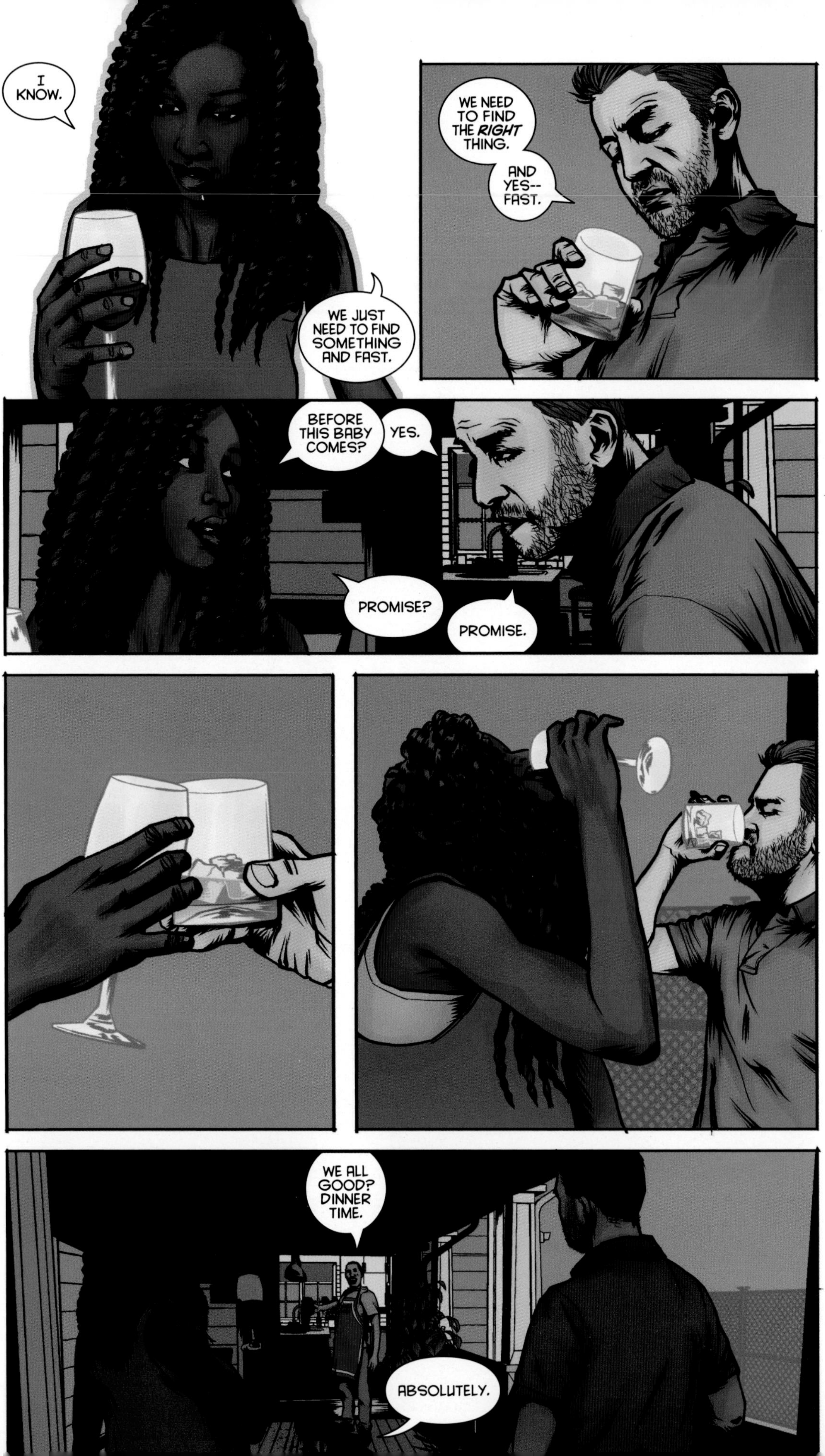
I KNOW.
WE NEED TO FIND THE *RIGHT* THING.
AND YES-- FAST.
WE JUST NEED TO FIND SOMETHING AND FAST.
BEFORE THIS BABY COMES?
YES.
PROMISE?
PROMISE.
WE ALL GOOD? DINNER TIME.
ABSOLUTELY.

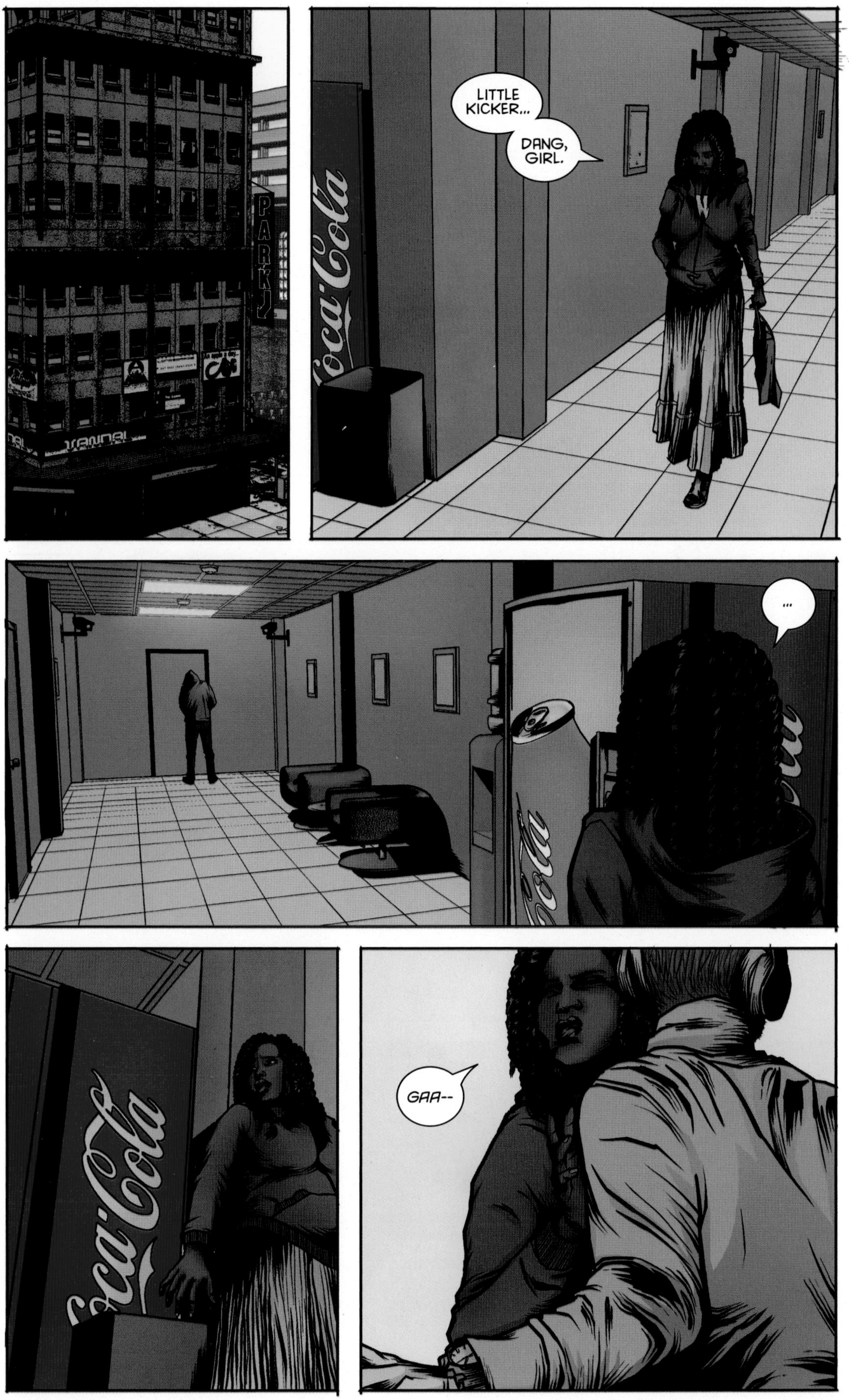
PARK
Coca-Cola
LITTLE KICKER...
DANG, GIRL.
...
GAA--

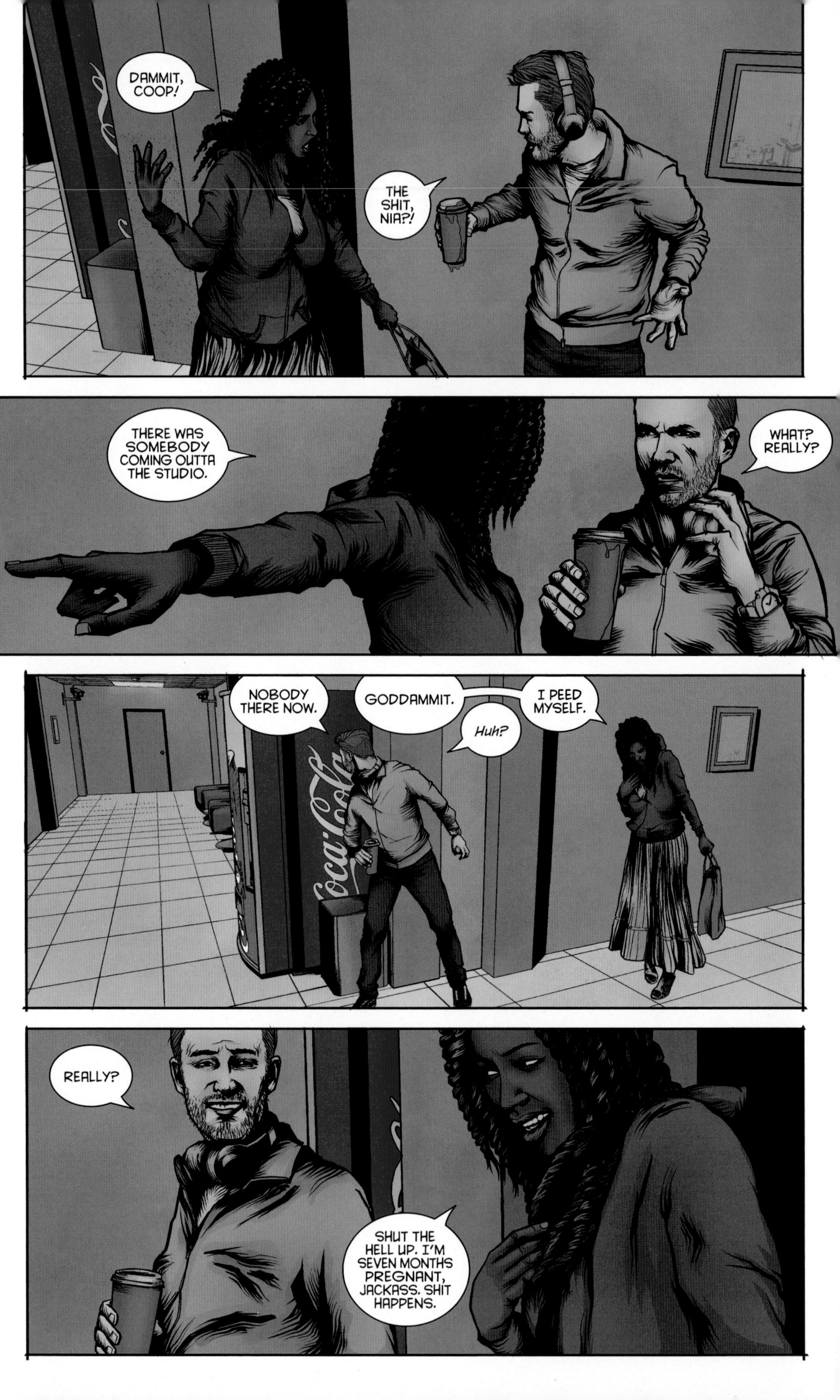

DAMMIT, COOP!
THE SHIT, NIA?!
THERE WAS SOMEBODY COMING OUTTA THE STUDIO.
WHAT? REALLY?
NOBODY THERE NOW.
GODDAMMIT.
I PEED MYSELF.
Huh?
REALLY?
SHUT THE HELL UP. I'M SEVEN MONTHS PREGNANT, JACKASS. SHIT HAPPENS.

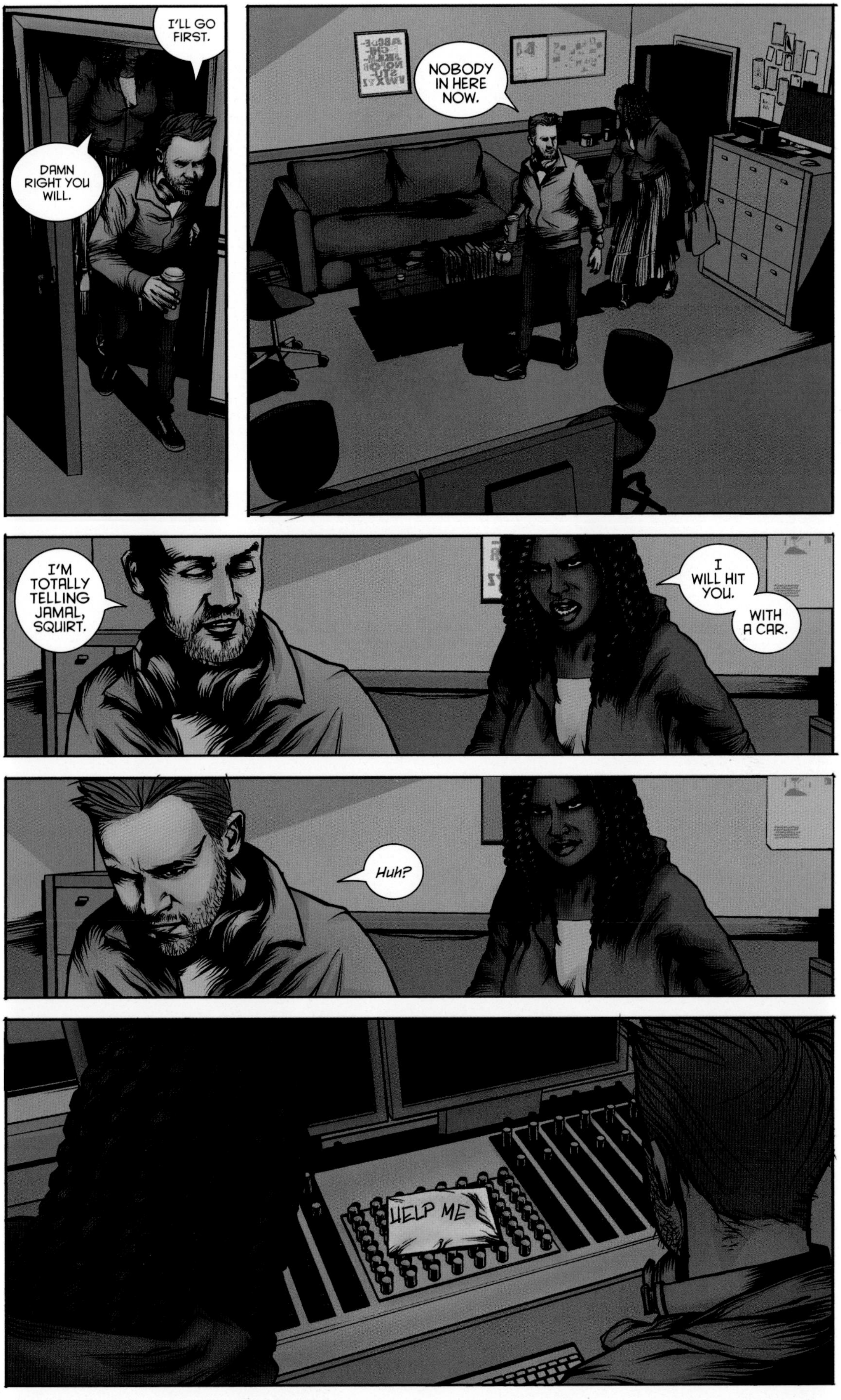
I'LL GO FIRST.
DAMN RIGHT YOU WILL.
NOBODY IN HERE NOW.
I'M TOTALLY TELLING JAMAL, SQUIRT.
I WILL HIT YOU.
WITH A CAR.
Huh?
HELP ME

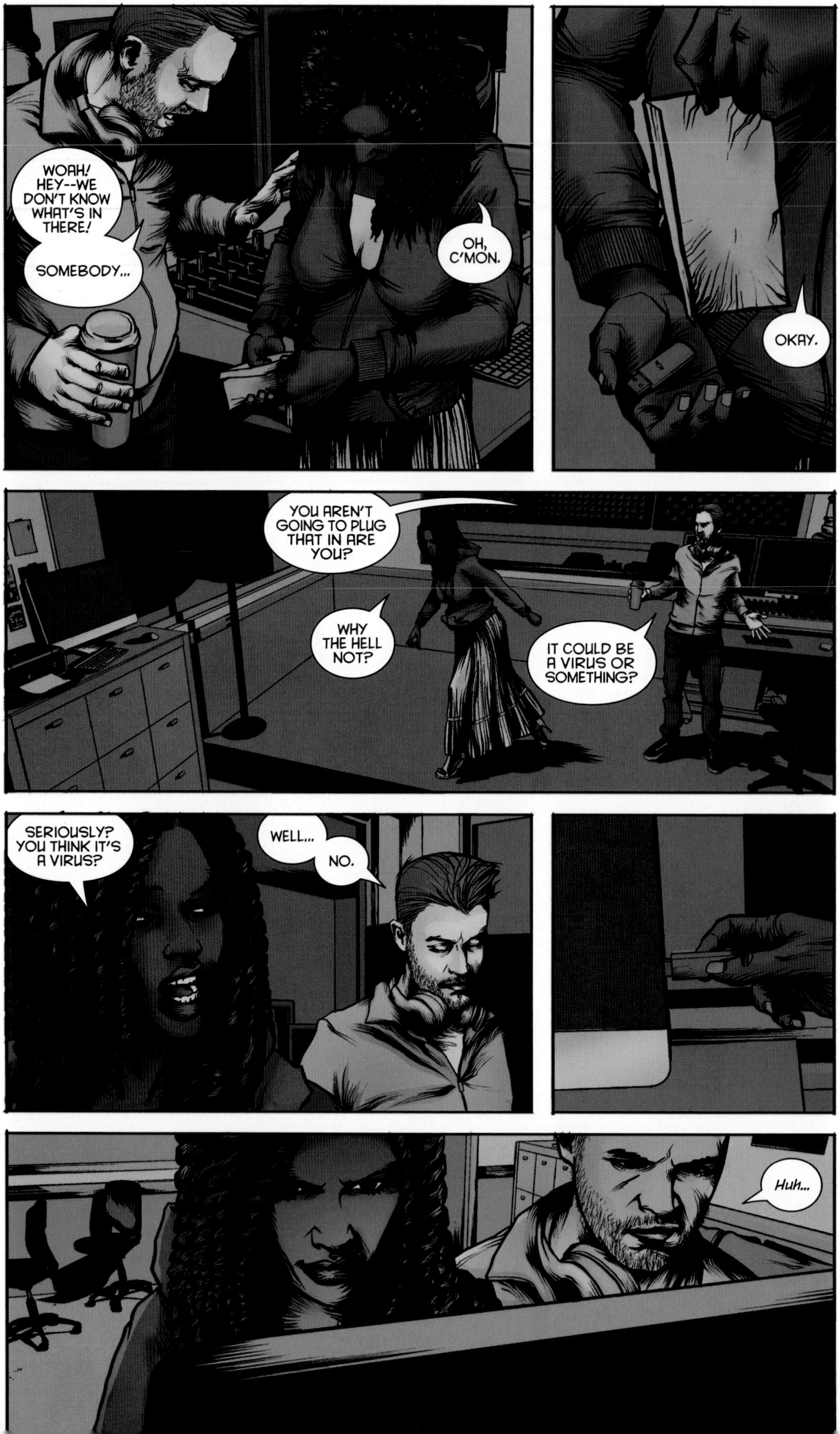
WOAH! HEY--WE DON'T KNOW WHAT'S IN THERE!
SOMEBODY...
OH, C'MON.
OKAY.
YOU AREN'T GOING TO PLUG THAT IN ARE YOU?
WHY THE HELL NOT?
IT COULD BE A VIRUS OR SOMETHING?
SERIOUSLY? YOU THINK IT'S A VIRUS?
WELL...
NO.
Huh...

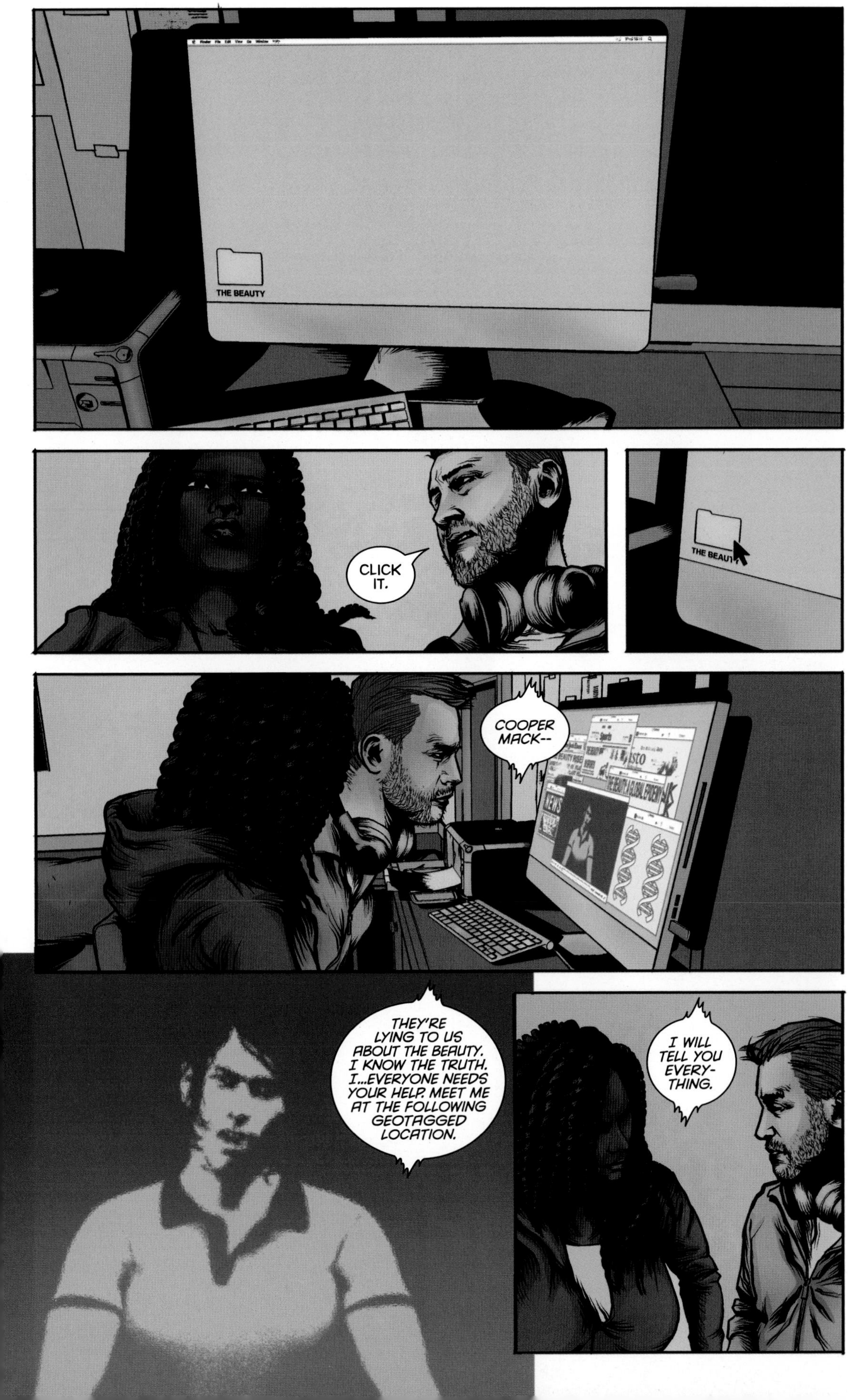
THE BEAUTY
CLICK IT.
COOPER MACK--
THEY'RE LYING TO US ABOUT THE BEAUTY. I KNOW THE TRUTH. I...EVERYONE NEEDS YOUR HELP. MEET ME AT THE FOLLOWING GEOTAGGED LOCATION.
I WILL TELL YOU EVERY-THING.

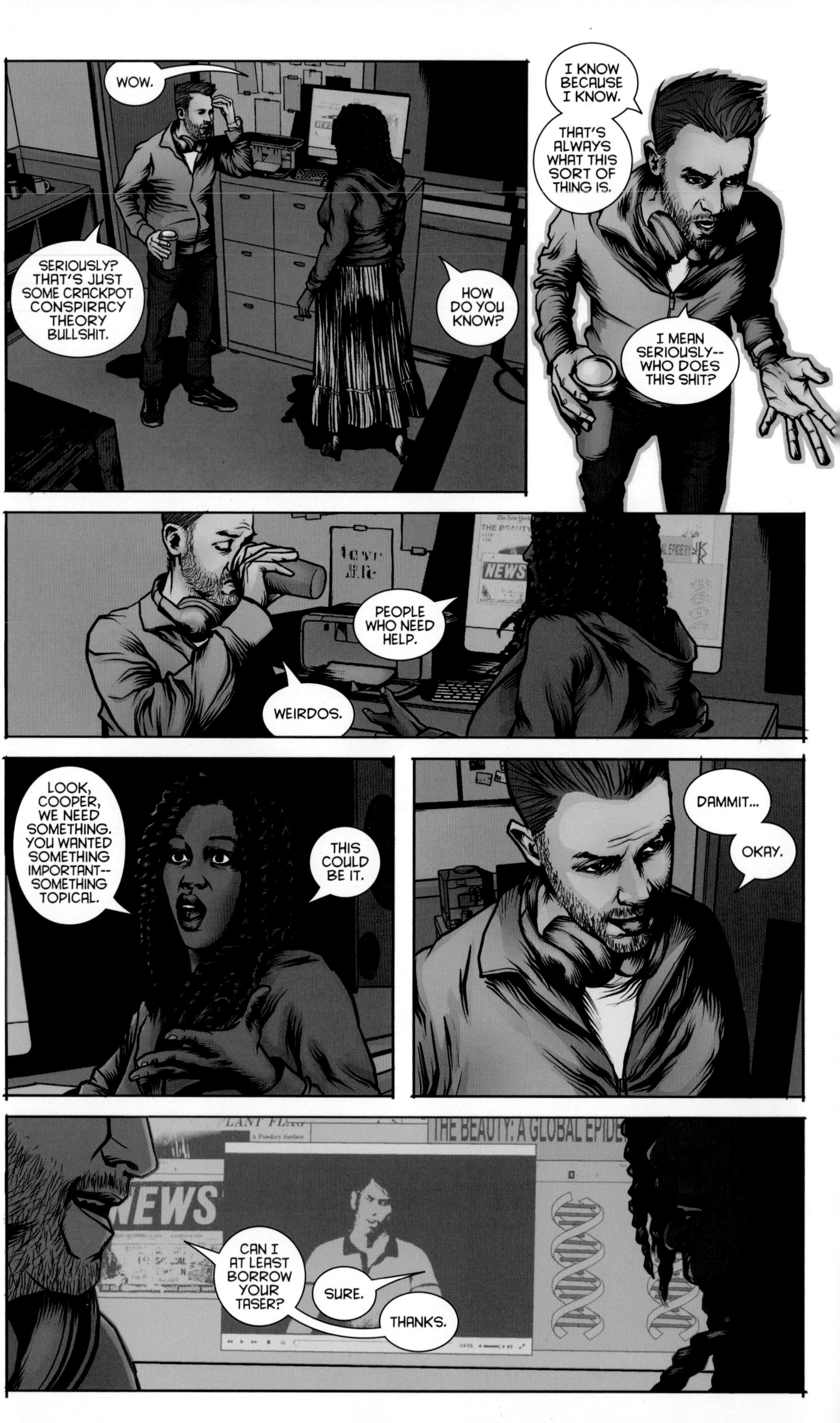
WOW.
SERIOUSLY? THAT'S JUST SOME CRACKPOT CONSPIRACY THEORY BULLSHIT.
HOW DO YOU KNOW?
I KNOW BECAUSE I KNOW.
THAT'S ALWAYS WHAT THIS SORT OF THING IS.
I MEAN SERIOUSLY-- WHO DOES THIS SHIT?
PEOPLE WHO NEED HELP.
WEIRDOS.
NEWS
LOOK, COOPER, WE NEED SOMETHING. YOU WANTED SOMETHING IMPORTANT-- SOMETHING TOPICAL.
THIS COULD BE IT.
DAMMIT...
OKAY.
THE BEAUTY: A GLOBAL EPIDE
A Powdery Surface
NEWS
CAN I AT LEAST BORROW YOUR TASER?
SURE.
THANKS.

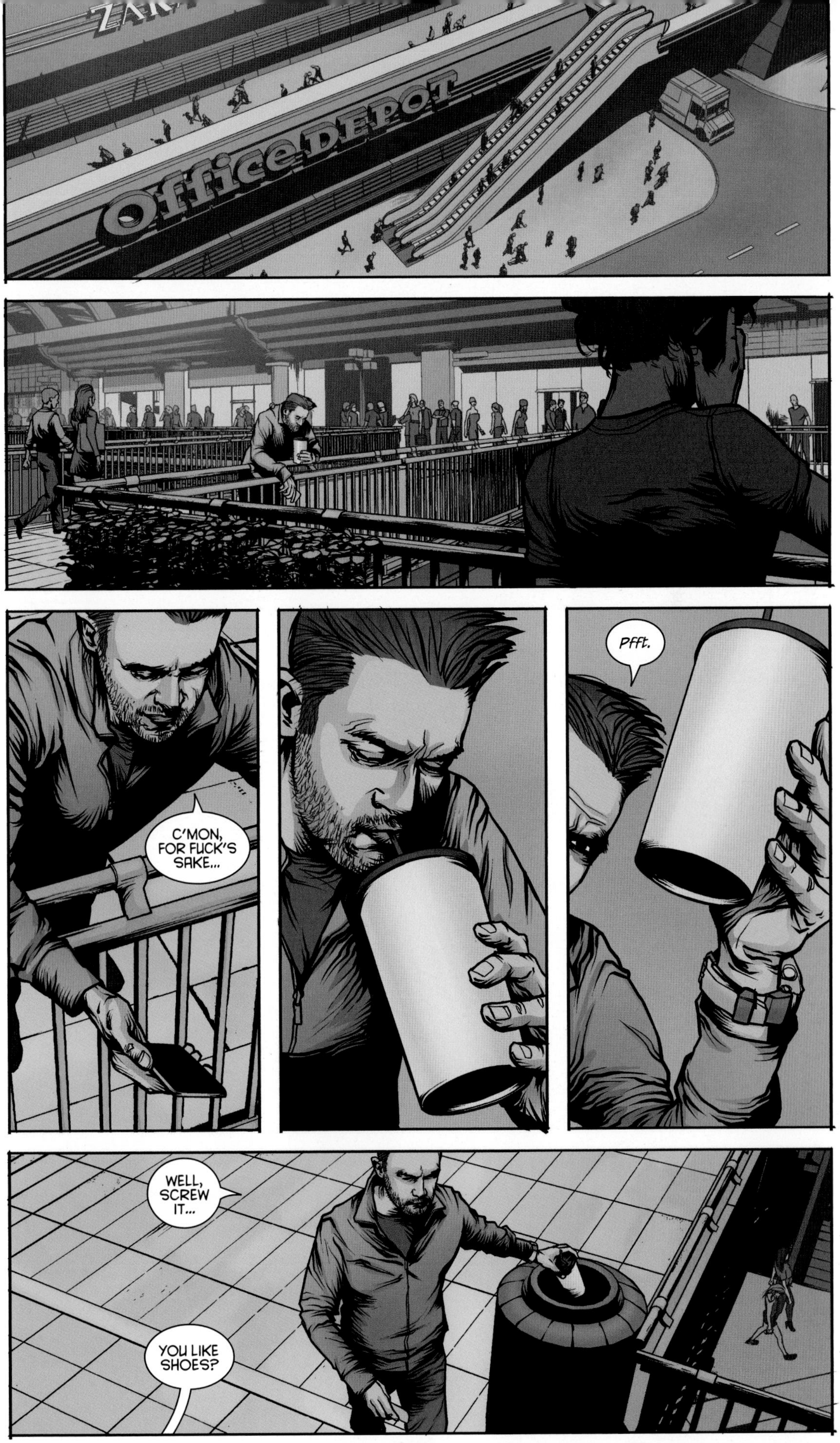

Office DEPOT
C'MON, FOR FUCK'S SAKE...
Pfft.
WELL, SCREW IT...
YOU LIKE SHOES?

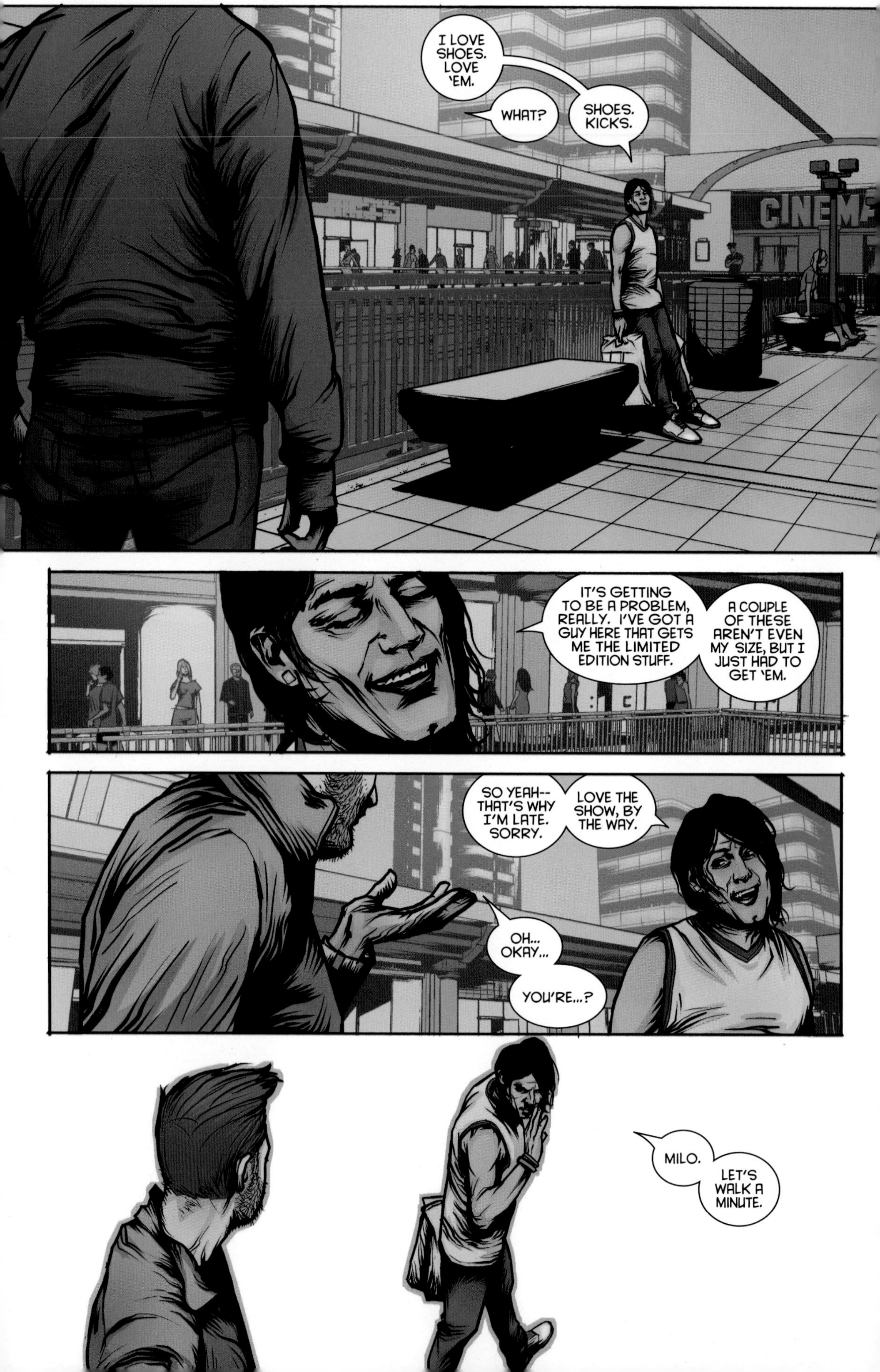
I LOVE SHOES. LOVE 'EM.
WHAT?
SHOES. KICKS.
IT'S GETTING TO BE A PROBLEM, REALLY. I'VE GOT A GUY HERE THAT GETS ME THE LIMITED EDITION STUFF.
A COUPLE OF THESE AREN'T EVEN MY SIZE, BUT I JUST HAD TO GET 'EM.
SO YEAH-- THAT'S WHY I'M LATE. SORRY.
LOVE THE SHOW, BY THE WAY.
OH... OKAY...
YOU'RE...?
MILO.
LET'S WALK A MINUTE.
CINEMA

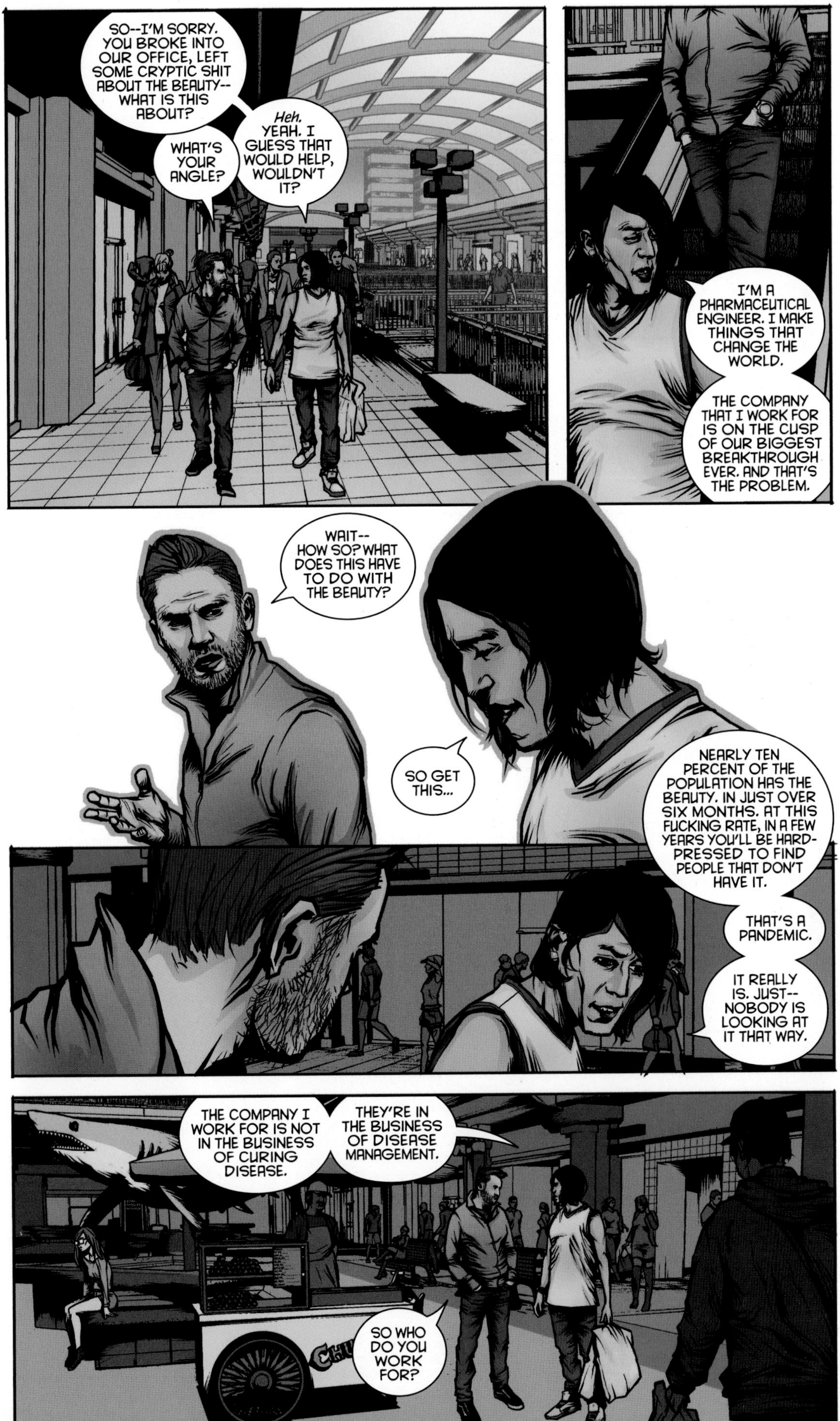
SO--I'M SORRY. YOU BROKE INTO OUR OFFICE, LEFT SOME CRYPTIC SHIT ABOUT THE BEAUTY--WHAT IS THIS ABOUT?
WHAT'S YOUR ANGLE?
Heh. YEAH. I GUESS THAT WOULD HELP, WOULDN'T IT?
I'M A PHARMACEUTICAL ENGINEER. I MAKE THINGS THAT CHANGE THE WORLD.
THE COMPANY THAT I WORK FOR IS ON THE CUSP OF OUR BIGGEST BREAKTHROUGH EVER. AND THAT'S THE PROBLEM.
WAIT--HOW SO? WHAT DOES THIS HAVE TO DO WITH THE BEAUTY?
SO GET THIS...
NEARLY TEN PERCENT OF THE POPULATION HAS THE BEAUTY. IN JUST OVER SIX MONTHS. AT THIS FUCKING RATE, IN A FEW YEARS YOU'LL BE HARD-PRESSED TO FIND PEOPLE THAT DON'T HAVE IT.
THAT'S A PANDEMIC.
IT REALLY IS. JUST--NOBODY IS LOOKING AT IT THAT WAY.
THE COMPANY I WORK FOR IS NOT IN THE BUSINESS OF CURING DISEASE.
THEY'RE IN THE BUSINESS OF DISEASE MANAGEMENT.
SO WHO DO YOU WORK FOR?

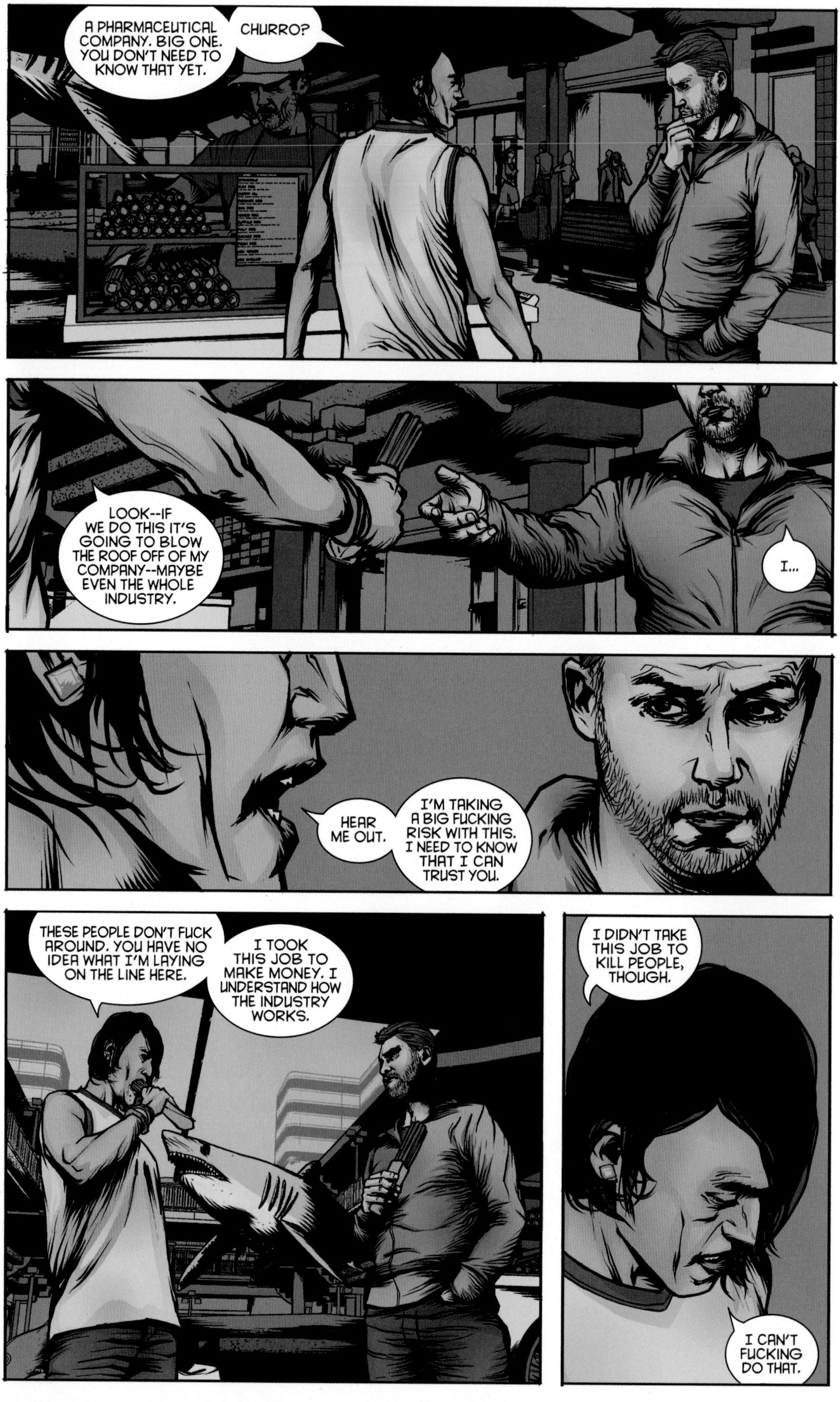
A PHARMACEUTICAL COMPANY. BIG ONE. YOU DON'T NEED TO KNOW THAT YET.
CHURRO?
LOOK--IF WE DO THIS IT'S GOING TO BLOW THE ROOF OFF OF MY COMPANY--MAYBE EVEN THE WHOLE INDUSTRY.
I...
HEAR ME OUT.
I'M TAKING A BIG FUCKING RISK WITH THIS. I NEED TO KNOW THAT I CAN TRUST YOU.
THESE PEOPLE DON'T FUCK AROUND. YOU HAVE NO IDEA WHAT I'M LAYING ON THE LINE HERE.
I TOOK THIS JOB TO MAKE MONEY. I UNDERSTAND HOW THE INDUSTRY WORKS.
I DIDN'T TAKE THIS JOB TO KILL PEOPLE, THOUGH.
I CAN'T FUCKING DO THAT.

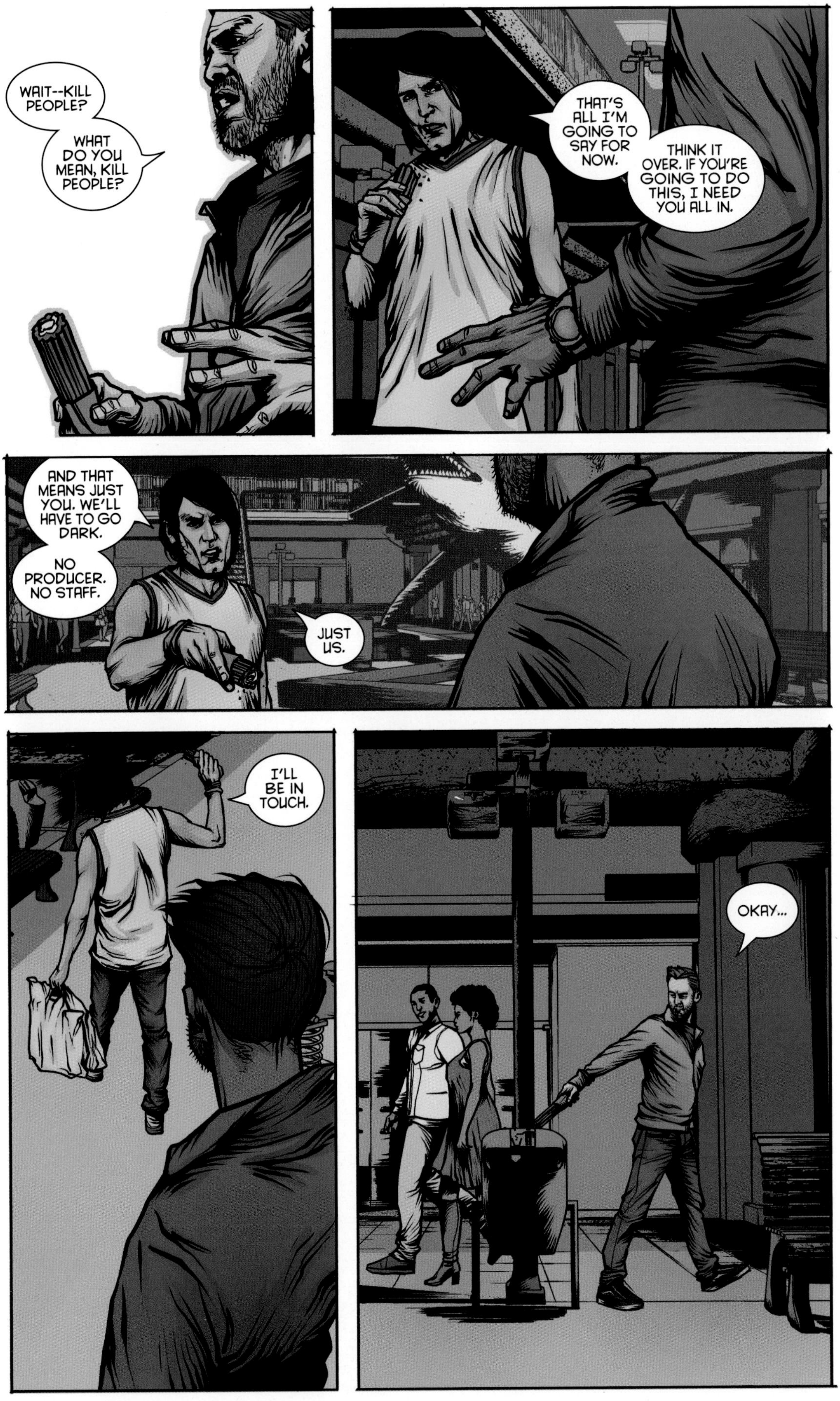
WAIT--KILL PEOPLE?
WHAT DO YOU MEAN, KILL PEOPLE?
THAT'S ALL I'M GOING TO SAY FOR NOW.
THINK IT OVER. IF YOU'RE GOING TO DO THIS, I NEED YOU ALL IN.
AND THAT MEANS JUST YOU. WE'LL HAVE TO GO DARK.
NO PRODUCER. NO STAFF.
JUST US.
I'LL BE IN TOUCH.
OKAY...

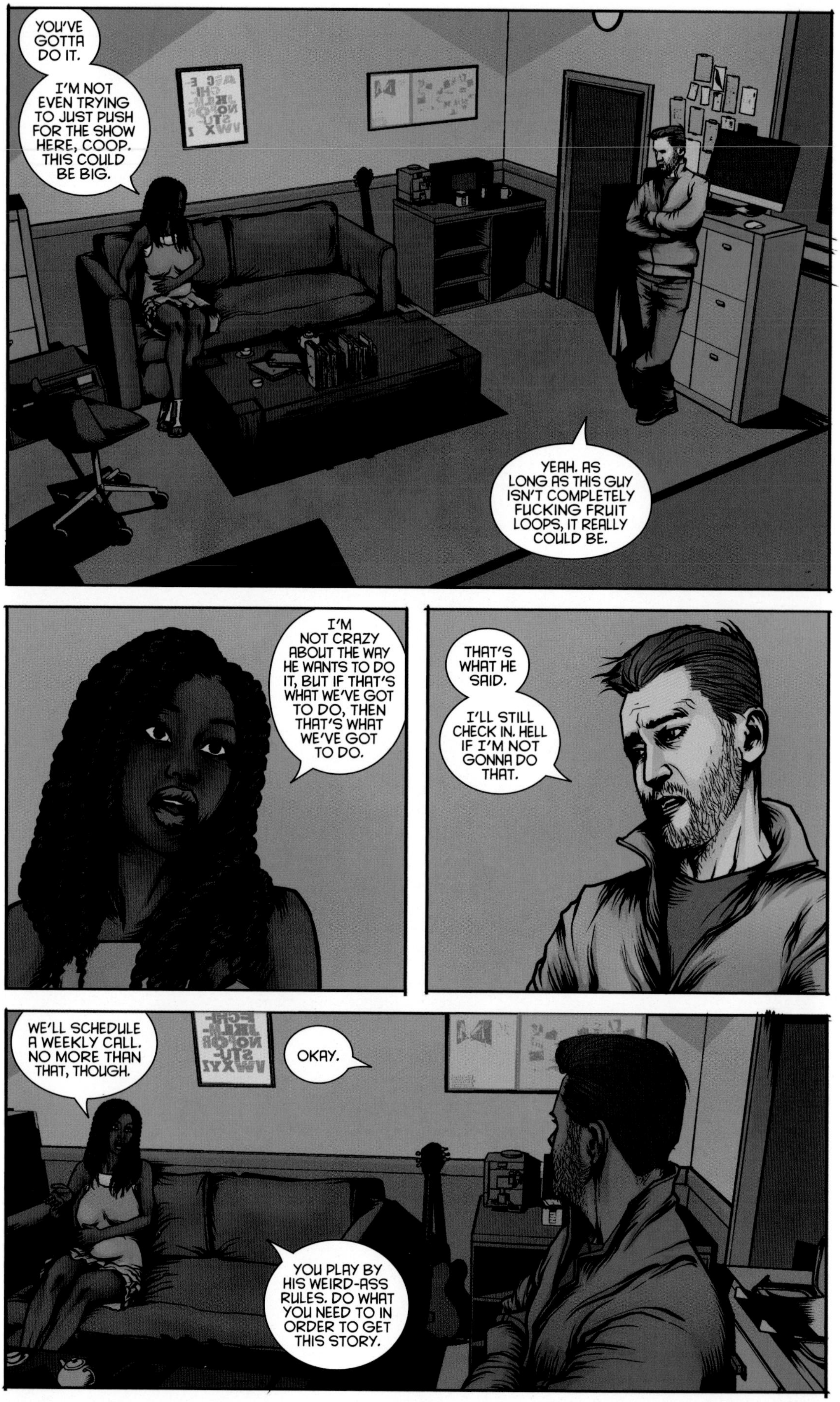
YOU'VE GOTTA DO IT.
I'M NOT EVEN TRYING TO JUST PUSH FOR THE SHOW HERE, COOP. THIS COULD BE BIG.
YEAH. AS LONG AS THIS GUY ISN'T COMPLETELY FUCKING FRUIT LOOPS, IT REALLY COULD BE.
I'M NOT CRAZY ABOUT THE WAY HE WANTS TO DO IT, BUT IF THAT'S WHAT WE'VE GOT TO DO, THEN THAT'S WHAT WE'VE GOT TO DO.
THAT'S WHAT HE SAID.
I'LL STILL CHECK IN. HELL IF I'M NOT GONNA DO THAT.
WE'LL SCHEDULE A WEEKLY CALL. NO MORE THAN THAT, THOUGH.
OKAY.
YOU PLAY BY HIS WEIRD-ASS RULES. DO WHAT YOU NEED TO IN ORDER TO GET THIS STORY.

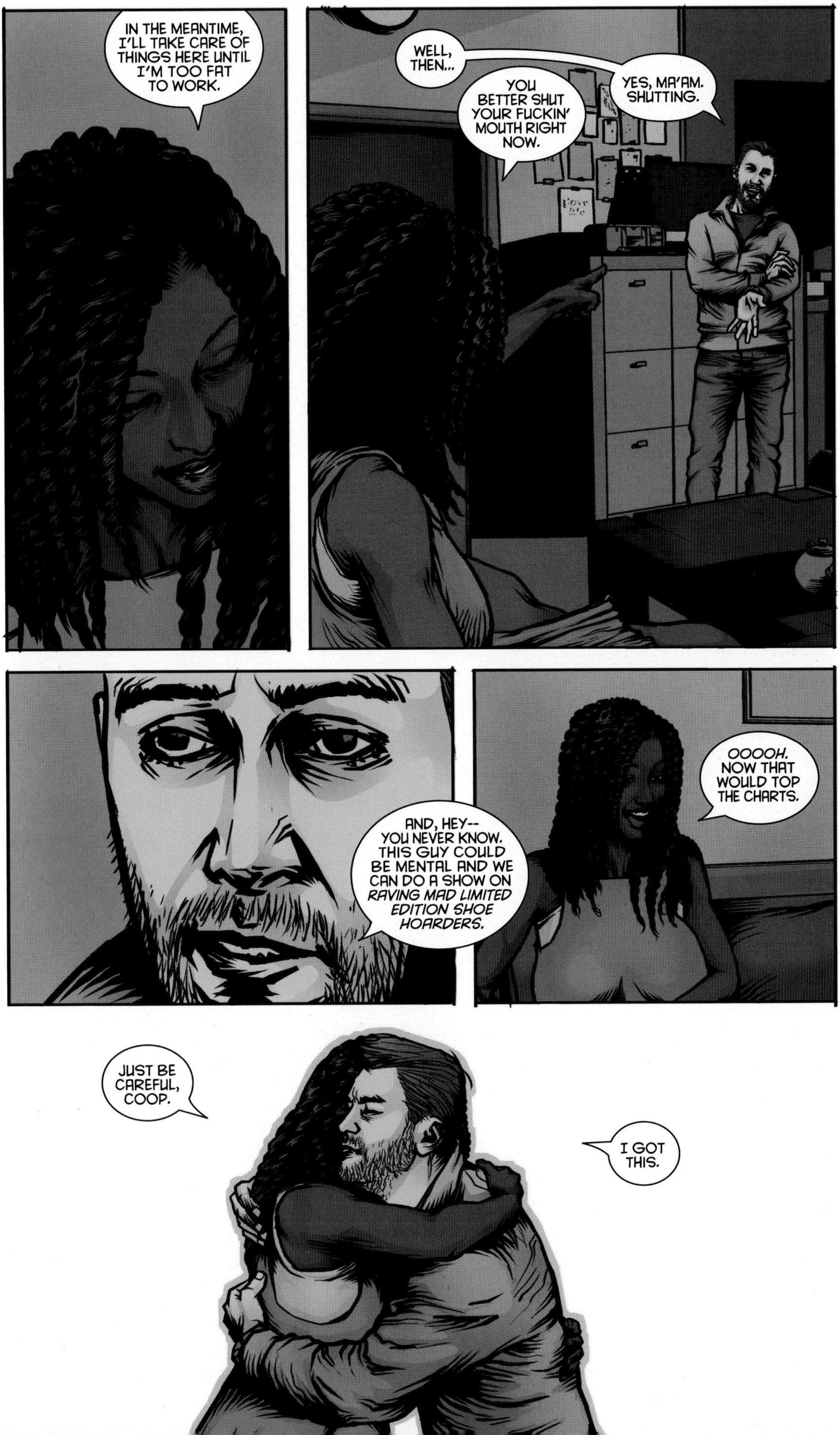
IN THE MEANTIME, I'LL TAKE CARE OF THINGS HERE UNTIL I'M TOO FAT TO WORK.
WELL, THEN...
YOU BETTER SHUT YOUR FUCKIN' MOUTH RIGHT NOW.
YES, MA'AM. SHUTTING.
AND, HEY-- YOU NEVER KNOW. THIS GUY COULD BE MENTAL AND WE CAN DO A SHOW ON *RAVING MAD LIMITED EDITION SHOE HOARDERS.*
OOOOH. NOW THAT WOULD TOP THE CHARTS.
JUST BE CAREFUL, COOP.
I GOT THIS.

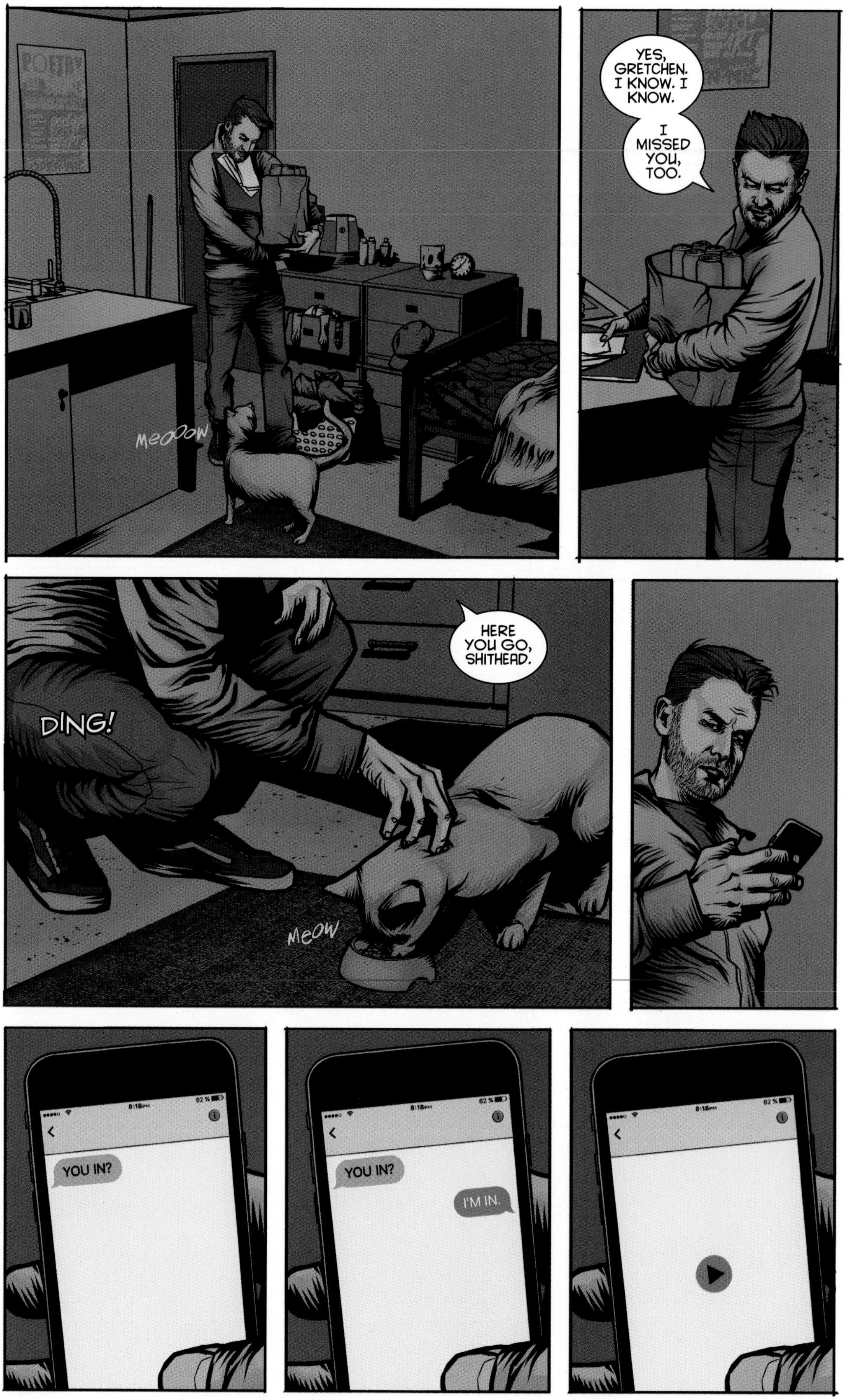
MEOOOW
YES, GRETCHEN. I KNOW. I KNOW.
I MISSED YOU, TOO.
DING!
HERE YOU GO, SHITHEAD.
MEOW
8:18PM
62 %
YOU IN?
8:18PM
62 %
YOU IN?
I'M IN.
8:18PM
62 %

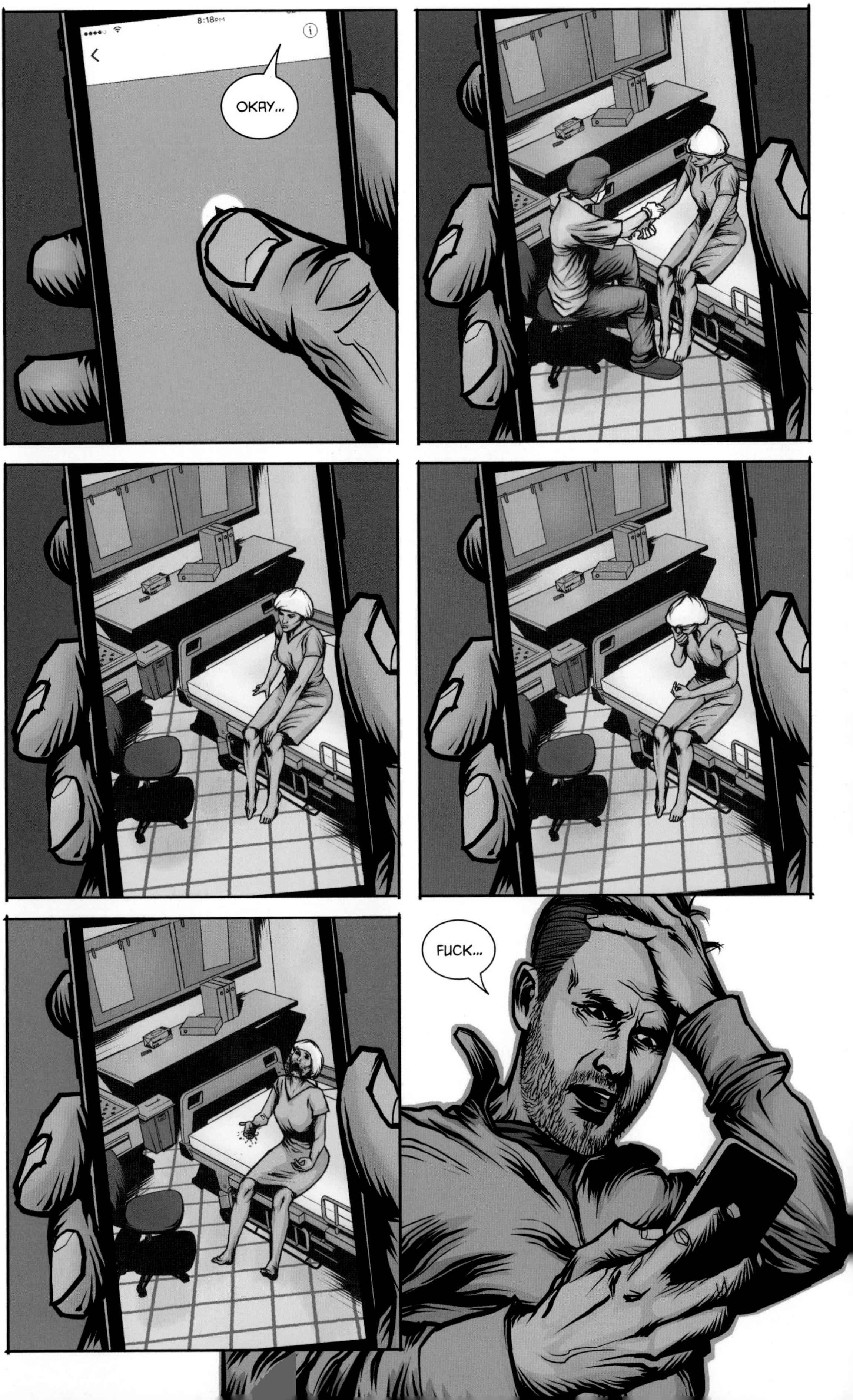
8:18PM
OKAY...
FUCK...

CHAPTER

19

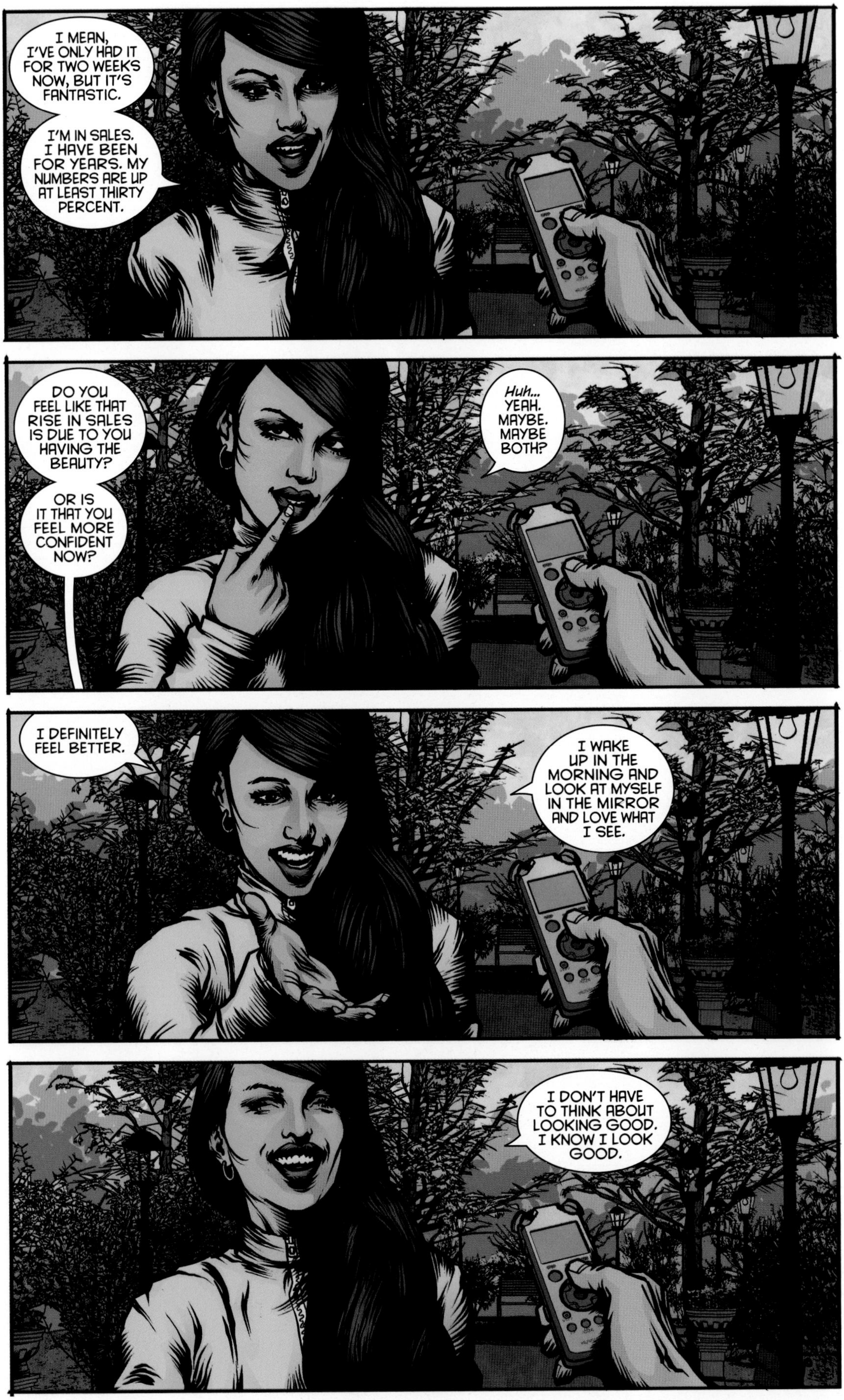
I MEAN, I'VE ONLY HAD IT FOR TWO WEEKS NOW, BUT IT'S FANTASTIC.
I'M IN SALES. I HAVE BEEN FOR YEARS. MY NUMBERS ARE UP AT LEAST THIRTY PERCENT.
DO YOU FEEL LIKE THAT RISE IN SALES IS DUE TO YOU HAVING THE BEAUTY?
OR IS IT THAT YOU FEEL MORE CONFIDENT NOW?
Huh... YEAH. MAYBE. MAYBE BOTH?
I DEFINITELY FEEL BETTER.
I WAKE UP IN THE MORNING AND LOOK AT MYSELF IN THE MIRROR AND LOVE WHAT I SEE.
I DON'T HAVE TO THINK ABOUT LOOKING GOOD. I KNOW I LOOK GOOD.

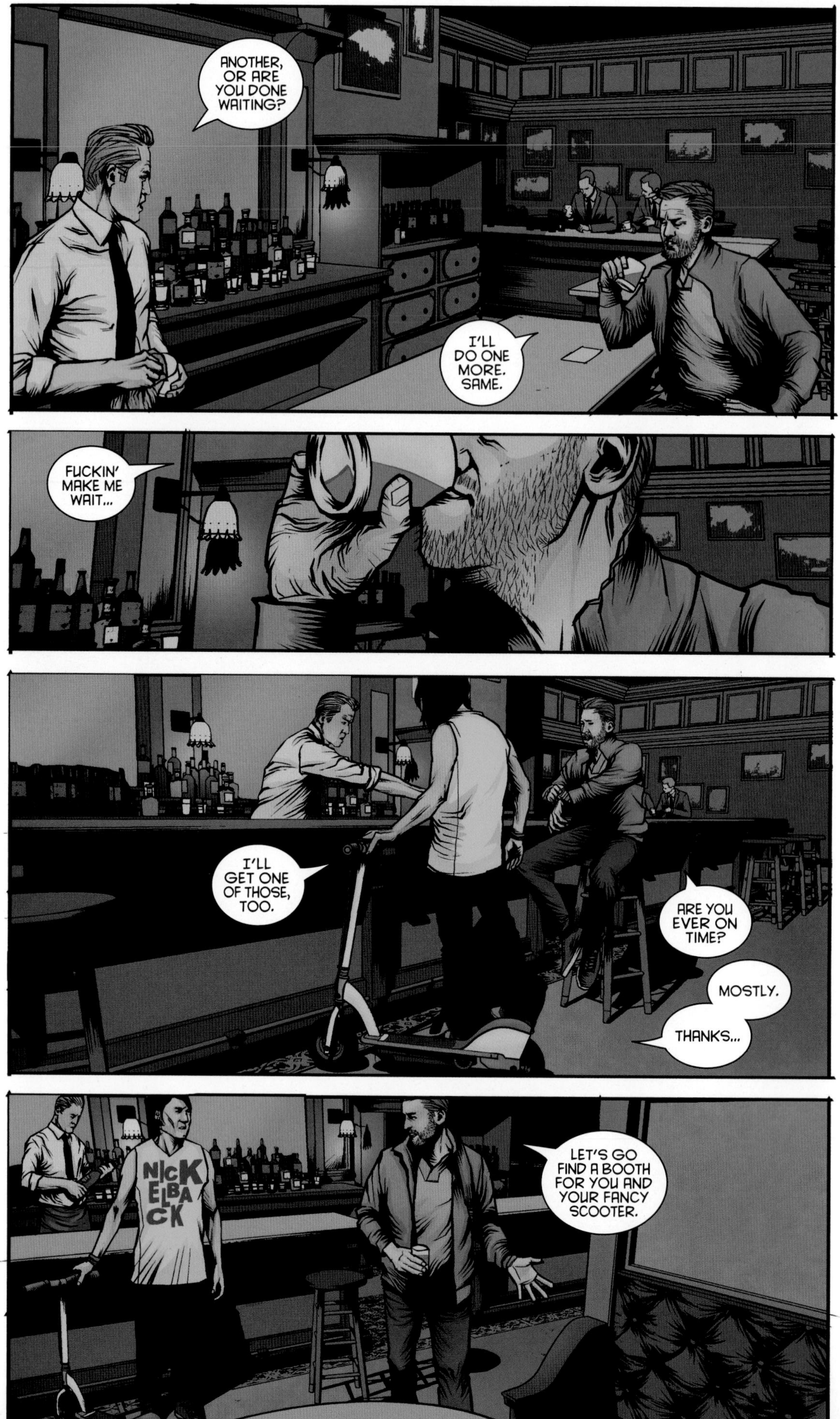
ANOTHER, OR ARE YOU DONE WAITING?
I'LL DO ONE MORE. SAME.
FUCKIN' MAKE ME WAIT...
I'LL GET ONE OF THOSE, TOO.
ARE YOU EVER ON TIME?
MOSTLY.
THANKS...
NICKELBACK
LET'S GO FIND A BOOTH FOR YOU AND YOUR FANCY SCOOTER.

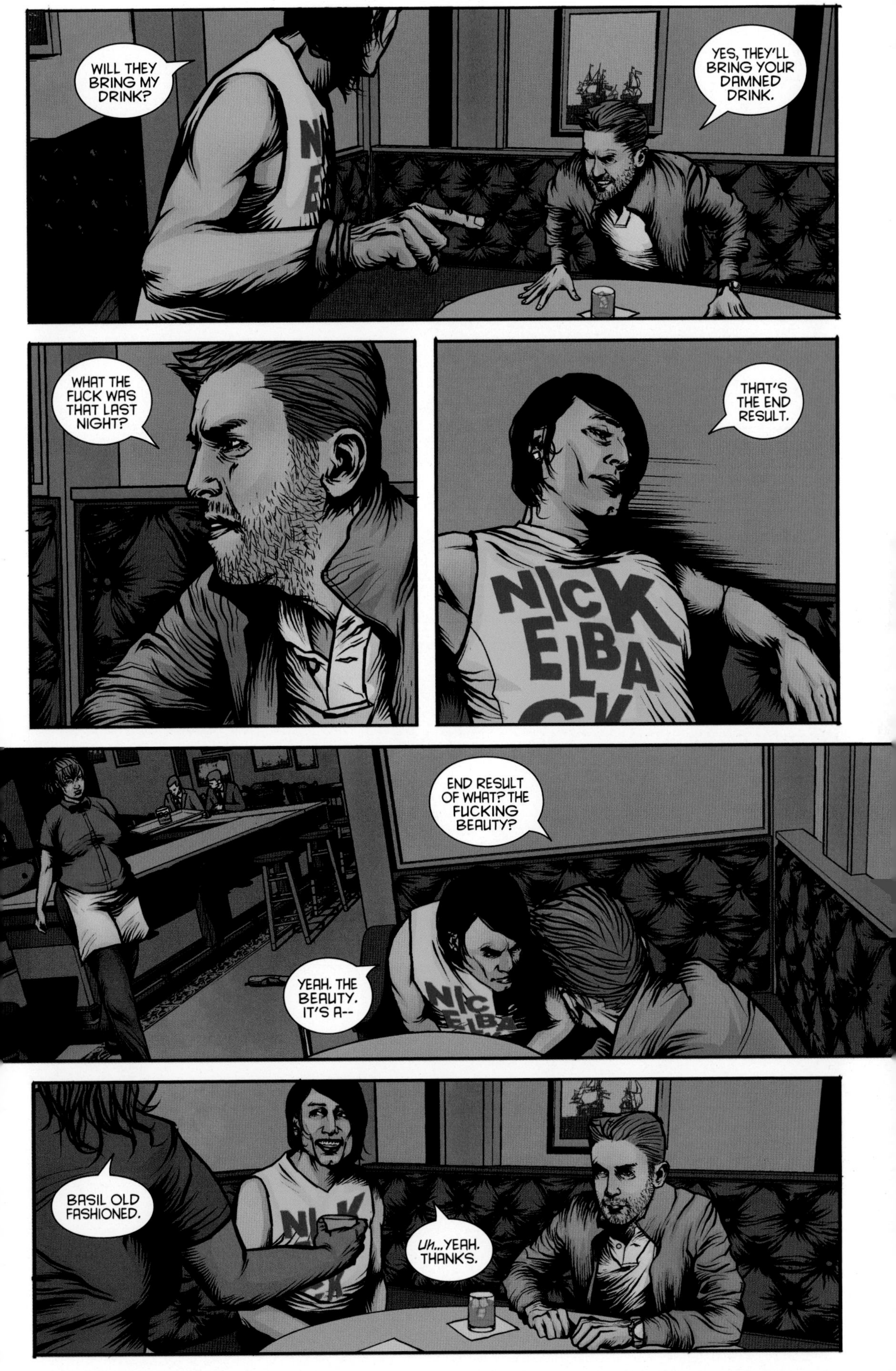
WILL THEY BRING MY DRINK?
YES, THEY'LL BRING YOUR DAMNED DRINK.
WHAT THE FUCK WAS THAT LAST NIGHT?
THAT'S THE END RESULT.
END RESULT OF WHAT? THE FUCKING BEAUTY?
YEAH. THE BEAUTY. IT'S A--
BASIL OLD FASHIONED.
UH...YEAH. THANKS.

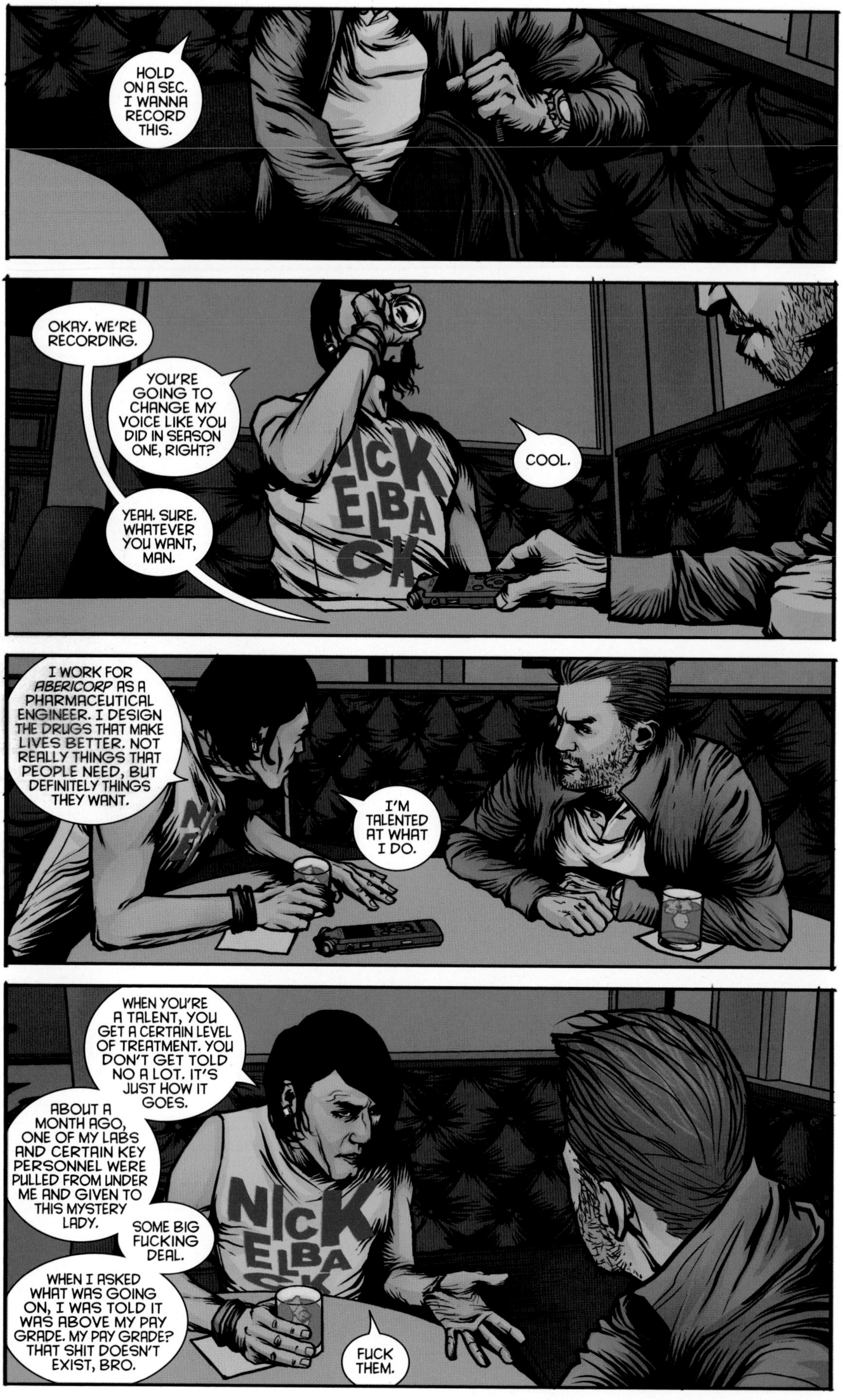
HOLD ON A SEC. I WANNA RECORD THIS.
OKAY. WE'RE RECORDING.
YOU'RE GOING TO CHANGE MY VOICE LIKE YOU DID IN SEASON ONE, RIGHT?
YEAH. SURE. WHATEVER YOU WANT, MAN.
COOL.
NICKELBACK
I WORK FOR *ABERICORP* AS A PHARMACEUTICAL ENGINEER. I DESIGN THE DRUGS THAT MAKE LIVES BETTER. NOT REALLY THINGS THAT PEOPLE NEED, BUT DEFINITELY THINGS THEY WANT.
I'M TALENTED AT WHAT I DO.
WHEN YOU'RE A TALENT, YOU GET A CERTAIN LEVEL OF TREATMENT. YOU DON'T GET TOLD NO A LOT. IT'S JUST HOW IT GOES.
ABOUT A MONTH AGO, ONE OF MY LABS AND CERTAIN KEY PERSONNEL WERE PULLED FROM UNDER ME AND GIVEN TO THIS MYSTERY LADY.
SOME BIG FUCKING DEAL.
WHEN I ASKED WHAT WAS GOING ON, I WAS TOLD IT WAS ABOVE MY PAY GRADE. MY PAY GRADE? THAT SHIT DOESN'T EXIST, BRO.
FUCK THEM.

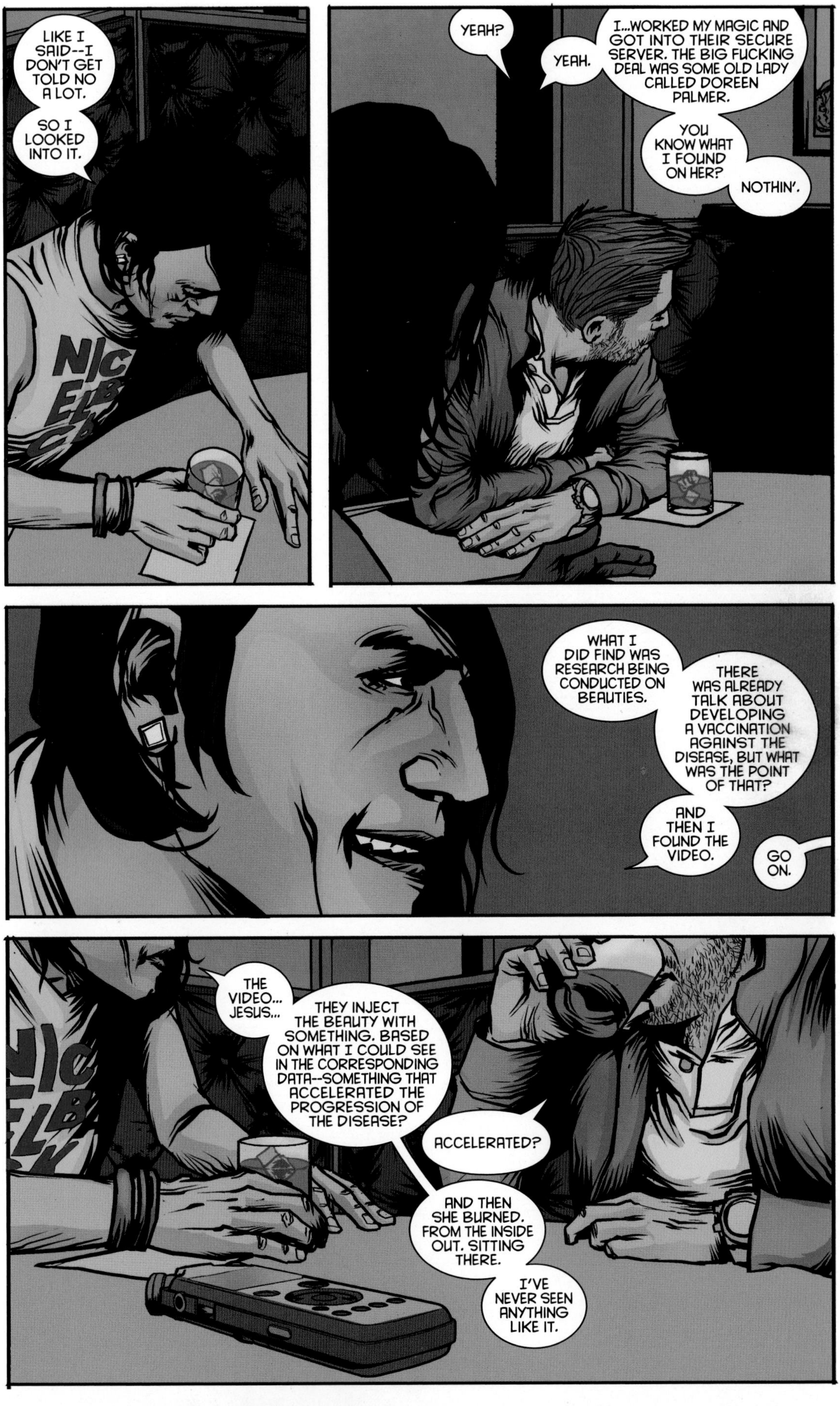

LIKE I SAID--I DON'T GET TOLD NO A LOT.
SO I LOOKED INTO IT.
YEAH?
YEAH.
I...WORKED MY MAGIC AND GOT INTO THEIR SECURE SERVER. THE BIG FUCKING DEAL WAS SOME OLD LADY CALLED DOREEN PALMER.
YOU KNOW WHAT I FOUND ON HER?
NOTHIN'.
WHAT I DID FIND WAS RESEARCH BEING CONDUCTED ON BEAUTIES.
THERE WAS ALREADY TALK ABOUT DEVELOPING A VACCINATION AGAINST THE DISEASE, BUT WHAT WAS THE POINT OF THAT?
AND THEN I FOUND THE VIDEO.
GO ON.
THE VIDEO... JESUS...
THEY INJECT THE BEAUTY WITH SOMETHING. BASED ON WHAT I COULD SEE IN THE CORRESPONDING DATA--SOMETHING THAT ACCELERATED THE PROGRESSION OF THE DISEASE?
ACCELERATED?
AND THEN SHE BURNED. FROM THE INSIDE OUT. SITTING THERE.
I'VE NEVER SEEN ANYTHING LIKE IT.

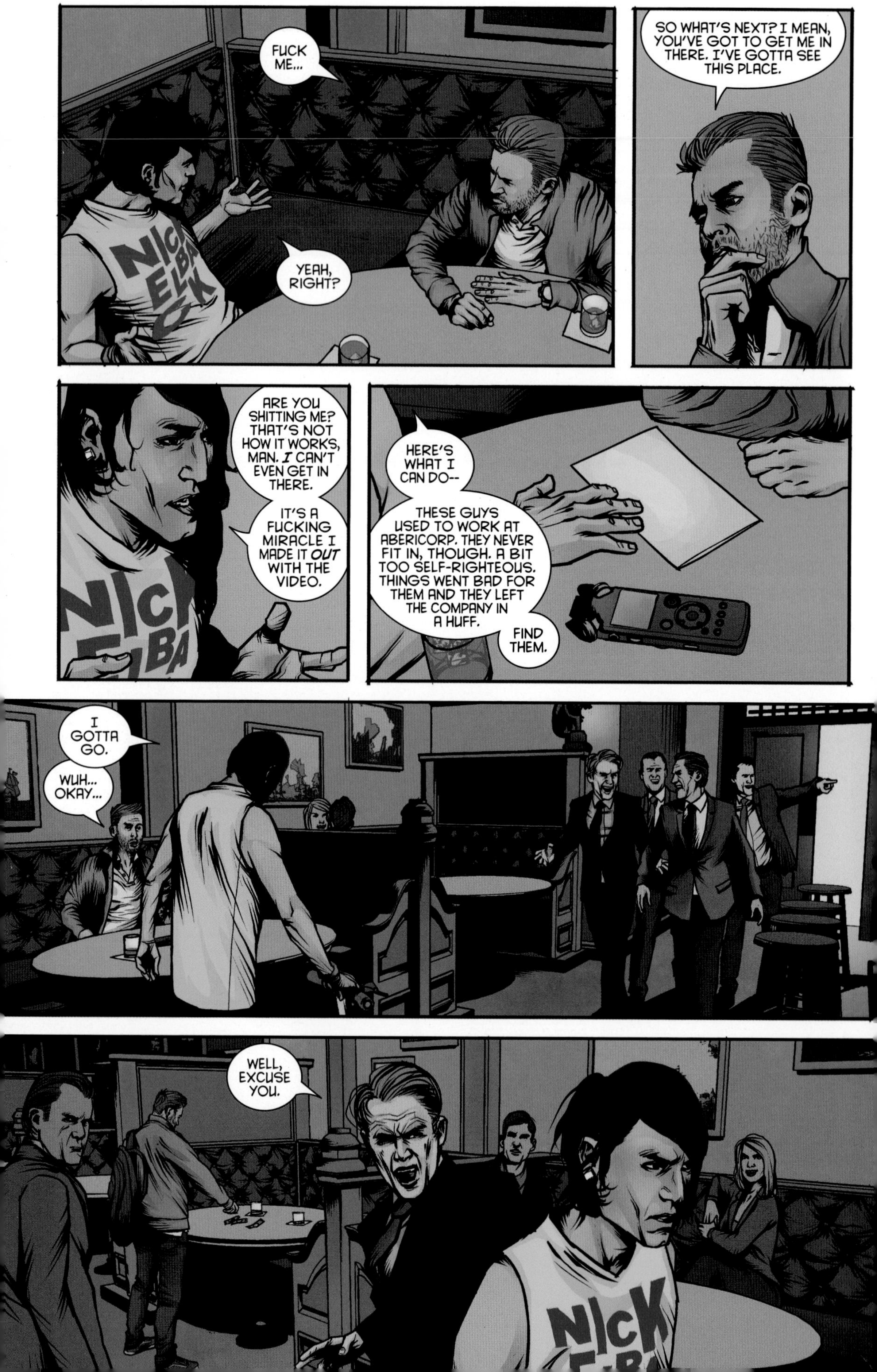
FUCK ME...
YEAH, RIGHT?
SO WHAT'S NEXT? I MEAN, YOU'VE GOT TO GET ME IN THERE. I'VE GOTTA SEE THIS PLACE.
ARE YOU SHITTING ME? THAT'S NOT HOW IT WORKS, MAN. I CAN'T EVEN GET IN THERE.
IT'S A FUCKING MIRACLE I MADE IT OUT WITH THE VIDEO.
HERE'S WHAT I CAN DO--
THESE GUYS USED TO WORK AT ABERICORP. THEY NEVER FIT IN, THOUGH. A BIT TOO SELF-RIGHTEOUS. THINGS WENT BAD FOR THEM AND THEY LEFT THE COMPANY IN A HUFF.
FIND THEM.
I GOTTA GO.
WUH... OKAY...
WELL, EXCUSE YOU.

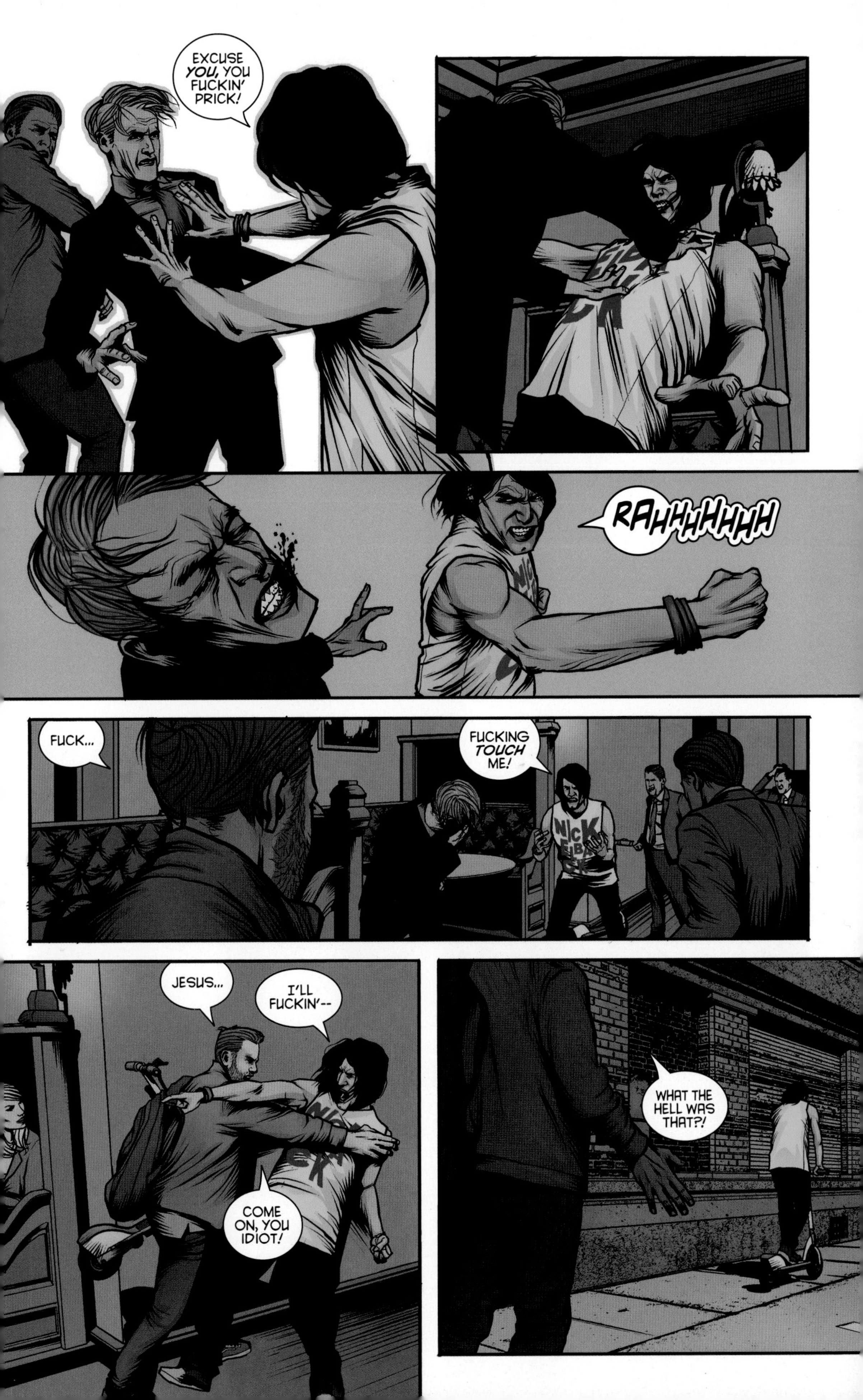
EXCUSE YOU, YOU FUCKIN' PRICK!
RAHHHHHHH
FUCK...
FUCKING TOUCH ME!
JESUS...
I'LL FUCKIN'--
COME ON, YOU IDIOT!
WHAT THE HELL WAS THAT?!

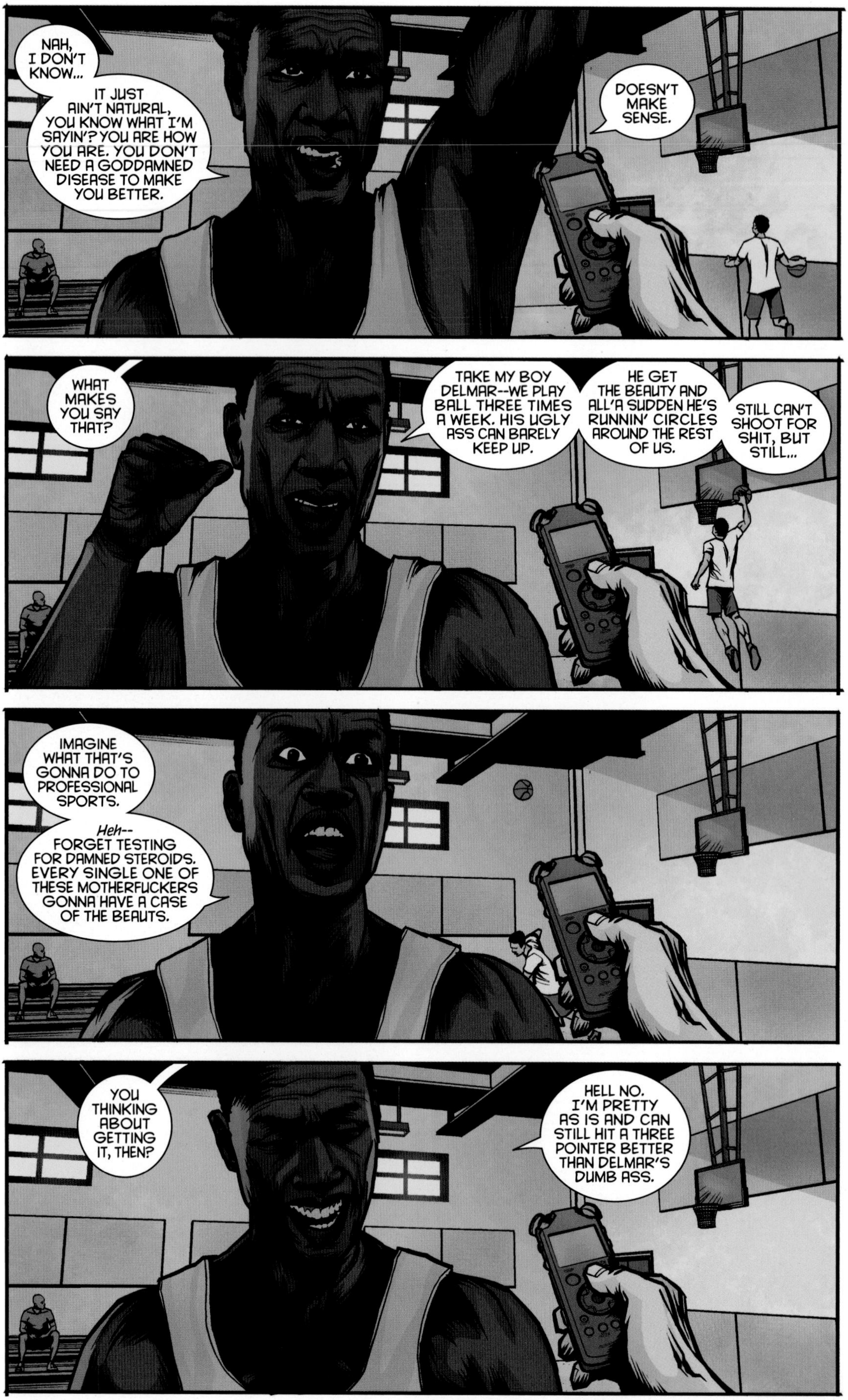
NAH, I DON'T KNOW...
IT JUST AIN'T NATURAL, YOU KNOW WHAT I'M SAYIN'? YOU ARE HOW YOU ARE. YOU DON'T NEED A GODDAMNED DISEASE TO MAKE YOU BETTER.
DOESN'T MAKE SENSE.
WHAT MAKES YOU SAY THAT?
TAKE MY BOY DELMAR--WE PLAY BALL THREE TIMES A WEEK. HIS UGLY ASS CAN BARELY KEEP UP.
HE GET THE BEAUTY AND ALL'A SUDDEN HE'S RUNNIN' CIRCLES AROUND THE REST OF US.
STILL CAN'T SHOOT FOR SHIT, BUT STILL...
IMAGINE WHAT THAT'S GONNA DO TO PROFESSIONAL SPORTS.
Heh-- FORGET TESTING FOR DAMNED STEROIDS. EVERY SINGLE ONE OF THESE MOTHERFUCKERS GONNA HAVE A CASE OF THE BEAUTS.
YOU THINKING ABOUT GETTING IT, THEN?
HELL NO. I'M PRETTY AS IS AND CAN STILL HIT A THREE POINTER BETTER THAN DELMAR'S DUMB ASS.

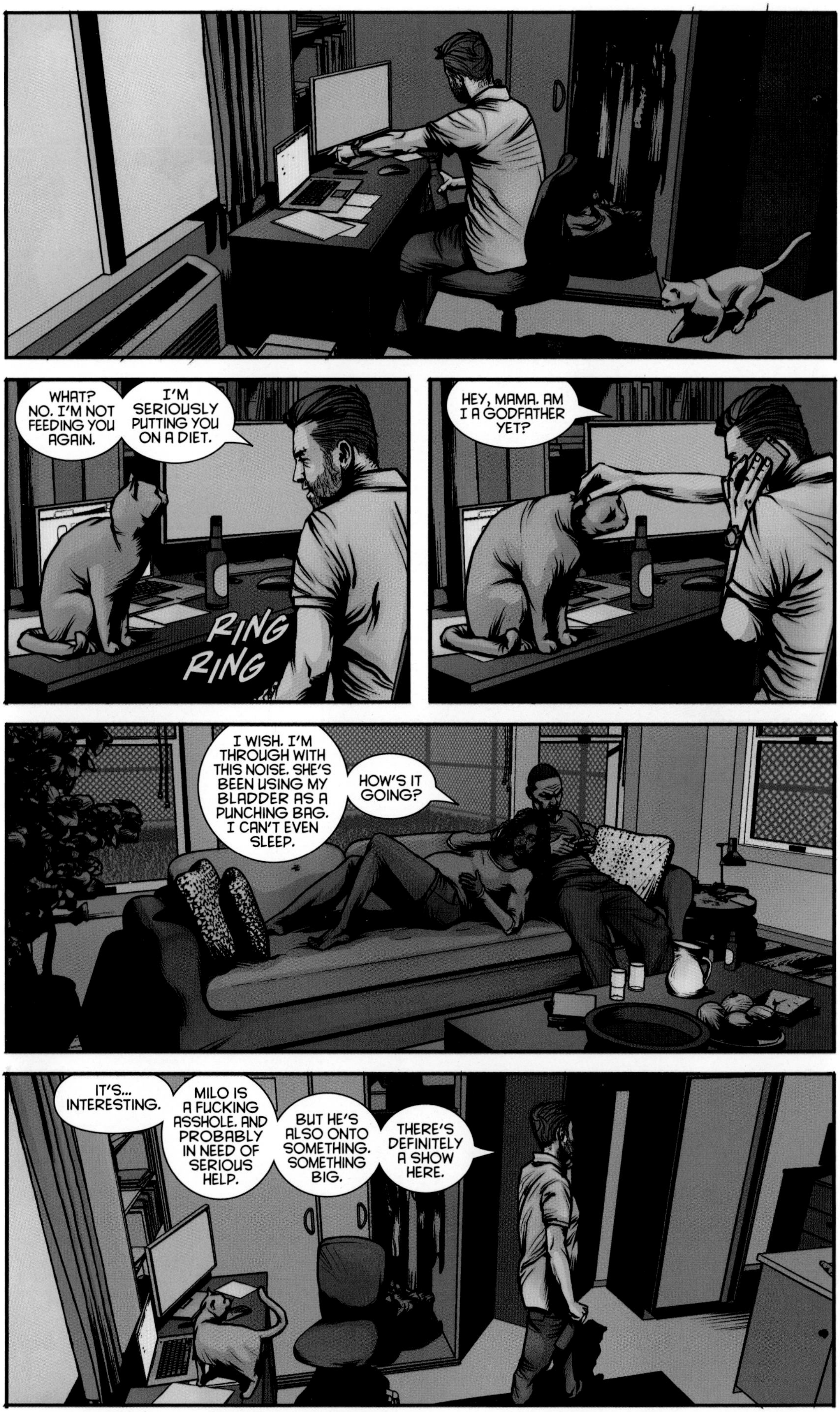
WHAT? NO. I'M NOT FEEDING YOU AGAIN.
I'M SERIOUSLY PUTTING YOU ON A DIET.
RING RING
HEY, MAMA. AM I A GODFATHER YET?
I WISH. I'M THROUGH WITH THIS NOISE. SHE'S BEEN USING MY BLADDER AS A PUNCHING BAG. I CAN'T EVEN SLEEP.
HOW'S IT GOING?
IT'S... INTERESTING.
MILO IS A FUCKING ASSHOLE. AND PROBABLY IN NEED OF SERIOUS HELP.
BUT HE'S ALSO ONTO SOMETHING. SOMETHING BIG.
THERE'S DEFINITELY A SHOW HERE.

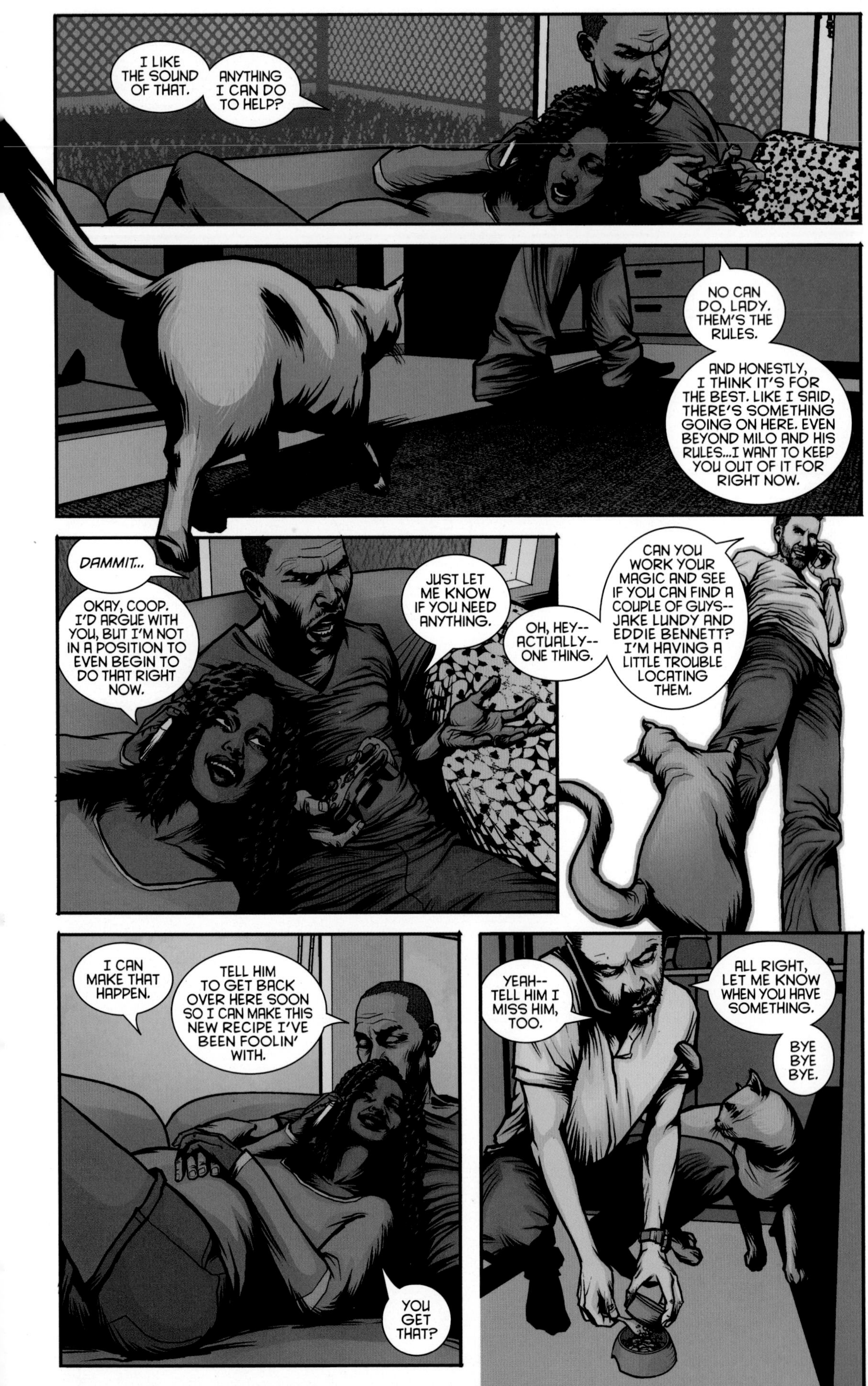
I LIKE THE SOUND OF THAT.
ANYTHING I CAN DO TO HELP?
NO CAN DO, LADY. THEM'S THE RULES.
AND HONESTLY, I THINK IT'S FOR THE BEST. LIKE I SAID, THERE'S SOMETHING GOING ON HERE. EVEN BEYOND MILO AND HIS RULES...I WANT TO KEEP YOU OUT OF IT FOR RIGHT NOW.
DAMMIT...
OKAY, COOP. I'D ARGUE WITH YOU, BUT I'M NOT IN A POSITION TO EVEN BEGIN TO DO THAT RIGHT NOW.
JUST LET ME KNOW IF YOU NEED ANYTHING.
OH, HEY-- ACTUALLY-- ONE THING.
CAN YOU WORK YOUR MAGIC AND SEE IF YOU CAN FIND A COUPLE OF GUYS-- JAKE LUNDY AND EDDIE BENNETT? I'M HAVING A LITTLE TROUBLE LOCATING THEM.
I CAN MAKE THAT HAPPEN.
TELL HIM TO GET BACK OVER HERE SOON SO I CAN MAKE THIS NEW RECIPE I'VE BEEN FOOLIN' WITH.
YOU GET THAT?
YEAH-- TELL HIM I MISS HIM, TOO.
ALL RIGHT, LET ME KNOW WHEN YOU HAVE SOMETHING.
BYE BYE BYE.

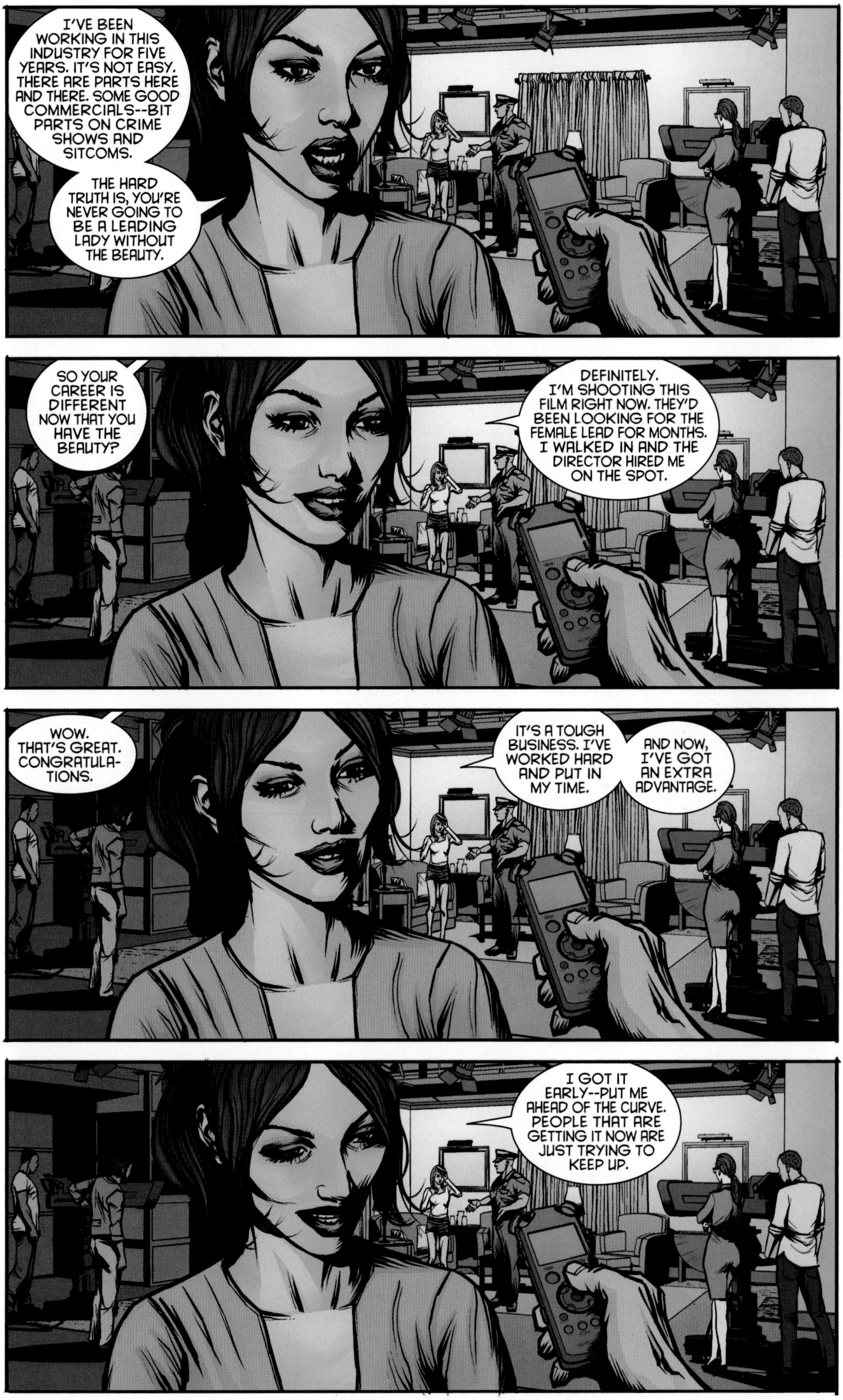
I'VE BEEN WORKING IN THIS INDUSTRY FOR FIVE YEARS. IT'S NOT EASY. THERE ARE PARTS HERE AND THERE. SOME GOOD COMMERCIALS--BIT PARTS ON CRIME SHOWS AND SITCOMS.
THE HARD TRUTH IS, YOU'RE NEVER GOING TO BE A LEADING LADY WITHOUT THE BEAUTY.
SO YOUR CAREER IS DIFFERENT NOW THAT YOU HAVE THE BEAUTY?
DEFINITELY. I'M SHOOTING THIS FILM RIGHT NOW. THEY'D BEEN LOOKING FOR THE FEMALE LEAD FOR MONTHS. I WALKED IN AND THE DIRECTOR HIRED ME ON THE SPOT.
WOW. THAT'S GREAT. CONGRATULA-TIONS.
IT'S A TOUGH BUSINESS. I'VE WORKED HARD AND PUT IN MY TIME.
AND NOW, I'VE GOT AN EXTRA ADVANTAGE.
I GOT IT EARLY--PUT ME AHEAD OF THE CURVE. PEOPLE THAT ARE GETTING IT NOW ARE JUST TRYING TO KEEP UP.

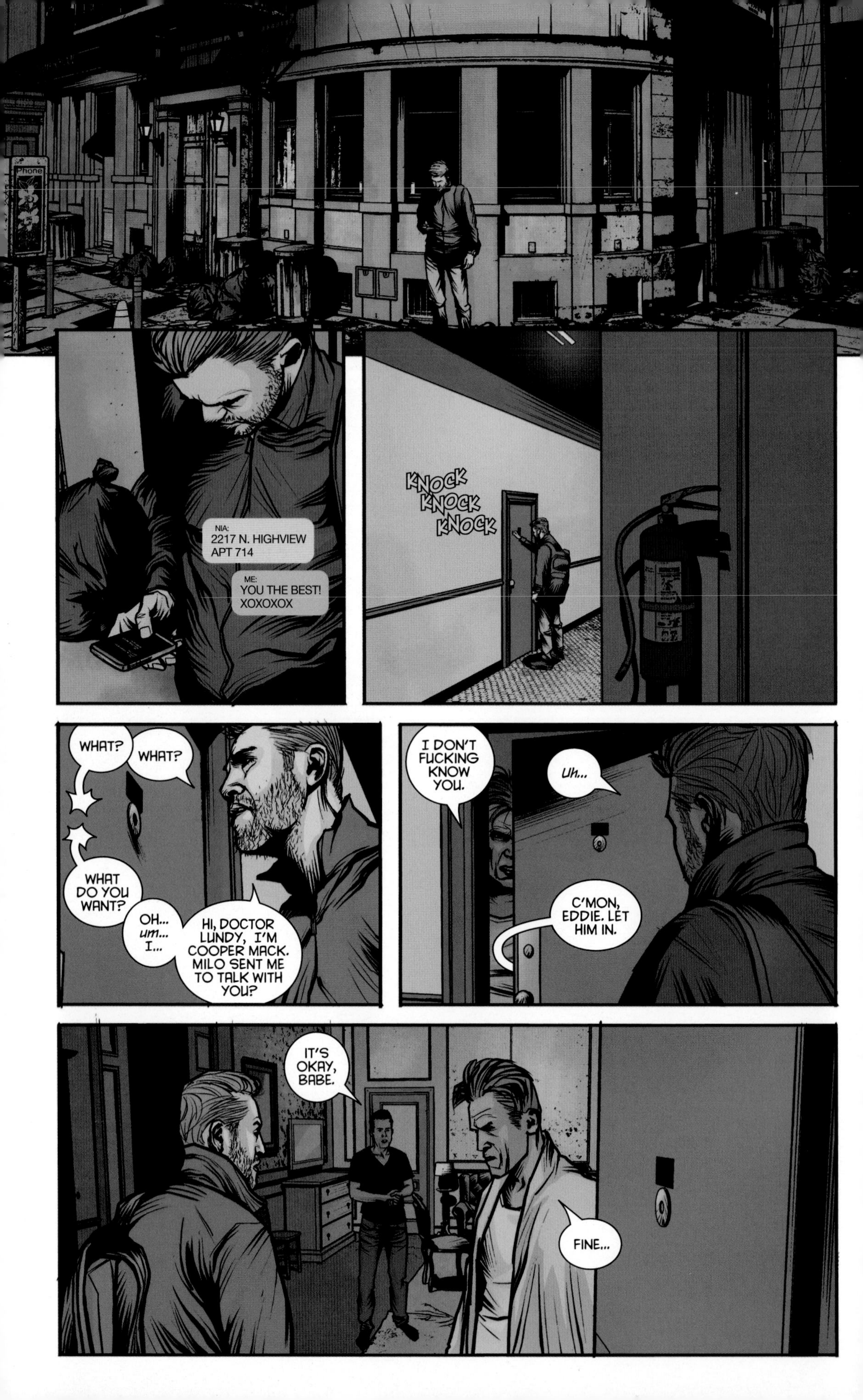

NIA:
2217 N. HIGHVIEW
APT 714
ME:
YOU THE BEST!
XOXOXOX
KNOCK
KNOCK
KNOCK
WHAT?
WHAT?
WHAT DO YOU WANT?
OH... um... I...
HI, DOCTOR LUNDY, I'M COOPER MACK. MILO SENT ME TO TALK WITH YOU?
I DON'T FUCKING KNOW YOU.
Uh...
C'MON, EDDIE. LET HIM IN.
IT'S OKAY, BABE.
FINE...

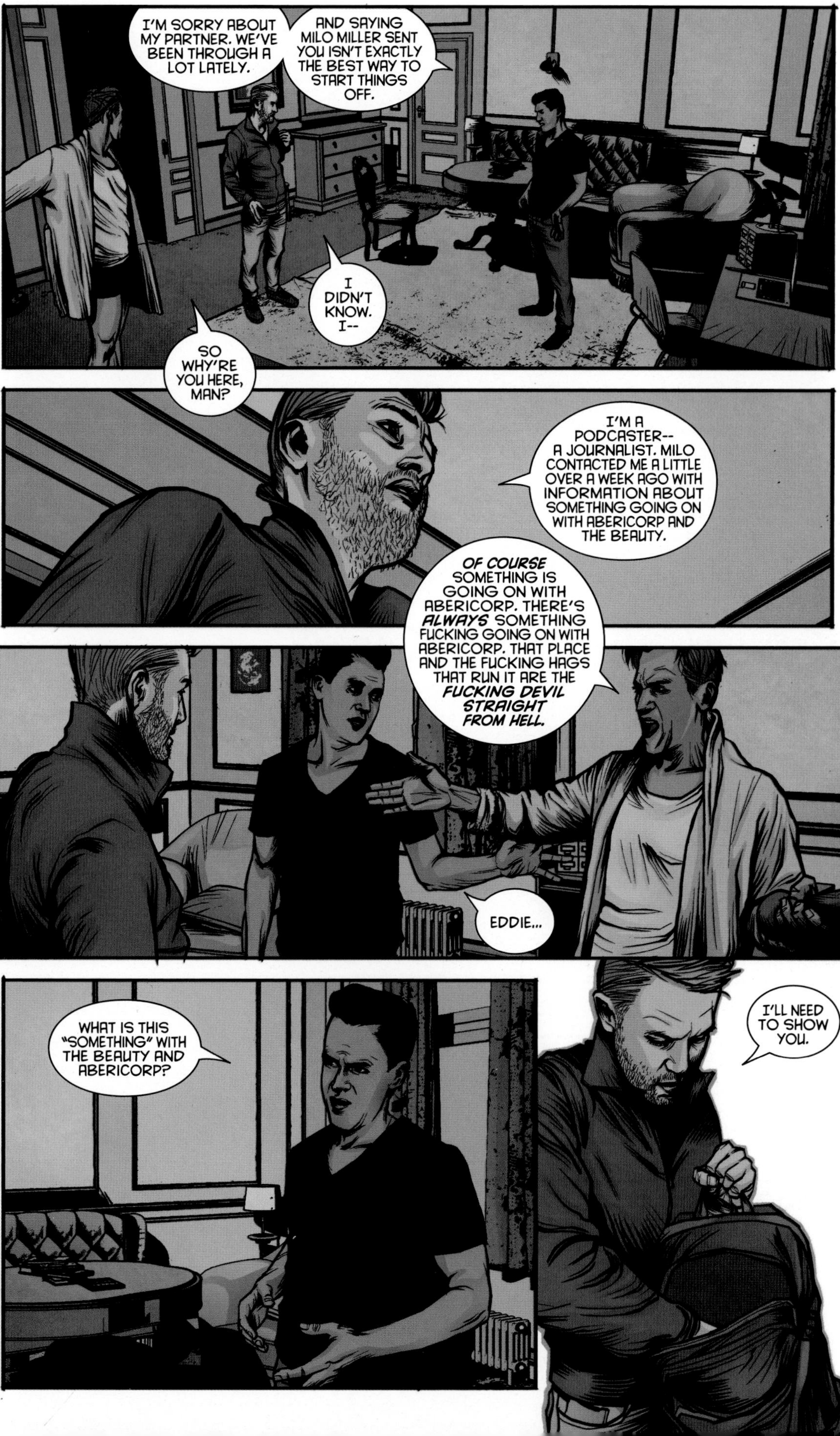
I'M SORRY ABOUT MY PARTNER. WE'VE BEEN THROUGH A LOT LATELY.
AND SAYING MILO MILLER SENT YOU ISN'T EXACTLY THE BEST WAY TO START THINGS OFF.
I DIDN'T KNOW. I--
SO WHY'RE YOU HERE, MAN?
I'M A PODCASTER-- A JOURNALIST. MILO CONTACTED ME A LITTLE OVER A WEEK AGO WITH INFORMATION ABOUT SOMETHING GOING ON WITH ABERICORP AND THE BEAUTY.
OF COURSE SOMETHING IS GOING ON WITH ABERICORP. THERE'S ALWAYS SOMETHING FUCKING GOING ON WITH ABERICORP. THAT PLACE AND THE FUCKING HAGS THAT RUN IT ARE THE FUCKING DEVIL STRAIGHT FROM HELL.
EDDIE...
WHAT IS THIS "SOMETHING" WITH THE BEAUTY AND ABERICORP?
I'LL NEED TO SHOW YOU.

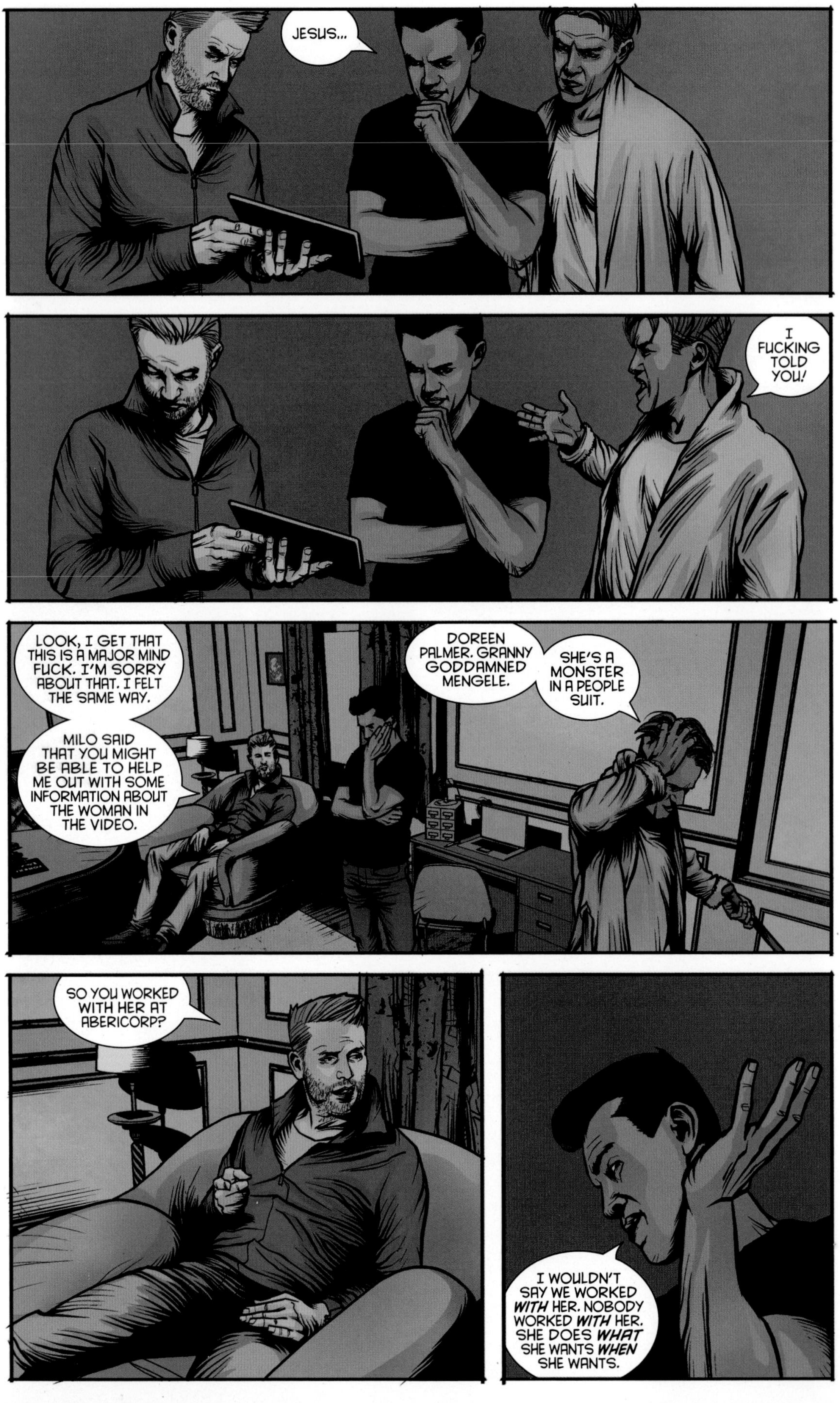
JESUS...
I FUCKING TOLD YOU!
LOOK, I GET THAT THIS IS A MAJOR MIND FUCK. I'M SORRY ABOUT THAT. I FELT THE SAME WAY.
MILO SAID THAT YOU MIGHT BE ABLE TO HELP ME OUT WITH SOME INFORMATION ABOUT THE WOMAN IN THE VIDEO.
DOREEN PALMER. GRANNY GODDAMNED MENGELE.
SHE'S A MONSTER IN A PEOPLE SUIT.
SO YOU WORKED WITH HER AT ABERICORP?
I WOULDN'T SAY WE WORKED *WITH* HER. NOBODY WORKED *WITH* HER. SHE DOES *WHAT* SHE WANTS *WHEN* SHE WANTS.

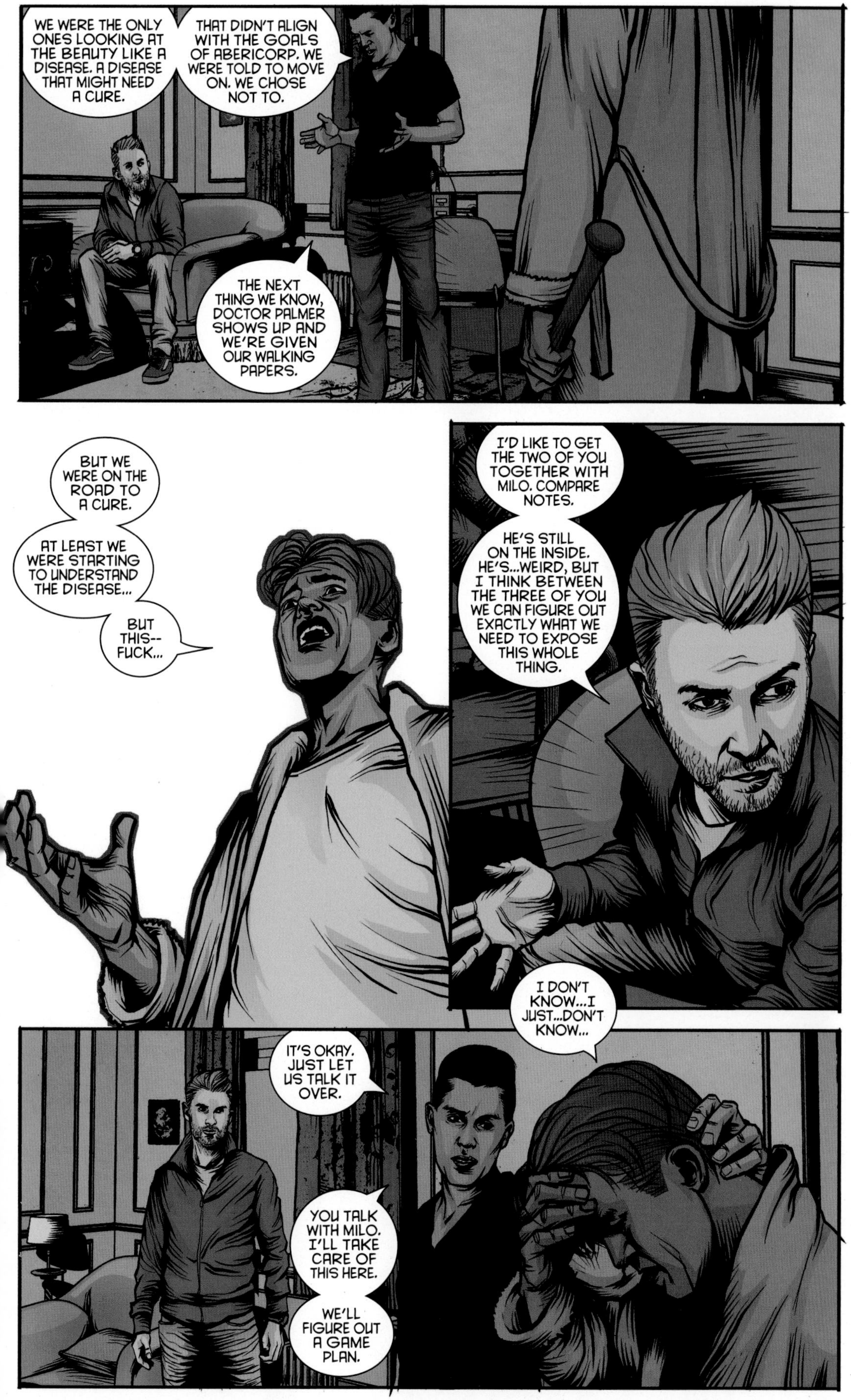
WE WERE THE ONLY ONES LOOKING AT THE BEAUTY LIKE A DISEASE. A DISEASE THAT MIGHT NEED A CURE.
THAT DIDN'T ALIGN WITH THE GOALS OF ABERICORP. WE WERE TOLD TO MOVE ON. WE CHOSE NOT TO.
THE NEXT THING WE KNOW, DOCTOR PALMER SHOWS UP AND WE'RE GIVEN OUR WALKING PAPERS.
BUT WE WERE ON THE ROAD TO A CURE.
AT LEAST WE WERE STARTING TO UNDERSTAND THE DISEASE...
BUT THIS-- FUCK...
I'D LIKE TO GET THE TWO OF YOU TOGETHER WITH MILO. COMPARE NOTES.
HE'S STILL ON THE INSIDE. HE'S...WEIRD, BUT I THINK BETWEEN THE THREE OF YOU WE CAN FIGURE OUT EXACTLY WHAT WE NEED TO EXPOSE THIS WHOLE THING.
I DON'T KNOW...I JUST...DON'T KNOW...
IT'S OKAY. JUST LET US TALK IT OVER.
YOU TALK WITH MILO. I'LL TAKE CARE OF THIS HERE.
WE'LL FIGURE OUT A GAME PLAN.

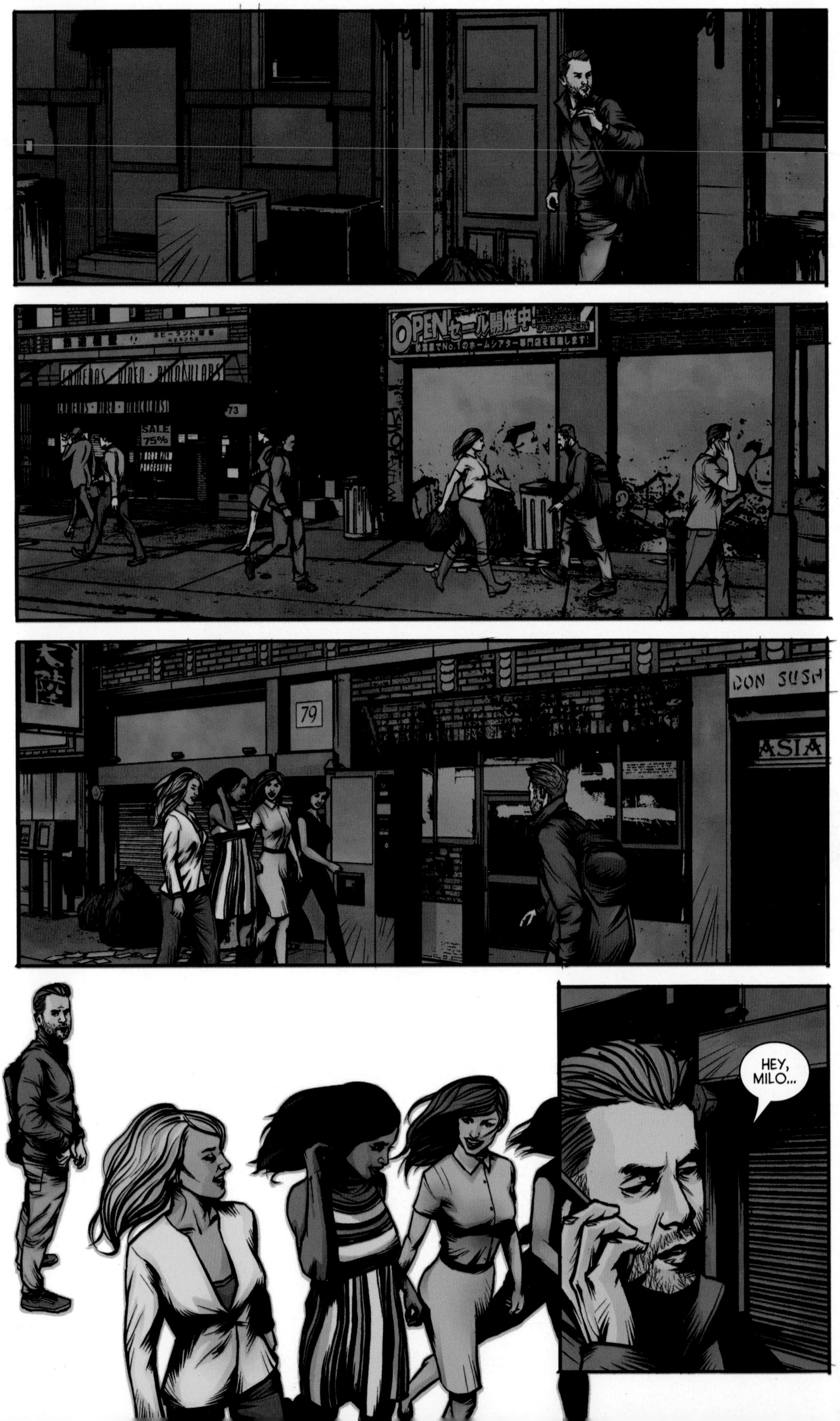
OPEN セール開催中!
SALE 75%
1 HOUR FILM PROCESSING
73
79
DON SUSH
ASIA
HEY, MILO...

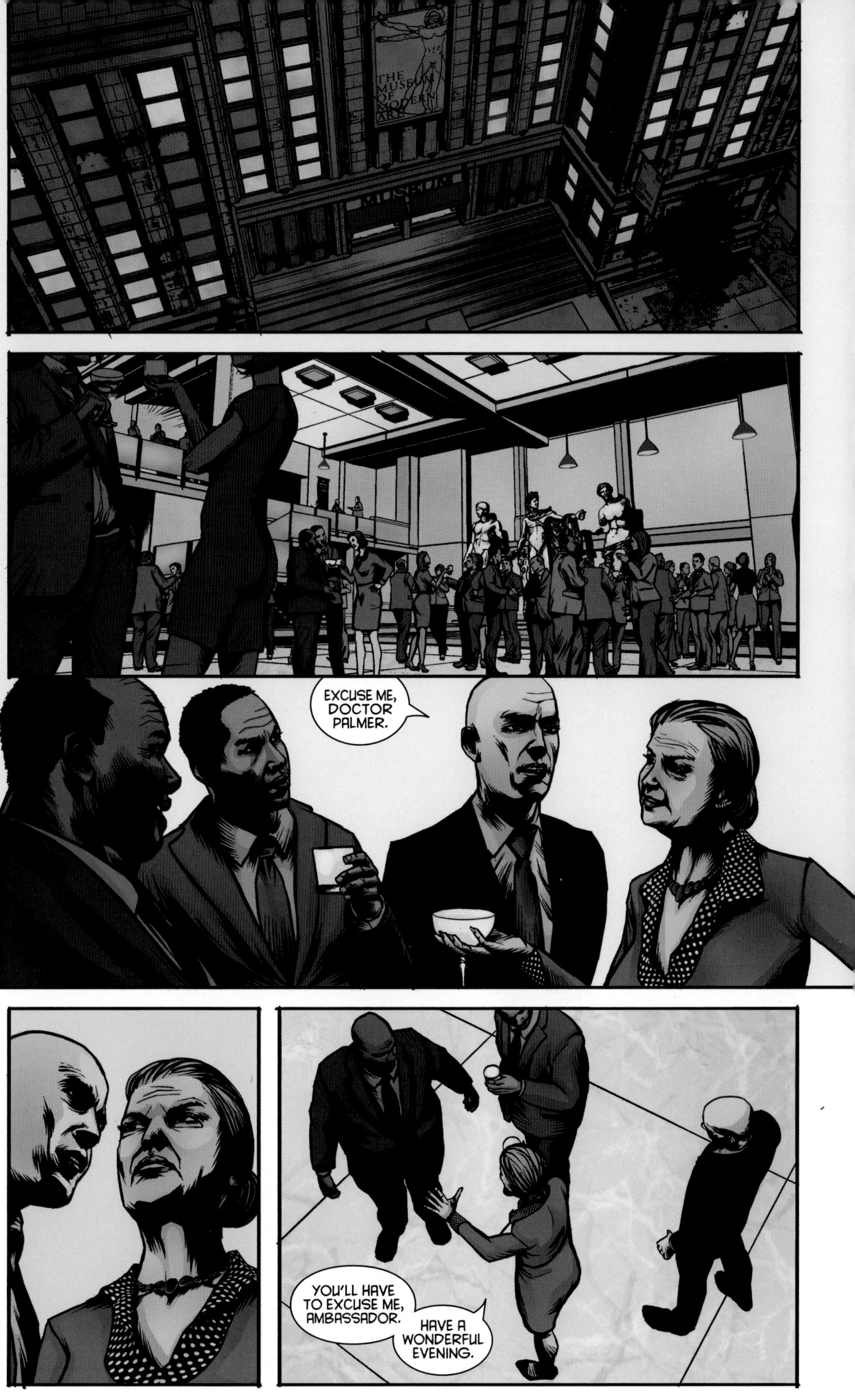
THE MUSEUM OF MODERN ART
MUSEUM
EXCUSE ME, DOCTOR PALMER.
YOU'LL HAVE TO EXCUSE ME, AMBASSADOR.
HAVE A WONDERFUL EVENING.

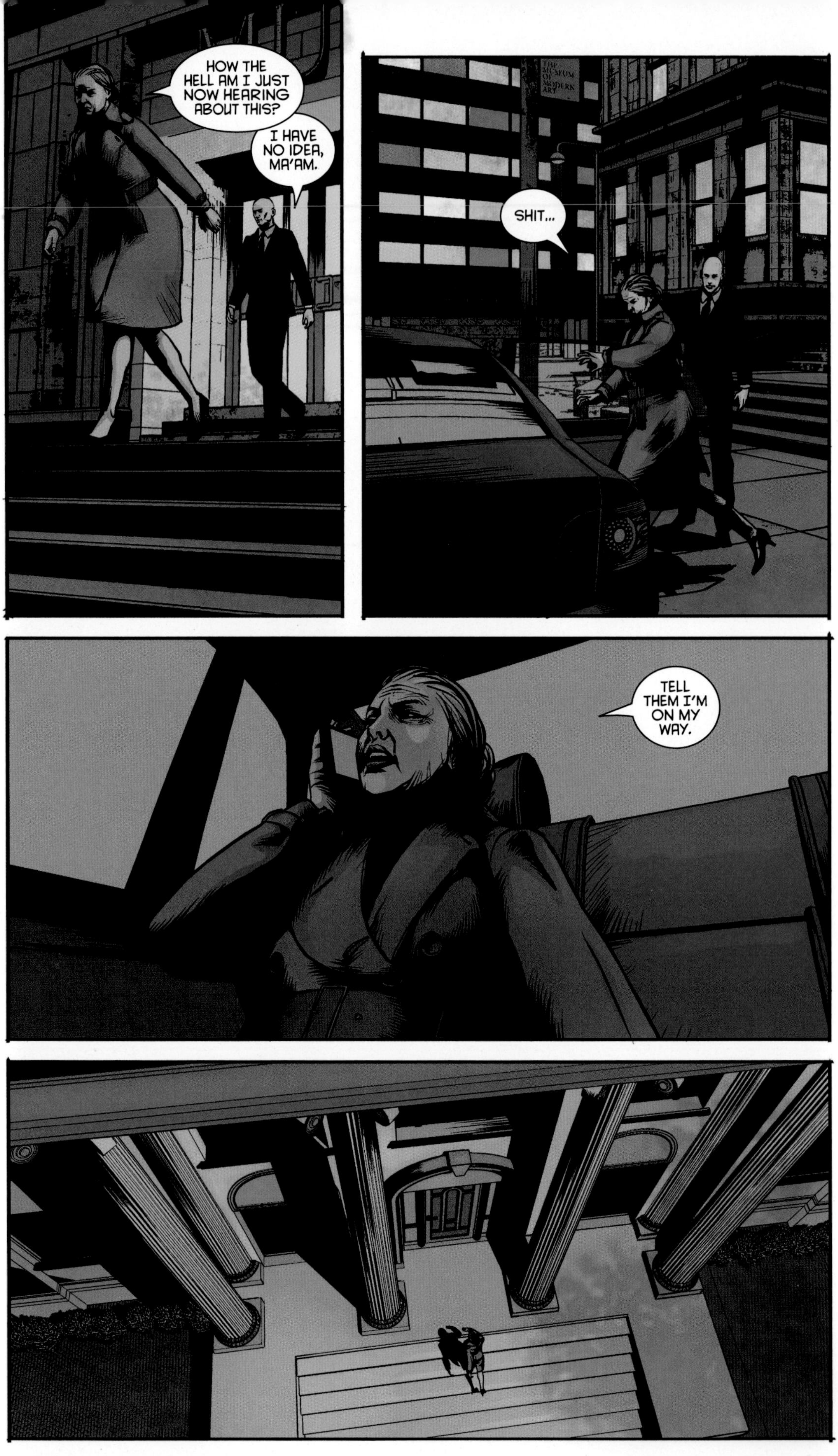
HOW THE HELL AM I JUST NOW HEARING ABOUT THIS?
I HAVE NO IDEA, MA'AM.
THE MUSEUM OF MODERN ART
SHIT...
TELL THEM I'M ON MY WAY.

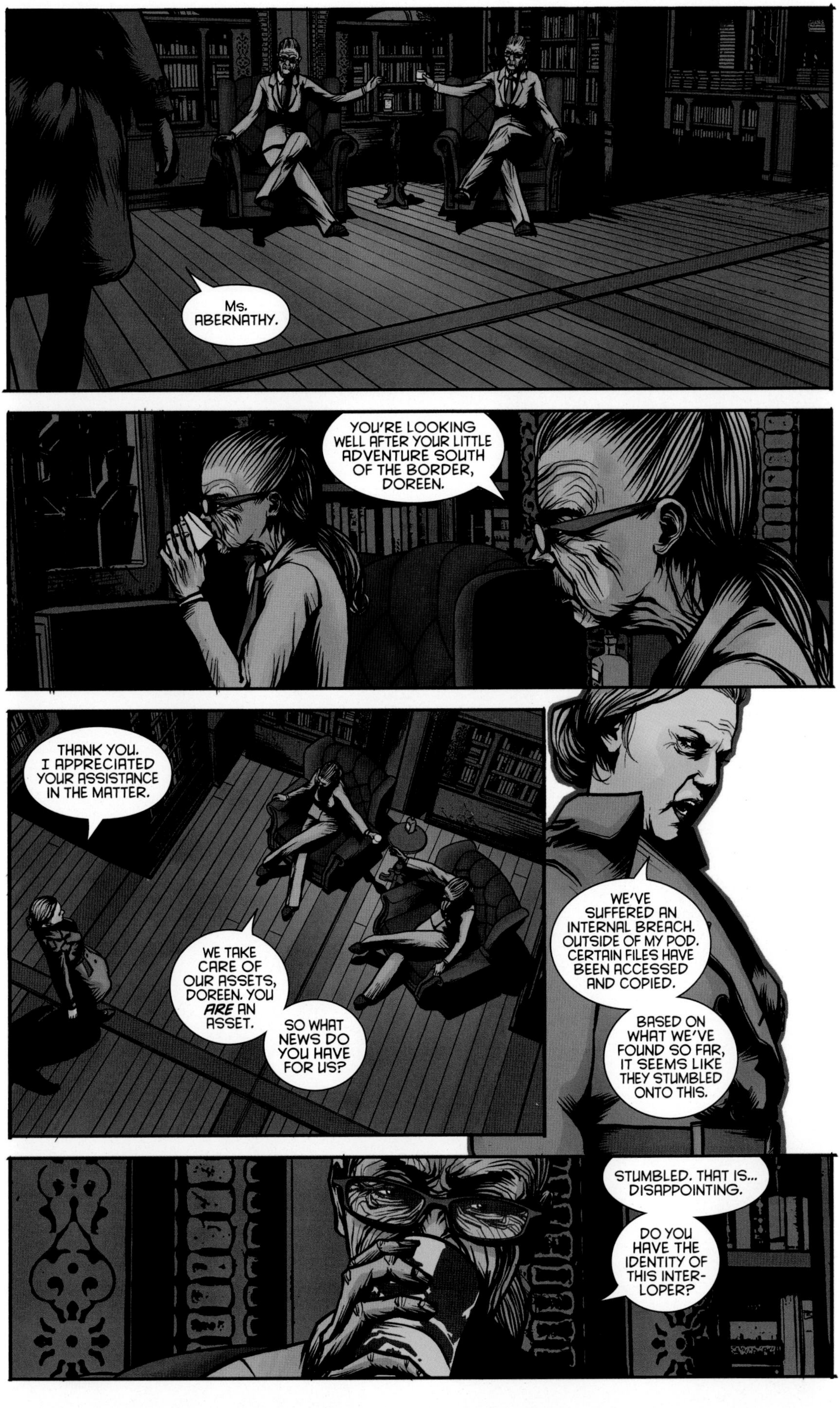
Ms. ABERNATHY.
YOU'RE LOOKING WELL AFTER YOUR LITTLE ADVENTURE SOUTH OF THE BORDER, DOREEN.
THANK YOU. I APPRECIATED YOUR ASSISTANCE IN THE MATTER.
WE TAKE CARE OF OUR ASSETS, DOREEN. YOU *ARE* AN ASSET.
SO WHAT NEWS DO YOU HAVE FOR US?
WE'VE SUFFERED AN INTERNAL BREACH. OUTSIDE OF MY POD. CERTAIN FILES HAVE BEEN ACCESSED AND COPIED.
BASED ON WHAT WE'VE FOUND SO FAR, IT SEEMS LIKE THEY STUMBLED ONTO THIS.
STUMBLED. THAT IS... DISAPPOINTING.
DO YOU HAVE THE IDENTITY OF THIS INTER-LOPER?

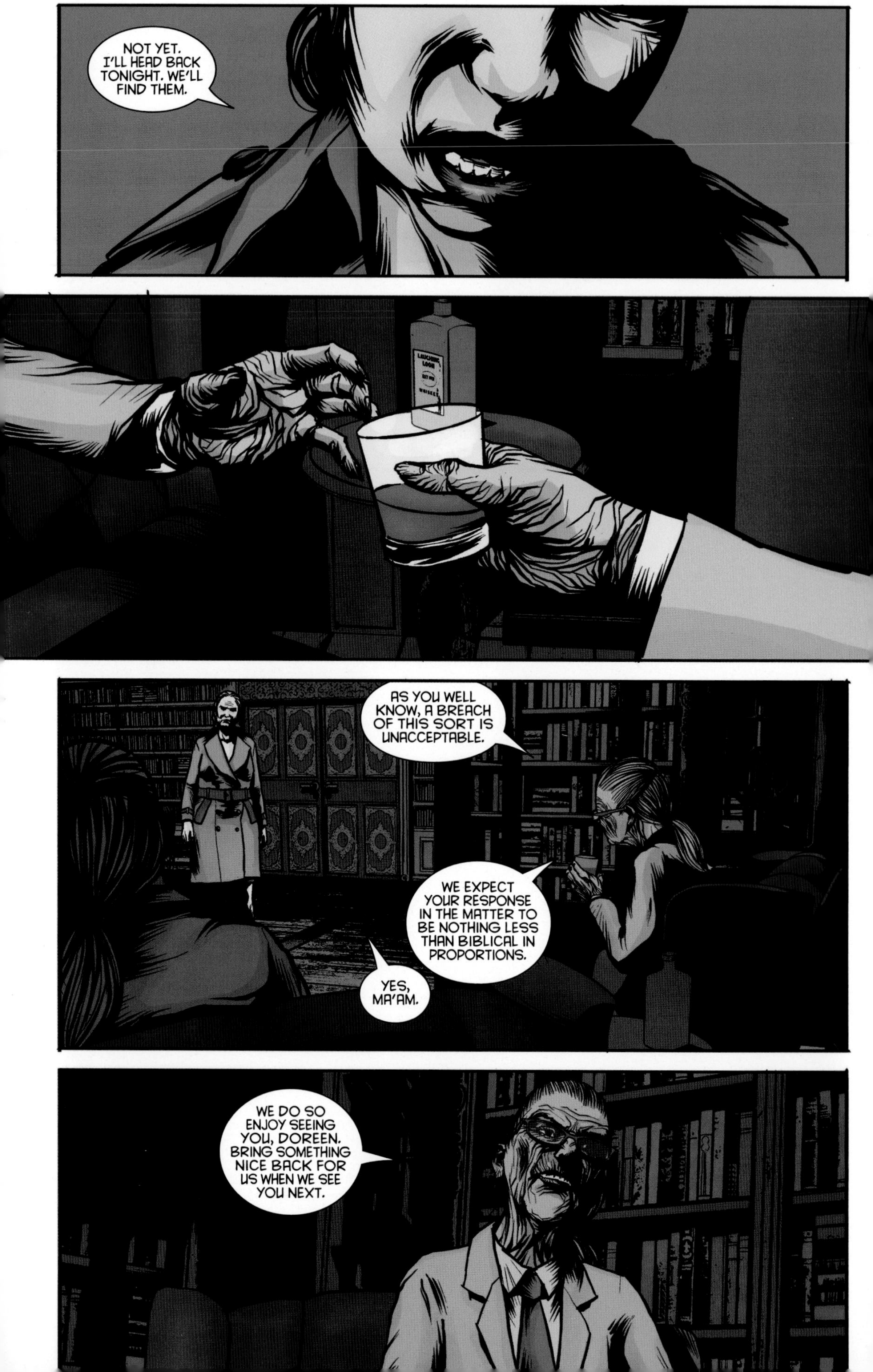
NOT YET. I'LL HEAD BACK TONIGHT. WE'LL FIND THEM.
AS YOU WELL KNOW, A BREACH OF THIS SORT IS UNACCEPTABLE.
WE EXPECT YOUR RESPONSE IN THE MATTER TO BE NOTHING LESS THAN BIBLICAL IN PROPORTIONS.
YES, MA'AM.
WE DO SO ENJOY SEEING YOU, DOREEN. BRING SOMETHING NICE BACK FOR US WHEN WE SEE YOU NEXT.

CHAPTER

20

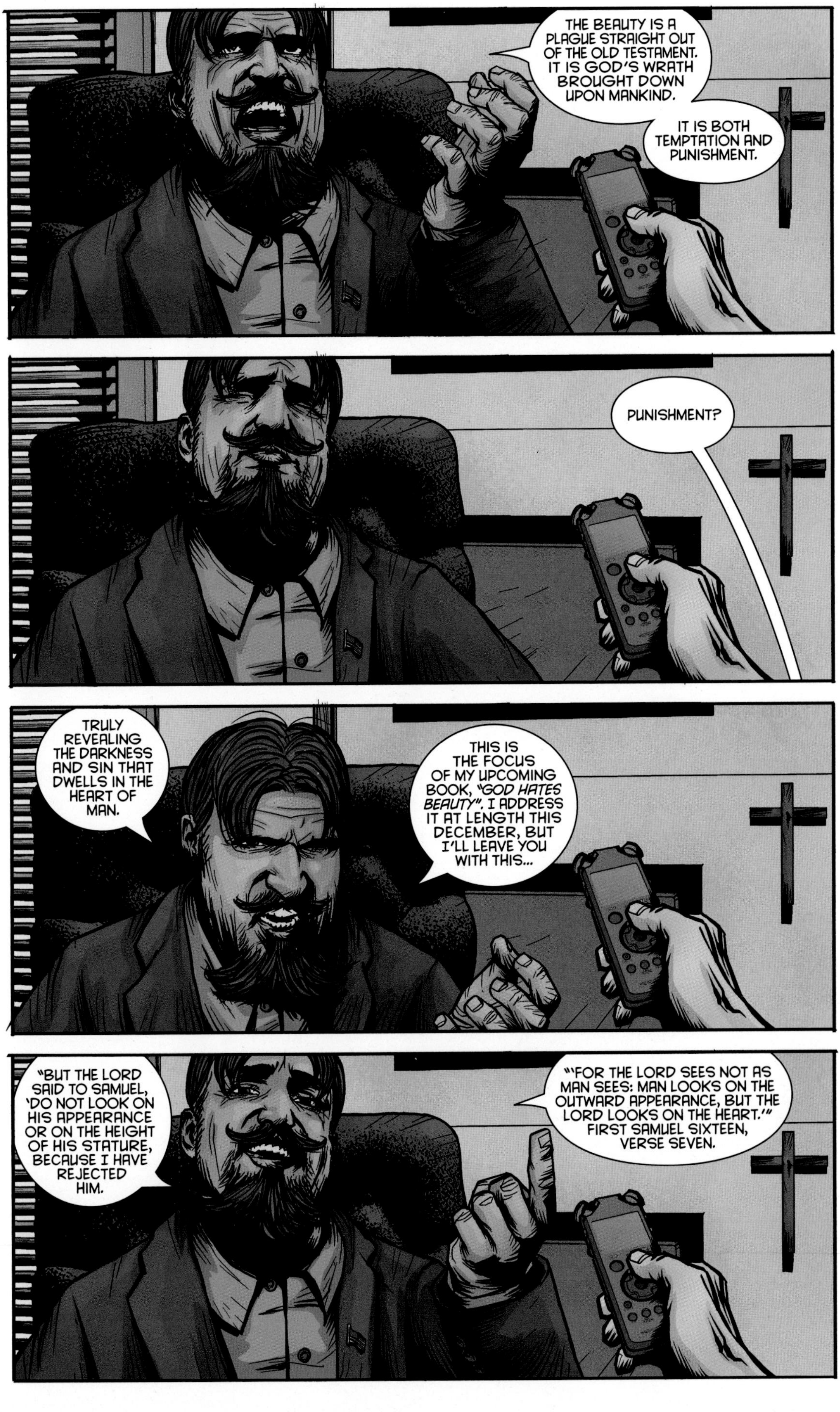
THE BEAUTY IS A PLAGUE STRAIGHT OUT OF THE OLD TESTAMENT. IT IS GOD'S WRATH BROUGHT DOWN UPON MANKIND.
IT IS BOTH TEMPTATION AND PUNISHMENT.
PUNISHMENT?
TRULY REVEALING THE DARKNESS AND SIN THAT DWELLS IN THE HEART OF MAN.
THIS IS THE FOCUS OF MY UPCOMING BOOK, *"GOD HATES BEAUTY"*. I ADDRESS IT AT LENGTH THIS DECEMBER, BUT I'LL LEAVE YOU WITH THIS...
"BUT THE LORD SAID TO SAMUEL, 'DO NOT LOOK ON HIS APPEARANCE OR ON THE HEIGHT OF HIS STATURE, BECAUSE I HAVE REJECTED HIM.
"'FOR THE LORD SEES NOT AS MAN SEES: MAN LOOKS ON THE OUTWARD APPEARANCE, BUT THE LORD LOOKS ON THE HEART.'" FIRST SAMUEL SIXTEEN, VERSE SEVEN.

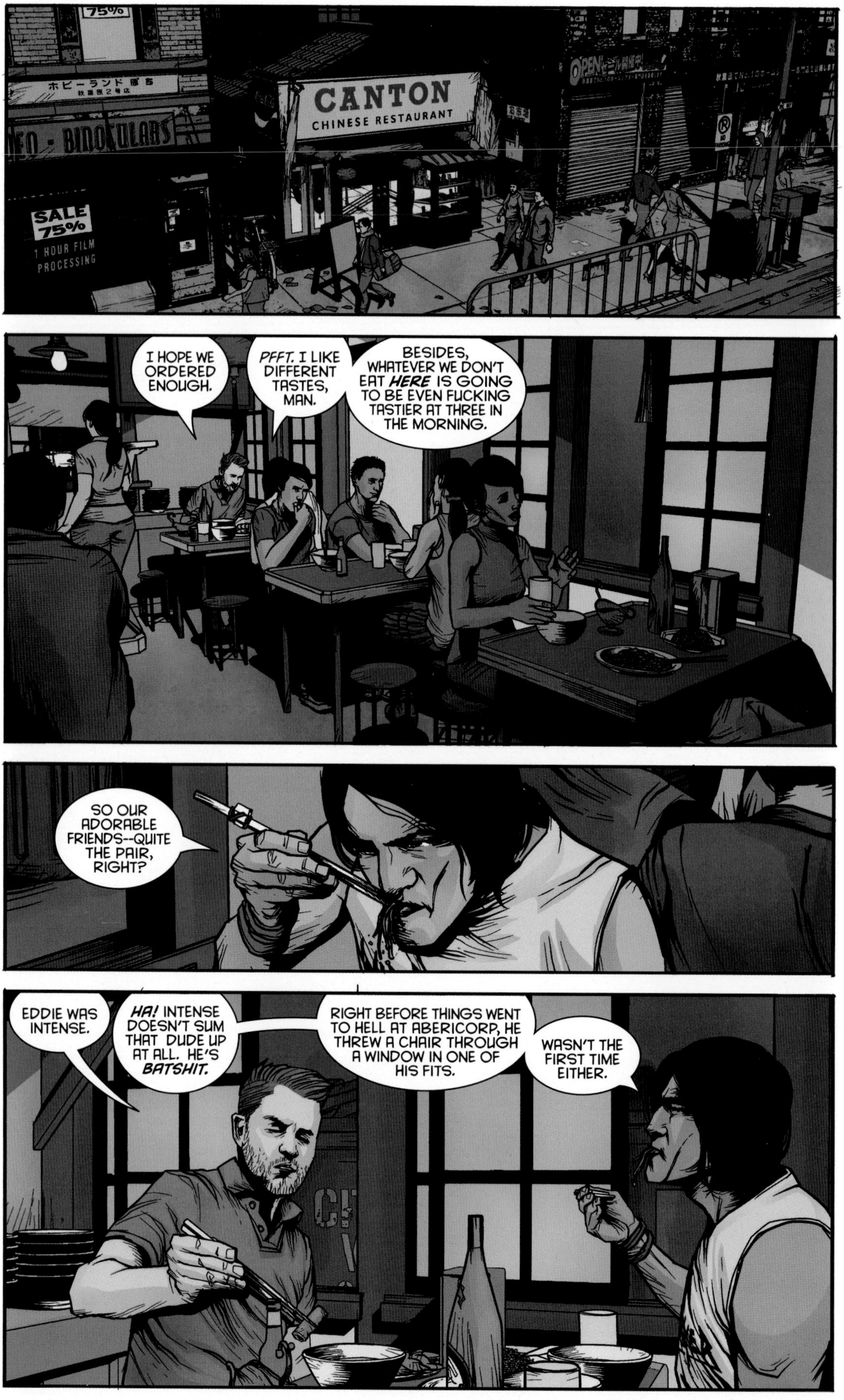
75%
CANTON
CHINESE RESTAURANT
BINOCULARS
SALE 75%
1 HOUR FILM PROCESSING
OPEN
I HOPE WE ORDERED ENOUGH.
PFFT. I LIKE DIFFERENT TASTES, MAN.
BESIDES, WHATEVER WE DON'T EAT HERE IS GOING TO BE EVEN FUCKING TASTIER AT THREE IN THE MORNING.
SO OUR ADORABLE FRIENDS--QUITE THE PAIR, RIGHT?
EDDIE WAS INTENSE.
HA! INTENSE DOESN'T SUM THAT DUDE UP AT ALL. HE'S BATSHIT.
RIGHT BEFORE THINGS WENT TO HELL AT ABERICORP, HE THREW A CHAIR THROUGH A WINDOW IN ONE OF HIS FITS.
WASN'T THE FIRST TIME EITHER.

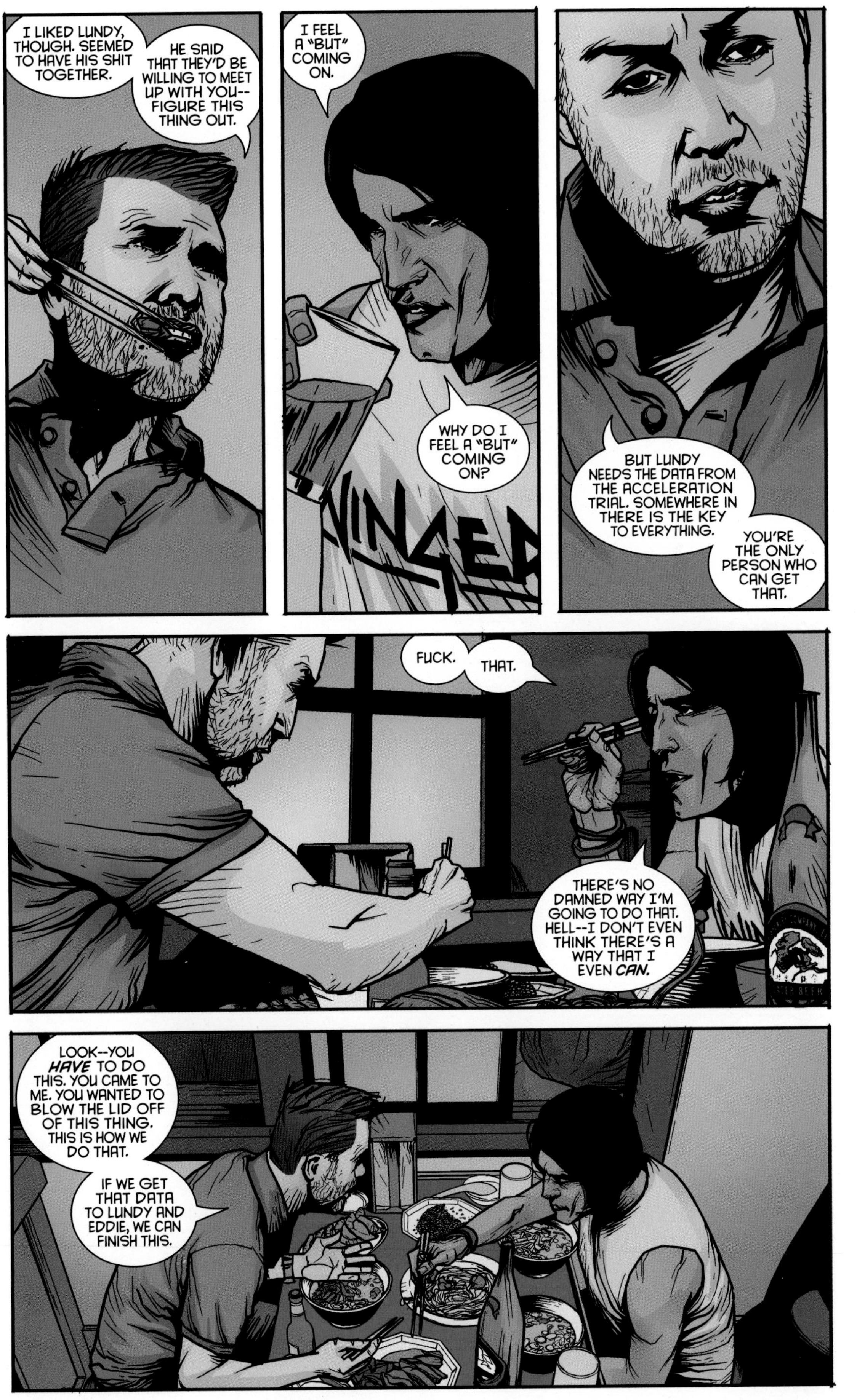
I LIKED LUNDY, THOUGH. SEEMED TO HAVE HIS SHIT TOGETHER.
HE SAID THAT THEY'D BE WILLING TO MEET UP WITH YOU--FIGURE THIS THING OUT.
I FEEL A "BUT" COMING ON.
WHY DO I FEEL A "BUT" COMING ON?
BUT LUNDY NEEDS THE DATA FROM THE ACCELERATION TRIAL. SOMEWHERE IN THERE IS THE KEY TO EVERYTHING.
YOU'RE THE ONLY PERSON WHO CAN GET THAT.
FUCK.
THAT.
THERE'S NO DAMNED WAY I'M GOING TO DO THAT. HELL--I DON'T EVEN THINK THERE'S A WAY THAT I EVEN *CAN.*
LOOK--YOU *HAVE* TO DO THIS. YOU CAME TO ME. YOU WANTED TO BLOW THE LID OFF OF THIS THING. THIS IS HOW WE DO THAT.
IF WE GET THAT DATA TO LUNDY AND EDDIE, WE CAN FINISH THIS.

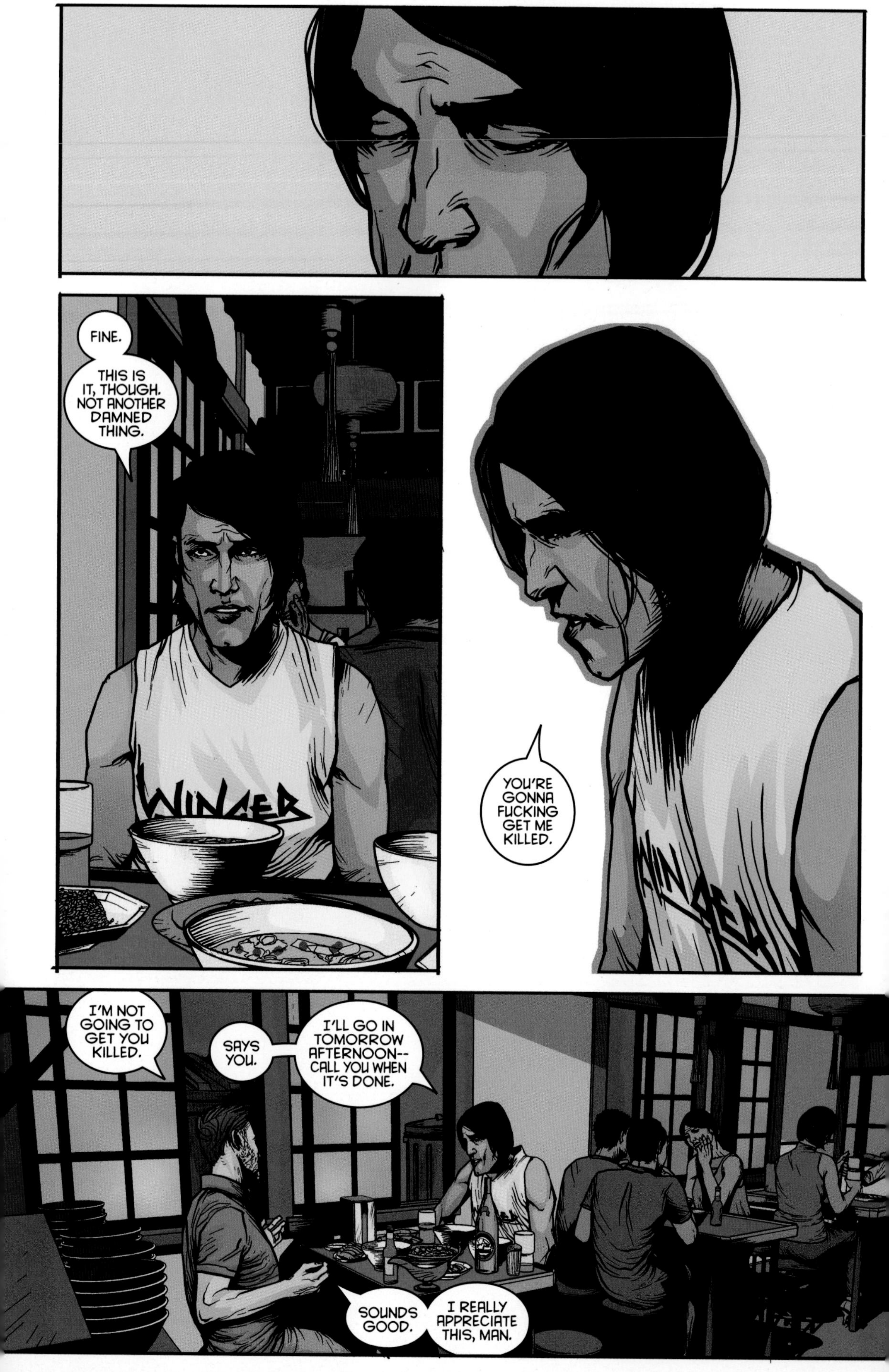
FINE.
THIS IS IT, THOUGH. NOT ANOTHER DAMNED THING.
YOU'RE GONNA FUCKING GET ME KILLED.
I'M NOT GOING TO GET YOU KILLED.
SAYS YOU.
I'LL GO IN TOMORROW AFTERNOON-- CALL YOU WHEN IT'S DONE.
SOUNDS GOOD.
I REALLY APPRECIATE THIS, MAN.

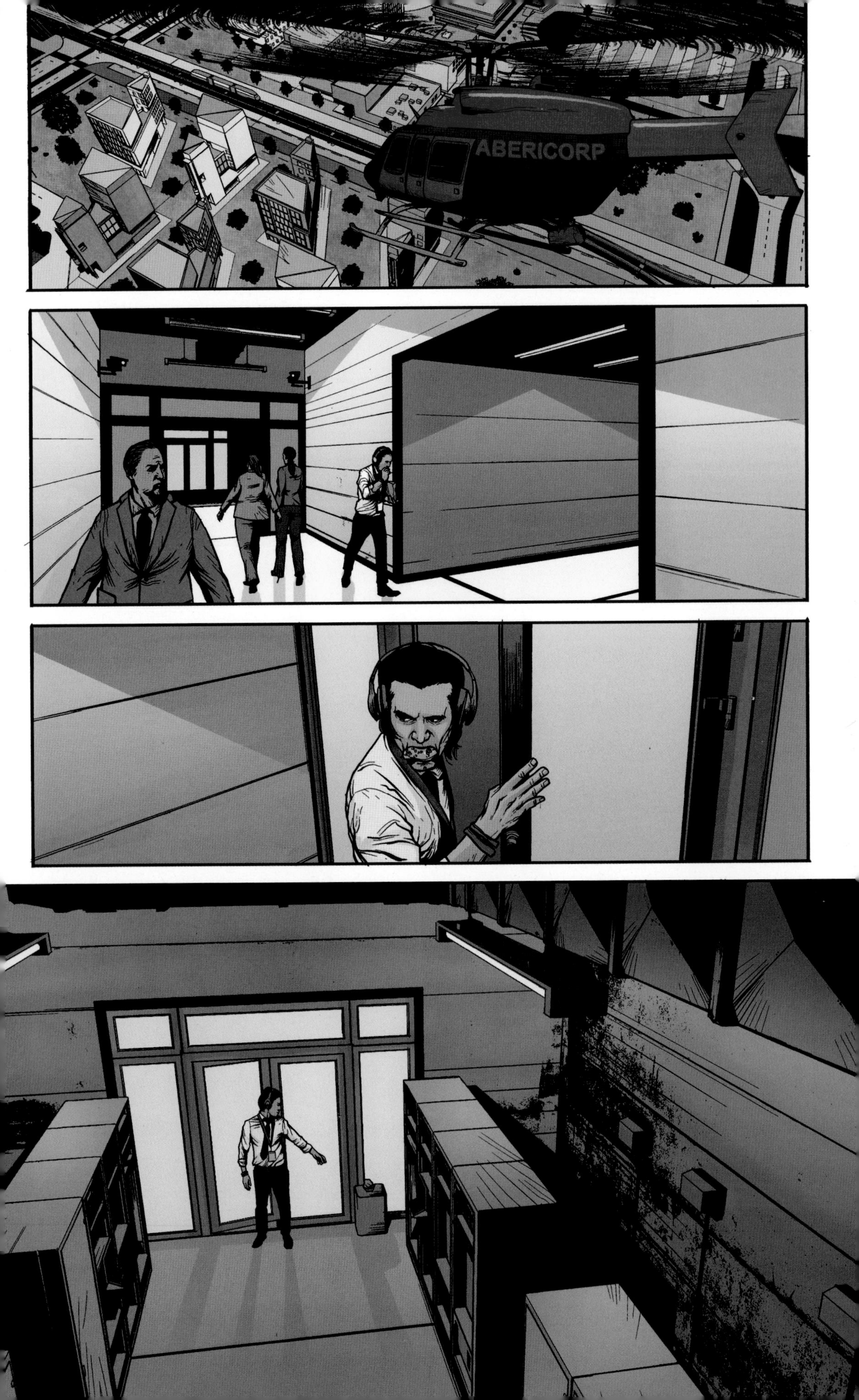
ABERICORP

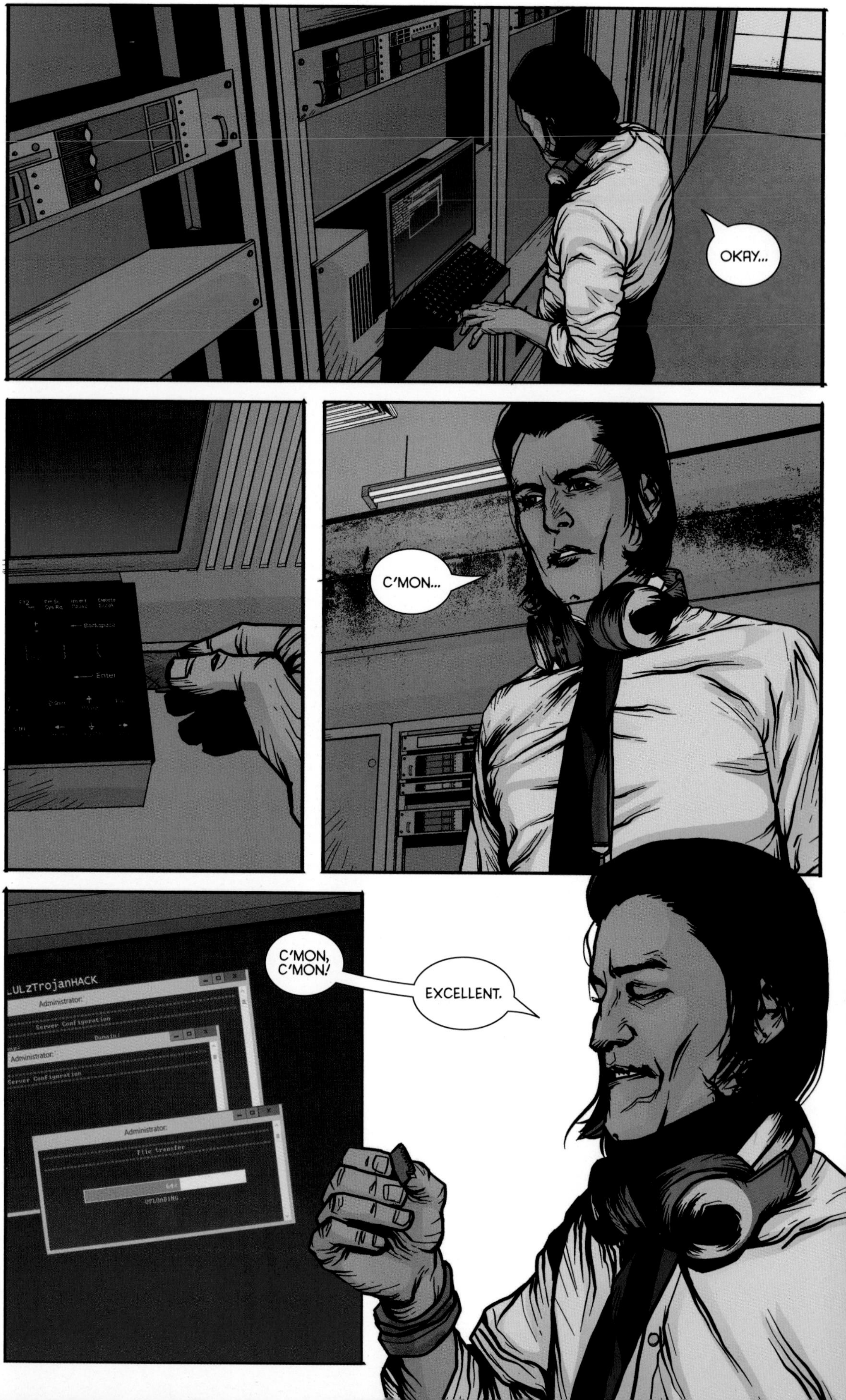
OKAY...
C'MON...
C'MON, C'MON!
EXCELLENT.
Administrator:
Server Configuration
Administrator:
Server Configuration
Administrator:
File transfer
UPLOADING...

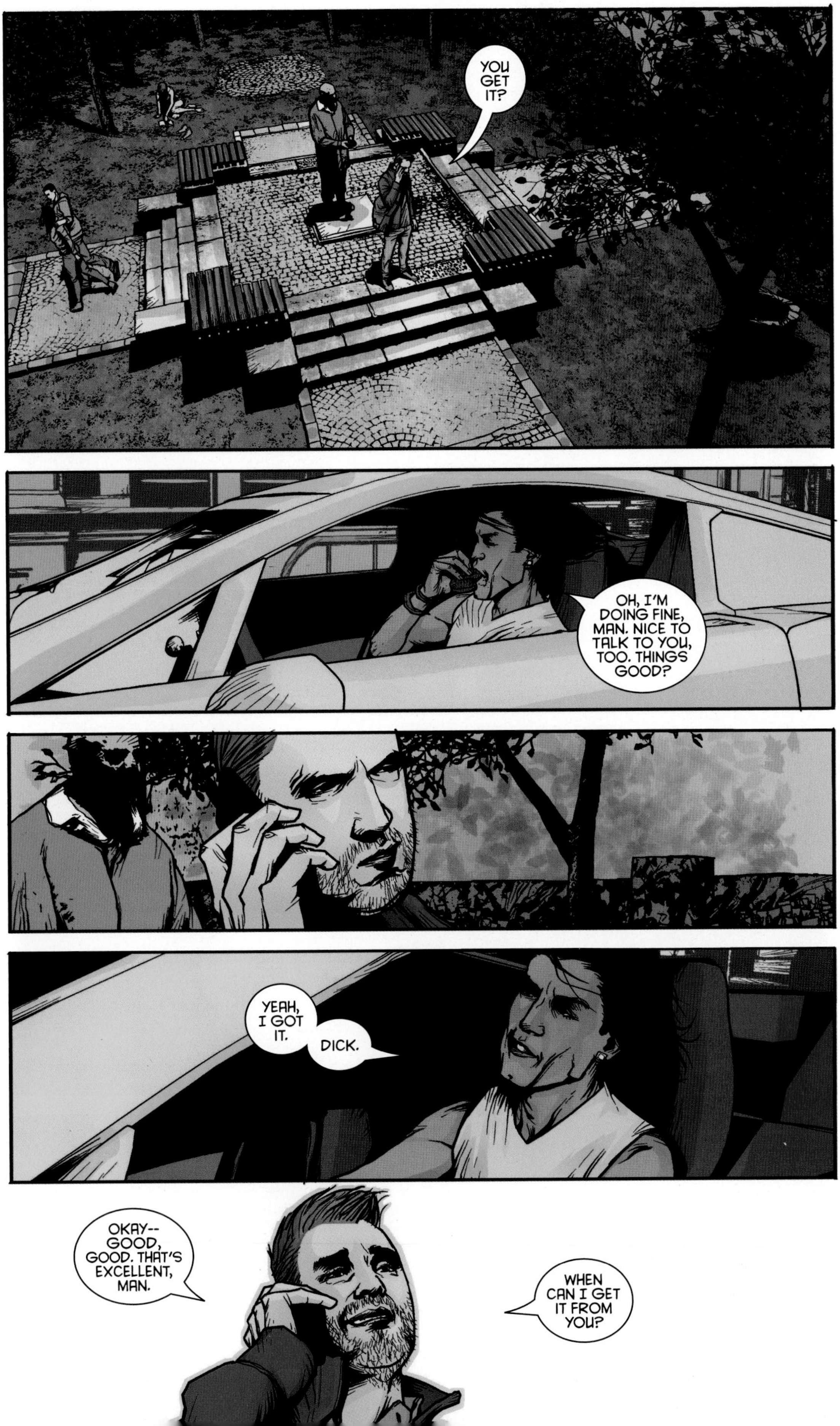
YOU GET IT?
OH, I'M DOING FINE, MAN. NICE TO TALK TO YOU, TOO. THINGS GOOD?
YEAH, I GOT IT.
DICK.
OKAY-- GOOD, GOOD. THAT'S EXCELLENT, MAN.
WHEN CAN I GET IT FROM YOU?

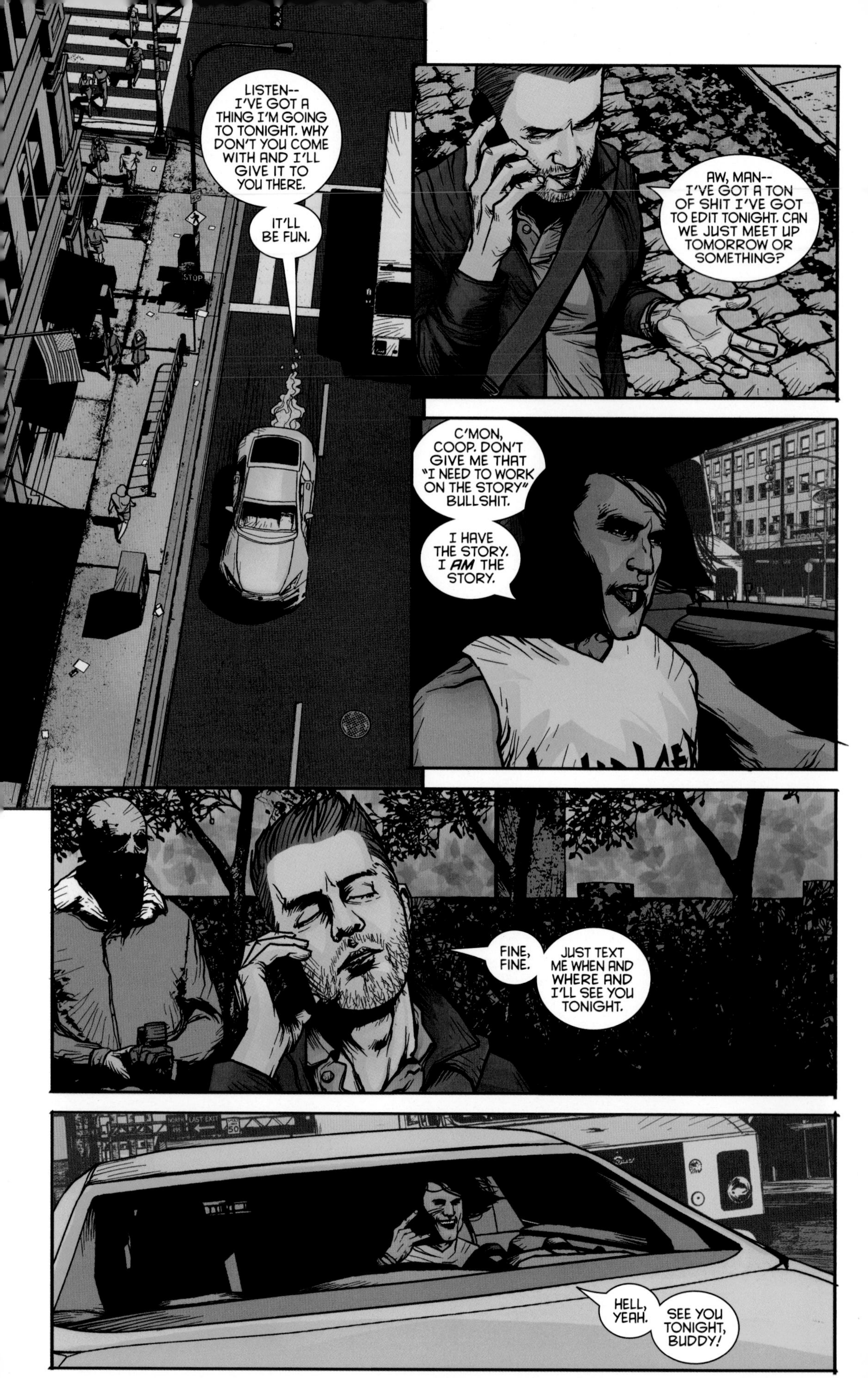
LISTEN-- I'VE GOT A THING I'M GOING TO TONIGHT. WHY DON'T YOU COME WITH AND I'LL GIVE IT TO YOU THERE.
IT'LL BE FUN.
AW, MAN-- I'VE GOT A TON OF SHIT I'VE GOT TO EDIT TONIGHT. CAN WE JUST MEET UP TOMORROW OR SOMETHING?
C'MON, COOP. DON'T GIVE ME THAT "I NEED TO WORK ON THE STORY" BULLSHIT.
I HAVE THE STORY. I *AM* THE STORY.
FINE, FINE.
JUST TEXT ME WHEN AND WHERE AND I'LL SEE YOU TONIGHT.
HELL, YEAH.
SEE YOU TONIGHT, BUDDY!

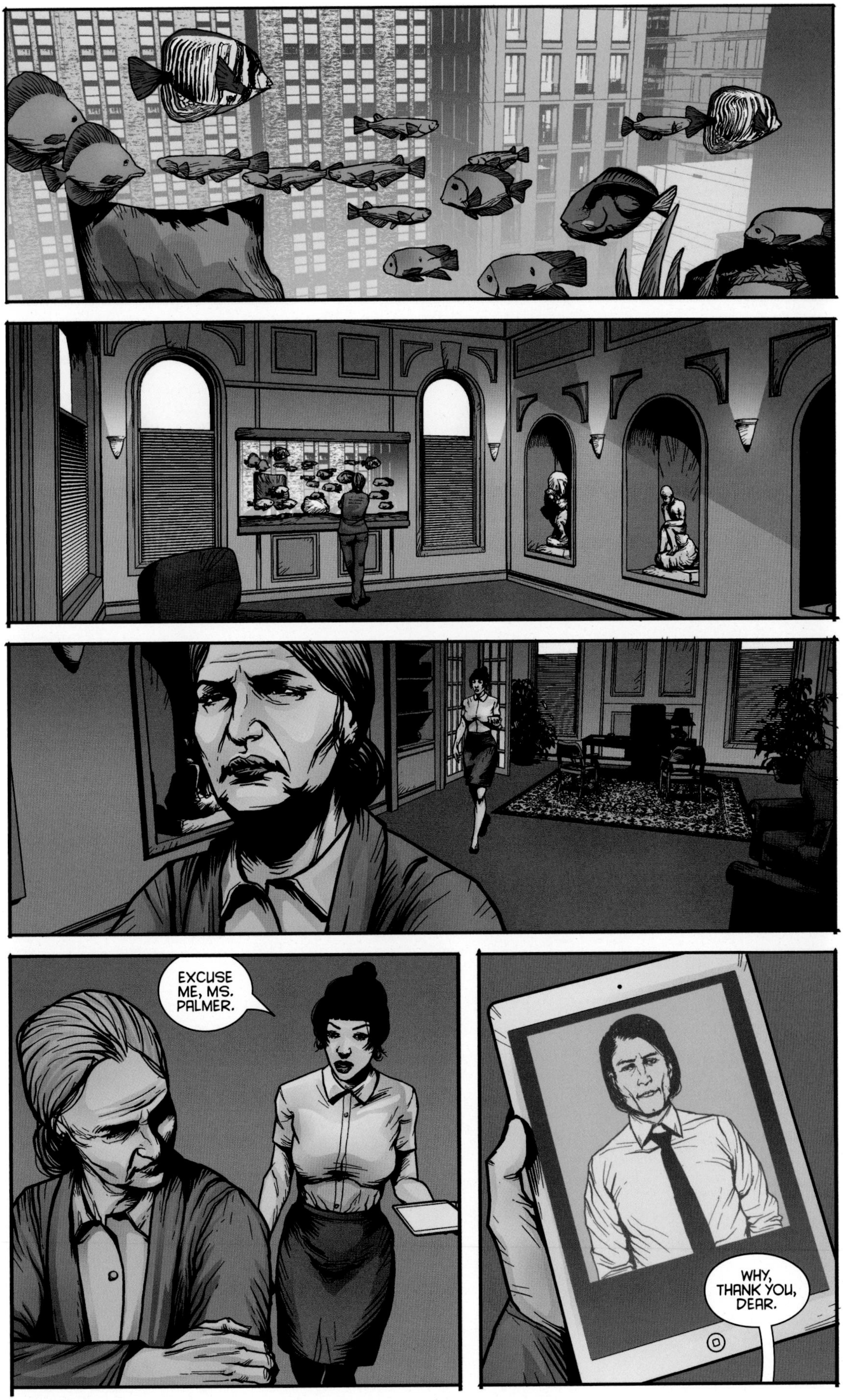
EXCUSE ME, MS. PALMER.
WHY, THANK YOU, DEAR.

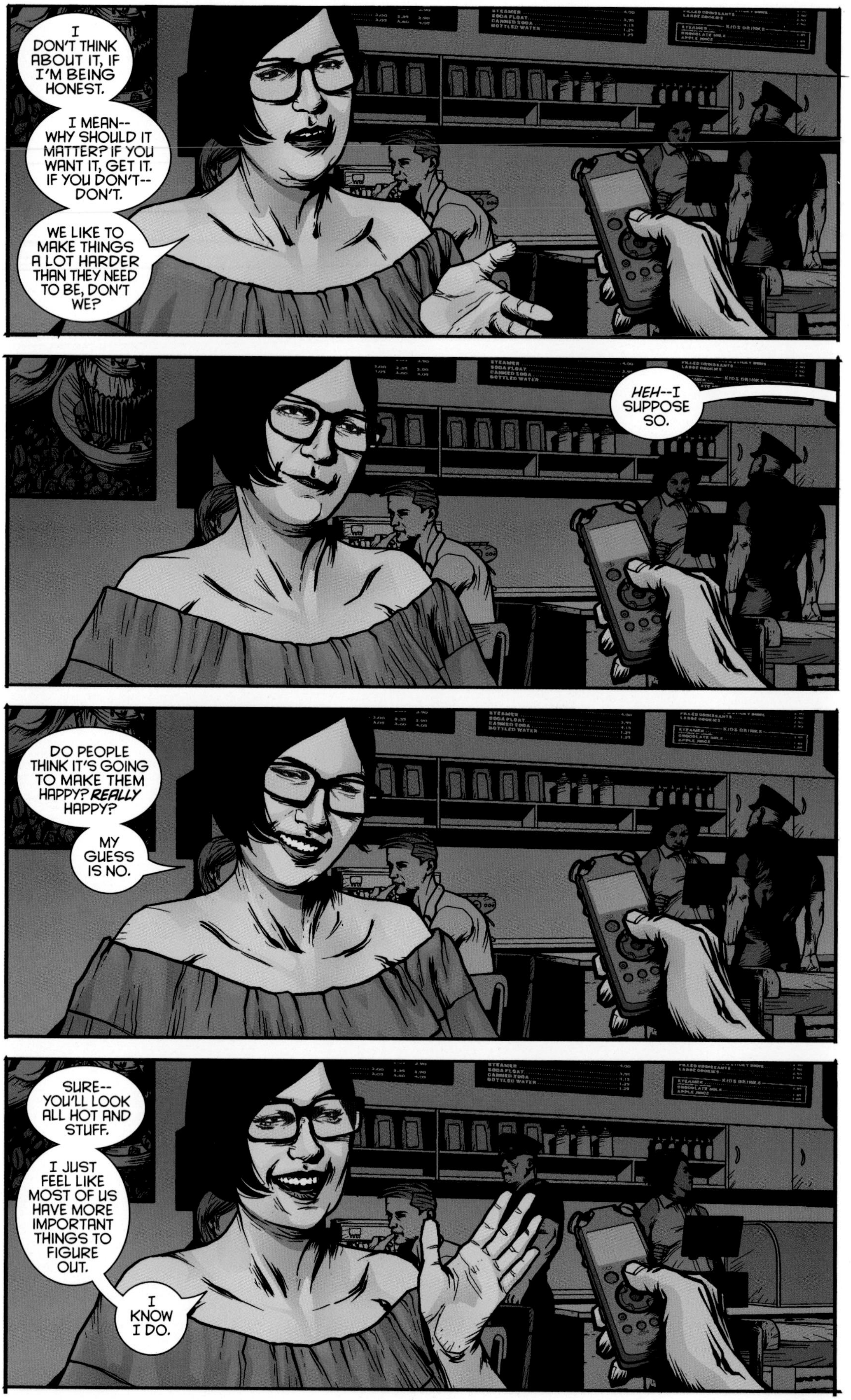
I DON'T THINK ABOUT IT, IF I'M BEING HONEST.
I MEAN-- WHY SHOULD IT MATTER? IF YOU WANT IT, GET IT. IF YOU DON'T-- DON'T.
WE LIKE TO MAKE THINGS A LOT HARDER THAN THEY NEED TO BE, DON'T WE?
HEH--I SUPPOSE SO.
DO PEOPLE THINK IT'S GOING TO MAKE THEM HAPPY? ***REALLY*** HAPPY?
MY GUESS IS NO.
SURE-- YOU'LL LOOK ALL HOT AND STUFF.
I JUST FEEL LIKE MOST OF US HAVE MORE IMPORTANT THINGS TO FIGURE OUT.
I KNOW I DO.

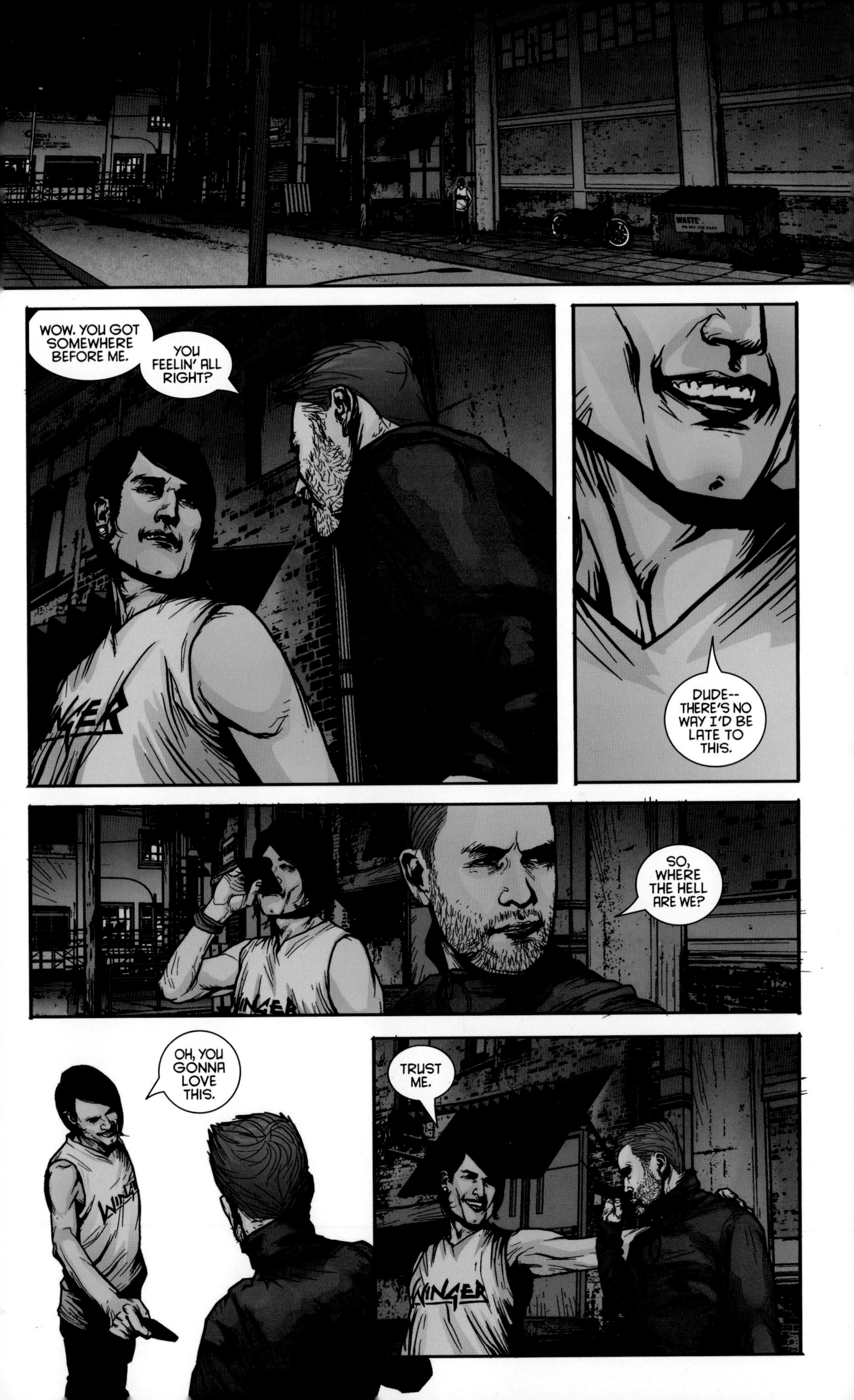

WOW. YOU GOT SOMEWHERE BEFORE ME.
YOU FEELIN' ALL RIGHT?
DUDE-- THERE'S NO WAY I'D BE LATE TO THIS.
SO, WHERE THE HELL ARE WE?
OH, YOU GONNA LOVE THIS.
TRUST ME.
WASTE

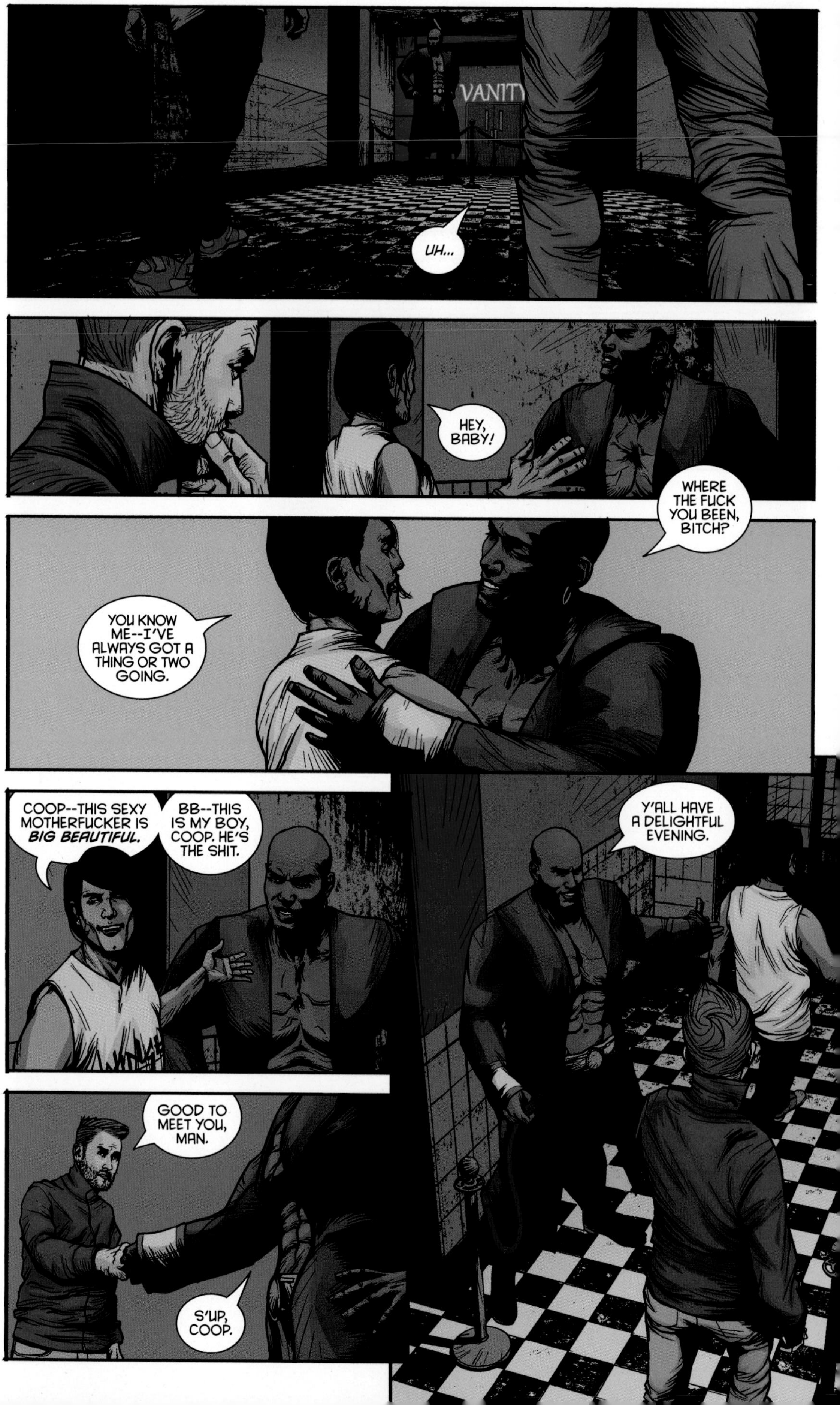
VANITY
UH...
HEY, BABY!
WHERE THE FUCK YOU BEEN, BITCH?
YOU KNOW ME--I'VE ALWAYS GOT A THING OR TWO GOING.
COOP--THIS SEXY MOTHERFUCKER IS *BIG BEAUTIFUL.*
BB--THIS IS MY BOY, COOP. HE'S THE SHIT.
GOOD TO MEET YOU, MAN.
S'UP, COOP.
Y'ALL HAVE A DELIGHTFUL EVENING.

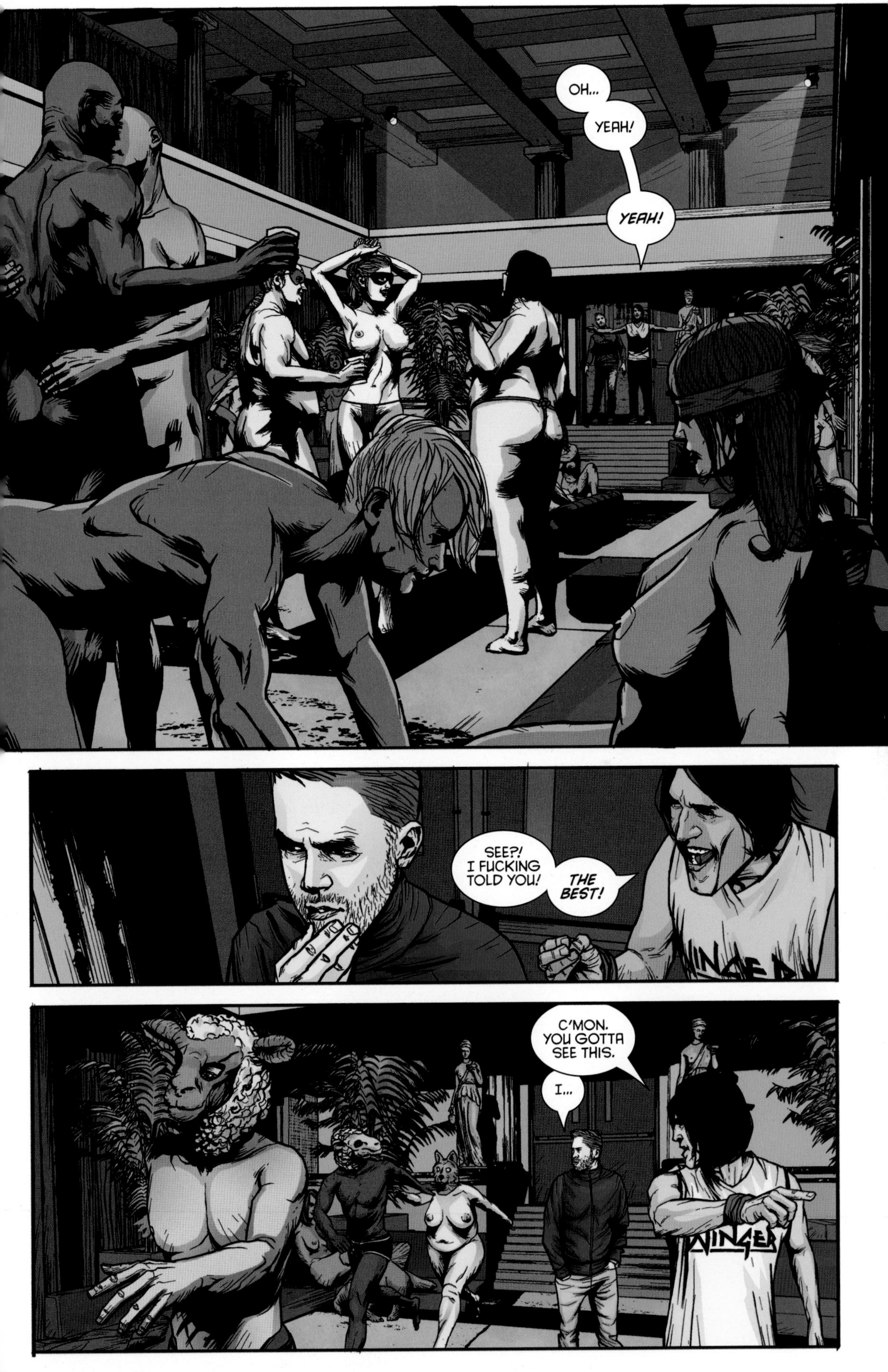
OH...
YEAH!
YEAH!
SEE?! I FUCKING TOLD YOU!
THE BEST!
C'MON. YOU GOTTA SEE THIS.
I...

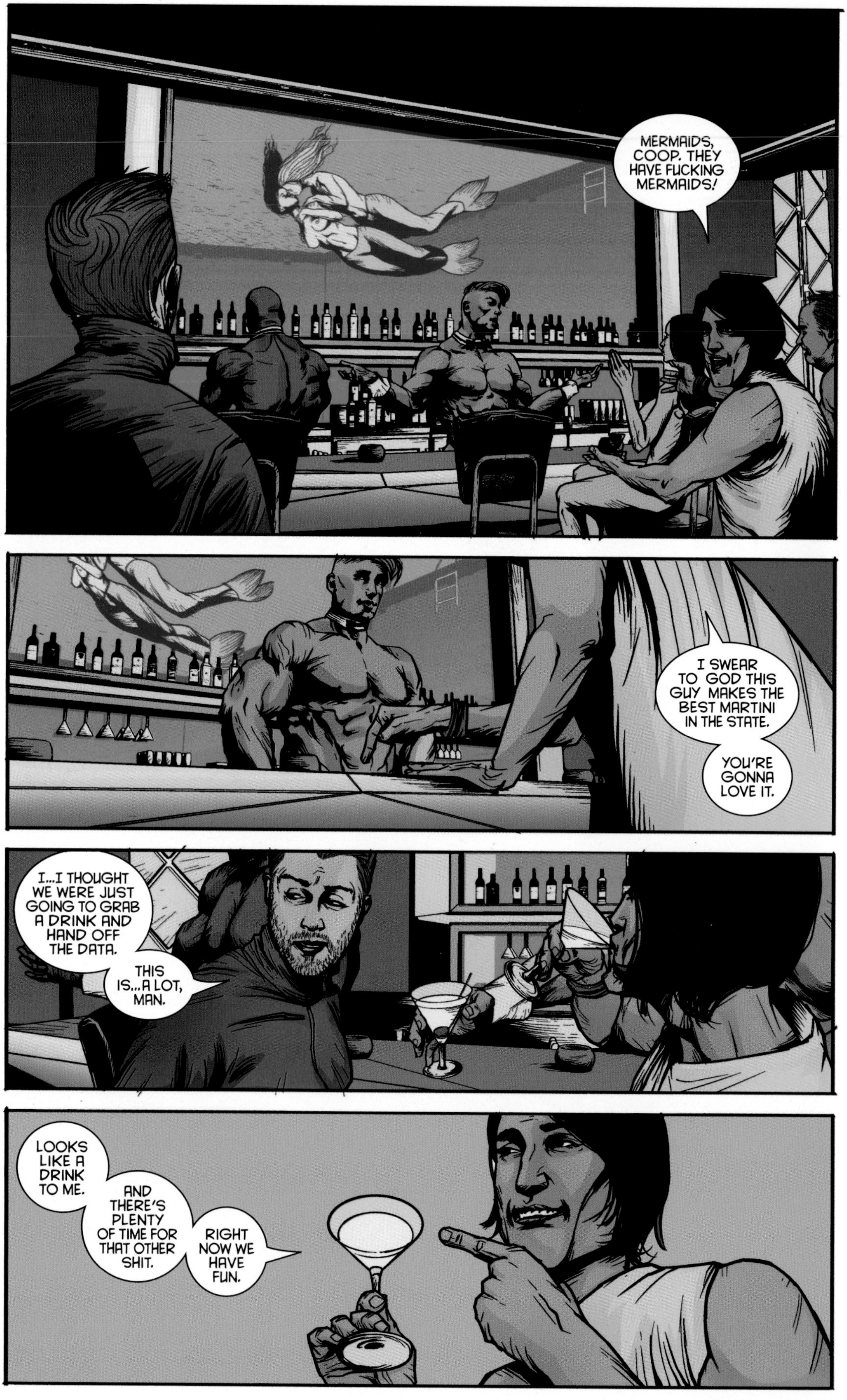
MERMAIDS, COOP. THEY HAVE FUCKING MERMAIDS!
I SWEAR TO GOD THIS GUY MAKES THE BEST MARTINI IN THE STATE.
YOU'RE GONNA LOVE IT.
I...I THOUGHT WE WERE JUST GOING TO GRAB A DRINK AND HAND OFF THE DATA.
THIS IS...A LOT, MAN.
LOOKS LIKE A DRINK TO ME.
AND THERE'S PLENTY OF TIME FOR THAT OTHER SHIT.
RIGHT NOW WE HAVE FUN.

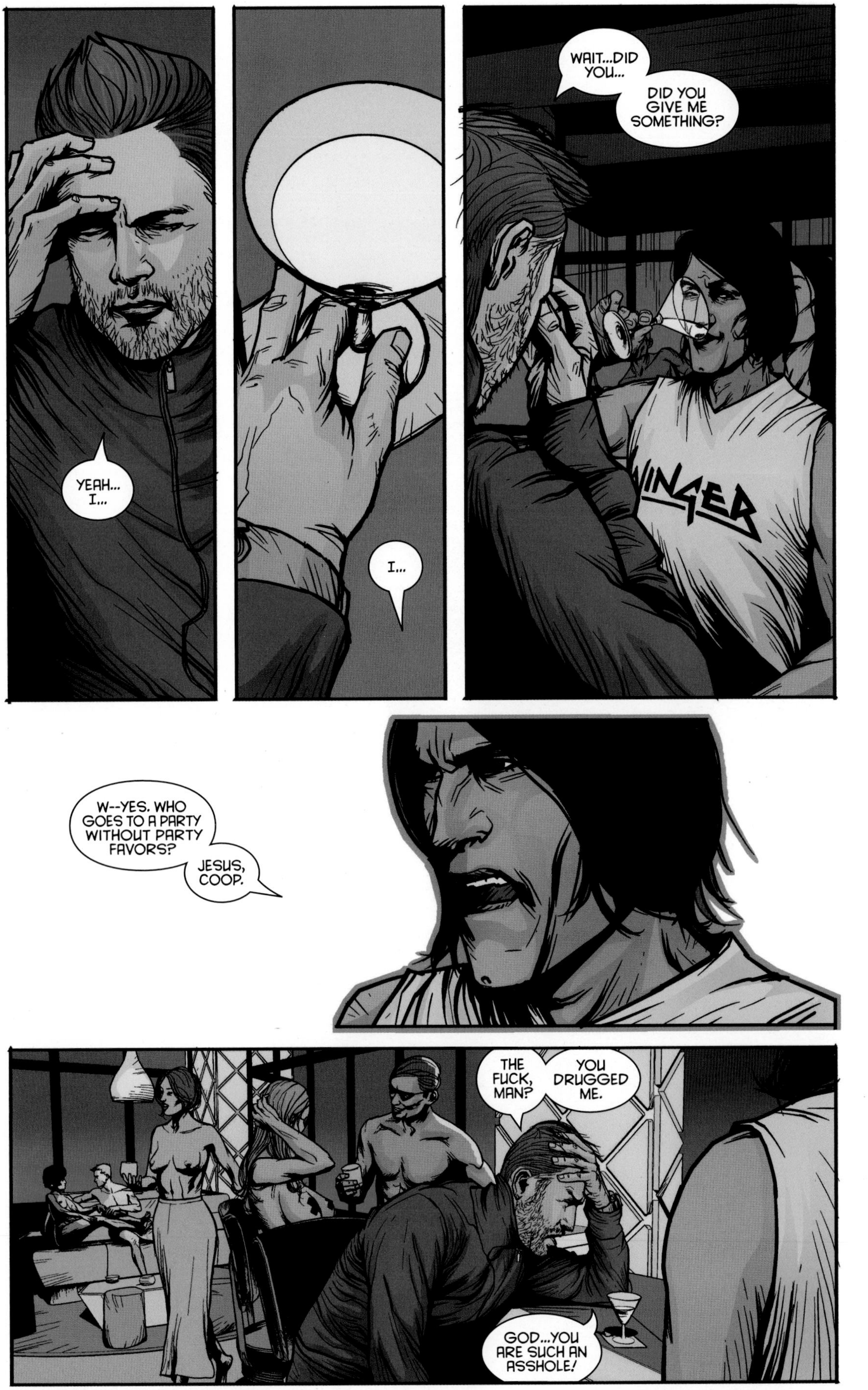
YEAH... I...
I...
WAIT...DID YOU...
DID YOU GIVE ME SOMETHING?
WINGER
W--YES. WHO GOES TO A PARTY WITHOUT PARTY FAVORS?
JESUS, COOP.
THE FUCK, MAN?
YOU DRUGGED ME.
GOD...YOU ARE SUCH AN ASSHOLE!

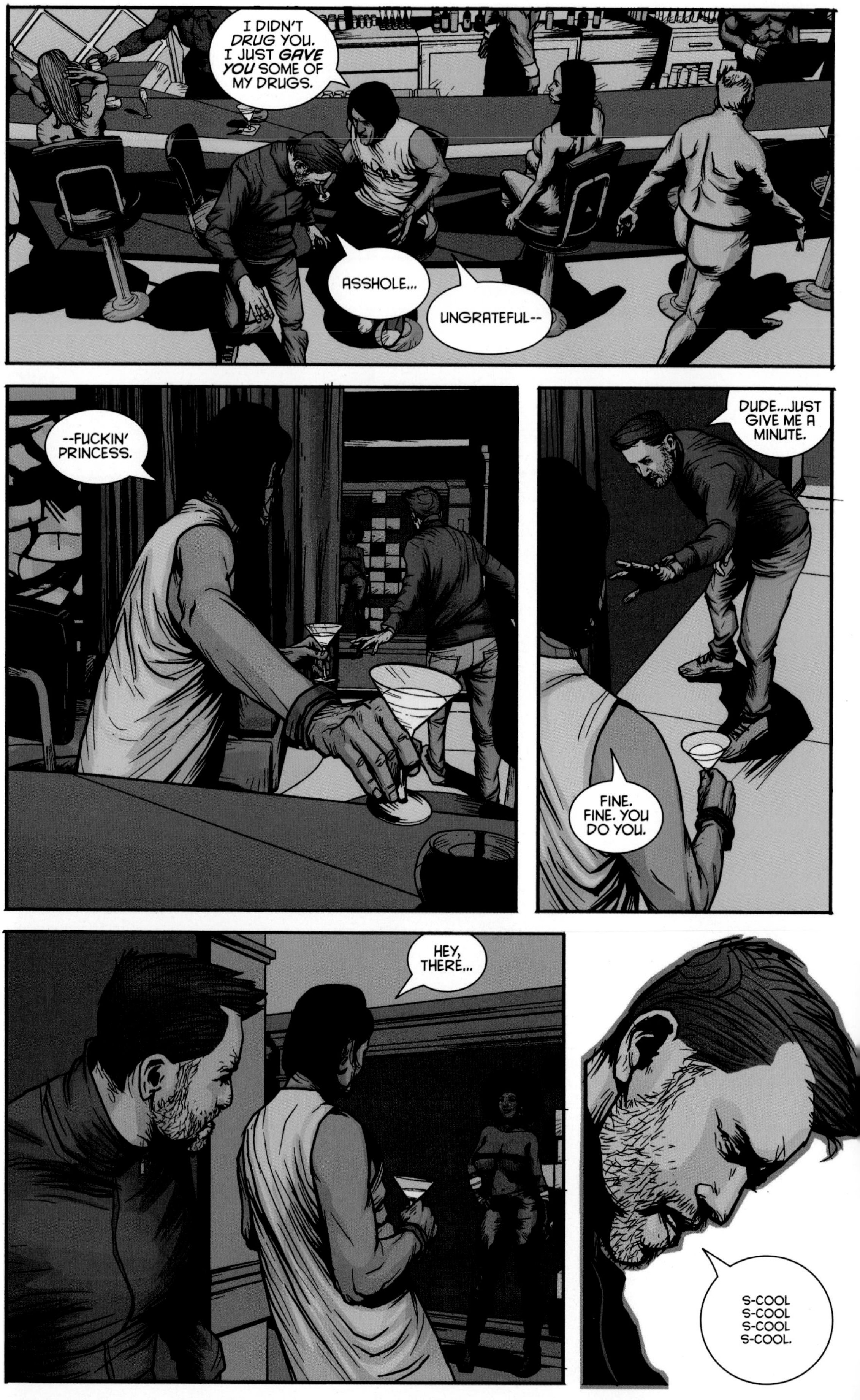
I DIDN'T *DRUG* YOU. I JUST ***GAVE YOU*** SOME OF MY DRUGS.
ASSHOLE...
UNGRATEFUL--
--FUCKIN' PRINCESS.
DUDE...JUST GIVE ME A MINUTE.
FINE. FINE. YOU DO YOU.
HEY, THERE...
S-COOL
S-COOL
S-COOL
S-COOL.

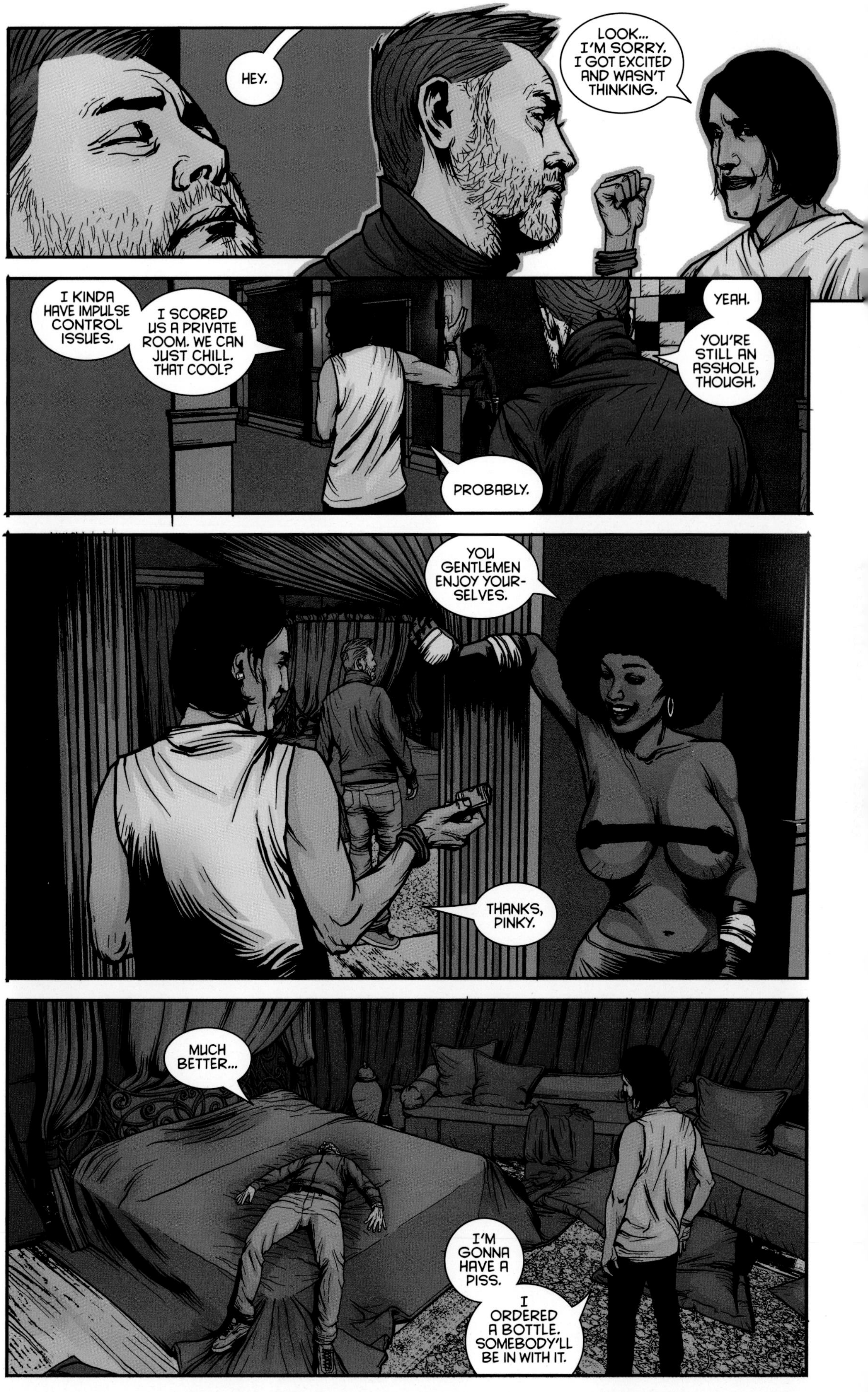
HEY.
LOOK... I'M SORRY. I GOT EXCITED AND WASN'T THINKING.
I KINDA HAVE IMPULSE CONTROL ISSUES.
I SCORED US A PRIVATE ROOM. WE CAN JUST CHILL. THAT COOL?
YEAH.
YOU'RE STILL AN ASSHOLE, THOUGH.
PROBABLY.
YOU GENTLEMEN ENJOY YOUR-SELVES.
THANKS, PINKY.
MUCH BETTER...
I'M GONNA HAVE A PISS.
I ORDERED A BOTTLE. SOMEBODY'LL BE IN WITH IT.

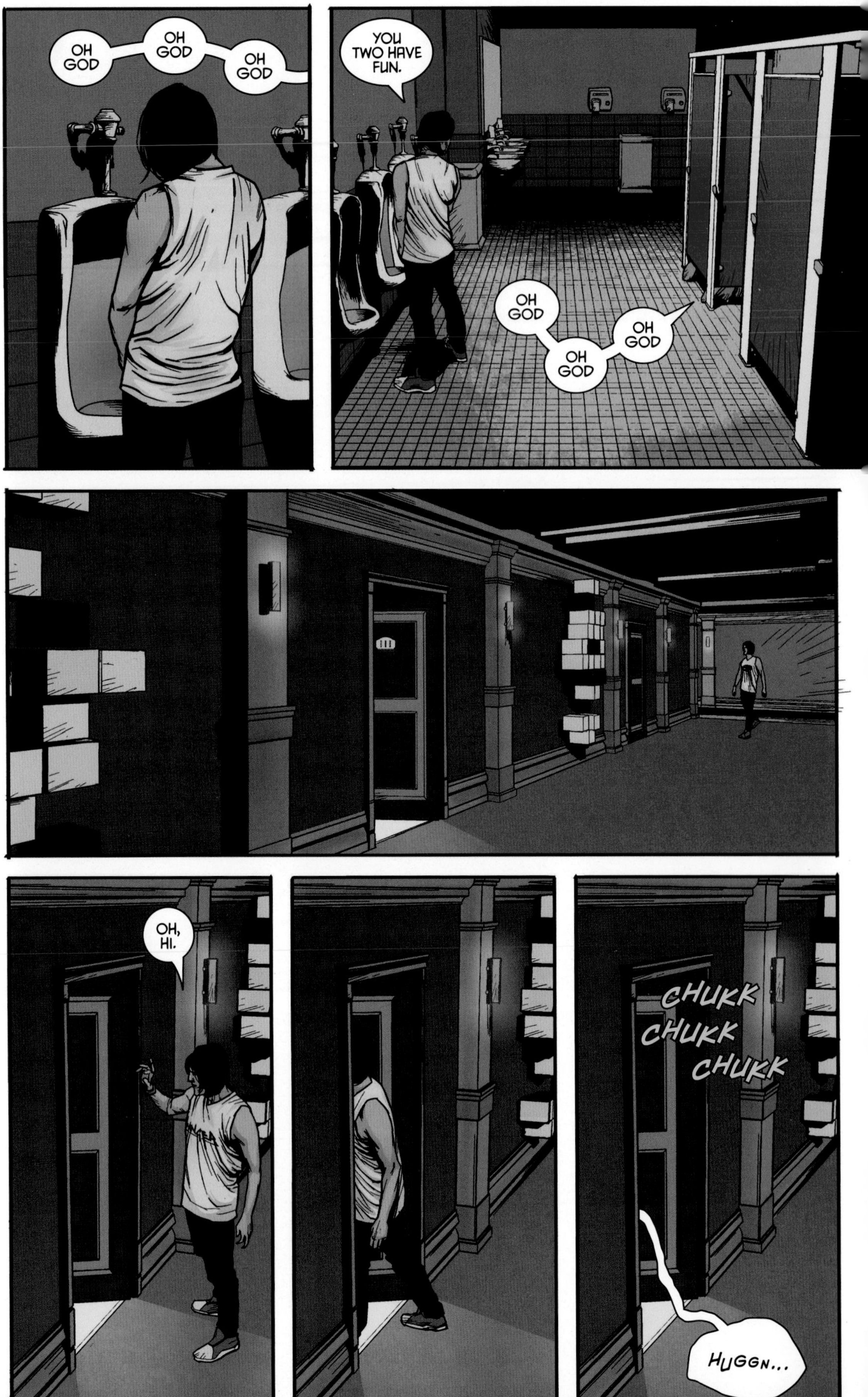
OH GOD
OH GOD
OH GOD
YOU TWO HAVE FUN.
OH GOD
OH GOD
OH GOD
OH, HI.
CHUKK
CHUKK
CHUKK
HUGGN...

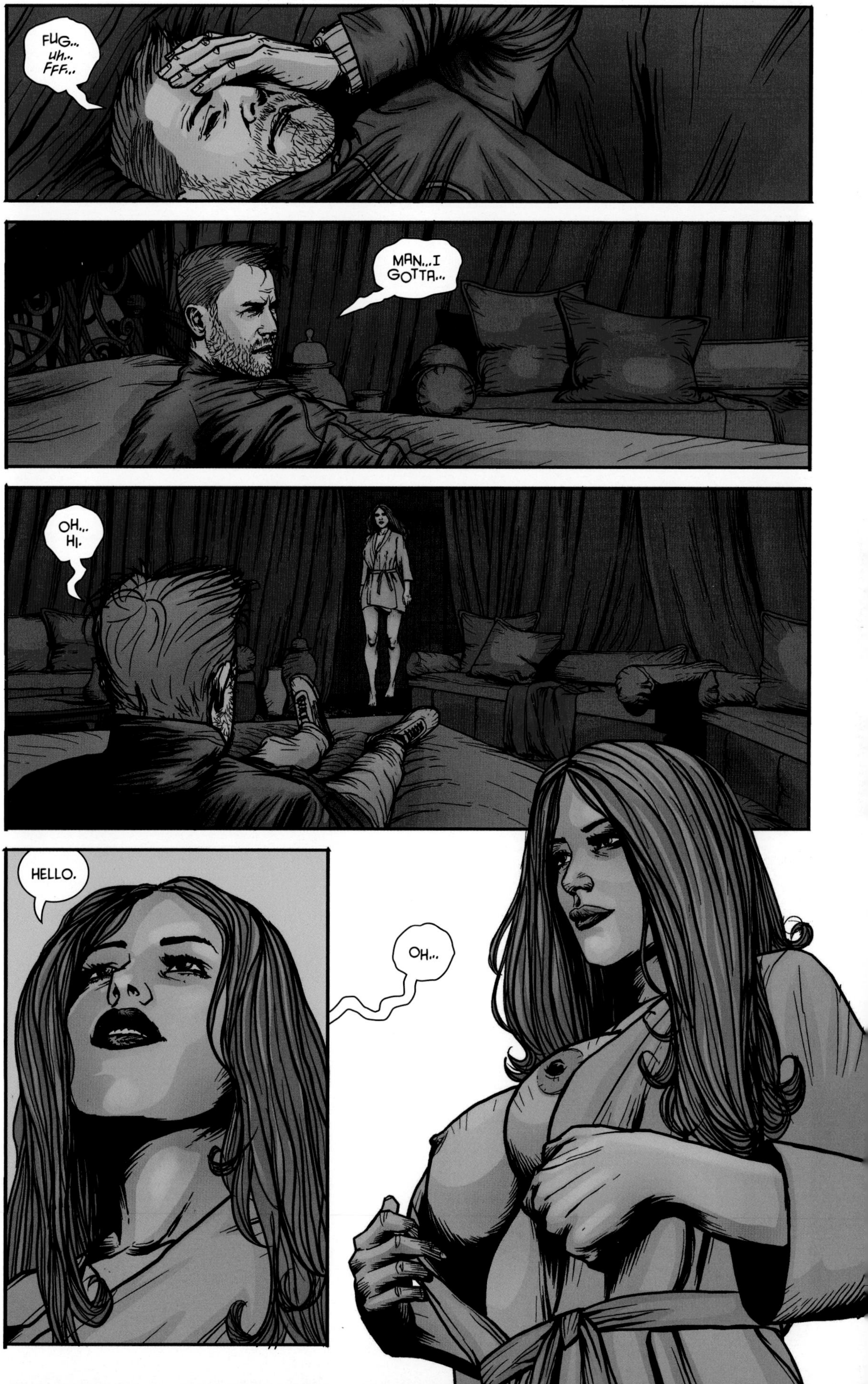
FUG...
UH...
FFF...
MAN...I GOTTA...
OH...
HI.
HELLO.
OH...

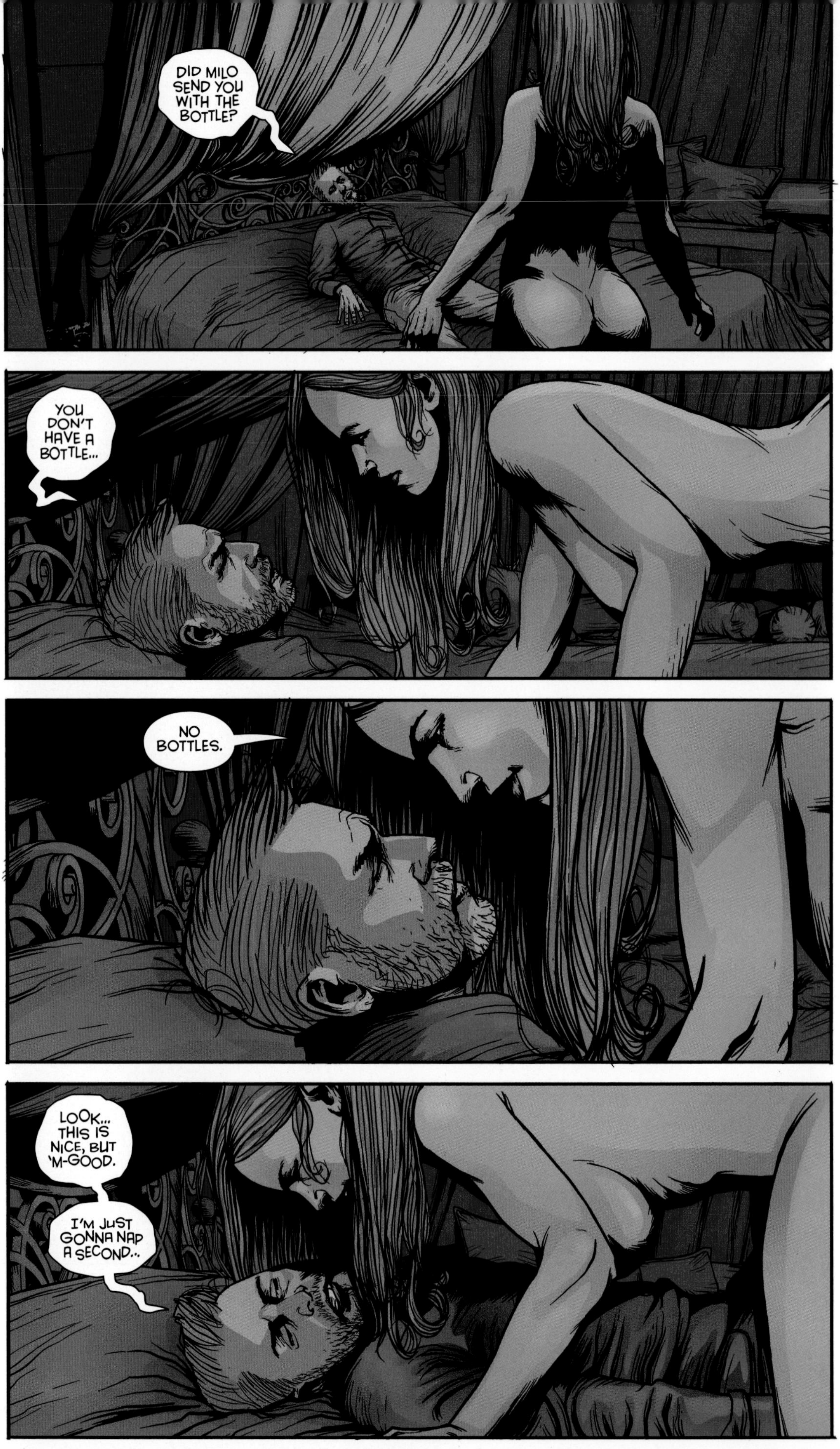
DID MILO SEND YOU WITH THE BOTTLE?
YOU DON'T HAVE A BOTTLE...
NO BOTTLES.
LOOK... THIS IS NICE, BUT 'M-GOOD.
I'M JUST GONNA NAP A SECOND...

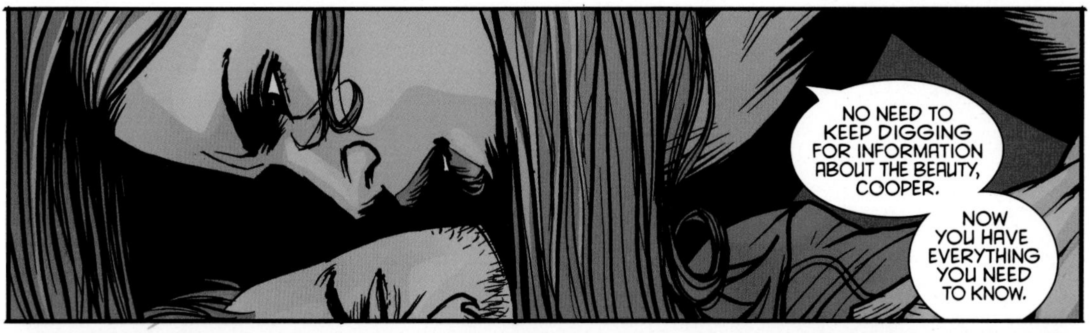
NO NEED TO KEEP DIGGING FOR INFORMATION ABOUT THE BEAUTY, COOPER.
NOW YOU HAVE EVERYTHING YOU NEED TO KNOW.

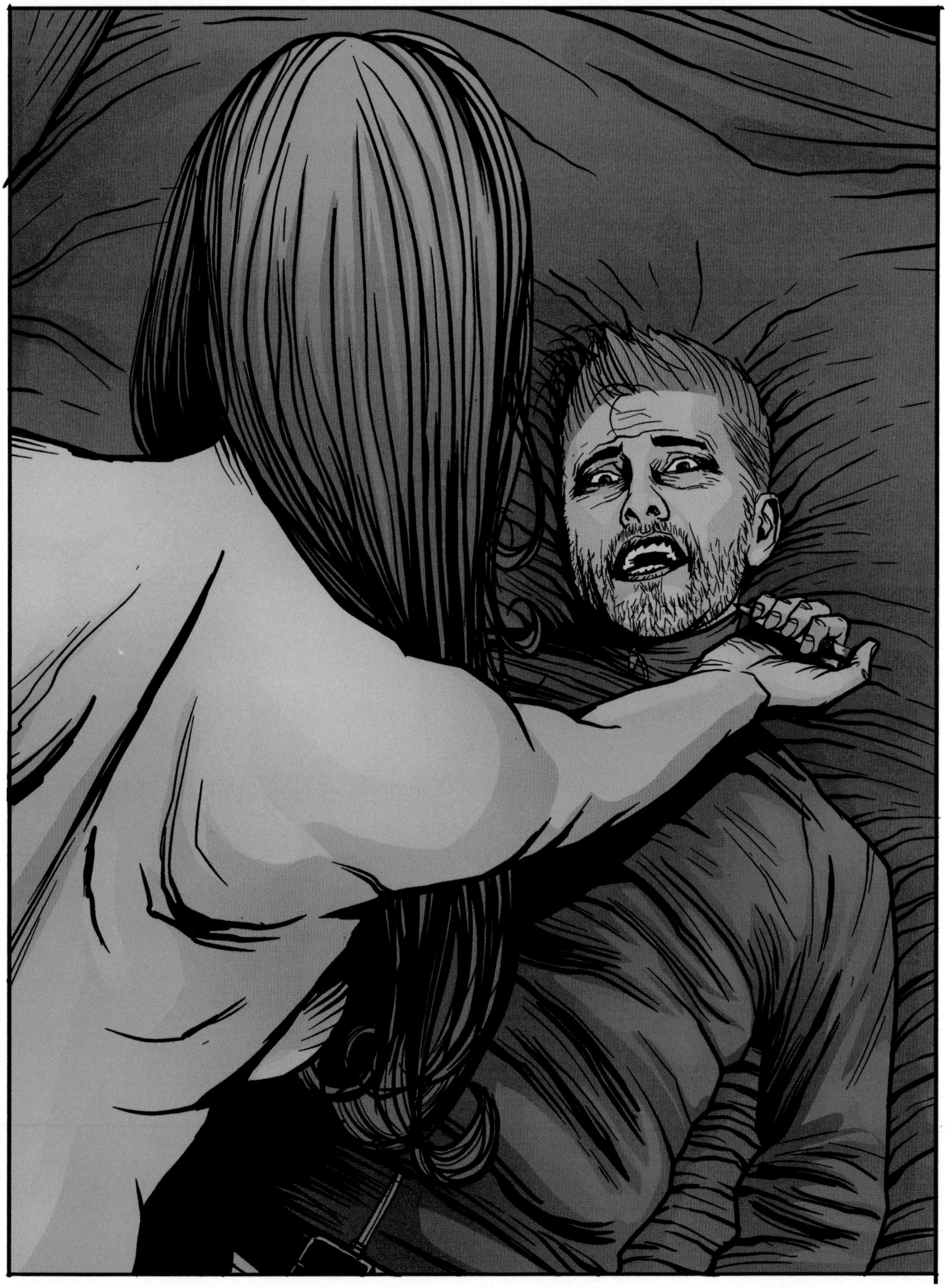

CHAPTER

21

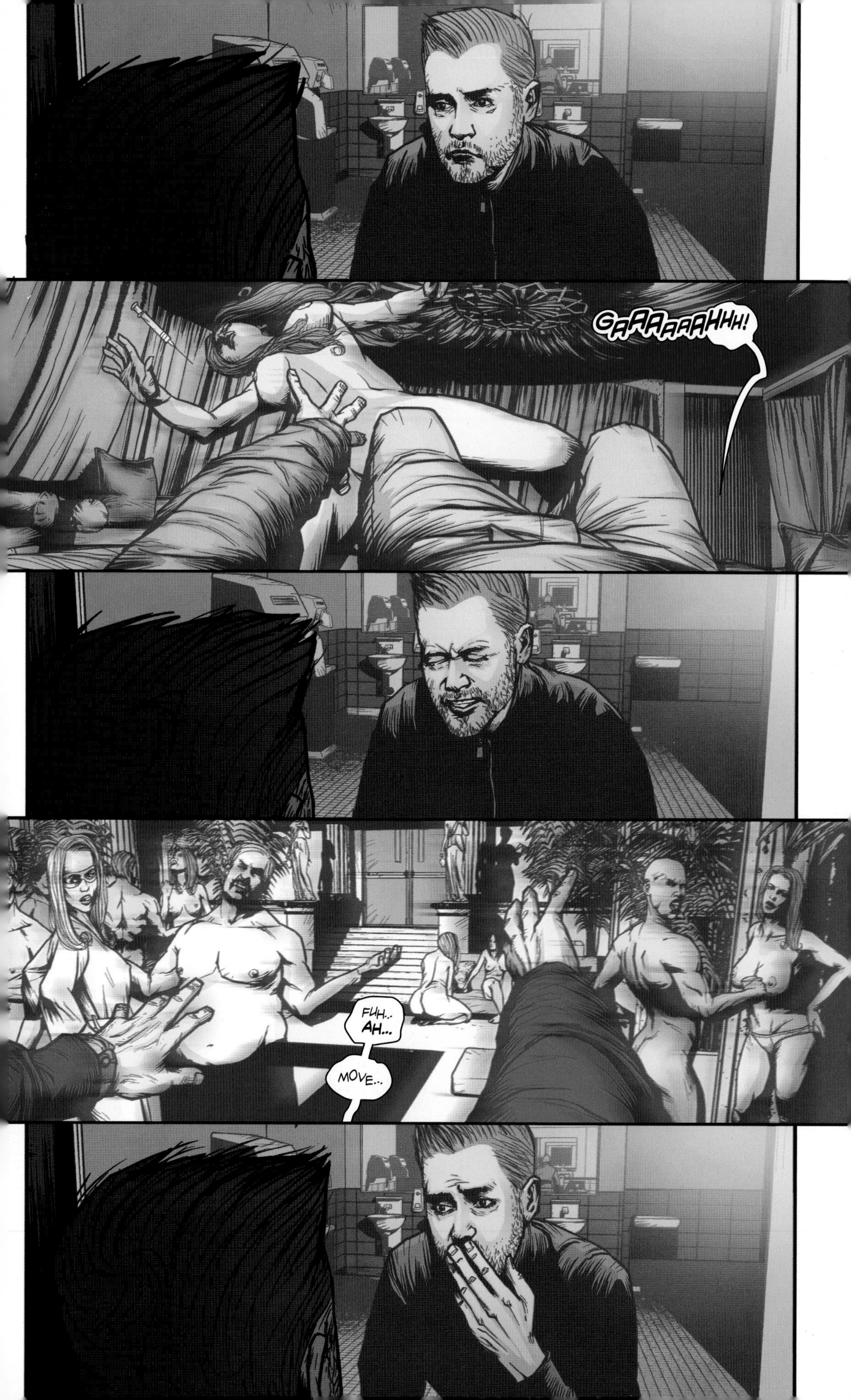
GAAAAAAAHHH!
FUH...
AH...
MOVE...

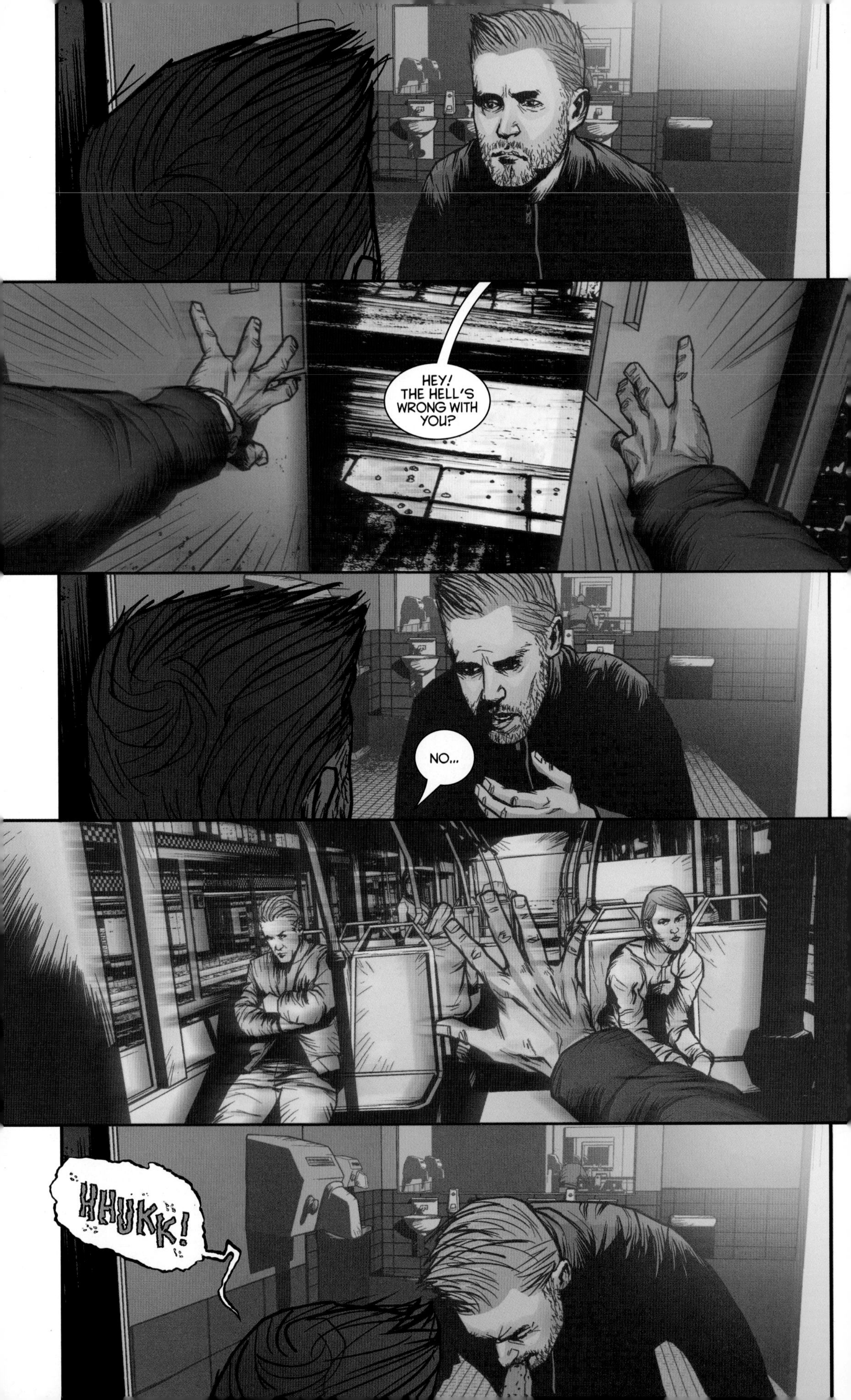
HEY! THE HELL'S WRONG WITH YOU?
NO...
HHUKK!

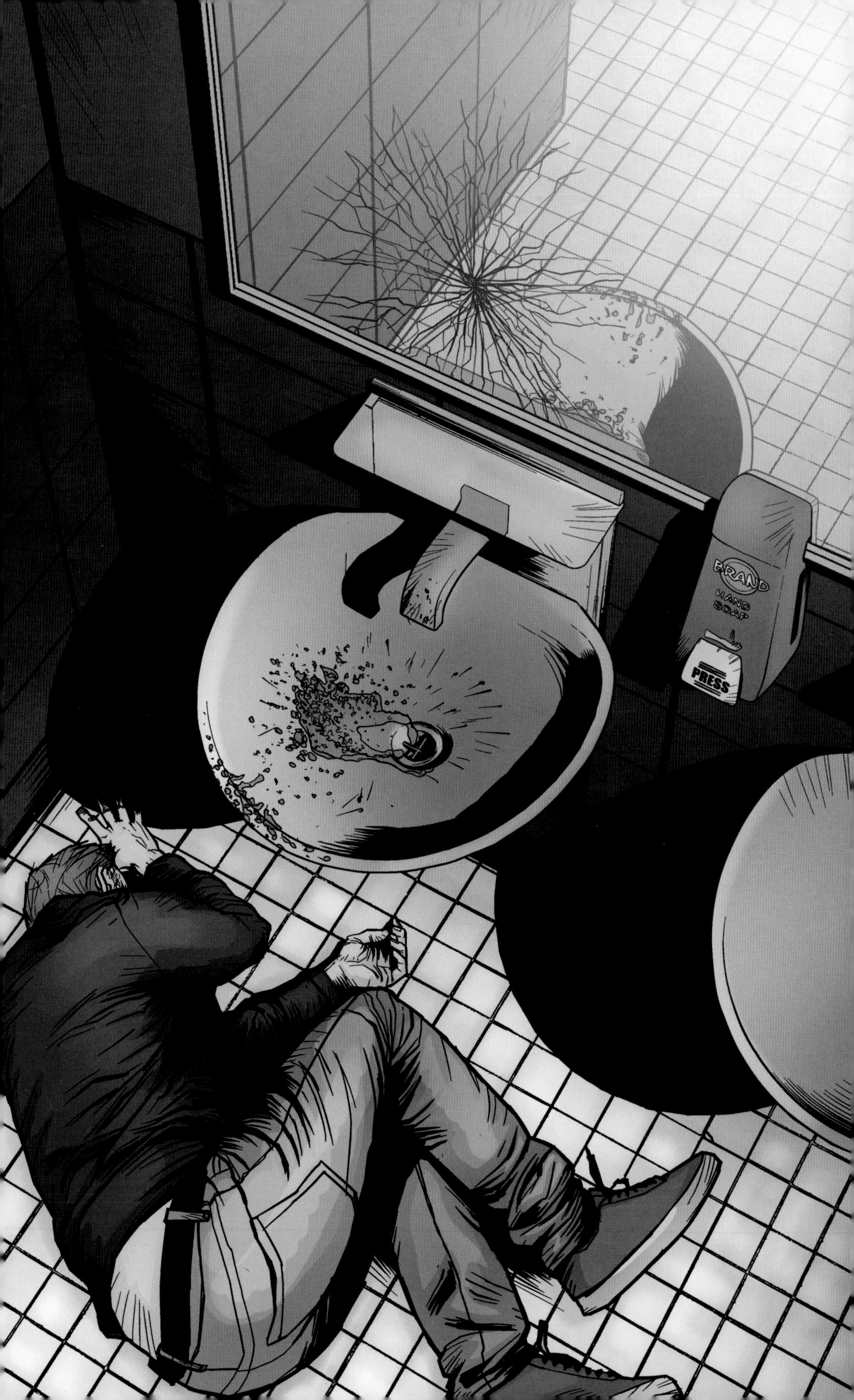
BRAND
HAND
SOAP
PRESS

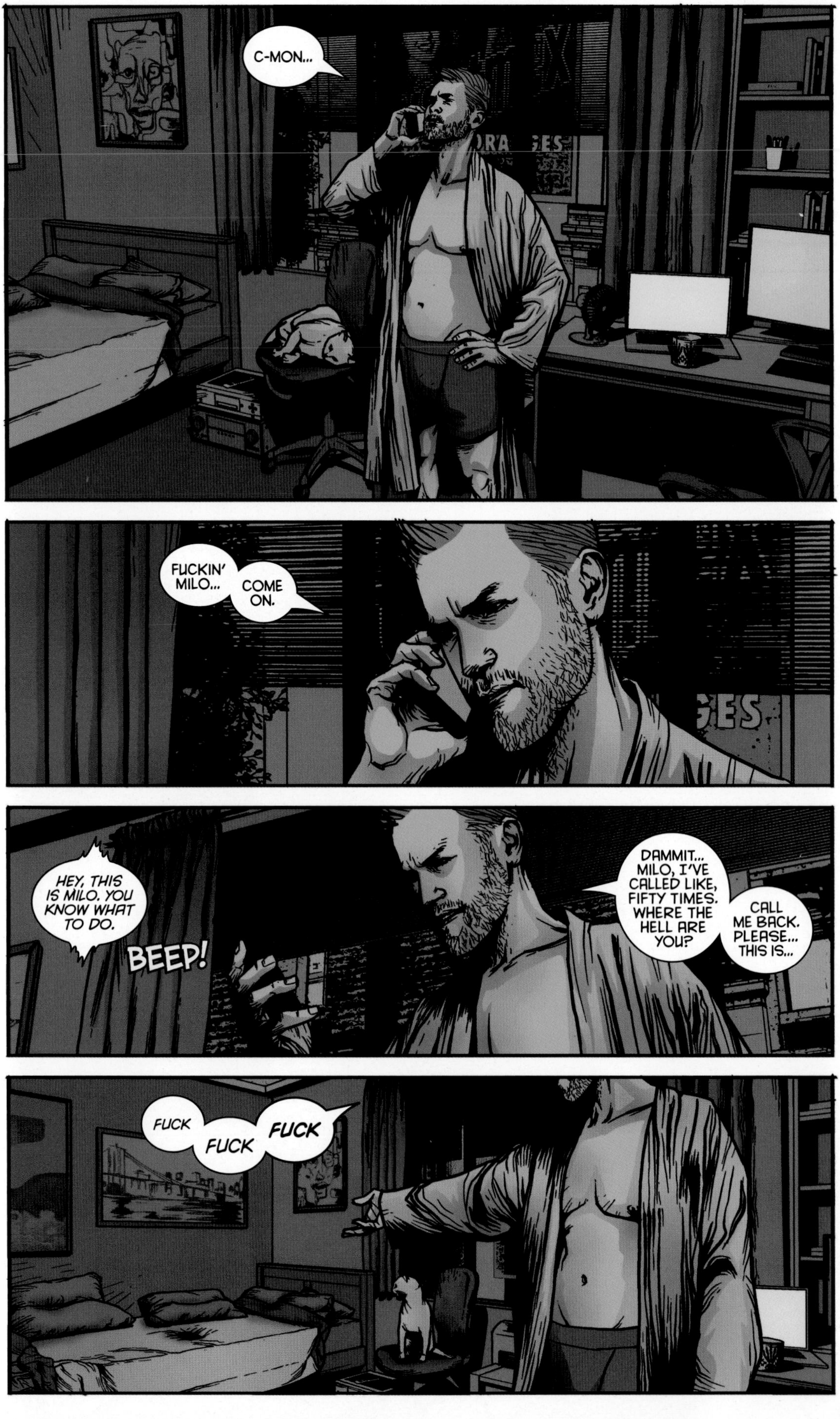
C-MON...
FUCKIN' MILO...
COME ON.
HEY, THIS IS MILO. YOU KNOW WHAT TO DO.
BEEP!
DAMMIT... MILO, I'VE CALLED LIKE, FIFTY TIMES. WHERE THE HELL ARE YOU?
CALL ME BACK. PLEASE... THIS IS...
FUCK
FUCK
FUCK

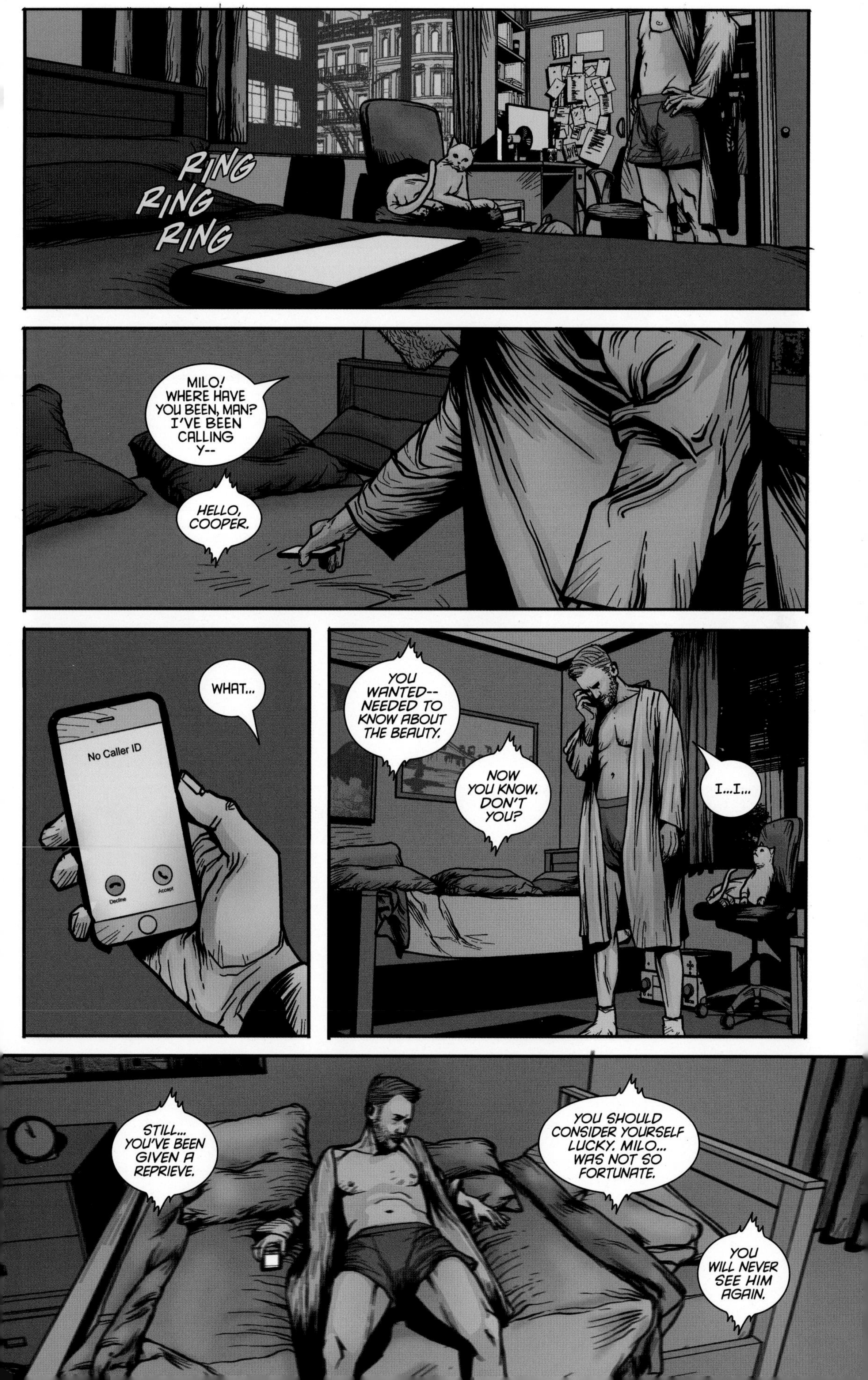
RING
RING
RING
MILO! WHERE HAVE YOU BEEN, MAN? I'VE BEEN CALLING Y--
HELLO, COOPER.
WHAT...
No Caller ID
Decline
Accept
YOU WANTED-- NEEDED TO KNOW ABOUT THE BEAUTY.
NOW YOU KNOW. DON'T YOU?
I...I...
STILL... YOU'VE BEEN GIVEN A REPRIEVE.
YOU SHOULD CONSIDER YOURSELF LUCKY. MILO... WAS NOT SO FORTUNATE.
YOU WILL NEVER SEE HIM AGAIN.

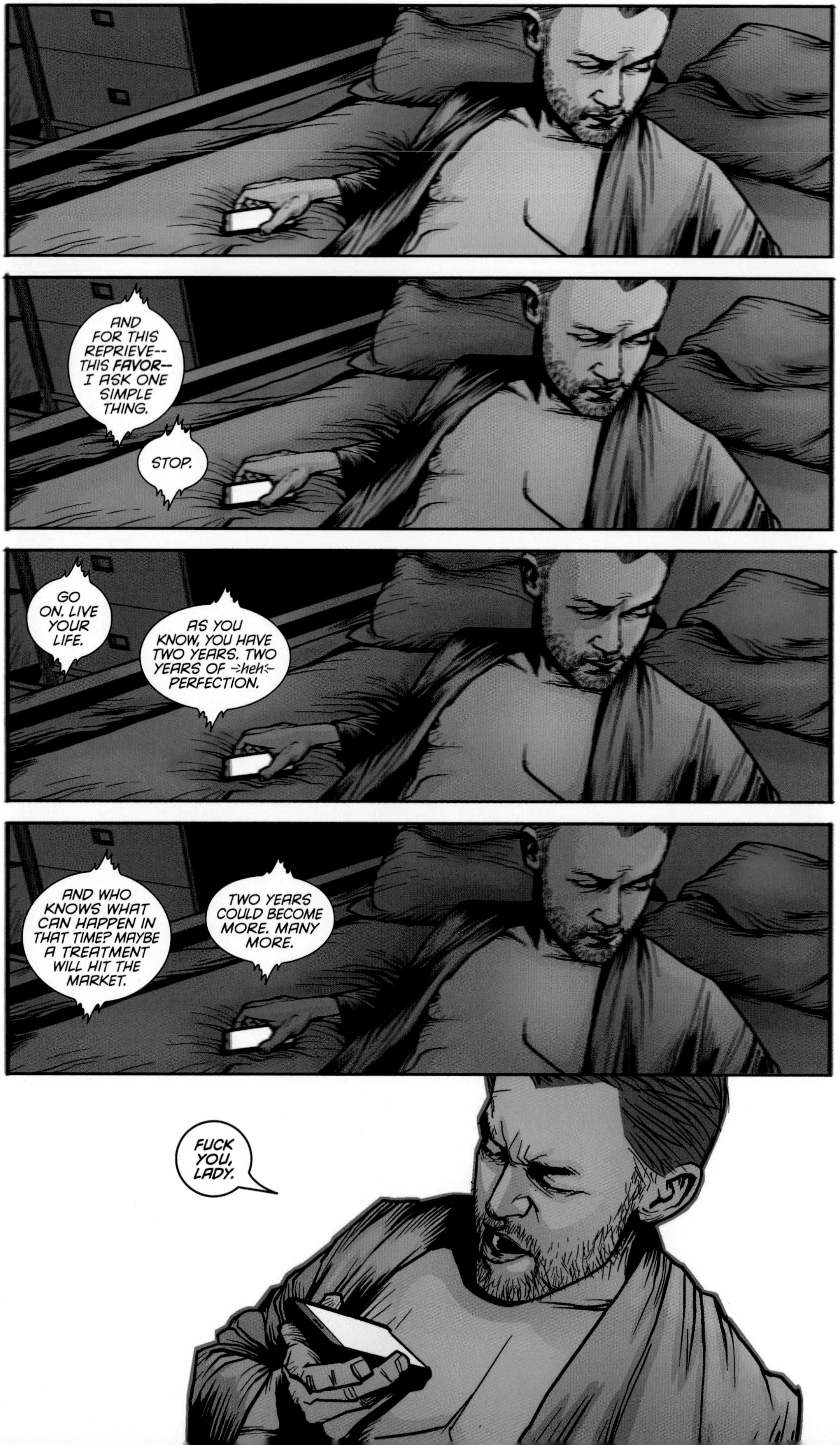
AND FOR THIS REPRIEVE-- THIS FAVOR-- I ASK ONE SIMPLE THING.
STOP.
GO ON. LIVE YOUR LIFE.
AS YOU KNOW, YOU HAVE TWO YEARS. TWO YEARS OF ~heh~ PERFECTION.
AND WHO KNOWS WHAT CAN HAPPEN IN THAT TIME? MAYBE A TREATMENT WILL HIT THE MARKET.
TWO YEARS COULD BECOME MORE. MANY MORE.
FUCK YOU, LADY.

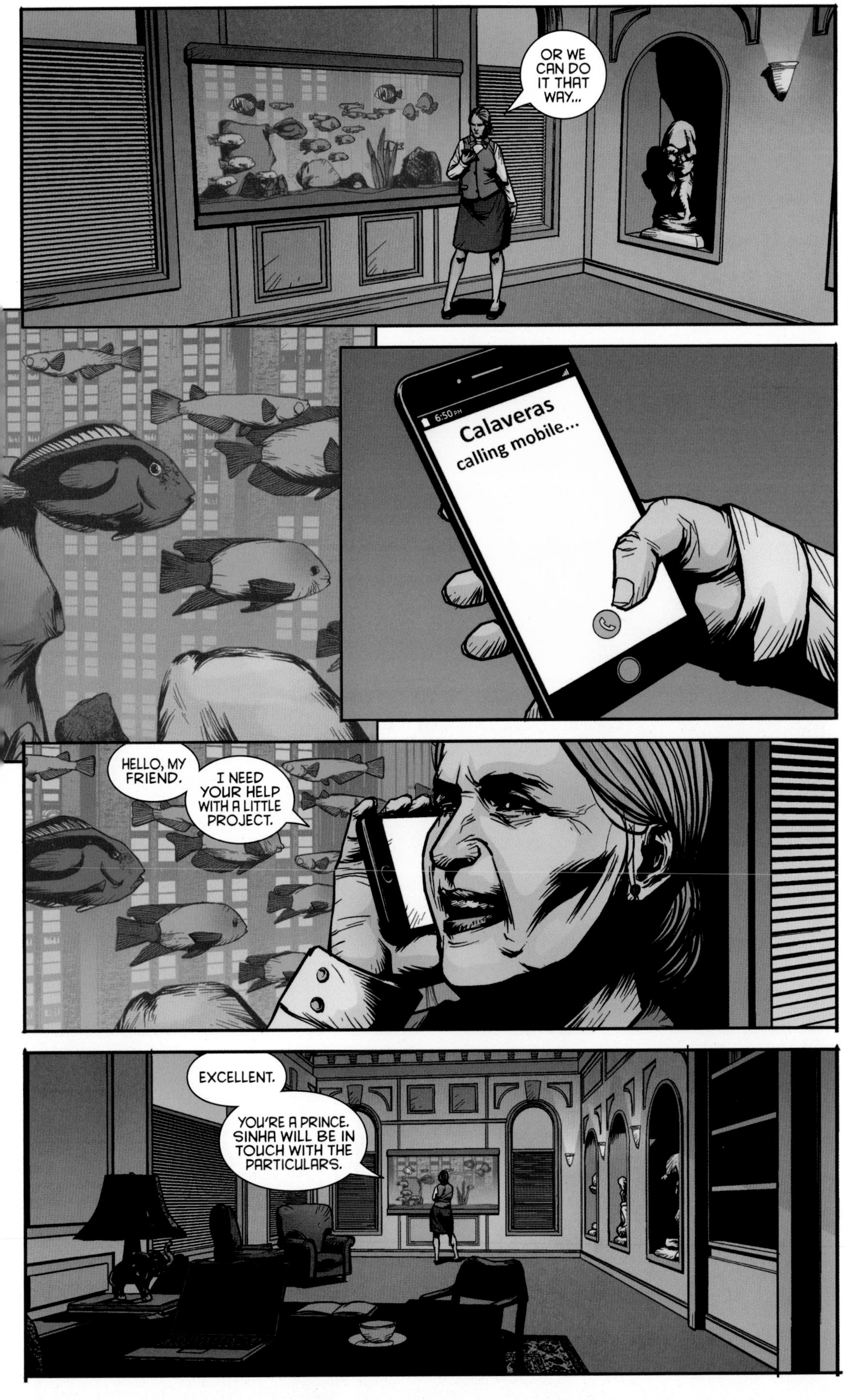
OR WE CAN DO IT THAT WAY...
6:50 PM
Calaveras
calling mobile...
HELLO, MY FRIEND.
I NEED YOUR HELP WITH A LITTLE PROJECT.
EXCELLENT.
YOU'RE A PRINCE. SINHA WILL BE IN TOUCH WITH THE PARTICULARS.

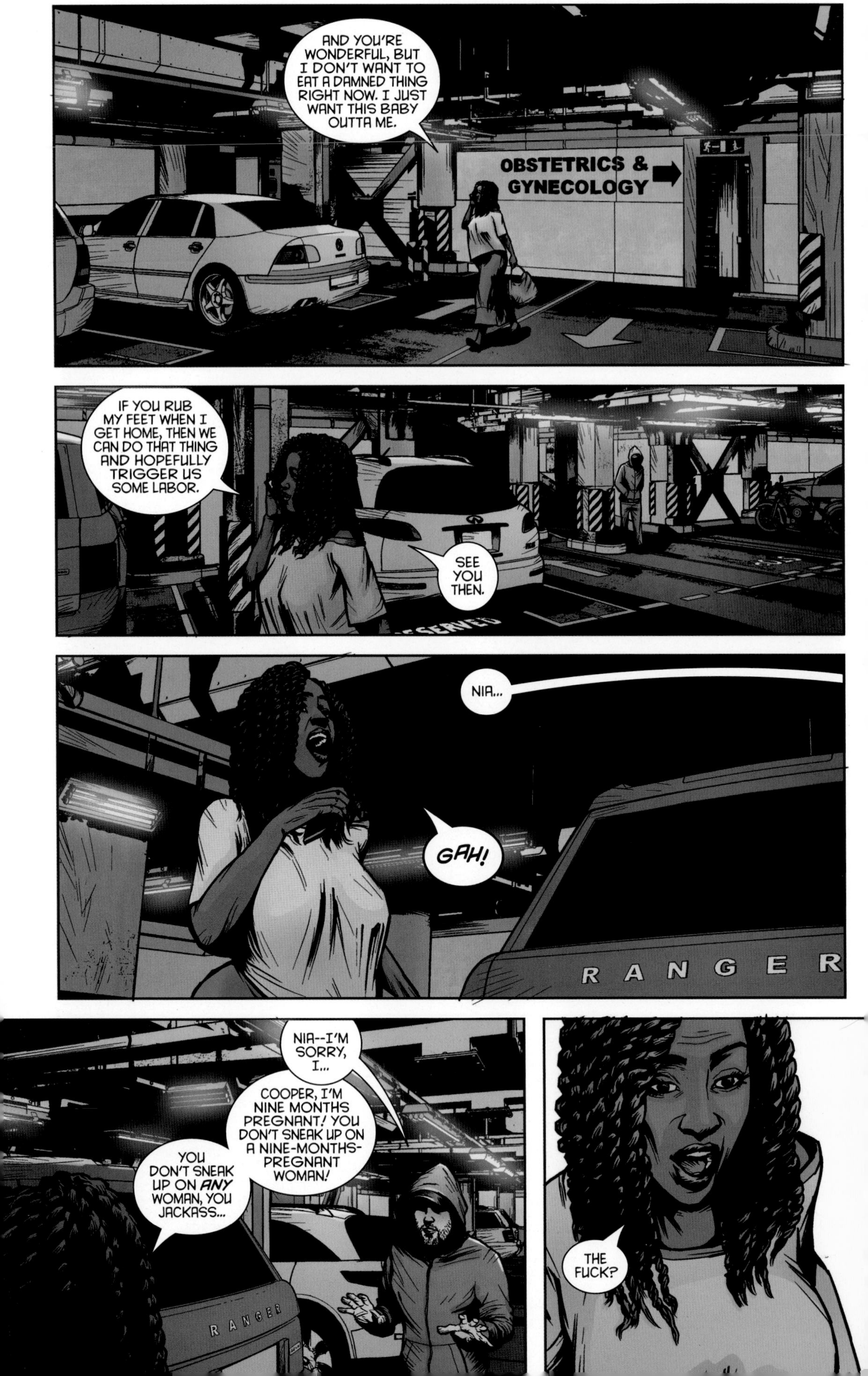
AND YOU'RE WONDERFUL, BUT I DON'T WANT TO EAT A DAMNED THING RIGHT NOW. I JUST WANT THIS BABY OUTTA ME.
OBSTETRICS & GYNECOLOGY
IF YOU RUB MY FEET WHEN I GET HOME, THEN WE CAN DO THAT THING AND HOPEFULLY TRIGGER US SOME LABOR.
SEE YOU THEN.
NIA...
GAH!
RANGER
NIA--I'M SORRY, I...
COOPER, I'M NINE MONTHS PREGNANT! YOU DON'T SNEAK UP ON A NINE-MONTHS-PREGNANT WOMAN!
YOU DON'T SNEAK UP ON ANY WOMAN, YOU JACKASS...
RANGER
THE FUCK?

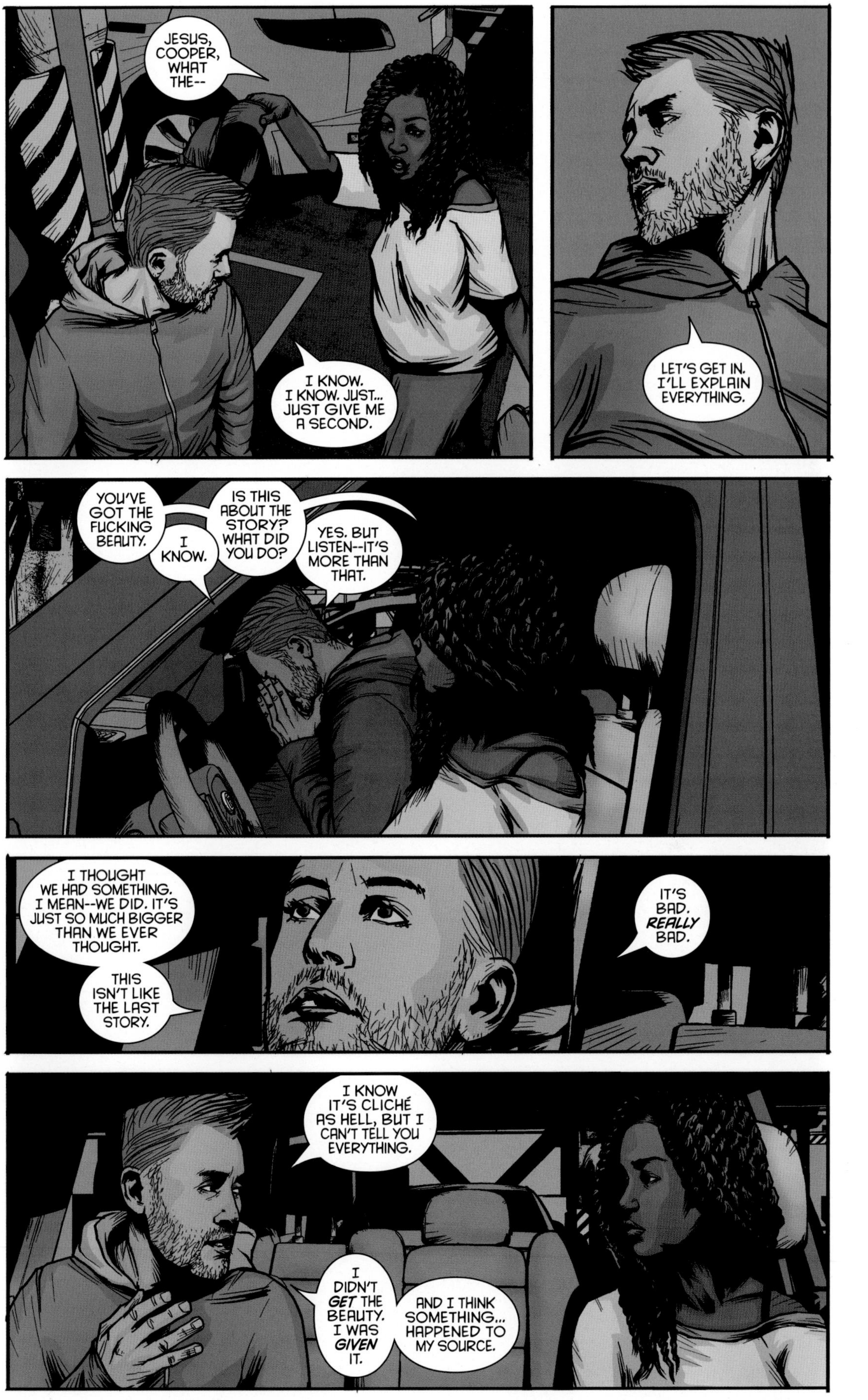
JESUS, COOPER, WHAT THE--
I KNOW. I KNOW. JUST... JUST GIVE ME A SECOND.
LET'S GET IN. I'LL EXPLAIN EVERYTHING.
YOU'VE GOT THE FUCKING BEAUTY.
I KNOW.
IS THIS ABOUT THE STORY? WHAT DID YOU DO?
YES. BUT LISTEN--IT'S MORE THAN THAT.
I THOUGHT WE HAD SOMETHING. I MEAN--WE DID. IT'S JUST SO MUCH BIGGER THAN WE EVER THOUGHT.
THIS ISN'T LIKE THE LAST STORY.
IT'S BAD. REALLY BAD.
I KNOW IT'S CLICHÉ AS HELL, BUT I CAN'T TELL YOU EVERYTHING.
I DIDN'T GET THE BEAUTY. I WAS GIVEN IT.
AND I THINK SOMETHING... HAPPENED TO MY SOURCE.

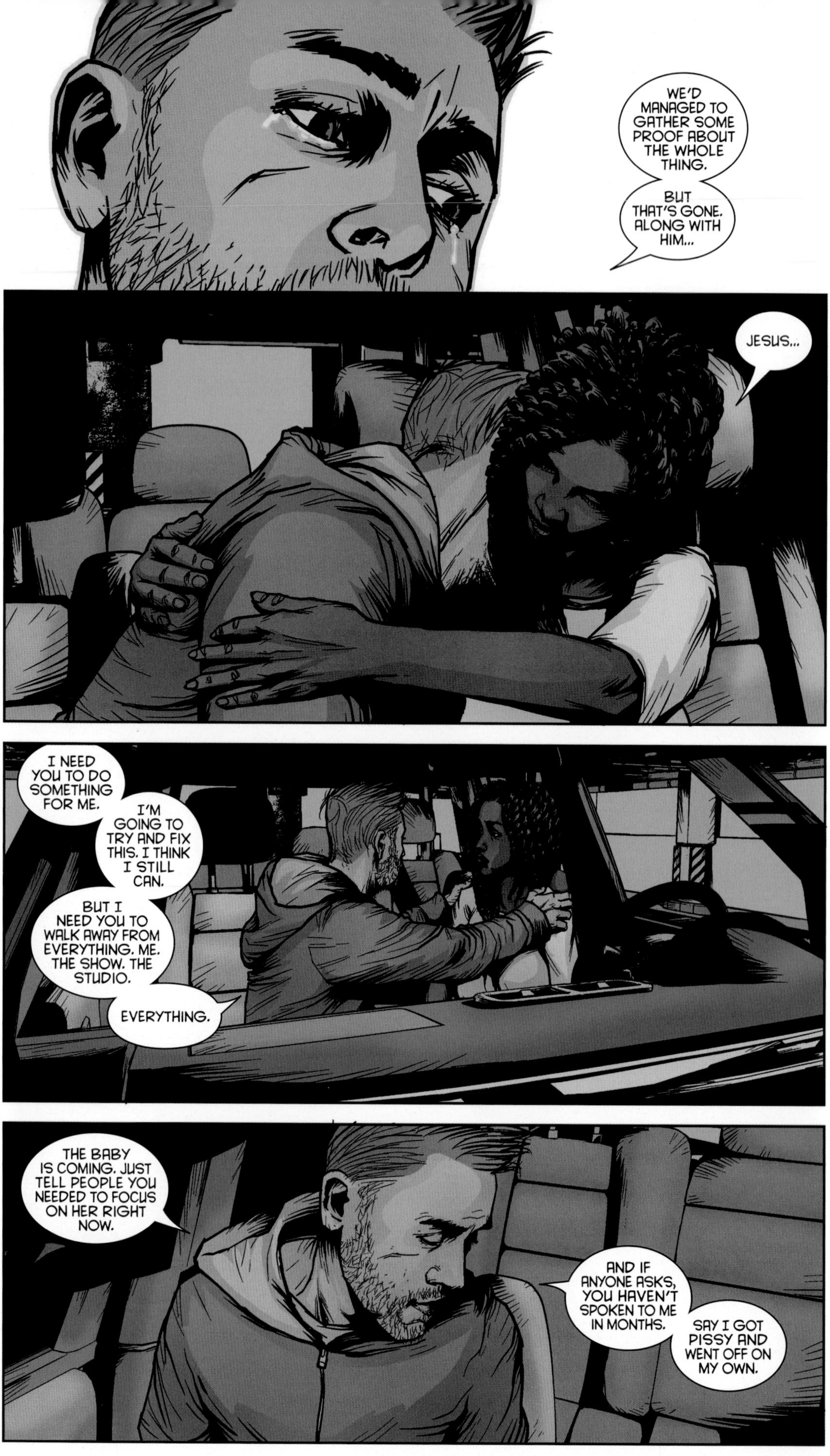
WE'D MANAGED TO GATHER SOME PROOF ABOUT THE WHOLE THING.
BUT THAT'S GONE. ALONG WITH HIM...
JESUS...
I NEED YOU TO DO SOMETHING FOR ME.
I'M GOING TO TRY AND FIX THIS. I THINK I STILL CAN.
BUT I NEED YOU TO WALK AWAY FROM EVERYTHING. ME. THE SHOW. THE STUDIO.
EVERYTHING.
THE BABY IS COMING. JUST TELL PEOPLE YOU NEEDED TO FOCUS ON HER RIGHT NOW.
AND IF ANYONE ASKS, YOU HAVEN'T SPOKEN TO ME IN MONTHS.
SAY I GOT PISSY AND WENT OFF ON MY OWN.

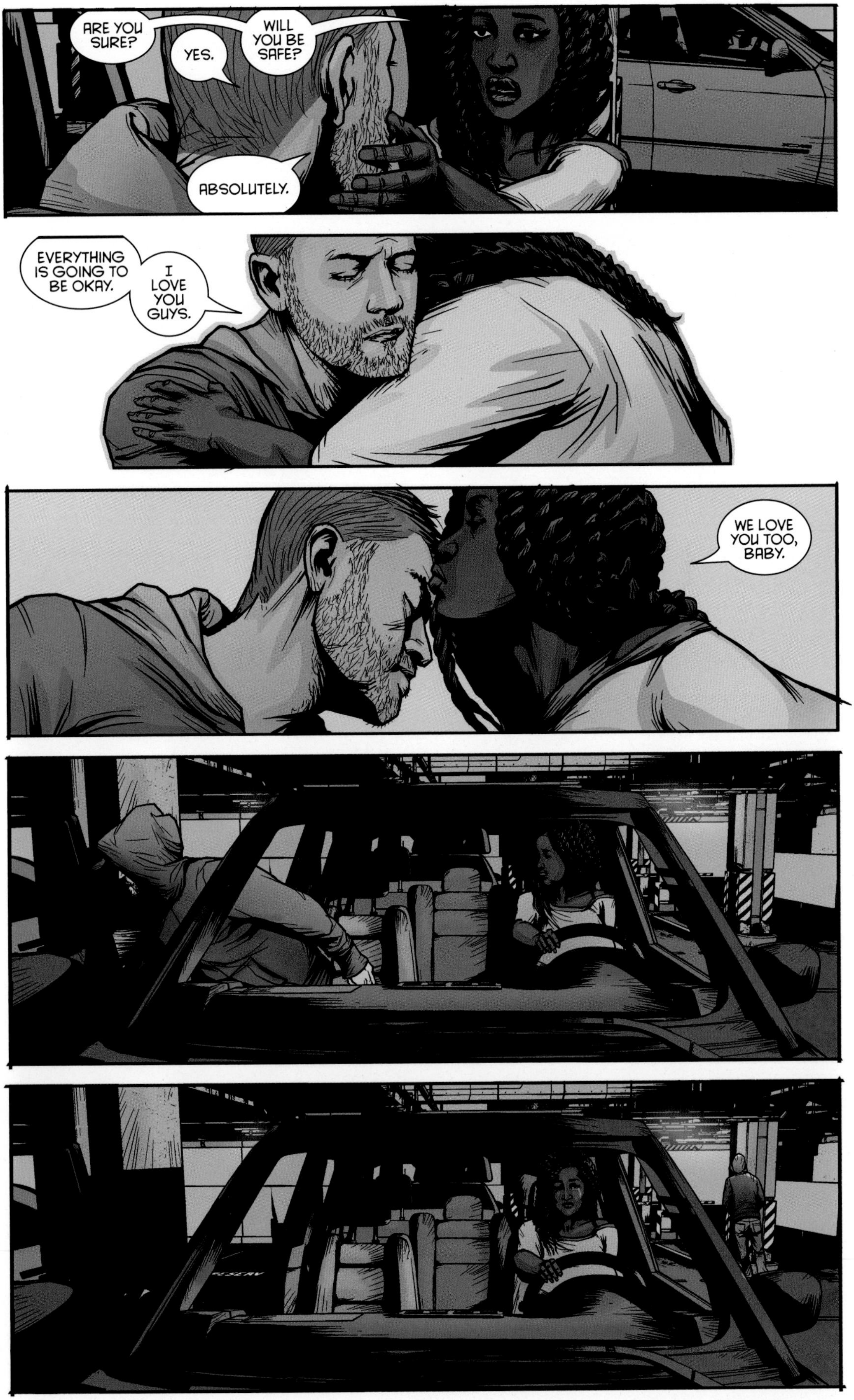
ARE YOU SURE?
YES.
WILL YOU BE SAFE?
ABSOLUTELY.
EVERYTHING IS GOING TO BE OKAY.
I LOVE YOU GUYS.
WE LOVE YOU TOO, BABY.

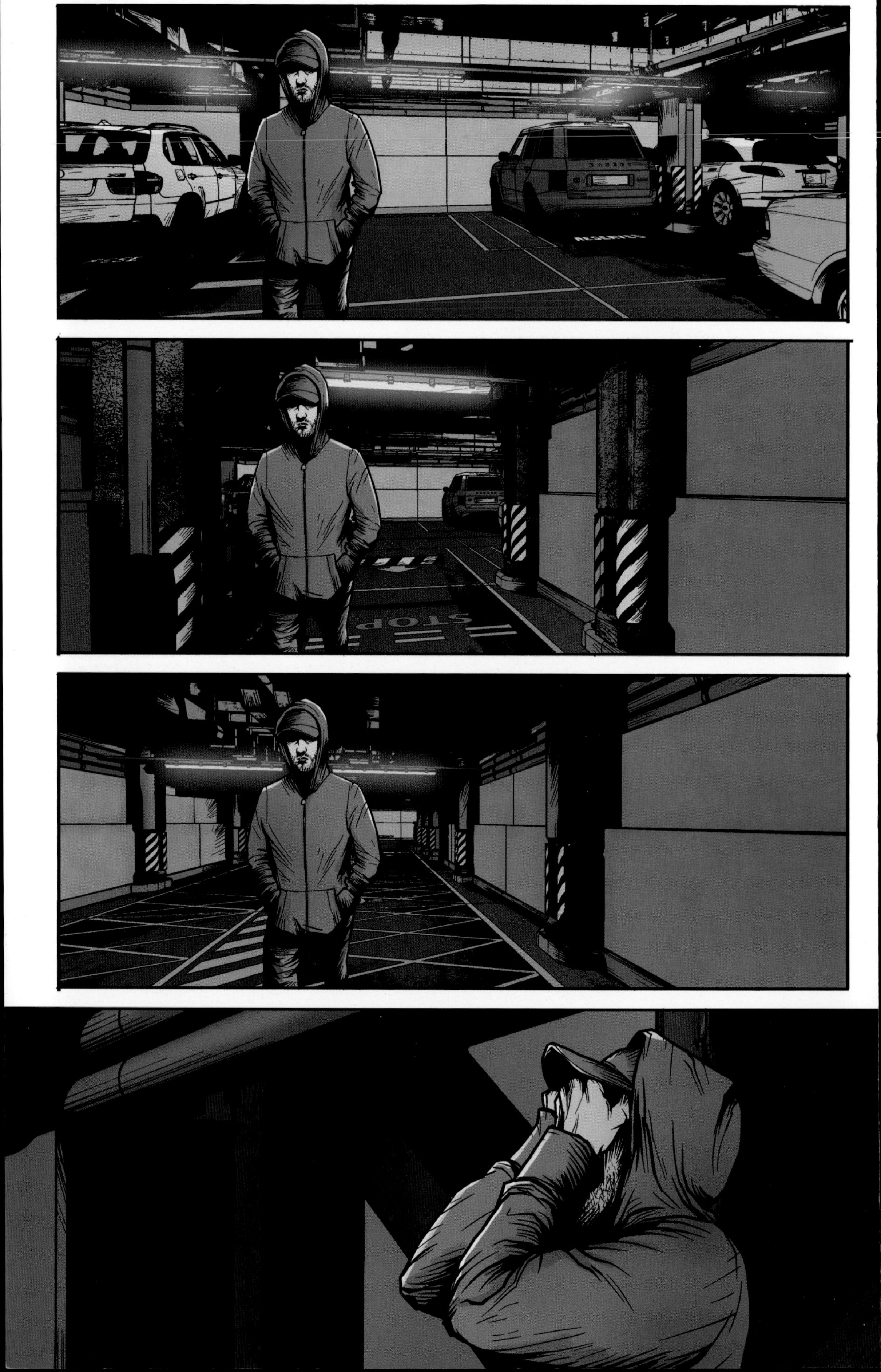
STOP

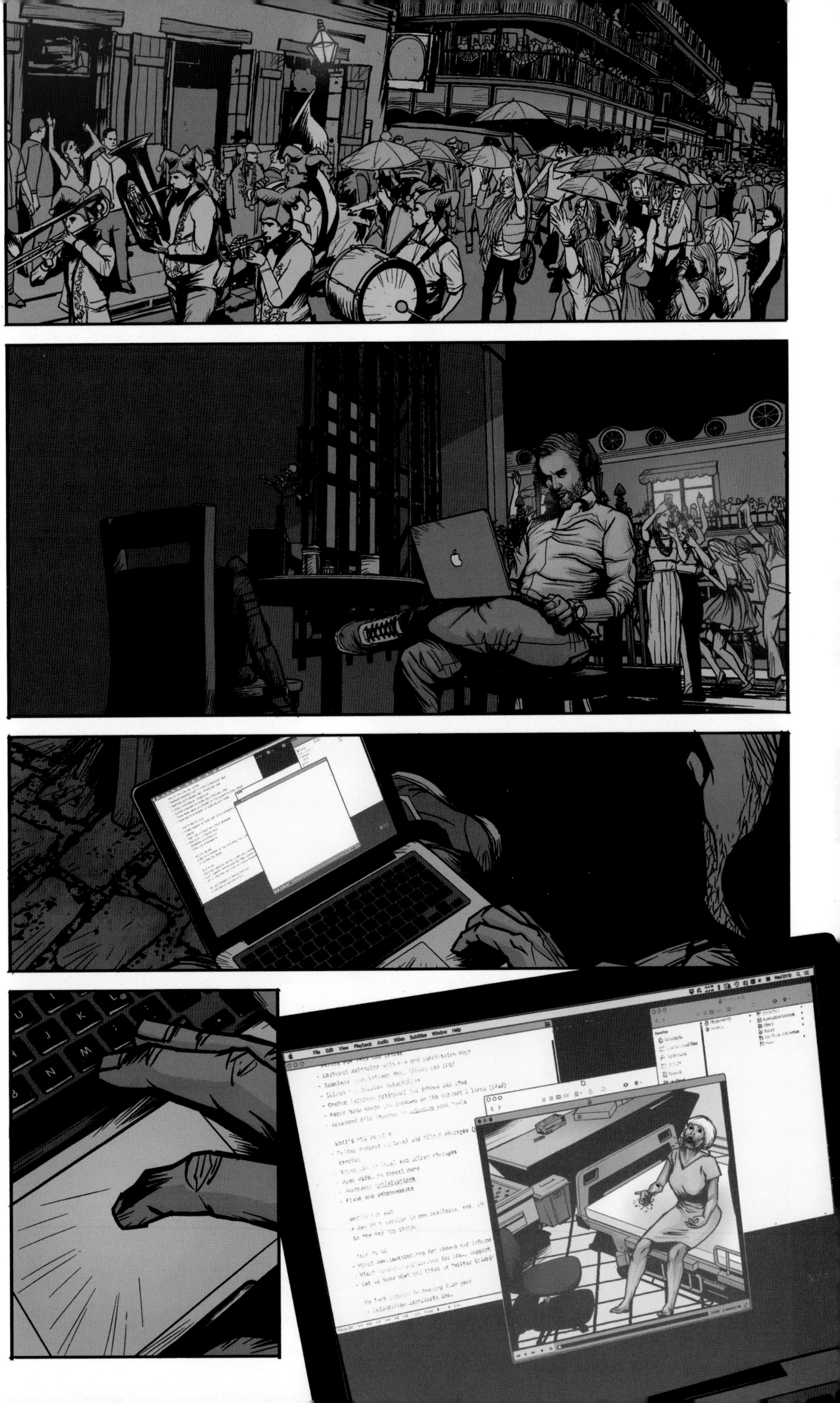
File Edit View Playback Audio Video Subtitles Window Help

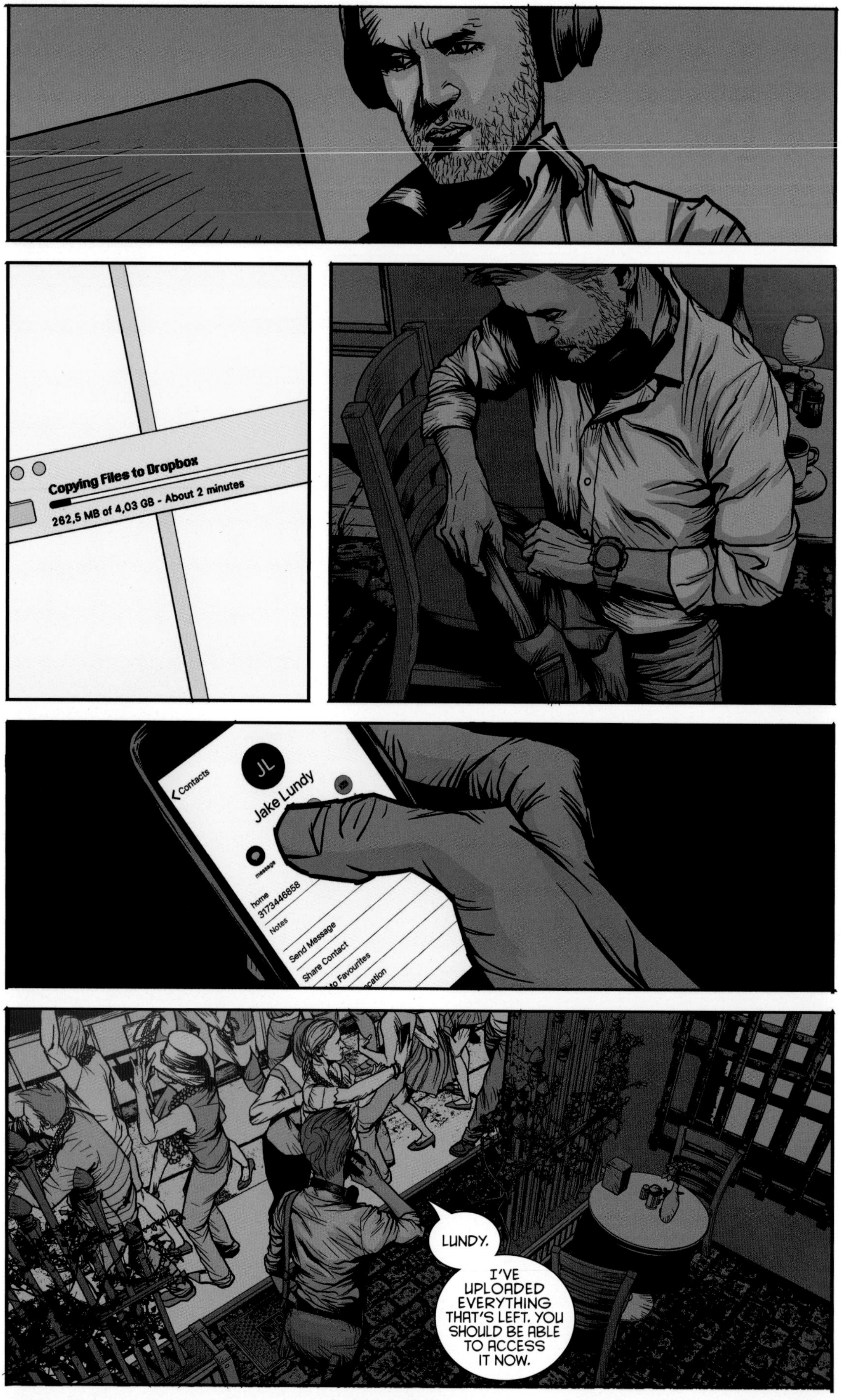
Copying Files to Dropbox
262,5 MB of 4,03 GB - About 2 minutes
Contacts
JL
Jake Lundy
message
home
3173446858
Notes
Send Message
Share Contact
LUNDY.
I'VE UPLOADED EVERYTHING THAT'S LEFT. YOU SHOULD BE ABLE TO ACCESS IT NOW.

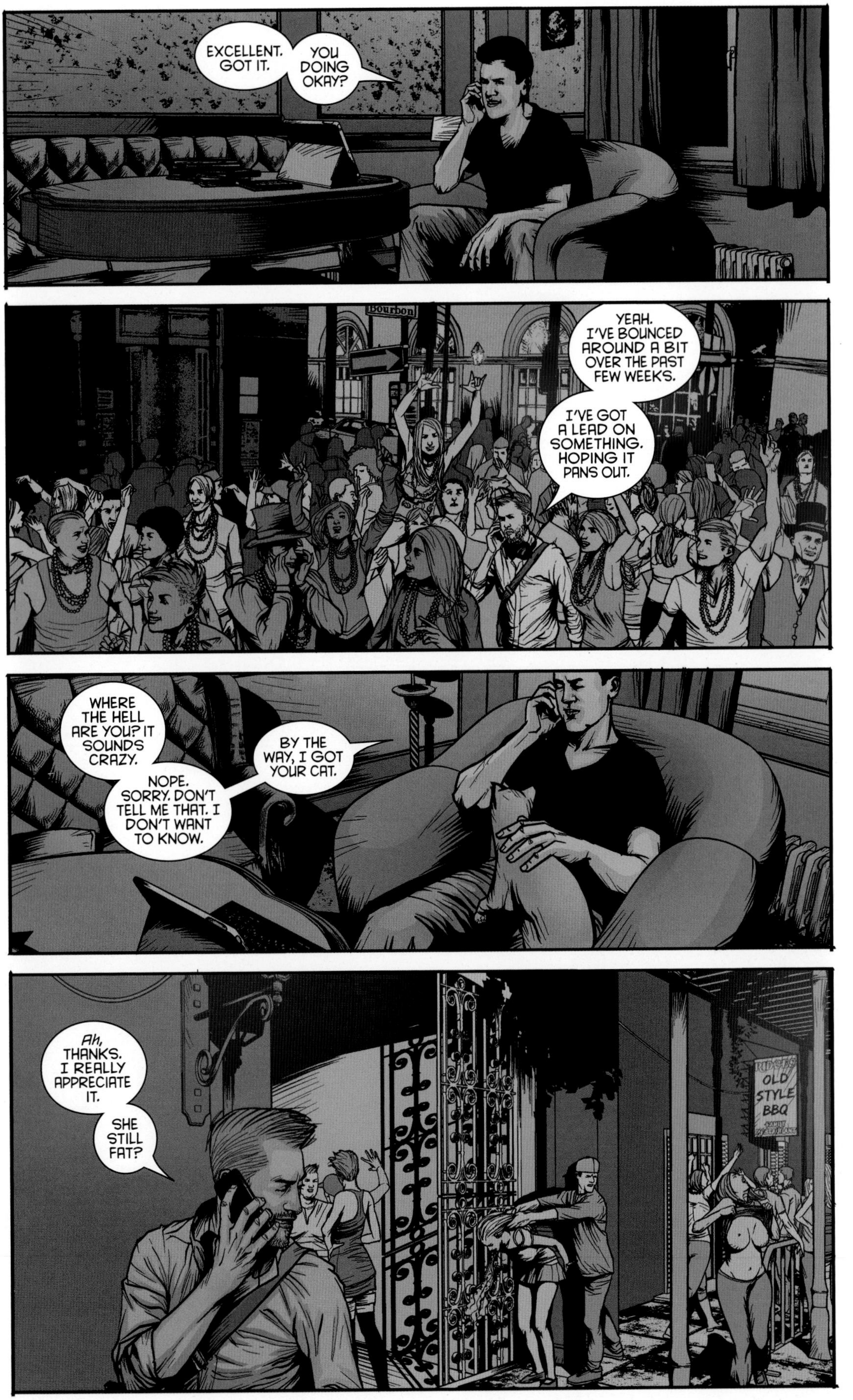
EXCELLENT. GOT IT.
YOU DOING OKAY?
Bourbon
YEAH. I'VE BOUNCED AROUND A BIT OVER THE PAST FEW WEEKS.
I'VE GOT A LEAD ON SOMETHING. HOPING IT PANS OUT.
WHERE THE HELL ARE YOU? IT SOUNDS CRAZY.
NOPE. SORRY. DON'T TELL ME THAT. I DON'T WANT TO KNOW.
BY THE WAY, I GOT YOUR CAT.
Ah, THANKS. I REALLY APPRECIATE IT.
SHE STILL FAT?
OLD STYLE BBQ

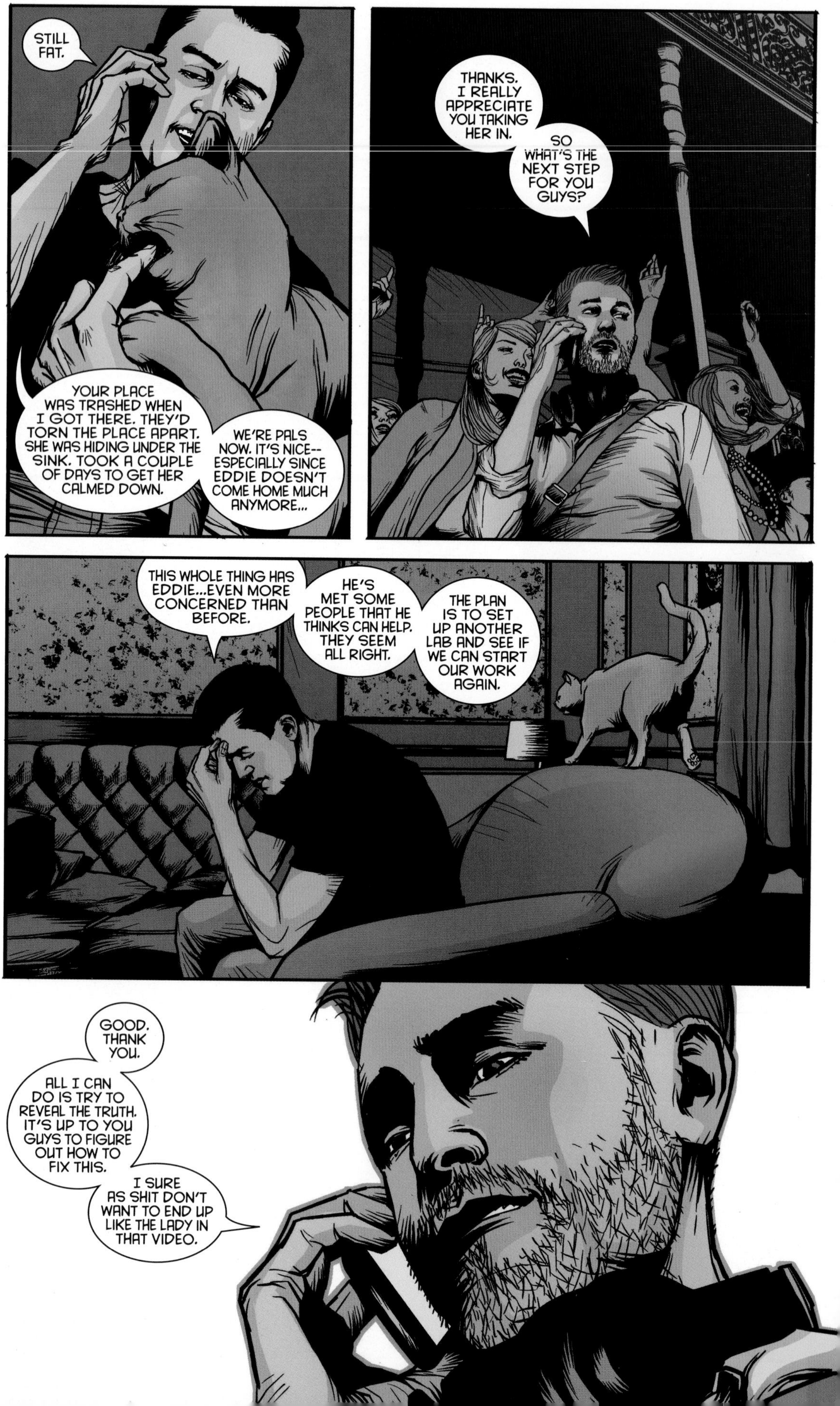
STILL FAT.
YOUR PLACE WAS TRASHED WHEN I GOT THERE. THEY'D TORN THE PLACE APART. SHE WAS HIDING UNDER THE SINK. TOOK A COUPLE OF DAYS TO GET HER CALMED DOWN.
WE'RE PALS NOW. IT'S NICE-- ESPECIALLY SINCE EDDIE DOESN'T COME HOME MUCH ANYMORE...
THANKS. I REALLY APPRECIATE YOU TAKING HER IN.
SO WHAT'S THE NEXT STEP FOR YOU GUYS?
THIS WHOLE THING HAS EDDIE...EVEN MORE CONCERNED THAN BEFORE.
HE'S MET SOME PEOPLE THAT HE THINKS CAN HELP. THEY SEEM ALL RIGHT.
THE PLAN IS TO SET UP ANOTHER LAB AND SEE IF WE CAN START OUR WORK AGAIN.
GOOD. THANK YOU.
ALL I CAN DO IS TRY TO REVEAL THE TRUTH. IT'S UP TO YOU GUYS TO FIGURE OUT HOW TO FIX THIS.
I SURE AS SHIT DON'T WANT TO END UP LIKE THE LADY IN THAT VIDEO.

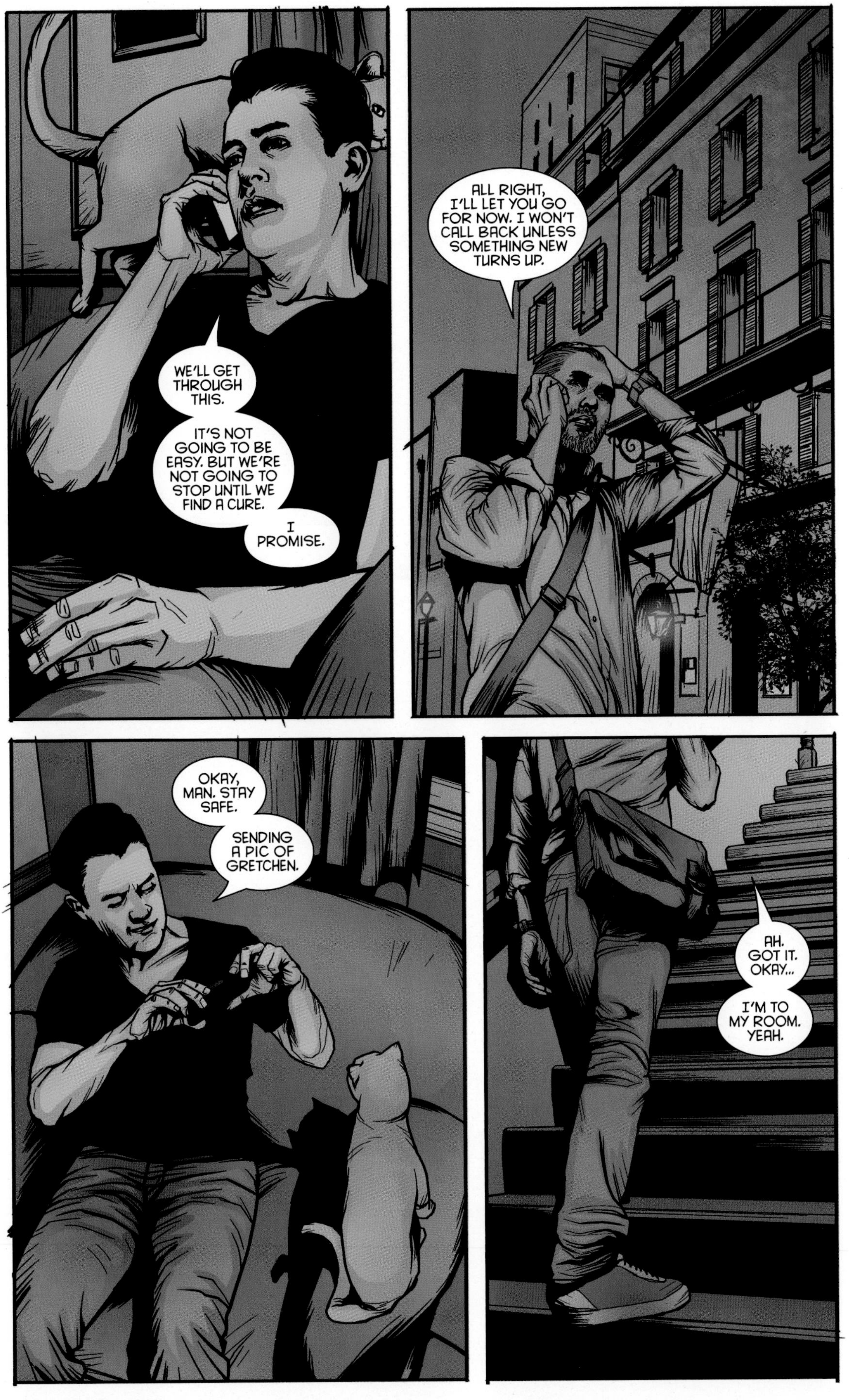
WE'LL GET THROUGH THIS.
IT'S NOT GOING TO BE EASY. BUT WE'RE NOT GOING TO STOP UNTIL WE FIND A CURE.
I PROMISE.
ALL RIGHT, I'LL LET YOU GO FOR NOW. I WON'T CALL BACK UNLESS SOMETHING NEW TURNS UP.
OKAY, MAN. STAY SAFE.
SENDING A PIC OF GRETCHEN.
AH. GOT IT. OKAY...
I'M TO MY ROOM. YEAH.

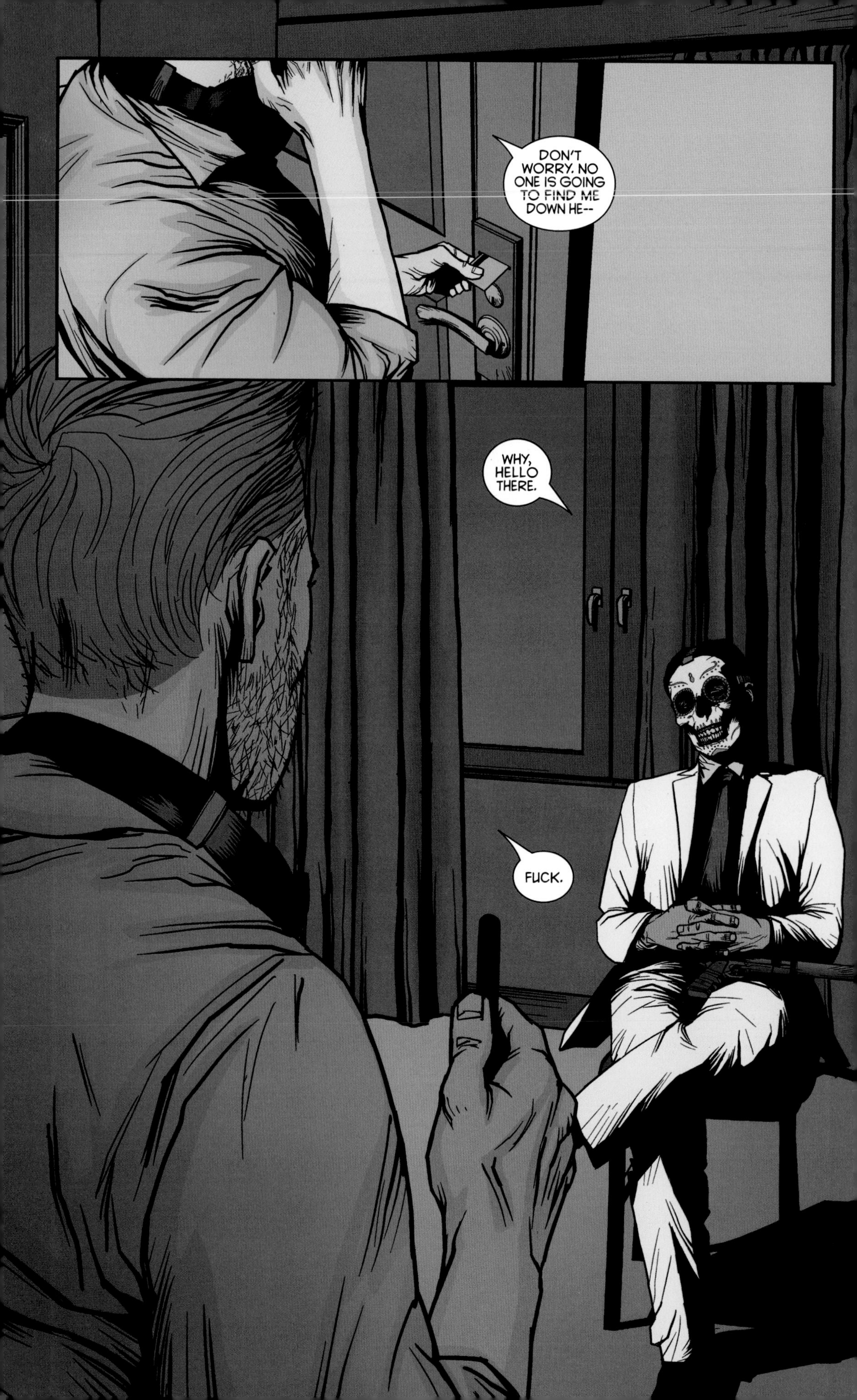
DON'T WORRY. NO ONE IS GOING TO FIND ME DOWN HE--
WHY, HELLO THERE.
FUCK.

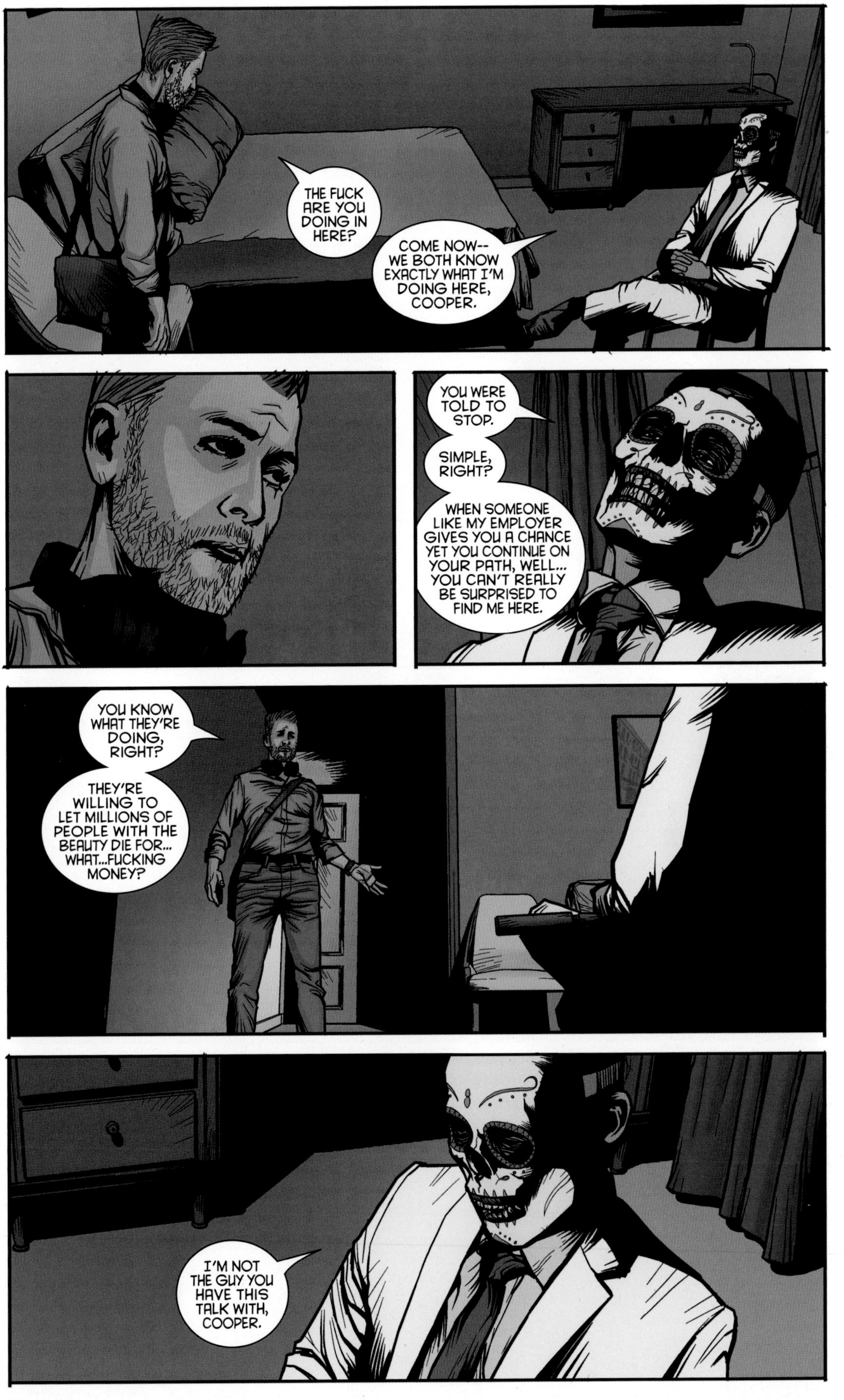
THE FUCK ARE YOU DOING IN HERE?
COME NOW-- WE BOTH KNOW EXACTLY WHAT I'M DOING HERE, COOPER.
YOU WERE TOLD TO STOP.
SIMPLE, RIGHT?
WHEN SOMEONE LIKE MY EMPLOYER GIVES YOU A CHANCE YET YOU CONTINUE ON YOUR PATH, WELL... YOU CAN'T REALLY BE SURPRISED TO FIND ME HERE.
YOU KNOW WHAT THEY'RE DOING, RIGHT?
THEY'RE WILLING TO LET MILLIONS OF PEOPLE WITH THE BEAUTY DIE FOR... WHAT...FUCKING MONEY?
I'M NOT THE GUY YOU HAVE THIS TALK WITH, COOPER.

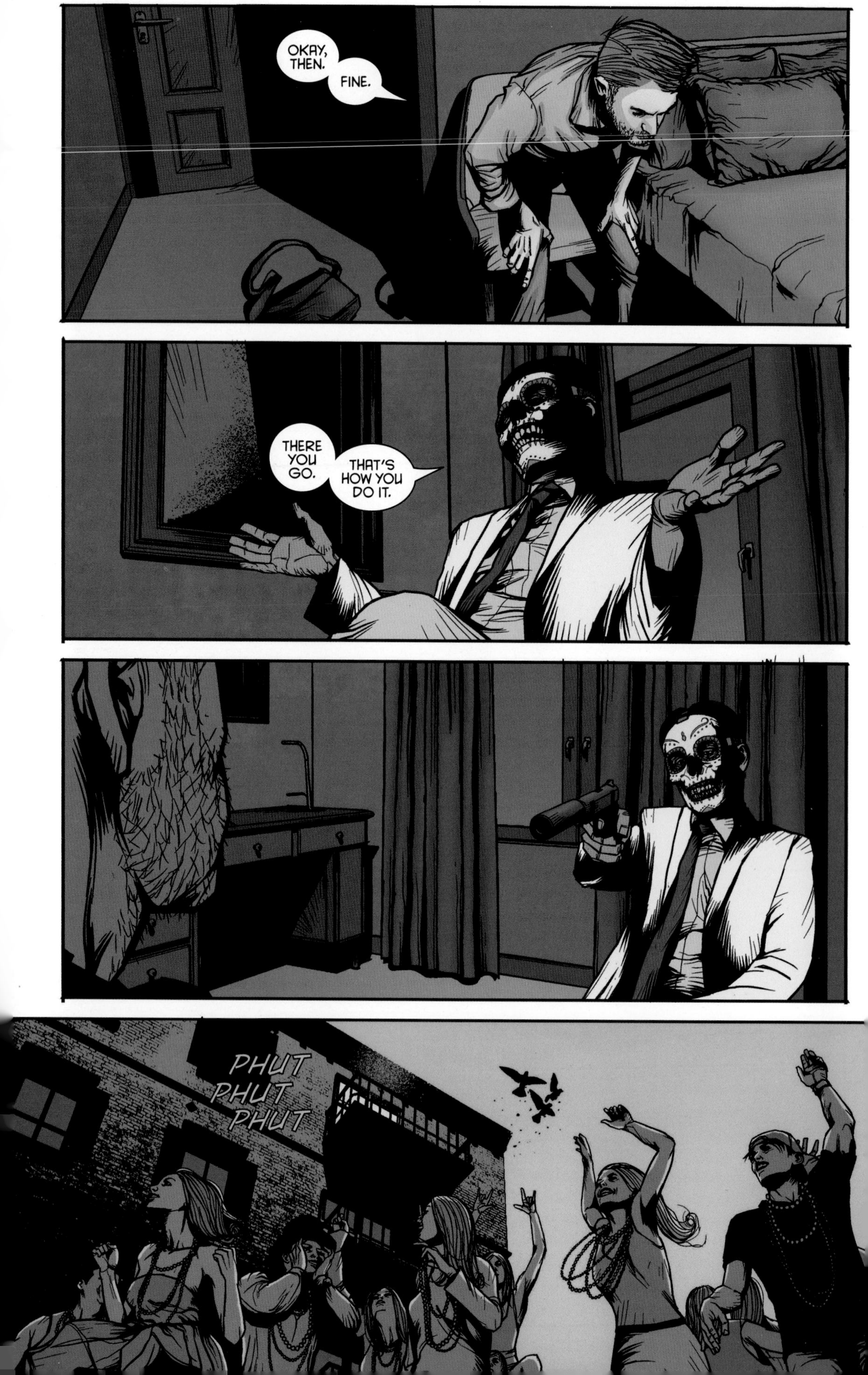
OKAY, THEN.
FINE.
THERE YOU GO.
THAT'S HOW YOU DO IT.
PHUT PHUT PHUT

COVERS

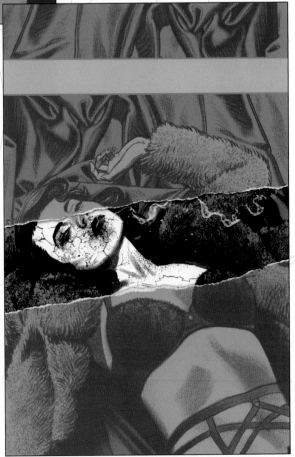

ISSUE #17
Cover B
Greg Smallwood

ISSUE #17
Cover A
Jeremy Haun
& Nick Filardi

ISSUE #18
Cover B
Andy MacDonald
& John Rauch

ISSUE #18
Cover A
Jeremy Haun
& Nick Filardi

ISSUE #19
Cover B
Baldemar Rivas

ISSUE #19
Cover A
Jeremy Haun
& Nick Filardi

ISSUE #20
Cover A
Jeremy Haun
& Nick Filardi

ISSUE #20
Cover B
Ray Fawkes

ISSUE #20
Cover C

Jeremy Haun
& Nick Filardi

ISSUE #21
Cover A
Jeremy Haun
& Nick Filardi

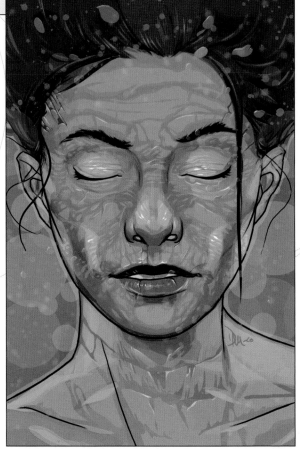

ISSUE #21
Cover B
Dave McCaig

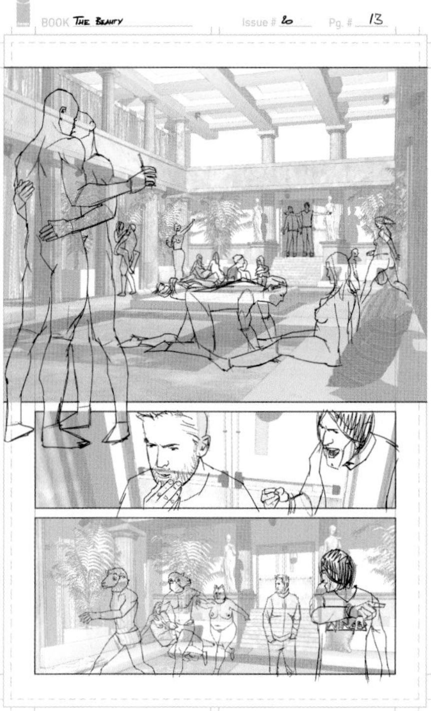
BOOK The Beauty
Issue # 20
Pg. # 13

PROCESS

"I don't pencil my pages traditionally because digital art allows me to work quicker and I have much more control over the quality of my artwork. This being said, I enjoy penciling on paper more than anything and decided to draw pages from time to time the traditional way.

"I chose these three particular pages because I liked them the most, and they reminded me of my nude drawing classes in college."

Thomas Nachlik

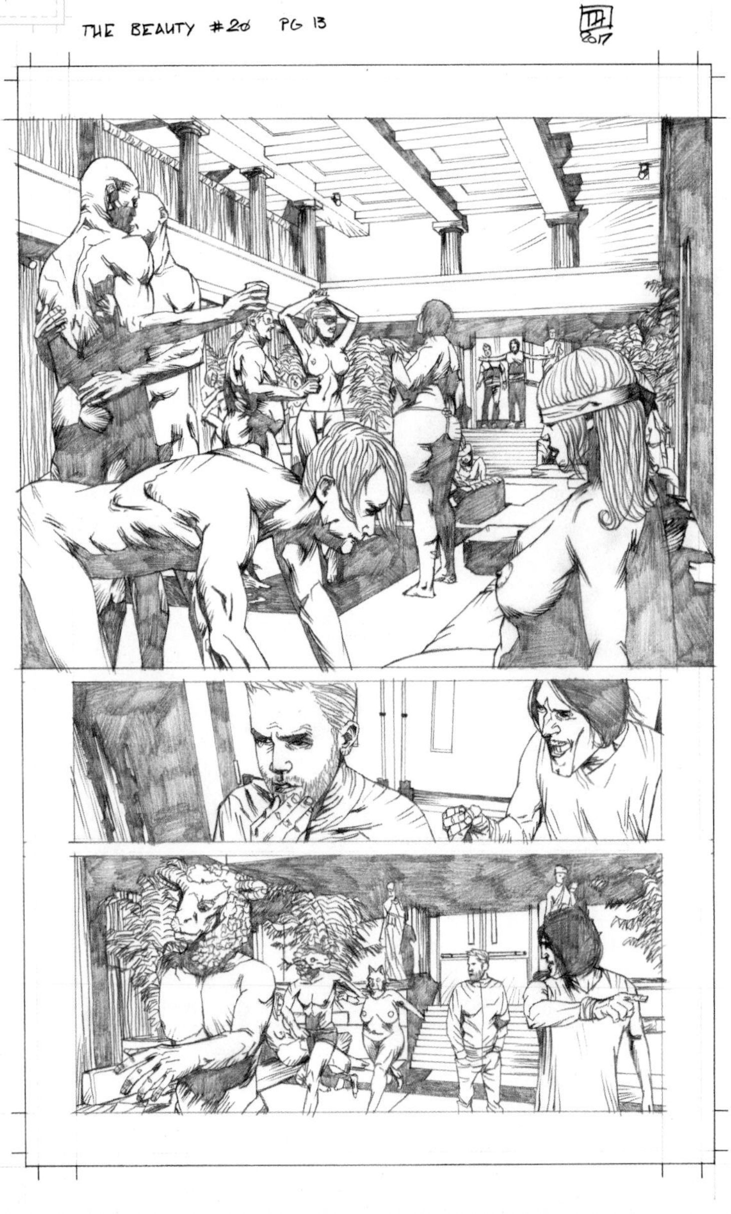
THE BEAUTY #20 PG 13
2017

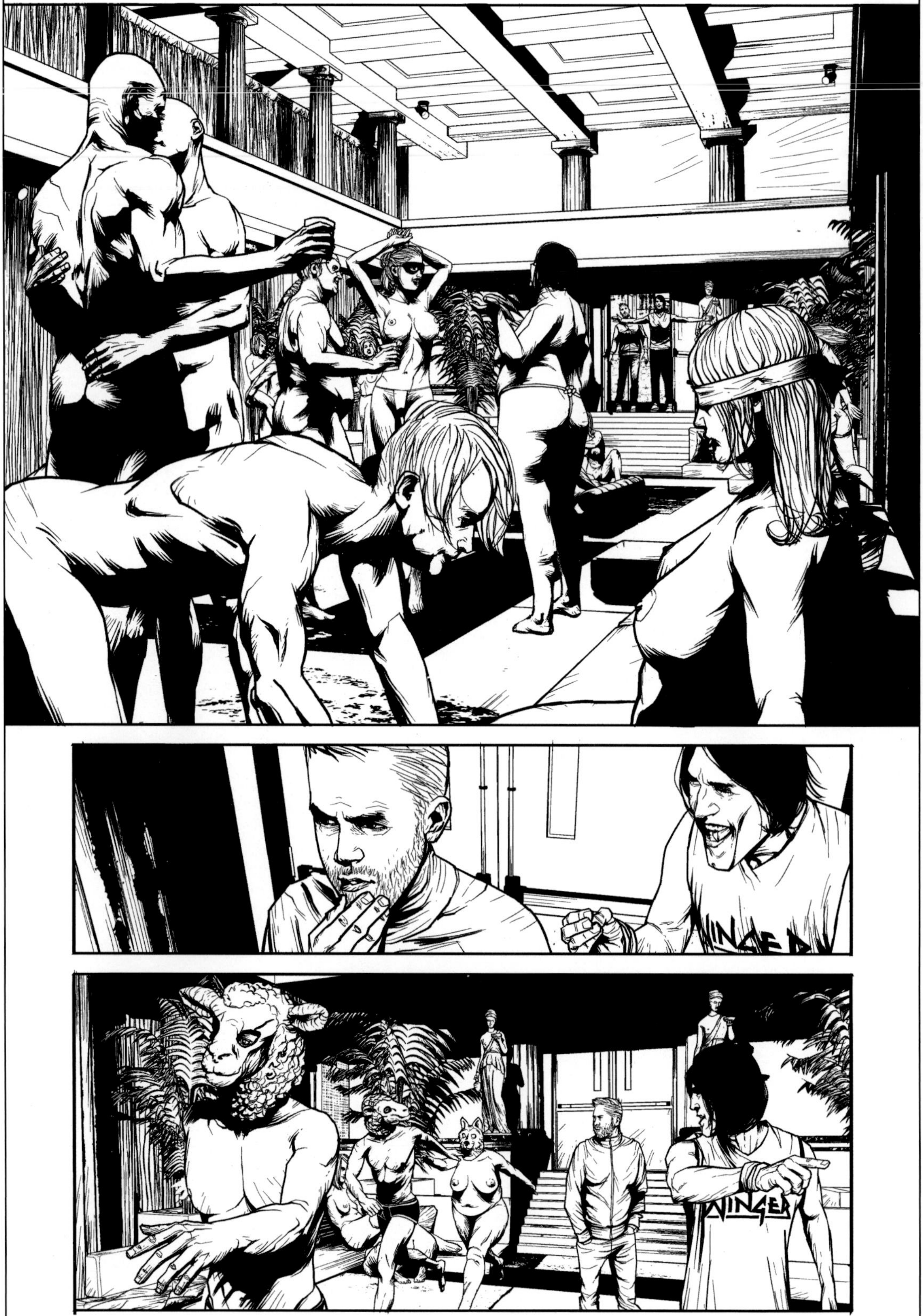
WINGER

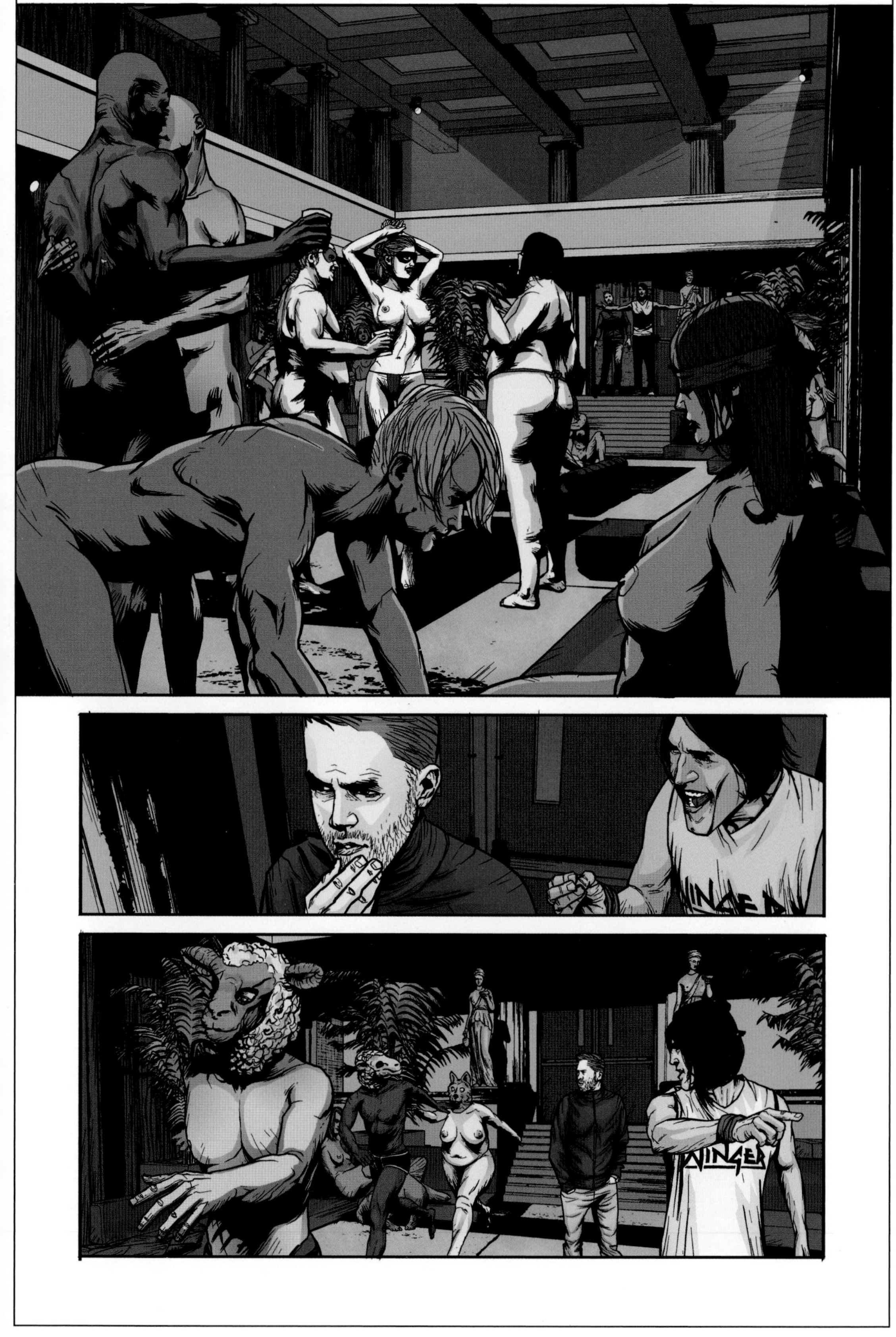
WINGER

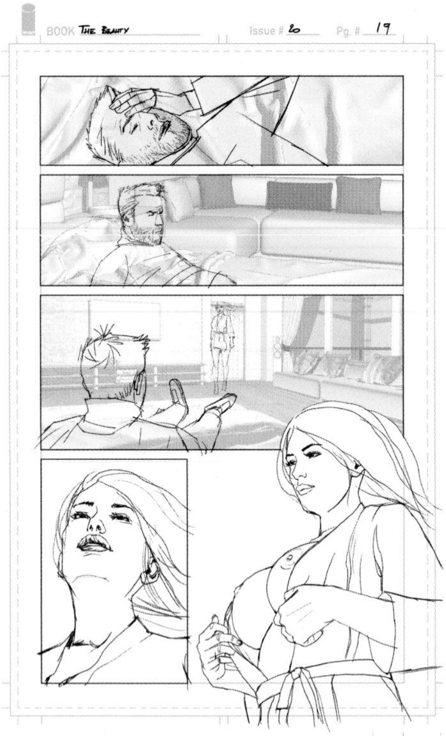
BOOK The Beauty
Issue # 20
Pg. # 19

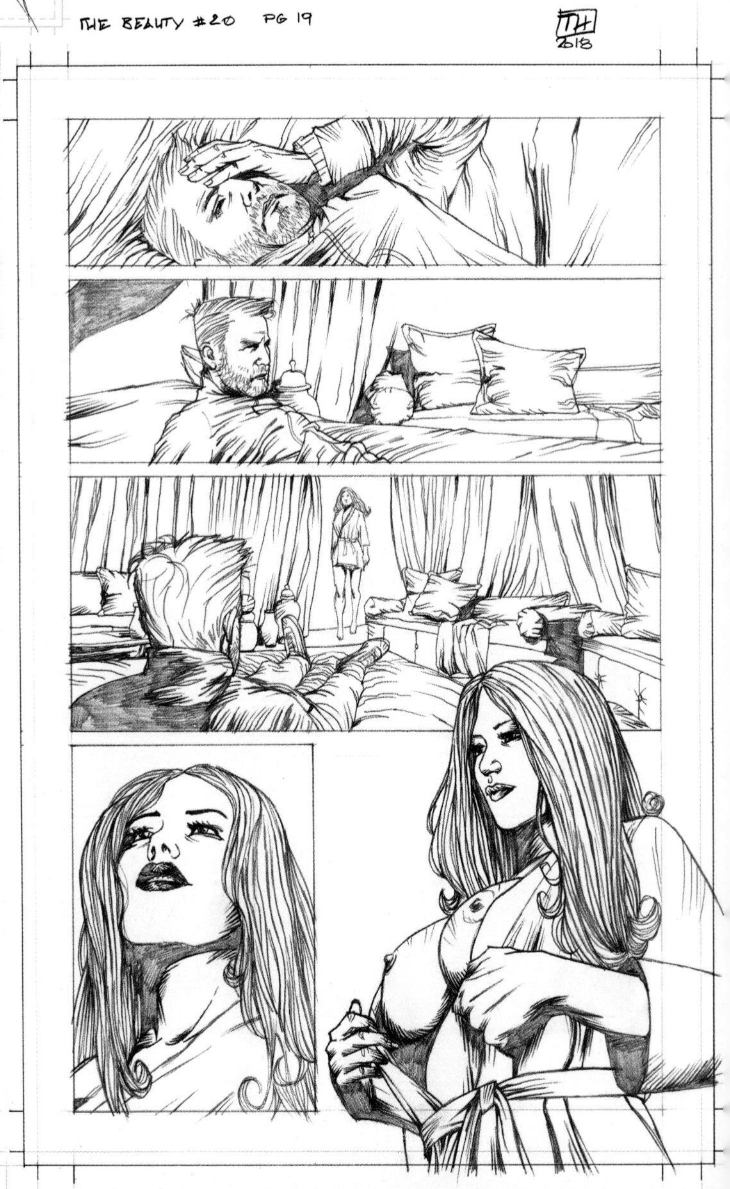
THE BEAUTY #20 PG 19
TH
2018

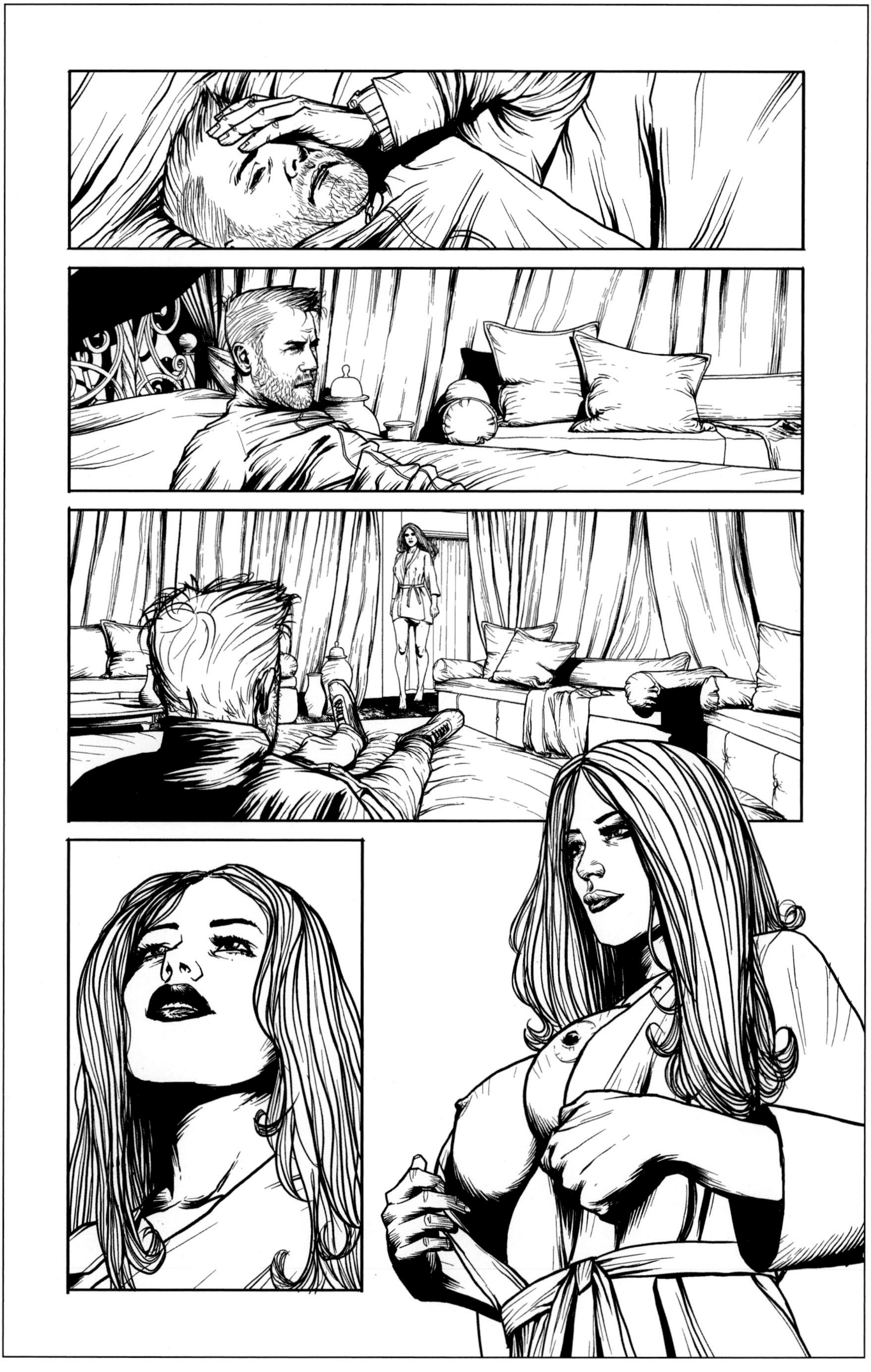

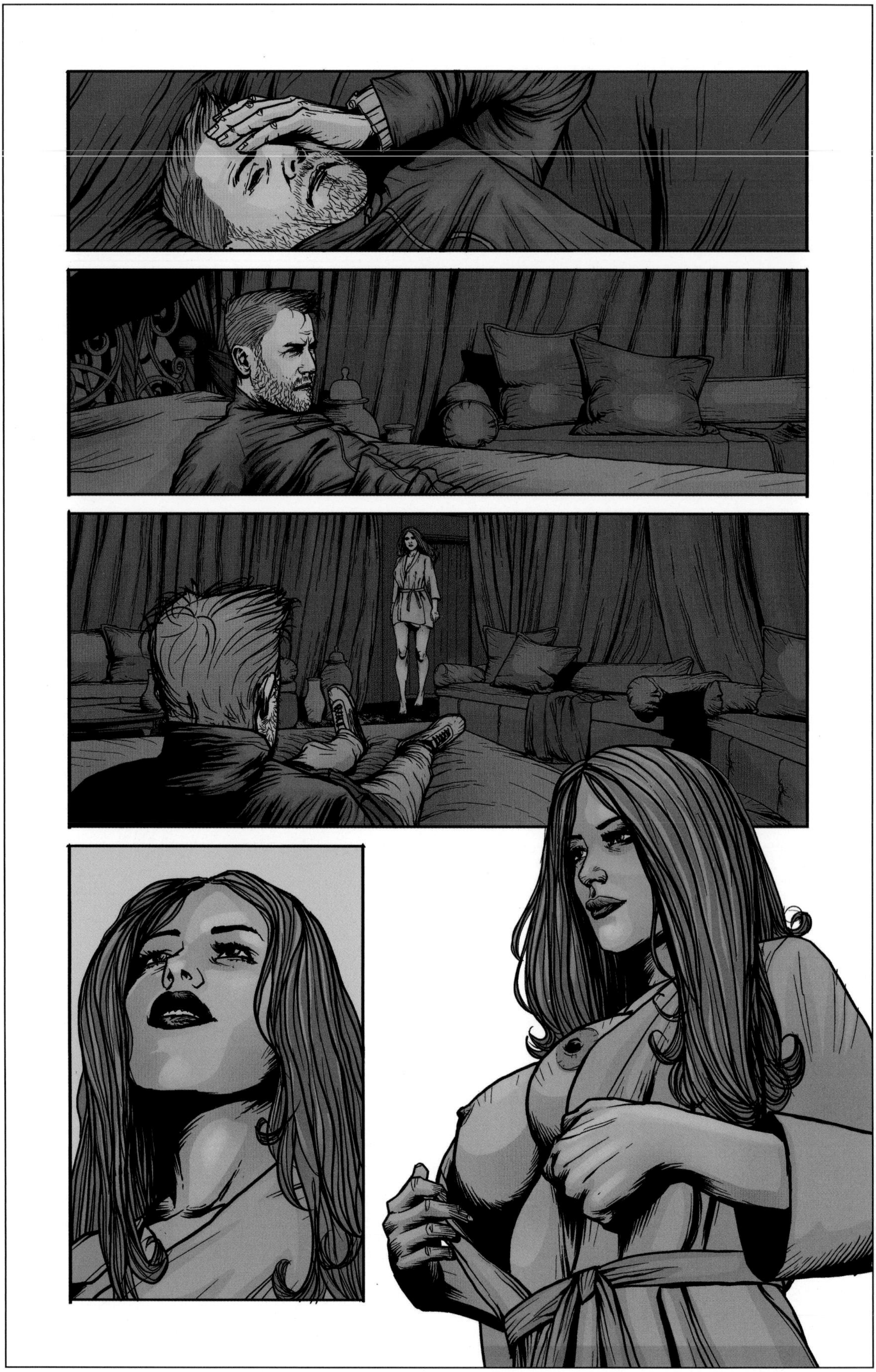

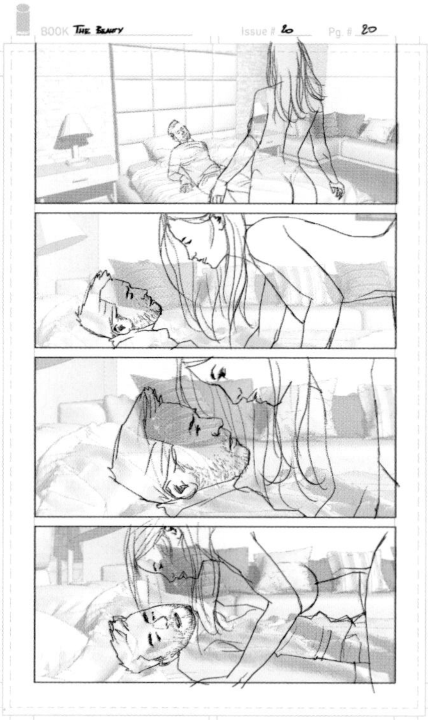
BOOK The Beauty
Issue # 20
Pg. # 20

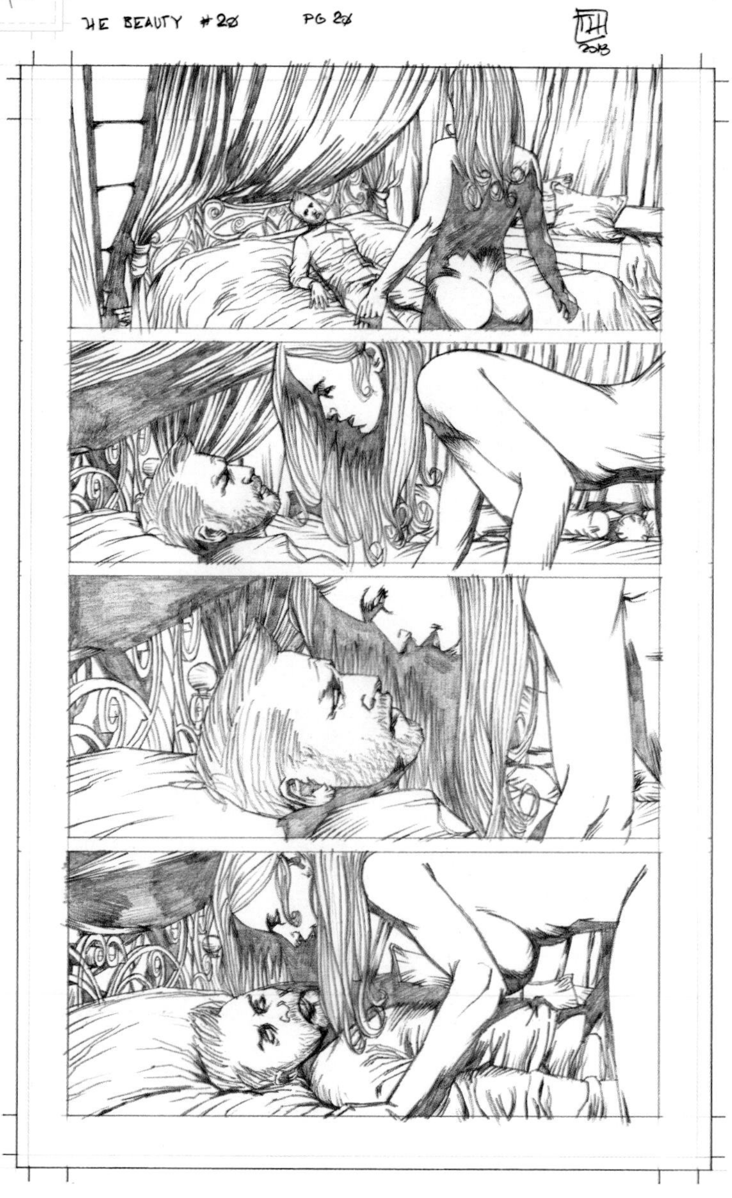
THE BEAUTY #20
PG 20
2013

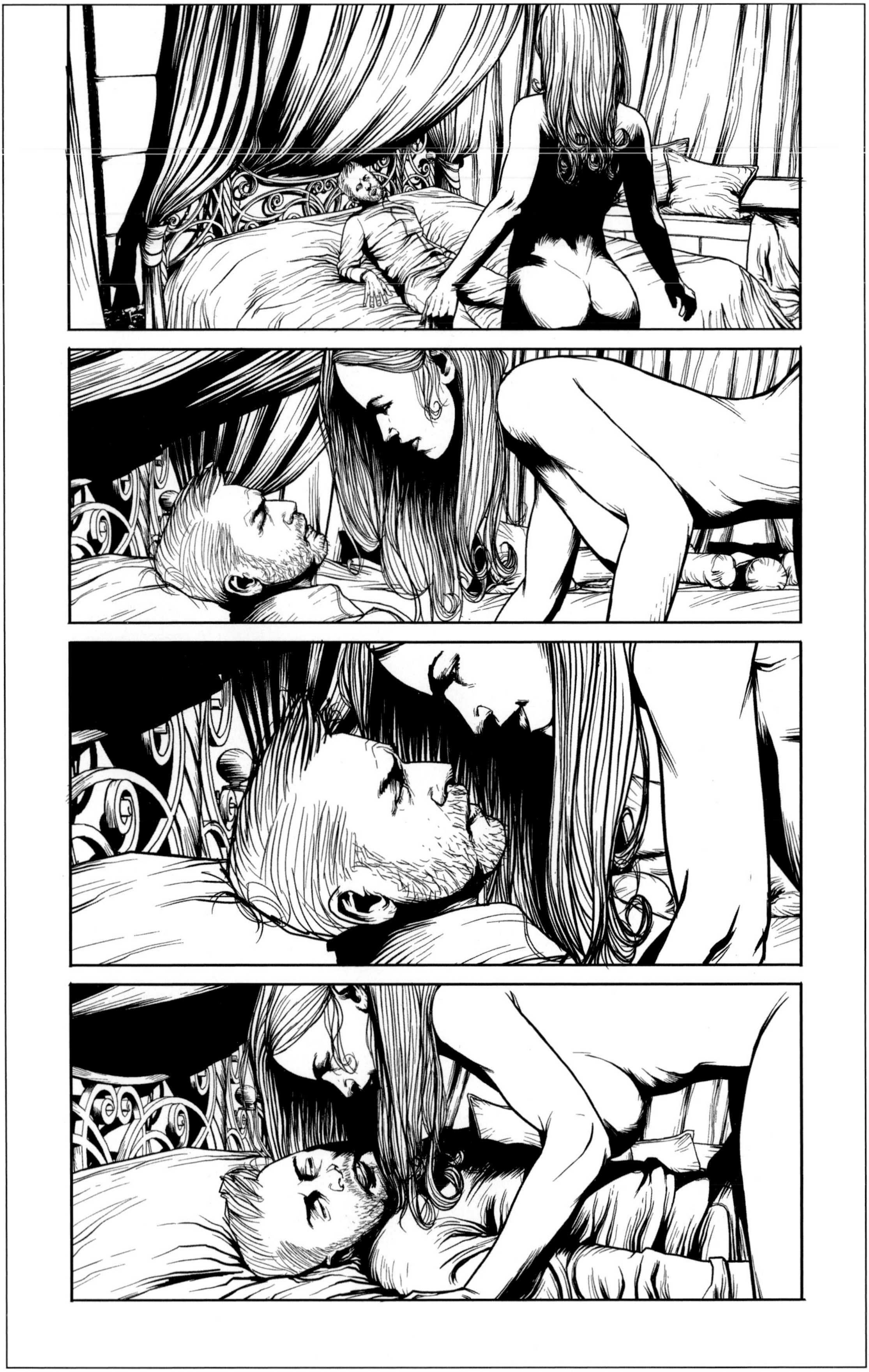

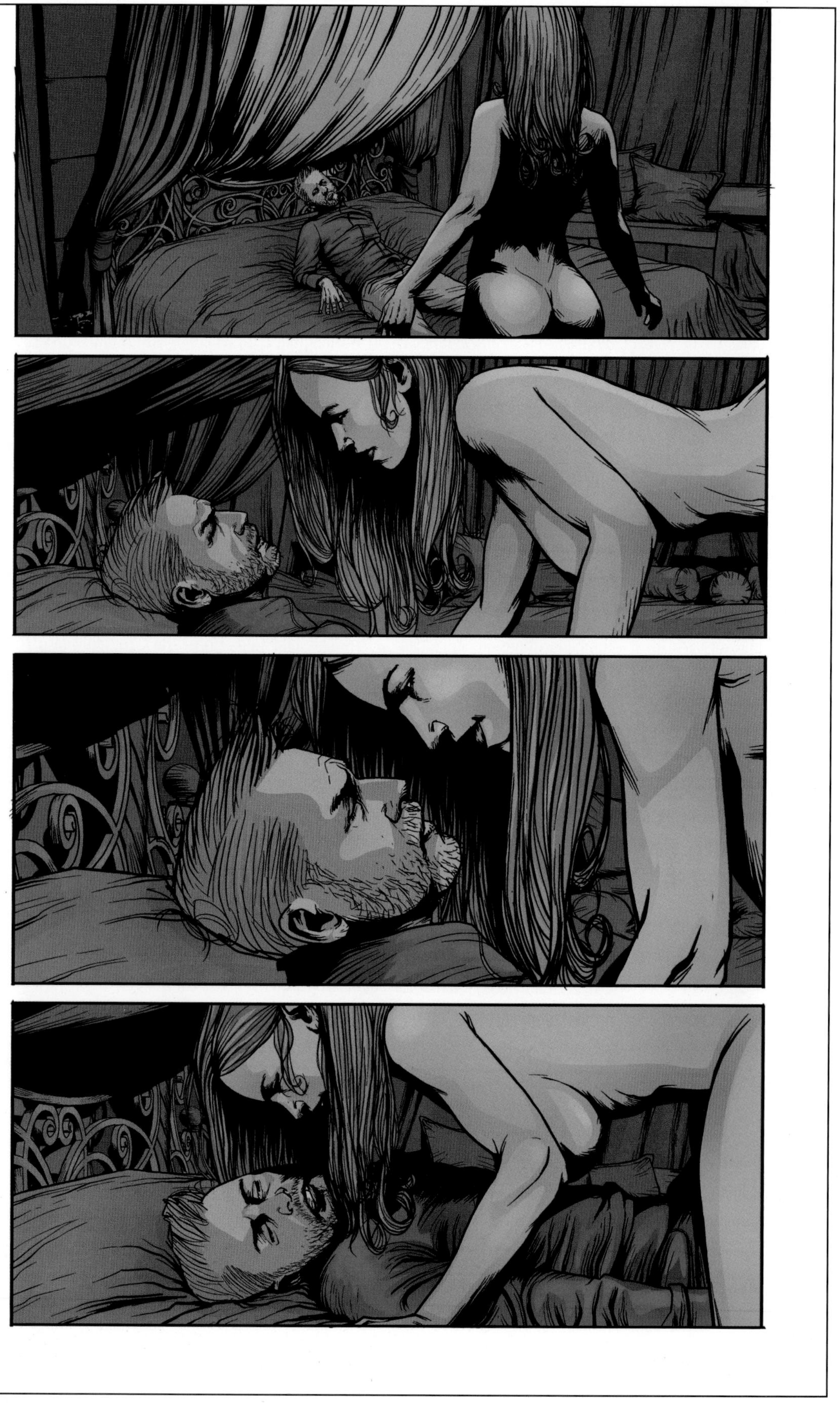

BIOGRAPHIES

Jeremy Haun, co-writer, co-creator and often artist for THE BEAUTY, has also worked on *Wolf Moon* from Vertigo, *Constantine* and *Batwoman* from DC. Over the past decade plus, along with wearing calluses on his fingers doing work for DC, Marvel, Image, and others, he has created and written several projects. Some you might know are graphic novel *Narcoleptic Sunday, Leading Man, Dino Day,* and most recently THE REALM. He is a part of the Bad Karma Creative group, whose *Bad Karma Volume One* debuted at NYCC 2013, thanks to Kickstarter funding.

Jeremy resides in a crumbling mansion in Joplin, Missouri, with his wife and two superheroes-in-training.

Jason A. Hurley has been in the comic book game for over fifteen years. However, none of you have ever heard of him because, until recently, he's been almost completely exclusive to the retail sector. In addition to comic books, he loves pro wrestling, bad horror movies, Freddy Mercury, hummingbirds, his parents, and pizza. While he's never actually tried it, he also thinks curling looks like a hell of a lot of fun. Hurley claims his personal heroes are Earl Bassett and Valentine McKee, because they live a life of adventure on their own terms. He also claims that he would brain anyone who showed even the most remote signs of becoming a cannibalistic undead bastard, including his own brother, without a second thought. He's lived in Joplin, Missouri, for most of his life, and never plans to leave.

Thomas Nachlik is a Polish-born illustrator, living in Germany with his wife and two cats. His client list includes Top Cow, Boom, Amazon Studios, and DC Comics.

Matthew Dow Smith is based in Washington, D.C., where he writes and draws comics.

Nayoung Kim got sucked into the world of comics by her husband from a graphic design career. They live outside Atlanta with two dogs and two cats— constantly fighting the urge to move west into the desert.

Nick Filardi has colored for just about every major comic book publisher including DC, Marvel, Oni Press, and Dark Horse. He's currently also coloring covers for THE BEAUTY. When he isn't buried in pages, you can find his digital likeness pulling up other colorists with tips and tricks at twitch.tv/nickfil, making dad jokes at twitter.com/nickfil, and just spreading dope art at instagram.com/nick_filardi. He lives in Florida with his 3-legged dog and fiancée.

Thomas Mauer has lent his lettering and design talent to award-winning books and obscure gems alike. Among his recent work are Black Mask Studios' *4 Kids Walk Into A Bank,* Image Comics' ELSEWHERE, COPPERHEAD, CRUDE, and THE REALM, as well as IDW's *Antar: The Black Knight,* and the World Food Programme's *Living Level-3* series.

Joel Enos is a writer and editor of comics and stories. His short stories have been published in *Flapperhouse, Bloodbond,* and *Year's Best Speculative YA Fiction.* He's currently the editor of THE BEAUTY, THE REALM, and REGRESSION, all published by Image Comics.